Made in the
U.S.A.

Also by Billie Letts

Where the Heart Is
The Honk and Holler Opening Soon
Shoot the Moon

Made in the U.S.A.

BILLIE LETTS

GRAND CENTRAL
PUBLISHING

NEW YORK   BOSTON

Grand Central Publishing
Hachette Book Group USA
237 Park Avenue
New York, NY 10017

Printed in the United States of America

Grand Central Publishing is a division of Hachette Book Group USA, Inc.
The Grand Central Publishing name and logo is a trademark of
Hachette Book Group USA, Inc.

Grateful acknowledgment is given to Shawn Letts to reprint portions of lyrics from "Nadia," music and lyrics by Shawn Letts. Copyright © 2005. All Rights reserved.
Used by permission.
ISBN-13: 978-1-60751-389-6

Book design by Charles Sutherland

To Dennis, my "Broadway Star,"
who trusted the wonder of love

ACKNOWLEDGMENTS

Humbled by how much I don't know, I want to thank the dozens of folks who provided me with information and encouragement as I worked on this book.

First, to those who know about circus life because they live it: Barbara Miller Byrd, Deedee McGarvey, Kristen Para, Katrina Perez, Obed Perez, and Ken Rawls, I am indebted.

With gratitude to the medical professionals who both answered my questions and tried to keep my body and mind functioning, Dr. Harold Battenfield, Dr. Jocelyn Idema, Dr. John Carletti, Dr. Bob Bruton, Dr. Scott Anthony, and Dr. Barry Eisen.

In Las Vegas, I was guided gently by Lenika Coleman and Mike Valenti.

Help in learning more about how the homeless of our country survive came from Sandra Lewis and Mary Battenfield.

Amy King shared with me her experience in gymnastics; Don Morrall knew all I needed to know about heavy equipment and construction sites; Jan Dougless gave me the great idea to include Draco; and Barbara Hendricks taught me about golf balls.

For the current jargon of teenagers, I turned to Malica Marlin,

Sam and Jack Stewart, Brad Cushman, and the Nicolo gang—Michael, Daniel, and Nic.

For Spanish translations, I followed the lead of Hector Uribe, Arturo Ruiz-Esparza, Miguel Figueroa, José Ramírez, and Selina McLemore.

Thanks to the good folks at Brookside Piercing & Tattoos.

A nod to David Hoffman, author of *Who Knew?*, a delightful collection of whimsical facts, which provided Fate with some of his offbeat trivia.

To my friends who offered encouragement: Molly Griffis, Renee Nicolo, Georgeann Vineyard, Teresa Miller, Russell Andrew, Arlene and Wes Johnson, I send my sincere gratitude.

And to my family, always pulling for me: Barbara Santee, Vicki Mooney, Dewey Dougless, Dana and Deborah Letts, Shawn and Shari Letts, Tracy Letts and Nicole Wiesner, I give my love.

I would never have finished this book without the help of Wilma Shires, special friend who put my work on disk (because I'm typewriter addicted); and to Blanche Jamison who proofed for Wilma, here's a big hug.

Finally, kisses to my editor, Jamie Rabb, and her assistants, Sharon Krassney and Sara Weiss; to my agent, Elaine Markson, and her assistant, Gary Johnson; and to my agent in Los Angeles, Lisa Callamaro—friends all . . . who guide me, support me, and nudge me ever so gently down the right road.

PART ONE

CHAPTER ONE

Lutie McFee struggled into the too tight red, sleeveless turtleneck, smoothed it across her ribs, then checked herself out in the mirror of the Wal-Mart dressing room.

She was almost pretty but still had the not quite finished look of a teenager—unlined skin dappled with sand-colored freckles, cheeks not quite shed of baby fat, frizzy hair too wild to be tamed by gel or spray. Her hips were as narrow as a boy's, and her feet looked too big for her tiny ankles and spindly legs.

But worst of all, she was convinced—not for the first time that day—that her breasts were never going to grow beyond the two walnut-size bumps on her chest. The best she could hope for was a Wonderbra, but she doubted even that would perform the miracle she needed.

After she got kicked off the gymnastics team, she was free to eat again—whenever, whatever, and as often as she wanted. So she began to satisfy her yearning for chili-cheese fries, chocolate malts, double-meat hamburgers, coconut cream pie, and banana-nut muffins slathered with warm butter.

She figured if she'd pile enough weight onto her stick-figure body, she'd eventually be able to replace her training bras with triple A's, or maybe even doubles.

But it didn't happen.

She jumped from one hundred and six pounds to one eleven and remained a size two. But most disappointing of all, the additional five pounds didn't go anywhere near the training bra, though if she used the right kind of socks for stuffing, she could pull off a size A.

One of the consolations for all the hours she spent in the gym before and after school was the shelf in her bedroom crowded with trophies, ribbons, and medals, all for her balance beam performances. Margie Holcomb, who replaced her, hadn't earned even an "also mention" certificate. Not one.

Coach Stebens had fought for her, taking on the entire school board, but like Lutie, she'd known from the beginning, the day the lie started circulating from classrooms to lockers, from the cafeteria to the parking lot, that it was a lost cause. Why? Because Superintendent Holcomb was Margie Holcomb's grandfather, who thought if Lutie lost her place on the gymnastics squad, then she—Margie—would win all those trophies. Of course, that plan didn't work out. Margie was a mediocre gymnast at best; but Lutie was the greatest ever produced not just in Spearfish, but in all of South Dakota. And many said she had a good chance of going to the Olympics. That's how her first dream of all her dreams was born.

The first time a judge placed the ribbon with a gold medal around her neck and her coach handed her a bouquet of roses, she had all she'd ever dreamed of.

Recognition!

But she'd been disqualified so many months ago and now, the summer before her junior year, the dream of competing in the Olympics had died. Not a painless death, either, not the kind that comes quietly in the night, stops the heart gently, and takes the next breath away with an unknowing comfort.

No, this death was shocking in its suddenness. Mourned. Buried. Grieved in lonely silence. Gone.

Replaced now with a more realistic goal. No longer a dream, actually, but more of a longing for the kind of attention so many other girls got seemingly without effort—popular girls with rounded hips and breasts that bounced like water balloons. But with little promise that she was destined to become the next Pamela Anderson, she thought she could be willing to settle for less.

If she could manage to give nature a boost, she would bleach her dark hair until it was the color of honey with streaks of gold. She would get more holes pierced in her ears and have a pair of kissing lips tattooed on her neck. She might even wear a nose ring.

But until she could find a way to get out of Spearfish, South Dakota, that was not likely to happen.

She took off the turtleneck, folded it into a neat square, then tucked it into the front of her underpants. She'd just rezipped her jeans when someone knocked at the dressing room door.

"This room is taken," she yelled.

"Lutie, let me in."

"I'll be out in a minute, Floy," she said, her voice edged with anger.

"Open the door."

Lutie pulled on her old sweatshirt, bloused it around her hips, then unlocked the door.

Floy Satterfield, at nearly three hundred pounds, filled the doorway. She had long ago given up on diets, counting instead on having her stomach stapled when she could put the money together. But that was a dim prospect given her four-hundred-dollar welfare check and the two extra mouths she had to feed.

"I need to go home," Floy said.

"Go? We just got here."

"I ain't feeling good."

"What's wrong now?" Lutie came down hard on the "now."

"Damned indigestion again." Floy fumbled a roll of Tums from her purse and popped two in her mouth. "You go find your brother and meet me out front."

"Well, I don't know where he is."

"He'll be where he always is. Now hurry."

Lutie waited until she could no longer hear the slap of Floy's rubber thongs before she slammed the door. She readjusted her sweatshirt, and then, satisfied no one would guess she had a turtleneck stuffed in her pants, she ran a comb through her hair and checked her mascara.

She stepped out of the fitting room carrying the ugly flannel nightgown and tweed jacket she'd used to conceal the turtleneck from the dressing room attendant.

Ignoring Floy's demand to hurry, Lutie made her way to the magazine rack, where she pulled out a couple of movie magazines, then sat cross-legged on the floor and began flipping pages. Each time she came across a picture of Brad Pitt, she ripped out the page, folded it so as to avoid creasing Brad's face, and slid it into her purse.

Fifteen minutes later, she found her brother, Fate, in the electronics department at the keyboard of a display computer, where he was trying to find out who invented shoelaces.

Though he was only eleven, he sometimes seemed to Lutie more like an old man than a child. He wore thick glasses with wire frames; worried about global warming and the endangerment of pandas; and moved like creeping Jesus. He liked plaid shirts, buttermilk, and old clocks. And he had a habit of running his fingers through his hair, which she predicted would make him bald before he finished eighth grade.

He spent most of his time reading, watching weird TV shows about lighthouses, Roman baths, prairie dogs, Jack Kerouac, and the Khmer Empire—subjects that nobody else would give two hoots about.

And he played games by himself—Trivial Pursuit, Scrabble, and Boggle.

He had no friends that she knew of—was never invited to sleepovers or slumber parties, campouts or even birthday parties. And he never invited boys to the places where he and Lutie happened to be living.

He went for long solitary walks at night and in the rain, he often talked in his sleep, but in strange languages she couldn't identify.

Lutie wouldn't be surprised if he grew up to be a shepherd.

"We gotta go," she said.

"I'm not ready yet."

"Floy's waiting on us."

"I just now got on the Net, Lutie. Some girl's been hogging it for the last half hour."

"So?"

"I need a few more minutes."

"Suit yourself. But Floy's gonna be pissed. Big-time."

As Lutie walked away, she saw several people rushing toward the front of the store, but she was too interested in getting to the cosmetics section to investigate what was going on.

A clerk restocking hand cream eyed her suspiciously as she began pulling tubes of lipstick from the Revlon rack. But when two older teenage girls came by and started opening bottles at the perfume counter, the clerk's attention was divided.

Lutie found a shade of Lightning Red she liked, palmed the

tube, and meandered to the other side of the aisle, where she slipped the lipstick into her purse.

Suddenly, the intercom blared. "Code blue. Code blue at register three."

The announcement sent the clerk hurrying away as Lutie moved on to a shelf of Maybelline makeup. She tried one shade of blush, then another, dabbing color onto her cheeks until her face looked bruised.

Finally, she settled on Purple Twilight, dropped it in her purse, then headed toward the front of the store, where she knew Floy would be fuming.

But she wasn't the only one going that way. People were rushing past her, and she could see a crowd forming at one of the checkouts.

The intercom crackled with static. "Attention, Wal-Mart shoppers, we need a doctor at register three. Uh . . . is there a doctor in the store?"

When a man in a cowboy hat bumped Lutie with his cart, she said, "Hey. Watch where you're going!" but he ignored her.

"What happened, Ida?" the man yelled to a skinny woman ahead of him.

"They said some woman dropped dead at the checkout."

"No shit?"

"Come on!"

Lutie had just reached the edge of the gathering crowd when a baby-faced boy wearing a starched blue shirt and a security badge pushed past her.

"Did someone die?" the skinny woman asked him.

"Looks like it."

"You know who it is?"

"Big fat woman's all I know."

Lutie felt a knot of dread building in her chest. She called

Floy's name, but with the noise and commotion inside and a siren blaring outside, she knew Floy couldn't hear her.

She tried to push her way through, but too many people were pushing back, so she circled around, trying to get in from the other side, but no one would budge.

Then she saw a policeman coming through the door.

"Okay," he shouted. "You folks move back and let me through."

The crowd grew quiet as they parted to make room for the policeman, who shouldered his way inside the group. Lutie fell in behind him.

And that's when she saw Floy.

She had pitched sideways when she fell, slamming into racks of batteries, disposable lighters, *TV Guide*s, and candy, spilling them onto the floor beside her. Her head was twisted at an angle that would have been painful had she been able to feel pain, and her glasses had slipped onto her cheeks. Her mouth was pulled into a perfect O, as if she had been about to whistle, and bits of the Tums she had been chewing clung to her bottom lip. Her fingers, adorned with rhinestone rings, still clutched the *National Enquirer* she had just paid for.

The policeman knelt beside her still body and dipped his fingers into the folds of flesh around her neck, probing for a pulse. Then he bent over her and put his cheek next to her opened mouth. Moments later, he straightened, pretending not to notice the urine seeping through the crotch of Floy's blue polyester pants and puddling beneath her buttocks.

He stood and faced the checker behind the register. "You know who she is?" he asked.

The checker shook her head. "I seen her in here before, though."

Then he turned to the crowd around him. "Do any of you know this woman?"

9

Those gathered craned their necks and waited.

"Is anyone here with this woman?" he yelled.

Then softly, her voice hardly more than a whisper, Lutie said, "I am."

CHAPTER TWO

Aᴀғᴛᴇʀ ᴛʜᴇ ᴍᴀɴᴀɢᴇʀ took Lutie to his office, he went to search for her brother. She hadn't seen Fate since she'd left him at the computer, so she didn't know if he had seen what happened to Floy.

While Lutie waited, a parade of Wal-Mart employees came by, taking stealthy glances at her as they passed. A couple of them even manufactured reasons to come inside, saying, "Excuse me, I just need to get a file" and "Sorry to disturb you, but I think I left my pen in here." Lutie never looked at any of them and never said a word, but she could hear them whispering outside the door.

When the manager returned, he had a hand clamped on Fate's shoulder as if he feared the boy might run. "I'll leave you two alone in here so you can talk," he said. "Take all the time you need."

As soon as the door was closed, Fate sat stiffly in a chair that dwarfed his small frame.

"Fate, do you know—"

"Lutie, I was gonna put it back. Honest." He dug in his

pocket, pulled out a packaged computer disk, and set it on the desk. "Here. You tell them that I—"

"Fate—"

"What're they gonna do to me? Am I going to jail?" Tears threatened, but he blinked them away. "A policeman's out there and—"

"That's not what this is about."

"You think they're gonna tell Floy?"

"Floy's . . . well, something happened."

"I know she's gonna be mad."

"Floy's dead."

"She'll spank me, but I don't care."

"Listen to me, Fate. Floy died."

He grew still, studied his sister for a moment, then flashed her a crooked grin. "Lutie, I know you're just trying to scare me, but you don't have to 'cause I'll never do it again. I promise."

"Shut up, Fate, and listen to what I'm telling you. Floy is dead."

His face settled into a puzzled look then, as if he'd just heard a joke he didn't understand. "Why?" he asked.

"Why? What do you mean, 'why'? That's a stupid question. I don't know why people die. They just do. I guess she might've had a heart attack."

Fate ran his hands through his hair. "You think she had a heart attack 'cause she was waiting for me? You think she got mad and—"

"She wasn't waiting. She was in the checkout line and she just died."

"But—"

A tap at the door made them both turn toward the sound.

"Miss McFee?"

"It's probably that policeman," Lutie whispered. "Don't say anything to him. You understand?"

Fate, eyes wide with fear, nodded.

"Come in," Lutie said.

The policeman opened the door and stepped inside. He was carrying Floy's brown imitation leather purse.

"You two doing okay?"

"Yeah."

"Good. My name is Sergeant Santos." He sat down, put the purse on the desk, and took a small notebook from his pocket. "This won't take long, but I need to ask some questions. Is that all right?"

"Uh-huh."

"Okay. You said your name is Lutie McFee. And you are . . . ?" He looked at Fate, waiting for an answer, but the boy was rigid and mute.

"His name's Fate. He's my brother."

"That's an unusual name."

"It was supposed to be Fale," Lutie said. "That was our mother's maiden name, but they got it wrong on his birth certificate. They crossed the *l*."

"Where do you live?"

"Out on Springer Road. Just east of the slaughterhouse."

"Was the deceased . . . the woman who passed away, was she your mother?"

"No," Lutie said.

"Are you related to her?" he asked.

"Not exactly. She and my daddy lived together, so she was sort of like our stepmother. But she wasn't. Not really."

The policeman wrote down everything Lutie said. She tried to read it upside down, but it was hard to make out.

"And you told me her name was . . . is Floy? Floy Satterfield?"

"Floy is what everyone calls her, but her real name is Florence."

"Where can we reach your father?" he asked.

"He's in Las Vegas."

"When will he be back?"

Lutie's hesitation prompted Sergeant Santos to look at Fate, but he wasn't talking.

"When did your father go to Las Vegas?"

"About a year ago," Lutie said.

"You know his phone number? His address?"

"No. We haven't heard from him."

"And your mother? Where is she?"

"She's dead."

"I'm sorry," he said, then he put down his pen, closed his eyes, and pinched the bridge of his nose.

"Do you have a migraine?" Fate asked, the first time he'd spoken since Lutie warned him to be quiet. "That's what Floy does when she gets her migraines."

"I'm just a little tired, I guess." Then he picked up his pen and looked at Lutie. "Do your grandparents live around here?"

"No. Grandpa Fale died a long time ago, and Grandma Fale's in a nursing home in Georgia. She has Oldtimers, or whatever it's called. Daddy's folks, they're divorced. I think his mom lives in Canada, but I don't know where his dad is."

"How do I get in touch with her? Your grandmother in Canada."

Lutie shrugged. "She got married again, and I don't know what her name is now."

"How about Ms. Satterfield. She have a family?"

"A sister. Milly Windout. She lives in Rapid City."

The policeman studied Lutie, then Fate. "Well, let me make a call to CPS and—"

"What's CPS?" Lutie asked.

"Child Protective Services. They help out in cases like this. They'll find you a place to stay and—"

"Oh, we don't need any help. See, we have an aunt who lives with us." Fate, dumbfounded, shifted in his chair, but Lutie pretended not to notice. "Our aunt Julia."

"What's her last name?" Sergeant Santos asked.

"Roberts."

"Like the movie star?"

"Yeah." Lutie smiled. "People are always making some joke about her being in the movies."

"Is she home?"

"You mean now?"

"Yes."

"Well . . ." Stalling, Lutie asked, "What time is it?"

"Almost six."

"She doesn't get off till nine. She's a nurse at the hospital."

"Then why don't we run over to Memorial and talk to her?"

"No!" Lutie said, a little too fast, a little too loud. "See, she has a bad heart. Just like Floy. And if she sees us come in with you . . . well, it might scare her so bad she'd drop dead, too."

"Then let me drive you home."

"Oh, I'll drive Floy's car." She grabbed Floy's purse, rummaged inside, and came up with a ring of keys. "Her car's parked right outside."

"You old enough to drive, Lutie?" he asked, his voice conveying suspicion.

"Sure. I have a license." Then, fearing he might ask to see it, she added, "Well, I don't have it with me. I left it at home. I mean, I didn't think I'd be driving tonight."

"I understand." He closed his notebook and slipped it back in his shirt pocket. "You don't mind if I drop by your place after your aunt gets home, do you? Might be a good idea if I talked to her for a few minutes."

"Okay."

"Then I'll see you later."

He nodded to them, opened the door, and walked into the hall, where the manager was waiting with another policeman.

Lutie signaled Fate to be quiet, then she shouldered her purse and Floy's and motioned Fate to follow her.

15

When they walked past the group in the hall, Lutie could hear the policemen talking, but she couldn't make out what they were saying.

Lutie and Fate slowed when they reached the checkouts, but all traces of Floy had been picked up, swept out, mopped up, and put back. And it was business as usual at register three, where a checker was dragging cans of Vienna sausage across the scanner.

CHAPTER THREE

L<small>UTIE, DO YOU</small> really know how to drive?"

"Sure," she said as she tried key after key in the ignition of Floy's car. "I took driver's ed."

"Yeah, but Mr. Edwards kicked you out before you ever got to drive."

"Mr. Edwards is a prick. Besides, I learned the basics."

"What does that mean?"

"The rules, stupid."

Lutie finally fitted the right key into the starter, turned it, and the engine fired, but when she mashed on the gas, the old Pontiac lurched forward and died.

"Are they watching us?" she asked. "And don't let them see you looking."

"How am I gonna know if they're watching us if I don't look?"

"Just do it!"

Fate took a quick peek out the rear window of the car, then slouched down in the passenger seat. "That policeman who talked to us is, but the other one went back into Wal-Mart."

When Lutie started the engine again, she stomped on the gas pedal, causing the car to shoot across the parking lot and bump across a curbed divider into the wrong lane.

"Watch out!" Fate yelled.

Lutie turned the wheel sharply, jumped the curbing again, and steered the car into the right lane.

"You're going too fast!"

"Be quiet, Fate. Let me concentrate."

When she reached the stop sign at the end of the exit lane, she hit the brakes and the car came to a squealing stop.

"Is he still looking?"

Fate glanced back. "Yeah."

"Dammit!"

"Can you get put in jail for reckless driving?"

The Pontiac's left front fender grazed a bumper guard at the side of the exit.

"I bet you'll go to jail if he finds out you don't have a driver's license."

"Will you stop talking about jail?"

Getting a feel for the pedals now, Lutie eased the car into the traffic as she pulled onto the roadway.

"He'll probably put us both in jail if he finds out we don't have an aunt named Julia Roberts."

"Fate, will you shut up about jail!"

"Why'd you tell him that, Lutie?"

Without warning, Lutie swerved into the left-turn lane, and the driver of the car she nearly sideswiped honked and gave her the finger.

"Dick-head!" she yelled, returning the gesture.

Oblivious to the yield sign, Lutie turned left when she reached the intersection, forcing one driver onto the shoulder and another to clip the center median. Relieved to have left the main thoroughfare and the traffic behind, she took a deep breath and rolled her head from side to side to ease the tension in her shoulders.

"Why'd you make up that story about Julia Roberts? Huh?"

"Christ alive, Fate. If you ask me one more question . . ."

"Floy says it's a sin to use the Lord's name in vain."

"I didn't say Lord. I said Christ."

"Same thing."

Fate was quiet until they neared the Buffalo Café, where Floy had taken them the first Friday of every month for the all-you-can-eat catfish special.

"Lutie, what's a heart attack like?"

"I don't know."

"You think it hurts a lot? You think Floy—"

"I said I don't know."

Fate stared at the café as they passed, then sniffed and wiped his nose on the sleeve of his plaid shirt.

"I know you didn't like her much, but Floy wasn't so bad."

"If you say so."

"I mean, she treated us okay. Better'n Gwen and Mona and Beverly."

"Gwen and Mona and Beverly were all drunks."

"Well, so is Daddy."

"Daddy's not a drunk. He's an alcoholic."

"What's the difference?"

"An alcoholic can quit. A drunk can't."

"Floy said Daddy was a drunk."

"That's because he walked out on her. She's been pissed at him ever since."

"Maybe she loved him."

"Floy? Hell, the only thing she loved about him was his paycheck. And she damn sure didn't love us. Always bitching because he ran off and left us for her to take care of. Said she knew he wouldn't come back for us like he promised."

"Well, he didn't."

Two miles past the café, Lutie turned onto the county road that led to Floy's place, a house trailer on a nearly treeless acre, land owned more by the bank than by Floy.

Lutie overshot the driveway by a couple of feet, the Pontiac coming to a stop with the two front tires on a scrawny bed of petunias.

"Come on," she said as she switched off the engine. "I got a lot to do, and you're gonna have to help me."

Lutie already had the car door open and one foot on the ground when Fate said, "Help you with what?"

She hesitated for a moment, then eased back into the driver's seat and turned to face her brother.

"Pack," she said.

"Where we going?"

"Fate, do you have any idea of the mess we're in here?"

He shook his head.

"Well, we're . . . Listen. You know why I told that policeman we had an aunt who lives with us?"

"No."

" 'Cause if I told him we didn't have no one but Floy, he'd have those welfare people out here in a flash and we'd get stuck in a foster home. And believe me, that's worse than living with Floy. It's even worse than jail."

At the word *jail*, Fate's eyes widened in alarm.

"I'm telling you the truth," Lutie said. "A girl in my class, Peggy Bellamy, she's in a foster home. Now, the people that took her, they got kids of their own, and they treat them just fine. But Peggy, she's like a slave to them. They slap her around, make her clean their toilets, feed her slop. That's not gonna happen to me."

"Me neither."

"Well, that's the thing. See, I'm going to Las Vegas to find Daddy. But I can't take you."

"Why not?"

" 'Cause when that policeman comes, I need you to tell him that me and Aunt Julia went to Rapid City to see Floy's sister, to tell her Floy died. He'll probably figure it out later, but by the time he does, I'll be hundreds of miles away."

"But what about me? I'll have to go to a foster home and eat slop and—"

"No. I been thinking about that. You can go stay with Floy's friend, the one she goes to bingo with. She don't have kids and she'll—"

"Miss Jacobs? No way, Lutie! She's about a hundred years old and she smells like mothballs and her hands shake and her dog hates me and—"

"You won't be there long. Soon's I find Daddy, we'll come back and get you."

"You don't even know where he is. After Floy got that letter, she tried to call him about a hundred times and all the operators said the same thing. He didn't have a phone."

"Yeah, but we have his address."

"Floy wrote to him there, but all her letters got returned."

"Look, Fate, I don't have time for this. For all I know that policeman might be calling the hospital right now, and if he finds out—"

"What are you gonna do when you get caught in a storm, huh? A storm with lightning and thunder?"

"I'll deal with it."

"You've never been able to deal with it before. And what'll happen if you have car trouble or if someone with a gun—"

"I'm old enough to take care of myself."

"You're only fifteen."

"So what."

"Well, if you're so old, why can't you take care of me?"

" 'Cause I can't, that's why," she said as she slid out of the car and headed for the trailer.

Following her, Fate said, "Please. Take me with you."

"Fate, I already told you—"

"You're the only one I got, Lutie. There ain't no one else."

Lutie turned then, angry enough to take a swing at him. Instead, she saw what she didn't want to see. A boy whose small, thin body was already bowed by loss . . . the brother whose face already bore the look of defeat and whose eyes, filling now with tears, had already seen too much disappointment.

"Well, hell." She tromped up three rickety steps before she said, "Come on. Let's get packed."

Lutie's history had taught her to avoid attachments . . . to people, to places, to almost everything. So packing for her was easy. She quickly crammed clothes, shoes, and cosmetics into black garbage bags and stuffed them in the trunk of the car.

She made few concessions to sentimentality.

One was Mr. PawPaw, a fourteen-year-old teddy bear made by her mother but disabled long ago when a puppy called Fizz chewed off and swallowed one of his eyes and the lobe of one ear. But now, despite his impairments, Mr. PawPaw would ride to Las Vegas on the dash of the Pontiac.

Her only other emotional ties fit into a floral hatbox secreted away in the back of the trunk, a hatbox filled with mementos from her gymnastic competitions: leotards carefully folded; medals and trophies wrapped in tissue paper; articles clipped from the *Rapid City Journal*; and photographs of Lutie and her teammates celebrating their victories.

The day Coach Stebens told her she'd been declared ineligible, Lutie had taken the box with its contents into the backyard, where she intended to burn it. Burn every damn bit of it in a ceremony of revenge.

But she couldn't do it. She couldn't destroy the evidence that the girl in the emerald green leotard with a gold medal suspended from a ribbon around her neck was the same girl who lived on the wrong side of town in a shabby trailer with a three-hundred-pound woman who came to all the events no matter how much the girl begged her not to; a father, the town drunk, who'd disappeared long ago; and a brother—the weirdest boy in school, and the smartest, too.

No, this girl needed proof, the "you can see it" and "you can touch it" kind of proof. Proof that she had been *somebody*. Even though her fame had been short-lived, she was the skinny, flat-chested girl who had completed a perfect back handspring, a flawless stepout, and an excellent dismount from the balance beam; then, clutching Mr. PawPaw, she waited for her score to be tallied—9.8; 9.9; 10; 9.9; 10. Two hundred spectators stomping in the bleachers, clapping, shouting her name: "Lu-tie, Lu-tie, Lu-tie . . ."

She could still hear it all, see it all. Live it again, but only for a few moments before Fate crowded in beside her with a bag of his plaid shirts and corduroy pants, which she squeezed into the trunk. He cared nothing about clothes, but even with Lutie pushing him to hurry, he agonized over his other possessions, wanting to leave nothing behind. He eventually settled on an encyclopedia, a dictionary, his *National Geographic*s, a collection of *Farmers' Almanac*s dating back to 1991, *The Book of Facts*, *Who Knew?*, and his *Trivial Pursuit* game.

Rejecting Lutie's demands, he wouldn't let her put these treasured belongings in the trunk; instead, he placed them in the backseat where he could reach them.

Finally, they set to work putting their funds together—money from Floy's billfold and the bingo stash she kept in her jewelry box, grocery money hidden in the sugar bowl, change from beneath the cushions of the couch, a few dollars from Fate's Christmas bank, and the cash Lutie had been saving for her Wonderbra.

Their total take was $112.47, and that, according to Fate, would hardly stretch all the way to Las Vegas. But just as Lutie started to back out of the driveway, he remembered the change in the coffee can under the kitchen sink, a cache of almost $40, all in quarters, which Floy had been squirreling away for an operation to have her stomach stapled.

Fate came out of the trailer handling his find like the Holy Grail and made a special place for the coffee can in the backseat next to his books.

"Okay," he said. "I guess I'm ready."

"Then we're out of here."

With the Pontiac gaining speed, Fate watched as the trailer grew smaller in the distance.

"I never seen a dead person, Lutie."

"Well, you're lucky."

"What about her funeral? There'll be a funeral, but we won't be there."

"Her sister will have to manage without us."

"Still, it doesn't seem right."

"Fate. Floy's gone. No sense in looking back now."

"Yeah, I know," he said, but he kept his eyes on the last place they'd called home until it was finally lost in the darkening night.

CHAPTER FOUR

By the time they crossed the state line, one hundred and seven miles from where they'd started, Lutie was convinced that driver's ed would have been a waste of her time. In just two hours she'd learned to keep the car inside the white lines of the right lane, discovered that the Pontiac was equipped with a turn signal, and mastered the intricacies of the horn.

Unfortunately for the drivers coming toward her, she had not learned how to dim the lights.

They made their first stop at a Texaco station, where a full tank of gas, two quarts of oil, a road atlas, beef jerky, and Gummi Bears made a sizable dent in their traveling money.

When the beef jerky and Gummi Bears ran out, Lutie pulled into a McDonald's.

Fate said they should get their order to go, reasoning that the more miles they put between them and home, the better. But Lutie thought the redheaded boy who worked behind the counter was cute, so they were eating inside.

She soon lost interest in her food, opting instead to go for the redhead's attention. She started pulling makeup from her purse, littering the table with lipstick, blush, mascara, and eyeliner, but Fate was too engrossed in the atlas to notice.

"You got a pen?" he asked.

"No, but I'll get you one," she said, thrilled to have an excuse to return to the counter.

Fate ate the last of his fries, then absently began to eat Lutie's while he flipped through pages of maps.

When she slid back into the booth, she said, "His name's Jason and he's a senior."

"Where's the pen?"

"Here."

Fate grabbed a napkin and began writing while Lutie went back to work on her face.

"Okay," he said, "I've got this figured out. We're about nine hundred miles from Las Vegas. Now, you paid almost twenty dollars to fill up the car, so—"

"Do I care?" She shot a smile at the redhead.

"Listen. If the Pontiac gets twenty miles to the gallon and gas costs a dollar twenty-nine, then—"

"Fate, that sounds like one of those stupid questions they ask on stupid tests at school." In a singsong voice she said, "If a train is traveling eighty miles an hour from New York to Chicago and you have three apples that weigh ten ounces each, how many can you eat before you get to Miami?"

"If a train is going from New York to Chicago, it's not going to Miami."

"Whatever."

"Lutie, we've got about a hundred and fifty dollars. That's all. And we're gonna spend at least eighty of it on gas. If we eat six times, and stay in a motel—"

"Fate, sometimes you sound like an old man."

"What if we have car trouble? What if—"

26

"Uh-oh." Lutie feigned a sudden interest in her cold hamburger. "Don't turn around," she whispered.

"Why?"

"Because a highway patrolman just walked in."

"You think he's looking for us?"

"Shh."

Lutie watched as the patrolman walked to the counter and spoke to the redheaded Jason.

"There's probably a warrant out for our arrest," Fate said.

"Fate, this isn't television."

"Yeah, but it happens. That policeman at Wal-Mart, he probably wrote down the license tag number of Floy's car. They do that, you know, when someone acts suspicious."

"We didn't act suspicious."

"Well, maybe not at the Wal-Mart. But by now he most likely knows you lied, and when he found out you took Floy's car, he probably called the highway patrol so they'd be on the lookout."

When the patrolman headed for the toilets, Lutie said, "Come on. Let's get out of here."

She raked her cosmetics into her purse while Fate grabbed the last of their food, and they ran to the car.

"Hurry, Lutie. Take off before he gets out of the bathroom."

"Fate, we don't know that he's looking for us. He probably just stopped to get something to eat."

But the more she thought about it, the more she figured there might be some truth to what Fate said.

Lutie had planned to stay at a Holiday Inn, but encountering the law had convinced her they should get off the highway in case the police really were looking for them, so they ended up at a place called the Cozy Up Motel. But it was hardly cozy.

Their room, cramped and airless, was lit by a forty-watt bulb in the lamp between their beds, and a fluorescent light in the bathroom blinked and made a hissing sound. The sheets were pocked with cigarette burns, the tub held one dead roach and one live one, and the carpet was sticky and stained with something that looked a lot like blood.

The billboard on the highway claimed that the Cozy Up was "loaded with amenities," but the amenities seemed limited to running water and dingy towels.

Still, the room was cheap, and the manager, a hairy man wearing plaid pajamas, hadn't seemed at all curious about two kids checking in at two o'clock in the morning. He was in too big a hurry to get back to bed.

After Lutie took a shower, she wanted to watch TV, but all they could get was a rerun of *Matlock* and a documentary on the Civil War, so she turned off the set and they both went to bed.

Ten minutes later, they heard a car door slam and Fate got up to peek out the window.

"Who is it?" Lutie whispered.

"A man going into the room next door."

"You think he's a policeman?"

"No. Looks more like a serial killer. One of those guys who strangles girls and cuts up their bodies."

"Stop it!"

After Fate settled down again, they heard the toilet flush in the adjoining room.

"He's probably getting rid of body parts. Fingers and toes and—"

"Dammit, Fate. Don't you say another word."

For the next half hour they listened to sounds coming through the wall—drawers closing, a man coughing, water running.

When finally their neighbor grew quiet, Fate guessed that Lutie had gone to sleep, but when he turned on his side facing her bed, he could see her face in the dim light coming through the window. Her eyes were open, staring at the ceiling.

"Lutie?"

"What?"

"Can you remember what Mama looked like?"

"Sure."

"I wish I could."

"You've seen pictures of her."

"Yeah, but a picture's not the same thing. I mean, a picture just shows the way she looked when it was taken. That very second. Like the one of her standing beside the car holding me. She was smiling 'cause she knew Daddy was gonna take her picture.

"But that doesn't tell me what she looked like when she was cooking breakfast, or how she looked when she was sad. I don't know what she looked like when she cried or when she was asleep.

"And those pictures don't show if she was left-handed like me or how she sounded when she laughed or the way she walked. They're just pictures."

A silence settled on them then as a train passed somewhere nearby. Minutes later, after the sound had faded, Lutie said, "Sometimes I'm not sure if I remember Mama the way she looked in real life . . . or the way she looked in a dream I had when I was little."

"What dream?"

"I was locked in a house and she was outside, trying to get in. She was going through the pockets of her coat, but she couldn't find the key. I was watching her through a window, and when she realized I was there, she started talking to me, but I couldn't hear what she was saying.

"The wind was blowing her hair across her face. She looked at me and she was crying. When I woke up, I could still see her like that. Still do. But I don't know if that's the exact same way she looked in real life . . . or just in that dream."

"Why didn't you tell me that before, Lutie? Why didn't you tell me about that dream?"

"I don't know."

"I never dream about her. Maybe if I did, I could remember what she looked like."

"Fate, you were only three when she died. When you're three, you're too young to remember anything at all. So I guess you shouldn't feel bad."

They were quiet for several minutes until Fate said, "Lutie?" He waited but could tell from her breathing that she was asleep. "I just wanted to tell you that I'm glad you let me come with you."

When she made a weak, whimpering sound, he whispered, "Good night, sister."

CHAPTER FIVE

Lutie had never been a cheerful riser. In fact, she hated almost everything about waking up. Hated to open her eyes, hated the taste in her mouth, the tangles in her hair. She did not engage in conversation for the first hour of the day, would not tolerate being touched, and refused to be hurried.

No one except her mother had ever been able to ease her through morning without encountering her wrath. Her father had endured her tirades by steeling himself with bourbon, and Fate had learned that his best defense was to stay out of her line of fire. Floy's approach, though, was to counterattack. She warned, she yelled, she threatened.

But unlike the others, Lutie's mother, a soft-spoken, patient woman, had known exactly how to mollify a cranky, sleepy child. She woke her with songs, wrapped her in blankets warmed by the fire, prepared hot chocolate with precisely eight small marshmallows—the only correct number, according to her young daughter. She fixed Lutie's favorite breakfast of peanut-butter pancakes, prepared tepid baths sprinkled with sweet-smelling oils, and made sure the clothes Lutie wanted were freshly pressed and ready to slip into.

But the Cozy Up Motel offered little promise of easing anyone into the day.

Lutie had had a bad night of troubling dreams punctuated by the hacking cough of the serial killer in the next room. Then, at nine o'clock, a motel maid had knocked on the door, an intrusion to which Lutie had responded by yelling, "Fuck off!" as she'd burrowed beneath her covers for more sleep.

Fate, hoping to avoid one of his sister's attacks, got up and dressed quietly, then turned on the TV, but not the sound, and watched a silent show about growing grapes.

An hour later, he nudged the unmoving lump of his sister hidden under her bedding and said, "Lutie, we have to check out pretty soon."

"Fate, if you touch me again, I'll kill you."

She finally crawled out of bed just before eleven and, still half-asleep, stumbled to the bathroom, where she discovered that shampoo was another of the amenities with which the Cozy Up was not "loaded." Having no other option, she washed her hair with a tiny bar of soap that broke into splinters just as the hot water gave out.

She dried herself on a towel so thin that she could see through it, pulled on yesterday's jeans and T-shirt, then came storming out of the bathroom as though she were being chased.

"This place is a dump," she shouted.

"Are you about ready to go?" Fate asked.

"Tonight we're staying at a Holiday Inn and I don't care what it costs."

"Lutie, we've spent nearly twenty-five for food, thirty for this room, more than that for gas, another—"

"We've still got that can of quarters. That ought to be plenty."

"Thirty-nine dollars isn't plenty. And we've got another seven hundred miles to go."

She ran a brush through her hair, then examined the slivers of soap caught on the bristles.

"Look at this shit," she said.

"Lutie, we need to get on the road."

"Don't rush me! I'm going to do my hair and put on my makeup, and if it takes an hour, then it takes an hour."

Just then, a terrific bolt of lightning struck, followed immediately by a deafening clap of thunder, causing Lutie to fall back on her bed, clamp her hands to her ears, and begin screaming.

Fate moved fast, jumped on the bed beside her, and wrapped her in his arms, whispering, "It's going to be okay, Lutie. It's over now. All over."

Minutes later, after the quick storm burst had moved on, Lutie's body relaxed enough that she disentangled herself from Fate and sat up.

"See?" he said. "Now, aren't you glad you had me with you?"

Lutie shot him a "hurry up and die" look, then headed for the bathroom.

"Fear of thunder," Fate said.

"If you say 'tonitrophobia' again, I'm gonna leave your ass here."

"Well, that's what it's called."

"I know!" she screamed from the bathroom. "You've told me a hundred times. I can even spell it. Now, let it go."

When they finally pulled out of the Cozy Up parking lot at noon, it was raining, which didn't improve Lutie's mood. She was mad at her hair, stoplights, the stain on her jeans, and the headache that was starting to throb in her temples.

And for everything that was wrong, she blamed her brother.

As she drove through town, she pushed the Pontiac over the speed limit, and before she reached the interstate, she was driving seventy.

"Lutie, you're driving too fast."

"Hey. You're the one who's been in such a damn hurry. I'm just trying to keep you happy."

Fate watched the needle on the speedometer. "Did you know that fifty-seven percent of all highway fatalities are caused by excessive speed?"

"That's the kind of crap you say to impress everyone, isn't it? That's why they put you in those weird classes."

"They're called accelerated studies."

"Oh, my! And everyone is so impressed with my brainy little brother. The nerd." Lutie made a look of disgust. "Sometimes I get sick of hearing about how smart you are."

"Well, sometimes I get sick of hearing about you."

"What do you hear about me?"

"That you're always in trouble at school."

"Sure I get in trouble. If you're not in trouble, you're not having fun."

"And I heard about you having sex with Tommy Holloway."

"Who told you that?" Lutie asked, her anger shifting into fury.

"Just some kids at school."

"Did they also tell you that I snorted cocaine, got drunk, danced naked at a party in Tommy Holloway's basement while his folks were out of town? And that I went down on both Tommy and his brother?"

"No." Fate looked stunned. "Did you?"

"I wasn't even invited to the party, but that's the lie Margie Holcomb and her crowd told all over school. That's why I got kicked off the gymnastics squad."

"I thought you quit because the school nurse said you'd damaged your rotator cuff."

"That's what I told Floy. If she'd heard the lie, she'd probably have believed it. Besides, I wouldn't have sex of *any* kind with Tommy Holloway or his brother or anyone else in that school."

"Then why did you hide condoms in your dresser drawer?"

"You crap-head! You snooped in my room!"

"Lutie, it's a fact that fifty-three percent of all eleventh graders have had sex at least once."

"You know what? I think you just make stuff up. Just say the first thing that pops into your pea-size brain so everyone will say how smart you are."

"I didn't make it up." He twisted around, leaned across his seat, and grabbed *The Book of Facts*. "I'll prove it."

"You're not gonna prove anything."

Fate flipped pages until he found what he was looking for. "Here it is!" He held the book so Lutie could see.

"I told you to knock it off."

"Look at it," he said, pointing to the lines.

Suddenly Lutie grabbed the book from his hands, then rolled down her window.

"Don't do it, Lutie. You throw that out and—"

"And what? Just what'll you do, smartass?"

Fate knew better than to go for the book, so in a defensive move, he grabbed her teddy bear from the dash and rolled his window down, too.

"Don't even think about it, Fate."

"Okay, you hand me the book and I'll give you your dumb bear."

Fate, more trusting than his sister, tentatively offered the bear. Just when he thought she was going to trade, she grabbed for the bear and then chucked the book out her window. But she was too late. Mr. PawPaw went flying.

"You shit! You little shit!" She slammed on the brakes and pulled onto the shoulder. "I'm going to kill you."

When the car stopped, they both jumped out and ran back down the highway. Fate found his book at the edge of a bar ditch, pages fluttering in the wind. Lutie retrieved her bear from a puddle in the middle of the road.

Both stomped back to the car, each trying to outdistance the other. When Lutie broke into a run, so did Fate, because he knew if she beat him, she'd drive away, leaving him behind.

When Lutie got in, she put the bedraggled Mr. PawPaw in her lap while Fate tried to smooth the wet and wrinkled pages of his book.

Barely able to control her rage, Lutie zipped back into the traffic and they rode in silence for the next half hour, both sullen, each wanting to hurt the other.

Lutie was stuck behind a slow-moving pickup when she spotted a man standing beside the highway gesturing for a ride. The late-model car parked on the shoulder behind him was missing its left rear tire.

When she slowed the Pontiac and pulled onto the shoulder fifty yards in front of the disabled car, Fate began to shake his head.

"No, Lutie. Don't do this!"

"What's wrong, little boy?" she taunted. "You scared?"

"You know this is stupid," he said, but by then she'd brought the Pontiac to a stop and the man, carrying a metal toolbox, was trotting toward them.

He was tall and powerfully built, his frame too large for the cheap leather jacket straining across his chest. He had a shock of curly black hair, and even though it was raining, he was wearing sunglasses.

When he reached the car, Lutie rolled down her window and smiled. "Looks like you've got a problem."

"Yeah. How about a ride?"

Without waiting for a response, he opened the door and slid into the passenger seat behind her.

"My name's Michael," he said as he took off the shades and caught Lutie studying him in her rearview mirror.

He was in his late thirties, years older than she'd first thought. And there was something about his eyes that made her uncomfortable.

"I'm Lutie," she said as she pulled back onto the highway.

"And who are you?" He jabbed a finger into the back of Fate's head. "You her boyfriend?"

Fate didn't answer, didn't turn, just sat rigidly facing front.

"My brother," Lutie said.

"Where you two going?" he asked.

"Las Vegas."

"Hey, what a break. That's where I'm headed. I'll ride along with you."

"What about your car?"

"Hell, that's not mine, I wouldn't be caught dead in a junker like that, I drive a Jag, so does Jodie Foster, I used to go out with her, did you see *Silence of the Lambs*, man, I loved that dude who skinned those girls alive." He spoke in machine-gun bursts, his words ricocheting from one thought to another. "See, there's some things you gotta know about hitching, little tricks like keepin' your shirttail tucked in your pants, let your shoulders droop like you're not expectin' anyone to stop for your ass, better luck when it's raining, or finding yourself a stalled car, broke down or wrecked, it don't matter, then you stand beside it and look real pitiful, you want me to drive?"

"No, uh . . ."

"Why, you think I'd crash this tanker into a slab of concrete,

37

throw you through the windshield, cut off your head, hell, I used to drive race cars, beat Richard Petty out down in Florida in '96, felt kind of bad about takin' the title away from him 'cause Rich's one of my best buds, but he can't win 'em all, that's the way I look at it , so I—"

"What race was that?" Fate asked. "The one in Florida?"

"Ain't but one race that counts down there, the Daytona."

Out of the corner of her eye, Lutie saw Fate begin to flip pages in his fact book.

"I got out of the racing game after I smashed up on the eighth lap of the Indy, lost a kidney, ruptured spleen, both lungs punctured, broken back, right leg snapped in two at the knee, they said I'd never walk again, they kept pumpin' blood into me, stopped breathing twice during surgery, let me tell you, once you look death in the face, nothin's ever the same again 'cause—"

"The '96 Daytona 500 was won by Dale Jarrett," Fate said. "You told us your name's Michael."

"Like you know what the fuck you're talking about," Michael said, raising his voice in anger. "I have the goddamned trophy and they don't hand those out to losers."

"Then why isn't your name here?" Fate held up his book.

"What the hell is that?"

"It's called a book."

Suddenly furious, Michael pushed himself to the edge of the seat and yelled into Fate's ear. "You're a smartass kid, ain't you, one of those faggy little nerds who—"

Lutie said, "He's just—"

"And why's a split-tail like you draggin' her faggy little brother along with her to Vegas, huh?"

When Lutie didn't respond, Michael poked her in the shoulder with his index finger. "Huh, why is that?"

"Our dad works in one of the casinos," she said.

And as quickly as his anger had ignited, it burned itself out. "They won't let me gamble in Vegas anymore," he said as he settled back in his seat. "Caught me counting cards at the Golden Nugget few years back, now I even get close to a casino, they call out security, but that don't bother me none 'cause I got other reasons to be there now, important reasons."

When neither Lutie nor Fate asked about his "reasons," he answered the question he had anticipated. "I'm meeting Céline Dion, Wayne Newton, couple other clients of mine."

Still no response from the front seat.

"I design jewelry for celebrities, Princess Diana loved my work, I had supper with her the day before she got killed, she was a sweetheart, recommended my work to some of the big-wigs in London—Boy George, Ringo, what's her name—the Mary Poppins gal."

Lutie and Fate exchanged a glance, but Michael didn't notice as he fiddled with the lock on the toolbox he balanced on his lap. When he finally opened the box, he was careful to shield the contents in case Fate got curious and turned to see what was inside.

"Now my designs are everywhere, keeps me so busy I don't have as much time as I need in my studio, the average person like you two has got no idea of what creative energy is." He leaned across the front seat and dangled a cheap gold chain in Lutie's face. "Made this for Donald Trump's fiancée, he wanted something simple, you like it?"

Before she could say anything, he draped the chain around her neck.

"Feels good, don't it, nothin' like the feel of gold against your skin, huh?"

"Yeah, it's . . . nice."

"Nice? What do you mean, nice?" he snarled, beginning to lose control again. "I don't make 'nice' jewelry, you can buy

39

'nice' in Wal-Mart." He pulled the chain tighter. "This is quality, twenty-four karat, unique design."

"Yes. It's . . . fabulous," Lutie said as he twisted the last bit of slack from the chain.

"You goddamn right it's fabulous, I was gonna give it to you, but you don't deserve it."

He gave the chain one hard jerk, causing it to bite into Lutie's flesh, then yanked it off and tossed it back into the toolbox.

Lutie rubbed at her throat where a fiery red welt began to rise.

"You all hungry?" Michael asked while he rummaged in the toolbox. "Huh, you want something to eat?"

"Yeah," Lutie said. "Why don't we stop for a pizza?"

"No!" Michael leaned forward again, holding a bruised apple in one hand . . . and in the other, a kitchen knife with a six-inch blade. "An apple a day keeps the doctor away."

"I just thought . . . well, we might find a Domino's or Pizza Hut."

"That's a lie. What you thought was that you'd run off and leave me at some shitty fast-food joint."

He leaned close to Lutie, his face two inches from her ear as he tapped the knife blade on her shoulder. "But that ain't gonna happen, is it?"

Lutie shook her head.

"So, let's share this apple."

He cut off a slice and handed it to Lutie, then offered one to Fate.

"I don't want any," Fate said.

"What, you think it's poisoned, that what you think? Hey, let me tell you something, if I kill you, it won't be with poison." He threw the apple on the floor, then put the tip of the knife to Fate's ear. "I'll do it with this."

Fate tried to lean away from the knife, but Michael grabbed a handful of his hair.

"But you know what you need more than killing? A haircut." Then, with a vicious swipe, Michael chopped off a hunk of Fate's hair.

"Stop it!" Lutie screamed.

Laughing, Michael slumped back in his seat.

Lutie's hands were shaking so badly, she could hardly hold on to the wheel. Moments later, when she looked in the mirror, Michael was grinning at her.

"When we drive out of this rain, we'll pull off on one of these county roads and get out and take ourselves a little walk, that's what we need, some exercise and fresh air, we'll all feel . . . Hey! Why are you slowing down?"

He sat up then and saw what Lutie and Fate saw. Traffic up ahead was slowing, and as the Pontiac crested a hill, they could see a long line of stopped vehicles and the flashing lights of police cars and ambulances.

"What the hell is going on?" Michael said.

In a single-line lane, ten, fifteen vehicles ahead of them, policemen were walking from one car to the next, speaking to drivers, working their way toward the Pontiac.

Then Michael went into motion. He slammed the lid of the toolbox and was halfway out the door before he said, "You say anything about me to that cop, they come after me, I'll tell them you're a couple of runaways in a stolen car." He ran across the median, darted across the road and down the steep slope of a culvert, then disappeared into scrub brush on the other side.

Lutie and Fate sat in stunned silence as the policeman made his way to their car.

"This traffic's not gonna be going anywhere for another hour, maybe longer. Follow the car in front of you, drive slow along the shoulder, and we'll have you out of here soon as we can."

Lutie said, "Thank you," but the policeman had already moved on.

"You okay?" she asked Fate, who was looking into the backseat.

"Yeah. But our quarters are gone."

Lutie pulled into the rest stop shortly after midnight and parked in a row taken up mostly by eighteen-wheelers and RVs. She wasn't happy about spending the night in the car, but she'd busted Floy's last twenty-dollar bill to pay for gas, and they still had hundreds of miles to cover.

Fate had hardly spoken since he'd discovered the hitchhiker had stolen their quarters. Lutie didn't know if he was mad about the money, his muddy book, or the nearly bald spot at the top of his head. And she didn't ask.

She found two afghans in the trunk of the car, products of one of Floy's yard sale runs. Fate had covered himself with one in the backseat, and Lutie had used the other to pad the console that divided the bucket seats in the front, but she could still feel the edges of it digging into her back as she fought to find a comfortable position.

Fate had started snoring only minutes after he settled, but she could do no more than reach the edge of sleep before she would be pulled back by the rumble of a big rig pulling in, or the sound of the wind rattling the pines that ringed the parking lot, or the smell of onions that came from the crushed McDonald's carton in the floorboard of the car.

Down to their last few dollars, she and Fate had shared a hot dog, the only meal they'd had all day, and her stomach was feeling the pinch.

But it was more than noise and hunger keeping her awake.

She knew, of course, that the chance of Michael showing up was next to nothing. She imagined that he was still in Wyoming, more than three hundred miles away. Still, she feared that if she looked in her rearview mirror, she would see his eyes staring back at her, like some scene from a slasher movie.

CHAPTER SIX

LUTIE WOKE UP near dawn when something thumped against the side of the car. She thought at first she had imagined the sound, but then she heard voices.

She raised herself to one elbow and peeked cautiously through the windshield to see a burly woman with magenta hair sitting on the front bumper, a bald man wedged between her fleshy thighs.

While the man worked his hands beneath the woman's short denim skirt, she unbuttoned her blouse and pulled it open, exposing one heavy, drooping breast. As the man bent and fastened his lips to her nipple, she laughed and, turning her head, caught Lutie staring. Then, looking right into the girl's eyes, she winked, as though she were sharing a joke.

Ducking down quickly, Lutie flattened herself against the seat, ignoring the console punishing her back as the car began to rock. A regular rhythm at first, then faster and faster, until, finally, the man made a sound like an animal yelping in pain.

Moments later, the woman slid off the car and Lutie listened

44

as footsteps and voices faded in the distance. Still, she waited, not daring to move until she heard the engine of an eighteen-wheeler start up, and when it rumbled past, she sat up in time to see the bald man behind the wheel.

She needed to go to the bathroom but put it off until her bladder just wouldn't wait any longer. She got out of the car as quietly as possible and crossed the grassy strip to the public toilet. It was empty when she entered, but minutes later when she came out of her stall, the woman with magenta hair was at the sink washing her hands.

She glanced at Lutie in the mirror. "Cheap bastard stiffed me out of five bucks," she said. "Take my advice, honey. Always get your money up front." Then she wheeled and walked out.

When Lutie got back to the car, Fate was still asleep, but when she fired up the Pontiac, he roused and sat up.

"Thought we'd get an early start," she said.

Fate only shrugged.

An hour later, Lutie stopped at a Get-N-Go, where she pumped exactly five gallons of gas into the near empty tank of the Pontiac. Inside, she picked up two cartons of chocolate milk and a package of powdered doughnuts. She had to pay for the milk because the cartons were too large to conceal in her purse, but the doughnuts fit just fine.

She left the station with sixty-two cents and a plan to ration the breakfast, but her plan evaporated five minutes later, and so did the milk and doughnuts.

Fate had stuck with the silent treatment all morning, but after he checked the map and did the math, he said, "We're not going to make it," the longest string of words he'd put together in the past fourteen hours.

"Sure we are," Lutie said.

"Look. We're getting right around twenty-two miles to the

gallon, so five gallons will take us approximately a hundred and ten miles. And as near as I can figure, we're two hundred miles from Las Vegas. No way we can make it."

"Fate, why do you always look on the dark side of everything?"

"I'm just telling you."

"Well, if we need more gas, we'll get it."

"How?"

"Haven't figured that out yet. But I'll take care of it."

And she did.

Just before they crossed the Nevada line, with the car running on little more than encouragement, Lutie pulled into an Amoco station in Enterprise, Utah, and pumped ten dollars' worth of gas.

At the counter inside the station, she put on a very convincing show of having lost the twenty-dollar bill with which she intended to pay. With her voice trembling and tears streaming, she went through her pockets and purse again and again, each time coming up empty. Then, breaking into sobs, she offered to sweep up, take out trash, and clean the toilet—work she had no intention of doing, work she'd never done before.

The clerk, a tiny gray-haired woman wearing a hearing aid, was so moved by the performance that she gave Lutie a sixteen-ounce bottle of Coke and the gentle admonition to be careful with her money.

"Great," Fate said as Lutie returned to the car, where he had witnessed her little drama. "You're a car thief, an unlicensed driver, a shoplifter. You've lied to the police, and now you're a con artist."

"You do what you have to do, Fate." She twisted the cap off the plastic Coke bottle. "That's what Floy always said."

"Yeah. And you always took Floy's advice, didn't you?"

"No. But I think it's time to start."

46

*   *   *

"Look, Lutie." Fate pointed first to one side of the street, then the other. All the tension and misgivings he'd been feeling for the past three days were dulled by the glitz of the Las Vegas Strip. "A pyramid! Did you see that?"

Lutie braked suddenly for two girls crossing against the traffic in the middle of the block. Then she got squeezed out of her lane by a taxi that almost clipped her fender as it zipped in front of her.

But she was too excited to feel nervous. She had brought them all the way from Spearfish, South Dakota, to this place that was more than she had ever imagined. Flashing neon. Blue waterfalls. Golden gods. Buildings taller than any she'd ever seen. Marquees with the names of stars she'd watched for years. And people—hundreds and hundreds of people jamming the sidewalks. Women carrying bags from Gucci and Prada, men wearing silk shirts, their arms encircling the waists of exotic beauties. College boys drinking from bottles of beer, girls strutting in short leather skirts and flashy heels.

She had arrived in the real world, the world she'd been waiting for.

It didn't matter then that she and her brother were hungry and broke. Didn't matter that they hadn't bathed in days or that they'd had nothing to call home but an old Pontiac. They had made it to Las Vegas, the most glamorous place on earth, the place where her life would finally begin.

"The Eiffel Tower!"

"That's Paris. I saw pictures of it in a magazine."

"Maybe that's where Daddy works. We could go in there and find out."

"Fate, look at all these casinos. It's stupid to think we can guess which one he works at."

"Well, I thought—"

"You just want to go up the Eiffel Tower."

"But—"

"We're going to Daddy's apartment first. If he's at work, we'll find out where."

"And let's go in and just walk right up and wait till he sees us. He'll be surprised, won't he?"

"Get that letter out for me."

Fate dug out the letter from the glove compartment and handed it to her. She glanced at the address, then at the next red light, she rolled down her window and yelled to the driver of a UPS truck pulled up beside her.

"Hey, can you tell me how to get to 105 Bonneville?"

"Yeah. Hang a right at the next corner. Keep going for seven or eight blocks. That'll put you at Sixth and Bonneville."

Lutie didn't have any trouble following his directions, but when she turned down Bonneville, she felt as though she'd made a mistake.

The street was a hodgepodge of pawnshops, shabby hotels, liquor stores, casinos, and bars.

"You think we're on the right street?" Fate asked.

"I guess."

"There's 105." Fate pointed to a narrow two-story building with a sign that said Hotel Nevada.

Lutie found a parking place in the next block, where she discovered that parallel parking wasn't her strong suit.

They stayed close together as they walked toward the hotel, sidestepping broken glass, fresh vomit, crushed beer cans.

They passed a man sleeping in the doorway of a boarded-up storefront, another drinking wine at the entrance to an alley. A little girl sitting on the curb in front of a bar watched them warily as they approached, then turned her attention back to a dead rat on a manhole cover.

They were only a few feet from the hotel when an old woman

wearing a bathrobe asked them for change, and across the street they saw two teenage boys waving at them and yelling, "Gotcha crack right here."

The hotel smelled of urine and cigarettes. The dim lobby was not brightened by potted plants filled with faded plastic flowers or dirty, mismatched torn chairs. An elderly man, sleeping on a couch, snored softly, a cigar butt resting in his opened palm.

"What can I do for you kids?"

The voice came from a man behind a registration desk where steel bars ran from the counter to the ceiling.

"We're here to see our daddy," Lutie said.

"Sure you are. A big family reunion, right?"

"No, we—"

"Rooms are ten bucks an hour. Cash before you get the key."

"Why would we want a room for an hour?" Fate asked.

"Here's what I figure, kid. You're too young to be her pimp or her john, so you two are figuring to find you a quiet place to shoot up. Those are the two most popular reasons to book a room at the quaint Hotel Nevada."

"Our daddy lives here."

"Sure he does."

"His name's McFee. Jim McFee."

"No, he ain't here."

"We've got to find him."

"Now, look. If you're snooping around for his stuff, forget it. He didn't leave nothing behind but a pile of dirty laundry and a busted hot plate. We got rules against cooking in the rooms."

"You mean he left?"

"You might say that."

"Can you tell us where we can find him?"

"Carson's what I heard."

"Is that a street?"

"Hell, no. It's a prison."

"What? What do you mean?"

"Prison, kid. Carson City Prison. Your old man's in the joint."

CHAPTER SEVEN

LUTIE AND FATE had nothing to say after they left the Hotel Nevada and started back to the car. They didn't even trade looks but kept their eyes on the sidewalk as if they might discover a message written there for them. Something like "Hi, kids. I love you, Daddy." Or maybe a phone number for them to call, the number of one of their father's women, somebody who might look out for them. Perhaps they'd find a secret code painted on a curb, a code unfathomable to everyone but Fate.

For some strange reason, Lutie remembered her daddy smoothing a freshly poured cement walkway to the back door of a house where they'd lived before her mother died. He'd had Lutie place her small hand in the mushy substance, then used his finger to write her name and the date. The memory was so vivid that for a moment she could recall the odor of the cement, could see every detail of her toddler-size handprint.

She started to tell Fate what she remembered but decided to keep it to herself. After all, she wasn't even sure that what she recalled was the actual memory or just the memory of an old photo her mother might have snapped. Either way, though, she found herself blinking back unexpected tears.

Finally, Fate broke the silence overpowering them since they'd heard the news about their father.

"Well, Lutie," he said, "what're we going to do now?"

"I wondered how long it would take for you to start in on me. Thought you might be able to hold off till we got to the car, but once again, I was wrong."

"What do you mean? Start in on you for what?"

"Go ahead. Say it. 'I told you so, Lutie,'" she said, trying for the whiny voice of a complaining child. "'Told you the letter from Floy came back, told you he didn't have a phone. Said we couldn't find him.' So go on, Fate, blame this on me just like I knew you would."

"No, Lutie, that's not what I meant. Coming here wasn't . . . well, it just didn't work out the way we hoped. So now we have to come up with a different plan. That's all. Really. I was only asking if you had an idea about what we should do."

"*We?*" She came to a sudden stop. "We, as in Batman and Robin? That kind of *we?* Oh, no, I don't know what *we* oughta do, but I'll tell you what *I'm* gonna do."

"What?"

"Leave your skinny ass right here, right on this street, right now. See how you'd make it without me, without no money. Nothing but a pile of stupid books containing nothing of value to no one in this whole damn city . . . except for maybe that guy across the street."

"That man in the alley? Why would he—"

"Who knows? He might have been the Trivial Pursuit champion of Nevada. Or maybe the Scrabble champion of the whole fucking world. But then the poor bastard stopped winning. Couldn't remember more than two words that started with *q*. So he—"

"I suppose you mean words beginning with *q* but not followed by *u*. See, those are the ones that trip players up."

Lutie continued, her anger made even more intense by Fate's ill-timed interjection. "So the pitiful old son of a bitch turns into a drunk eating out of Dumpsters, sleeping with alley rats.

"Then along comes Fate McFee, his brain bursting with words that start with *q* . . . but *not* followed by *u*. Now Fate gets some coffee down his new buddy's belly, wipes the vomit off his pants, gets him a clean shirt from Goodwill, and enters him in the Tournament of Scrabble Champions. And guess what? He wins! Gets a silver tray with his initials engraved on it and a check for a million dollars, which he splits with his bright young coach, McFee the Wonder Boy."

Fate waited to be sure his sister's rant had ended, then said, "Did you know rats can have sex twenty times a day, Lutie?"

After an interval of several moments of silence, Lutie said, "No, Fate," her voice flat, seemingly drained of hostility. "I didn't know that."

"Yes. They can multiply so fast that one pair of rats can have more than fifteen thousand descendants in a year."

Finally, Lutie shook her head—in either amazement at such a dramatic piece of information or at the bewilderment of her brother's total disconnect with reality.

The temperature inside the Pontiac was high and getting higher, but they slid in anyway, easing themselves onto the hot plastic seat covers with slow, deliberate movements.

"Maybe that guy at the hotel lied to us, Lutie," Fate said. "He didn't like Daddy, at least that's the way it seemed to me, so might be he just made up that story. About prison, I mean."

"Why would he do that?"

"Daddy might have left, moved out in the middle of the night without paying his bill. Or he could have gotten kicked out because he broke some hotel rule."

"I don't think hotels like that one have rules."

"Hey, what about this? We could call that prison in Carson City," Fate said with fresh enthusiasm, "ask them if Jim McFee's an inmate there. If he is, tell him the mess we're in here, see if he'll send us some money."

"I don't even know where Carson City is, Fate."

"And here's another thing. Maybe Daddy's not in for a great big crime, say like armed robbery or kidnapping . . . or murder." Fate's face suddenly drained of color. "You don't think they've electrocuted him, do you?"

"Hell, no! How do you come up with this shit, huh?"

"Listen, Lutie. When George Bush was governor of Texas, more prisoners were executed than—"

"Fate, Daddy is *not* a killer."

"No, he's not. I know that. He was probably just arrested for something minor, like stealing a pair of underwear, or—"

"Underwear! Why would he steal underwear?"

"Maybe he ran out of clean ones, didn't have money for the Laundromat, so—"

"For God's sake, Fate. They don't put people in prison for stealing underwear."

"Okay. Maybe he got in a fight. Remember, he did that before. Got in a bar fight, broke some guy's jaw, busted up the place. Floy couldn't get him out of jail for thirty days. Even then, it cost her five hundred dollars."

"That was jail. Not prison."

"What about this, then? What if he robbed a bank and hid the money before he got caught? What if he has five thousand . . . no, twenty-five thousand dollars buried somewhere here in Las Vegas? He could tell us where it is and we could dig it up, take it to the police, and get him out so he could take care of us."

"Fate, how can you be so clueless? You spend all your time learning facts, but you don't know anything about the world, how things work."

"Why don't you try, Lutie? What've we got to lose? Call Carson City, tell them if Daddy's there, you need to talk to him."

"Listen to me. You can't just call a prison, tell them to put your daddy on the phone."

Fate, exasperated and in a pout now, said, "Well, you got any brilliant ideas? You have any notion at all of what we're going to do?"

Lutie stared quietly out the window of the car, where she saw for the first time a parking ticket stuck beneath the windshield wiper. Finally, she said, "Yeah. Come on."

Following rigid instructions, Fate was letting Lutie do the talking when they returned to the Hotel Nevada.

"Look," the desk clerk said, "when the law came lookin' for him, they didn't stop to discuss their reasons with me. Besides, wasn't none of my business why he got busted, best to keep my nose out of it. Me and the police don't see each other socially, if you follow my drift. But if you kids got nothin' to hide, you could go down to central booking, ask around."

"No," Lutie said, "we can't do that."

The clerk grinned, exposing teeth stained brown as wormwood. "That's what I thought."

"Do you know where he worked while he stayed here? We know he had a job at a casino, but we don't know which one."

"Girlie, every asshole in Vegas has worked in a casino. Besides, that kind of information is private. I can't go givin' out personal intelligence on my guests. I have to operate on something like the client-lawyer privilege."

"But you're not a lawyer, and he's not a guest . . . not anymore."

"You're beginnin' to try my patience, sweetheart, so why don't you and your little mime move on and leave me the hell alone."

"Okay," Lutie said, "here's the truth. We're in trouble."

"Well, surprise, surprise."

"And we've got to find our dad, quick. So if you'll just give us the name of the place where he worked . . ."

"What's in it for me?"

"We don't have any money. That's why we're in trouble."

"You don't necessarily have to give me money."

"Then . . . what?"

"How about a half hour in my back office?"

"You mean for sex?"

"Whatever. You get what you want, I get what I want, we all walk away happy."

Fate, in a deep, measured tone that he hoped belied his age, said, "You know how old she is? My sister? How old you guess she is?"

"You think I really care?"

"She's twelve," he said, a comment that caused Lutie to do a double take of her brother. "You just offered to trade information for sex with a twelve-year-old girl. I believe that defines you as a child predator."

"So what're you gonna do? Go to the police now? All of a sudden, you're ready to walk into a station and—"

"How do you know we aren't here *because* of the police? How do you know this isn't a setup, that we're not wearing a wire? That the police aren't going to bust in here in thirty seconds and have you spread-eagled on the floor?"

"Kid, you watch too much television. Right?"

"And you're a registered sex offender. Right?"

*　　*　　*

Lutie's first pleasant experience of the day came in Harrah's where she discovered that minors were allowed inside the casino as long as they stayed on the nongaming walkway. So after getting directions to the office she was looking for, she made Fate come with her, then stationed him outside the office door, demanding that he wait there despite her having to pull him past a crap table, which seemed to fascinate him.

Lutie's second surprise came from a statuesque black woman named Nechia, according to her badge, who listened sympathetically to her story and agreed to help.

At her computer, Nechia determined within minutes that Jim McFee had indeed worked there as a janitor until more than a year ago, until mid-November, when he had been terminated. The document she pulled up provided a grainy black-and-white photograph of an unsmiling, unyielding man. And though the photo looked more like a mug shot than a personnel ID, Lutie smiled and said, "Yeah, that's my daddy," then reached out and touched his face on the screen.

The picture helped Nechia recall him vaguely only because he'd been taken off the floor in handcuffs following a police chase through the quarter slots; then, as he was led away, he'd let loose with a stream of obscenities that could be heard above the usual din of the place.

The scuttlebutt that circulated around the casino was that he'd been arrested for armed robbery at a liquor store. Sometime later, Nechia heard from one of the other janitors that McFee had ended up in the Nevada State Prison in Carson City. But that was a rumor that never took off, because by then nobody remembered the janitor who'd been arrested, and nobody there really cared to know where he was.

But Nechia knew someone who could find out.

Her brother-in-law, Foster, worked in the records department of a prison just outside Vegas. Ely State. And since both were state prisons, she bet Foster could find out more about Jim McFee. Nechia said she'd give him a call at home that night. Then she asked Lutie to come back late the next afternoon, sometime between five and six. She said she'd share whatever she learned . . . if anything.

Lutie was in such a good mood when she left the office that she wasn't even mad when she discovered that Fate had disappeared. She found him a few minutes later at the crap table where she'd almost lost him earlier. He was standing between a middle-aged woman screaming, "Come seven!" and a man blowing on a pair of dice just before he flung them the length of the table, where they landed to cheers and complaints from the crowd gathered there.

"Come on, Fate."

"Lutie, watch this. See the man with that stick? Well—"

"Fate! We've got to stay on the path for kids or—"

"It's called the nongaming walkway."

"Right. Now come on! I've got to come back here tomorrow, but if we get kicked out—"

"Lutie, did you know that on six-sided dice, the opposite sides always add up to seven?"

Once they were back on the walkway, headed toward the exit, Lutie said, "Guess what? That jerk at the Hotel Nevada told us the truth. I think you scared him with that business about him being a perv. That's why he told us about this place."

"So Daddy really did work here? Did you find out where he is? Did you ask if—"

"A woman's gonna try to help us, Fate, but she might not know anything for a day or two."

As they passed a snack bar, Fate said, "Lutie, I'm starving. How much money do we have left?"

"Not enough."

"I thought we might buy a hamburger. We could split it and—"

"We're not in Spearfish anymore, Toto. Look up there." She pointed to a menu posted over the grill. "Cheeseburger," she read. "Nine ninety-five."

"Wow. You think we've got enough to buy a bag of chips?"

"We'd still be hungry."

"Then . . ."

"We'll find a way. Let's go."

In the next block, Lutie led Fate up a winding staircase and into the Monte Carlo. "Now, stay behind me and keep quiet or we'll both starve."

At the first restaurant they came to, a place called the Garden Café, they stepped to the back of a line of people waiting to be seated. Lutie shot Fate a warning glance when they reached the front, where a hostess said, "Two for dinner?"

"Three, actually," Lutie said. "Our grandmother's playing poker, but she'll join us in a minute."

Lutie and Fate followed the hostess to a booth and took the menus she offered. "Your waitress will be with you soon."

Fate studied his menu for several minutes, then peeked over the top and whispered, "What can I have, Lutie?"

"Whatever you want. All you want. This might have to do us for a while."

"Hi, I'm Gail. I'll be your server today," the waitress said. "I understand there'll be three at your table. Would you like to wait until the other member of your party arrives before you order?"

"No, our grandmother told us what she wanted, so I guess we're ready." She cut her eyes at Fate. "Isn't that right, little brother?"

"I'll have the fried-chicken dinner," he said, "mashed potatoes and gravy, corn on the cob, a side order of green beans, and Texas toast. Three slices, please. Also, a piece . . . no, two pieces of chocolate pie."

"My," Gail said, "you've got a big appetite, don't you?"

"Boys," Lutie said with distaste in her voice. "They eat like pigs, don't they?" Then, without waiting for a comment, she ordered the same meal Fate had. "And our grandmother wants two supreme pizzas."

"Two? They're rather large."

"So's our grandmother. And Cokes. We'll all have Cokes."

"Okay. I'll get that turned in and have your drinks out in a jiffy," Gail said.

As soon as she left the table, Fate whispered, "You think she suspects anything? We ordered a lot of food. And why'd you make that stuff up about our 'grandmother'?"

"Fate, I told you to keep your mouth shut."

"But—"

"If you give this away, get us caught, we're probably gonna go to jail."

Lutie didn't have to repeat herself. The word *jail* made Fate shrink back into his side of the booth, his lips pressed together as if they were glued.

When Gail brought the tray containing their food and began to load dishes onto their table, she said, "Your grandmother's not here yet?"

"Oh, she came by," Lutie said. "Seems like she's having a run of good luck right now. Guess she'll eat later."

"Sure. If she's winning, she won't care if her pizza gets cold."

"No, she's funny that way. I think she'd rather win than eat."

"Okay. You kids need anything else, give me a wave."

"Thanks."

Fate dug into his food like a hungry hound. Before Lutie had finished with the salt and pepper, unwrapped her straw, and buttered her corn, Fate had eaten his fried chicken and most of his potatoes.

"Slow down, Fate. We don't have to hurry."

"I think we should eat fast and get out of here . . . if we can. But this sure is good," he said, his upper lip sporting a mustache of milk gravy. "What're we going to do with our 'grandmother's' pizza?" he asked.

"Why, we'll put it in a to-go box and take it to her."

"Good idea. She'll be hungry."

By the time Fate finished the last piece of chocolate pie, Lutie was coasting to a stop. "Now, here comes the waitress. Don't act surprised by anything I say."

"So, she never made it, huh? Your grandmother."

"No, but we'll take her pizza to her in a to-go box. She'll eat it later in our room."

"Oh, you're staying here in the hotel."

"Right."

"So will you be signing your check to your room, or—"

"To the room."

"All right. I'll be back with your ticket, a takeout box—"

"And another piece of chocolate pie," Fate said. "For my grandmother."

"Okay."

"Now, listen," Lutie said. "When she packs up the food, you take it and leave."

Fate began to fidget, looked stricken.

"Fate, goddammit, don't panic. You're gonna be fine. Leave the casino fast, but don't run. And try not to look like you've just committed murder. Understand?"

Fate nodded.

"Go the way we came in and meet me at the car."

"The car," he said, his courage wavering, his voice sound-

ing far less confident than when he'd ordered pie for his
"grandmother."

"You think you can find it?" Lutie asked.

"What?"

"The car, you idiot. The car."

"Yes."

Moments later, with his arms cradling Styrofoam boxes, Fate
strode toward the exit, making sure to stay on the nongaming
walkway and following Lutie's instructions exactly, although,
unaware of his own demeanor, he did move as if he'd just cut
someone's throat.

Lutie moved the Pontiac a little before midnight, surprised
it hadn't been towed despite new parking tickets papering the
windshield . . . and relieved the interior had cooled down to a
temperature that might not cook them in their sleep.

Because the gas gauge registered below empty, she couldn't
chance driving far, but as it turned out, she didn't have to. A few
blocks away, Fate spied a fenced construction site that, according
to what he could see as they circled the area twice, looked to be
unguarded.

He'd unlatched the gate without much trouble, then scouted
the grounds, creeping from spot to spot in the dark, peering
around corners of an unfinished building already stretching some
dozens of stories into the air, little more than a skeleton now of
what it would become.

He checked out the heavy equipment—one very large crane
and two smaller ones; motor-driven scissor lifts; several tractors
and backhoes; flatbed trailers loaded with steel beams, pipes,
concrete blocks; and two pickups, either of which could have a
night watchman sitting inside, but neither did. Good sign or
bad? Good if one watchman had walked off the job and a new one
hadn't been hired yet. Bad if the guy had slipped out to check

the perimeter or to visit a nearby bar, tossing back a few as Fate's father had done, causing him to be fired as regularly as a Friday paycheck.

Fate knew something about a construction site because his father had taken him to one just before he left Floy and the kids. Jim McFee, always a big talker who pretended to know more about everything than he actually knew, showed his boy the equipment and how it was used, throwing in a story here and there of some incident that made him seem, if not brave, at least important.

A few days later, a Friday payday, he was gone, headed to Las Vegas to make the fortune he felt awaited him there.

Finally, when Fate had completed his preliminary inspection, he motioned Lutie to pull in but warned her to keep the car lights off.

After he rewired the gate, he guided Lutie to a spot between the ground floor of the building and a huge pile of sand, a space almost entirely hidden from the street.

"What do you think?" Fate asked as he joined Lutie in the car.

"Perfect."

"It is unless you count the rats in the Dumpsters or the snakes that slither into cars with open doors."

"Stop it!" she said, already pushing debris from the seats onto the floorboards. "Get Floy's afghans from the trunk. We can use them for pillows."

As soon as they were bedded down, Fate said, "You know, Lutie, we'll have to be out of here early. These construction guys probably start work by seven."

"Yeah, I know."

"But if we stayed in a shelter—"

"How many times do I have to tell you, Fate? If we show up at a shelter, they're gonna call the police or some child welfare agency. Besides, we're not gonna live like this long. Let's find out about Daddy first, then we'll figure out the rest."

Despite the heat, the discomfort of his "bed," and his worry of being discovered, Fate—nearly asleep already—easily gave up the debate.

They'd had a long day. Even after hearing the bad news about their father, they'd found Las Vegas exciting, full of adventure, especially for a couple of kids from Spearfish, South Dakota.

They'd walked the Strip dozens of times, exploring the casinos and taking in the sights like a couple of carefree tourists. They'd strolled through the Forum Shops—a "forced march," according to Fate—and watched the talking statues come to "life" at Caesars Palace; conned a free gondola ride at the Venetian; watched the volcano erupt and observed the white tigers as they slept behind glass at the Mirage. They'd seen the water ballet at Bellagio; stood through three acts at Circus Circus as jugglers, clowns, and aerialists performed; and shared in the fun of the pirate fight and the sinking of the ship at Treasure Island.

Fate, of course, peppered his conversations with bits of trivia that seemed appropriate to the spectacles of Vegas. For instance, when they went to Paris, he announced that four hundred sixteen people had committed suicide by jumping from the real Eiffel Tower in the real Paris; and at the Flamingo, he told Lutie that there were more plastic flamingos in the United States than real ones, a fact that actually made her laugh.

But Lutie had paid more attention to the cocktail waitresses in the casinos than to any of the sights. She'd studied their tight, showy costumes; the attention they received—almost entirely from men; and the bills and chips they were given as tips.

Now, after finishing off the last of "Grandmother's" pizza and chocolate pie, both Lutie and Fate slept in Floy's Pontiac at the back of a half-constructed building, their bodies curled and bent to fit the confines of the car seats, their faces dampened with sweat, two kids unaware and unconcerned with the glamour of the Las Vegas Strip only blocks away.

But they would have been aware and concerned if they'd seen a pair of dark eyes watching them, eyes that had been following them since the moment Lutie had driven through the gate and parked two stories beneath where he stood.

CHAPTER EIGHT

THE SUN HAD just cleared Frenchman Mountain when Fate was half aroused from sleep by a popping sound that seemed to be coming from the roof of the Pontiac. Somehow he fitted the noise into his dream, a dream in which shots were being fired at him as he raced through darkened streets.

Moments later, as the sounds became more explosive, he awoke, sitting up in time to see several rocks bounce off the hood of the car.

He crawled out, shaded his eyes to scan the upper floors of the building beside him, but saw no one, nothing that looked out of the ordinary. However, just after he got back inside, another barrage of stones struck.

"Lutie," he whispered, "wake up. We have to get out of here. Now."

Since Lutie had slept through the noise of the riprap striking the automobile, Fate hadn't expected a response to his warning, especially on his first attempt.

Well aware of his sister's early morning tirades, he leaned over the front seat and nudged her shoulder, then pulled his hand back quickly before she had time to catch him and break one of his fingers.

But at that moment, another cluster of rocks, even larger and heavier than the last, bombarded the hood of the car, causing Lutie to bolt upright.

"What the hell's going on?" she yelled in alarm. "Is this an earthquake?"

"No. That rubblework's coming from one of those windows up there. I got out to look, didn't see anyone. But someone's there for sure. Might be the night watchman's seen us, trying to scare us off."

"Or maybe he's trying to kill us."

"Either way, we'd better get out of here."

"Yeah." Lutie started the car. "For once, I think you're right," she said as she raced across the lot.

She gunned the engine to show Fate her impatience as he worked to open the gate, then sped through after he succeeded, giving him only seconds to dive back in before she peeled out.

Once she was a safe distance away, she checked the rearview mirror to make sure they weren't being followed. "Guess we got out just in time," she said.

Fate turned to look back as a pickup followed by a panel truck pulled into the construction site.

"What do you think that was all about?" Lutie asked.

"I'm guessing the night watchman's got him a cot set up on the second or third floor so he can sleep on the job. He probably didn't hear us come in last night, but when he saw us this morning, he wanted us out of there before his boss showed up, figured out what was going on, and fired him."

"Maybe," Lutie said, but by then her attention had shifted. "What's that?" she asked.

"Where?"

"There." She pointed. "There on the hood."

Fate followed her gaze to a slip of paper partially covered by a brick. As Lutie pulled to the curb, the paper fluttered in the breeze.

"I'll get it," he said. He got out, freed the paper, then tossed the brick onto the floorboard when he crawled back in.

"What is it?" Lutie asked.

Fate held out a jagged half page of smudged and stained paper torn from a notebook. The handwriting, in dull pencil, was uneven, some of the letters printed, others in cursive, a few of the words misspelled.

Together, he and Lutie read the message silently:

"You can park at the clark co. liberry on flamingo just east of maryland prkway. Sekurity usually walks around the liberry but not at the back of the parking lot."

"Sounds like a trap to me," Lutie said.

"Who would try to trap us?"

"That guard back at the construction site."

"Lutie, if he'd wanted to catch us, he'd have done it there. Not at some library."

"It was you, then."

"Me? I was asleep. Besides, why would I do that?"

"Because you love libraries."

"So how did I get up in that building and throw stones down on the car while I was in it?"

"I don't know, but this note didn't just fall on the hood under a brick, did it?"

"No," he said as he stuffed the note in his pants pocket. "Someone put it there. Not me . . . but someone who wanted us to find it. You know, though, maybe we ought to go to this library, take a chance. See if—"

"Fate, we don't even know where it is. Probably clear across town . . . and we're out of gas. Out! Did you forget that little fact?"

"No, I didn't forget."

"Look, maybe it was some jerk who was trying to steer us wrong, get us in trouble."

"Yeah. Like we're not in enough trouble now."

Lutie had no comeback to Fate's comment. And the only person who knew at the moment just how much trouble this teenage girl and her little brother were in was the man with the dark, opaque eyes who watched the Pontiac until it turned a corner and disappeared from his sight.

Lutie squeezed into an unmetered parking space by pulling forward and back a half-dozen times, bouncing the Pontiac off a Toyota in front and a Mercedes behind, giving no thought to the damage she might have caused to either vehicle.

"I'm turned around," Fate said. "We're not close to where we parked yesterday, are we?"

"No, that's on the other side of the Strip. We have to keep moving, keep changing places so we don't draw attention. Big problem is gas. We're so out we probably don't even have enough left for a huffer to get high."

"You haven't ever done that, have you, Lutie?" Fate asked, unable to mask his apprehension. "You haven't huffed, have you?"

"You are such a dweeb-brain. Now, let's grab some clothes and get cleaned up."

"I'm not dirty."

"Then why do you smell like fungus feet?"

Lutie rummaged around in the plastic bags in the trunk until she came up with the least wrinkled clothes she could find for herself, along with a plaid shirt and almost clean jeans for Fate.

"Where are we going to get a shower?" Fate asked. "You thought of that?"

"We're not, but we can take a whore's bath in one of the casino restrooms."

"Floy used to say she took a 'whore's bath,' but I didn't know why. She wasn't a whore, was she?"

"You mean you couldn't find 'whore's bath' in one of your books of knowledge? No, she wasn't a whore, but she was so fat she had trouble getting in and out of the bathtub. And I wasn't about to help her. So she got naked, washed under her arms and between her legs with a wet, soapy rag, and called that a bath."

"Oh." Fate's face and neck reddened up with embarrassment.

"Found out more than you wanted to know, didn't you?" Lutie laughed at her brother's discomfort. "There. Up on the corner. Terrible's Casino. You can take your whore's bath at Terrible's."

"How wonderfully appropriate." Then he noticed a street sign, causing him to pull the note from his pocket. "Flamingo Road," he said with excitement. "That's where this library is." He shoved the note at Lutie. "Clark County Library. See?"

Without a glance, Lutie said, "Whoopee."

In the ladies' at Terrible's, she wet down a handful of paper towels at the sink, dousing some with hand soap from a wall dispenser. Inside a stall, she stripped, washed up, and changed into a pair of tight-fitting drawstring pants, pushing them so low that they barely covered her pubic hair. To avoid panty lines across her butt, she flushed her underwear down the toilet. After she padded her bra with wads of toilet paper, she pressed each cup until she had something on her chest resembling real breasts. Finally, she pulled on the sleeveless turtleneck she'd stolen from Wal-Mart the night Floy died, then went to the sinks to apply makeup.

A Mexican woman shining faucets watched Lutie for a few

moments, then she pointed to a piece of toilet paper protruding from the armhole of the red turtleneck before she silently turned away and resumed her work.

After Lutie wet her hair, she pulled it up and fastened it with a plastic claw clamp, believing the style made her appear older. She then applied more makeup than usual, darkening her eyes with mascara and eyeliner until she had that Avril Lavigne look she was going for.

When she finished, she stood back from the mirror to test the high-fashion model pout she'd seen in magazines, along with her sexiest pose . . . making sure her toilet paper breasts were in proper position and of more or less equal size.

Just outside the bathroom door, she found Fate waiting for her. He'd washed his face, "combed" his hair with his fingers, and changed into the clothes Lutie had pulled from the trunk for him.

"What now?" he asked.

"We have to go back to the car. I forgot my lip liner."

"Lutie, you've got on too much makeup now. You don't need lip liner."

"Yes, I do! And besides, I'm not going to carry around these dirty clothes all day. We can dump this stuff in the trunk so we won't have to mess with it."

"Then what?"

"I'm going to have my ears pierced and—"

"You had them pierced back in Spearfish. I remember because Floy had a fit when she saw them."

"Well, dong-head, Floy's dead, and we're not in Spearfish, and I'm having my ears pierced *again* because I want a pair of black crosses to go with these." She pulled out her earlobe to show him the tiny rhinestone studs she was wearing. "And I want a belly ring or a nose ring, I can't decide. I might get both. And a tattoo. I've always wanted a pair of kissing lips right here on my neck so they'll show."

"You think sixty-two cents'll cover three holes and a tattoo?"

"I'm going to get a Wonderbra, too, and a really awesome pedicure and a pair of lace thongs."

"Listen to yourself, Lutie. We don't have enough money for an order of fries, and the car is out of gas, we can't even make a long-distance phone call, and you're going to buy a pair of shoes."

"Thongs, stupid, not shoes. Besides, I didn't say I was going to buy them, did I?"

"Oh, I get it. You're not going shopping, you're going shop*lifting*."

"No, I'm going window shopping. Just looking, that's all. But when Daddy sends us some money—"

"*If* he sends us money."

"Well, I can't find out about him until late this afternoon. That's what the woman at Harrah's said. So let's go back to the Strip and—"

"And do what? See the volcano explode again, watch the white tigers sleep?"

"Let's go to that wedding chapel where Britney Spears got married. I'd like to see that. And we could go to the Elvis-A-Rama and the wax museum and the Hard Rock Cafe. Someone told me that—"

"And we can take our 'grandmother' with us. That's all she's talked about this whole vacation, eating at the Hard Rock Cafe."

"I got you fed, though, didn't I? And Granny, too."

"Yeah," Fate said grudgingly. "You did."

When they reached the Pontiac and got shed of their dirty

clothes, Lutie began to search for her lip liner. "So are you gonna go with me?" she asked.

"No. I think I'll try to find that library."

"Well, guess that's why millions flock to Vegas every year. To spend days in the damned library."

"Lutie, I'm not trying to be a hard case, but we did that tourist stuff yesterday and I don't want to—"

"You meet me at six o'clock. And don't be late because I won't wait for you. If you're here one minute past six, I'm gone."

The Clark County Library didn't open until nine, but Fate wasn't the first there. The steps leading to the entrance were peppered with readers waiting to get in.

A Hispanic woman with a girl who looked to be seven or eight sat on the top step, flipping through pages of *The Lorax.* Two fair-skinned, redheaded teenagers, a boy and girl, each wearing a backpack, chatted in a language Fate didn't recognize. An older man, dressed in baggy cargo pants, flip-flops, and a T-shirt with a faded peace sign, read a newspaper a couple of steps below where Fate was sitting.

A black woman in her thirties—obviously pregnant, hot, and tired—tried to corral a laughing toddler who was eating dirt as he ran circles around a palm tree growing near the stairs. An elderly white woman with a trickle of dried blood on her cheek sat on the bottom step beside a child's wagon filled with paper sacks, a deflated basketball, a man's worn work boot, a painted glass vase, and a small box of crumpled soda cans, glancing nervously about, guarding her possessions as if a thief might lurk nearby.

Fate studied the people around him from the oldest to the youngest, examined them as if he might be memorizing their images, wondering if one of them had left the note on Floy's Pontiac last night. But he saw nothing in their eyes or demeanor that suggested any interest in him, nothing that gave away an intent to either harm or help him.

The library, a three-story building the color of rose rock, looked as if it had been constructed of giant concrete blocks stacked one upon another. But Fate was much less aware of the structure than of the people and the parking lot, wide and deep, fourteen rows stretching two football fields before him, the back row already parked with several vehicles that, he surmised, belonged to the librarians and staff.

Then, the sound of metal against metal—bolts sliding at the front door—signaled the opening of the library, prompting all those waiting to head for the entrance.

Fate was third in line at the front desk, standing just behind the teenagers, both of whom pulled books from their backpacks and pushed them across the counter to the librarian.

"So, Sena, what did you think of our Mr. Steinbeck?"

"I love this book," the girl said with a strong European accent. "Now I will see the movie."

"Uh-oh. Another James Dean fan in the making, huh? Do you know who he is?"

"Yes. Everyone in the world know James Dean, a beautiful boy."

"And you, Josef? Did you read the book?"

"I tried," he said, "but many idioms."

When the teens' business ended, Fate stepped up to the counter.

"What can I do for you, young man?"

"I'd like to get a library card," he said.

"You have to be fourteen to get a card unless you have a parent or guardian sign our consent card. You're not fourteen, are you?"

Fate shook his head.

"Do you have a school ID?"

"I just moved here."

"Then . . ."

"Can I take the consent form with me? My dad's not . . . well, he's not in Las Vegas right now."

"No, I'm sorry. You'll need to have him or your mother with you so I can witness their signature."

"How about my sister? Can she sign for me?"

"Yes, if she's twenty-one."

"Oh." Unable to hide his disappointment, Fate turned away as if he intended to leave, but the librarian stopped him.

"You don't need a card to read here. Stay all day if you want to."

"Okay." Grinning, he said, "Thanks, thanks a lot."

He found the young people's library on the third floor, and inside the circle of a round counter was a woman wearing a construction paper crown with "jewels" cut from bright reds, blues, and greens.

"Hi," she said, flashing a smile. "Need any help?"

Fate would probably have said no, would probably have been content to wander around silently, running his fingers over the spines of books, reading their titles, loving the book smell that was, for him, sweeter than the smell of Floy's hot apple pies just out of the oven.

But by then, he'd spotted the computers. Six of them. Two taken by the redheaded teenagers, leaving four free.

"Yes. I'd like to use a computer."

"Great. Got plenty of room for you. If you'll let me swipe your card, I'll—"

"Oh, I don't have a card. Yet."

"No problem. I can give you a one-day pass. That okay?"

"Great. That's great."

"Here you go, but remember, it's only temporary."

"One day," he said. "Yes, I know."

75

As soon as he was settled, he Googled "newspapers" and pulled up the *Rapid City Journal*. In the archives, he started with the day after the night Floy had died. He found the story on the front page, all the details including his and Lutie's names.

He found Floy's obituary printed in the next day's paper as well as a story about his and Lutie's "disappearance." The article said the police "did not believe the children had been victims of a crime, but admitted that they were missing, as was the automobile belonging to Ms. Satterfield."

And there, just above the article, were last year's school pictures of Lutie and Fate McFee.

By the time Lutie reached the Strip, any feelings of guilt she had about leaving Fate had disappeared. He was, she figured, old enough to take care of himself in a library.

Besides, she was relieved he wasn't following her around, glad she didn't have to worry about finding him food. But most of all, she was happy not to hear his constant rattling on with his knowledge of trivia.

She had the day free. Las Vegas. All to herself.

As she headed for the Strip, she walked streets unlike those she and Fate had marveled at yesterday. Here she passed ratty little motels and rough-looking casinos with names like Easy Money and Finders-Keepers; liquor stores—Vegas Village Spirits and the Celebration Bottle Shack; adult bookstores and movie houses—Hard Reads, Tickle Your Fancy, Stroke Your Curiosity, and Sizzle Films.

She brushed by people pushing grocery carts, luggage pulls, rolling suitcases, a bicycle missing rubber on both tires—anything with wheels—all piled with plastic bags, filthy pillows and blankets, bottles of water, and toilet tissue, their detritus bound with belts, rope, neckties, chains and padlocks, bungee cords—whatever they could find to imply ownership.

One toothless man with a gray ponytail pushed a baby stroller filled with just about everything except a baby. A mutt, looking just a little less mangy than the man, was tethered to the handle of the buggy by a pink rhinestone–studded dog leash.

"Girlie," he said as Lutie passed, "can you spare some change? God will bless you if you can."

"Sorry, but I'm broke myself."

"Cunt!" he yelled over and over as she hurried away. "Only a cunt would refuse a man 'nuff money to feed his dog, ain't that right, Princess?" The dog, hearing her name, barked—seemingly in agreement.

Lutie passed all kinds of businesses for the down-and-out: Pay Day Liquor, Vegas on the Vine; AA Acceptance & Loan, Quick Cash; Big Al's Bail Bonds; pawnshops, their windows displaying jewelry, electronics, furs, musical instruments, guns, baby shoes, handcuffs, and Western boots of alligator and rattlesnake.

At a shop called Sexual Pleasures, Lutie went inside, partly because she was curious and partly because of the black lace thongs in the window. The clerk, a heavyset woman with purple hair, looked up when Lutie walked in, then went back to a book she was reading. Lutie walked the aisles, examining sex toys, hard-core DVDs, exotic lubricants, leather whips, wrist constraints of fake fur, flavored condoms, garter belts, and a black lace thong like the one in the window. But the minute she reached for the thong, the clerk was at her back.

"Twelve ninety-five," the purple-haired woman said, "and we don't bargain."

"I'm just looking." Lutie returned the underwear to the shelf.

"Yeah? Show me someone who's not."

As she left the shop, Lutie came to the conclusion that shoplifting in Vegas was going to be a bit harder than it was at the Wal-Mart back home.

When she reached the Strip with its flash and glitter, bright neon and sparkling waterfalls, dazzling buildings, thick tropical gardens, and gorgeous boys with bronze tans, she knew this was going to be a golden, unforgettable day in her life.

At a tattoo parlor called OUCH! she went in. A man at the counter with a split tongue, rings in his nose and lips, heavy earlobes hanging halfway to his shoulders with liquid glass tusks embedded in them, smiled when she stepped up to the counter.

"Hi," he said. "My name's Eddie. Can I help you?"

"Is it okay if I just look around?"

"Absolutely. Take your time."

The shop was, for Lutie, a complete surprise. In Spearfish, she'd had her ears pierced by a classmate in the girls' bathroom. Here she'd expected a dingy, sour-smelling room with crudely drawn biker tattoos taped to the walls, a trashy place where germs hid in bloody gauze and moist needles.

But this "studio of body maintenance," according to Eddie, glistened with bright blue tile floors, freshly painted walls hung with Asian art, pots of live plants, soothing sitar music, and the intoxicating aroma of hazelwood incense.

The body art room was furnished with a doctor's examination table covered with clean white paper, a tray with hand sanitizer, gauze, cotton balls, and swabs, and a table with herbal teas and bottles of distilled water.

"Are you interested in body art?" Eddie asked. "Tattoos?"

"Well, yes."

"Would you like to see some of our flash cards?"

"What are those?"

"Here." Eddie led her to a shelf containing books with laminated pages of lovely designs.

Lutie flipped through pages, then said, "What I've always

wanted is a pair of kissing lips right here." She pointed to a spot at the fleshy part of her neck, two inches above her collarbone.

"Like this?" he said, turning to a page of sketches, one exactly as she had described.

"Yes! That's it. In red. No, coral. How much would that cost?"

"I could do that for seventy-five dollars."

"I'll have to wait until payday."

"Here. Take one of my cards."

"And what do you charge for piercing, up here?" She ran her finger under the rounded loop at the top of her ear.

"Oh, the helix. We call that a cartilage piercing of the outer helix. I charge sixty dollars a pair."

"That's what I want, but . . ."

"I know." He grinned. "You have to wait until payday. But tell you what, I'll do your body art and the helix piercing for a hundred and twenty-five dollars. That sound about right?"

"Great. I'll be here."

"Look forward to it," he said, shaking her hand.

At the next corner, while she waited for the light to change, she saw an Elvis impersonator, more makeup than sweat rolling down his face as he signed autographs, posed for pictures, and took the tourists' money.

In an outdoor courtyard where vendors were set up selling T-shirts, maps of Las Vegas, ices, purses, beer, knockoff cologne, cheap jewelry, pretzels, and sunglasses, Lutie saw the pair she wanted: silver with black moons and stars on the earpieces.

The booth was crowded with teenagers, all pulling glasses from racks, pushing for space at two small mirrors . . . and being watched by only one clerk, a small Indian woman dressed in a gold-and-green sari, with a *bindi* on her forehead. She was having a difficult time watching her stock and was yelling at a boy, apparently her son, who was more interested in a girl with gigantic breasts bouncing beneath a sheer tank top than he was in helping his mother.

Lutie waited until the Indian woman was making change for a sale before she slipped the glasses into her purse, then turned and strolled away.

After a short walk to the Imperial Palace, she went into the ladies' room, where she let down her hair, freshened her makeup, and put on her new glasses.

They looked so fabulous. She felt so cool. And for one of the few times in her life, she believed she was pretty.

She hurried into a stall to pee, anxious to be back on the street, where one of the bronze boys might notice her, but while fumbling with a paper seat cover, she discovered a laptop sitting on a shelf above rolls of toilet paper.

She froze, waiting to hear some woman's desperate cry of loss or a frenzied pounding on the door or the face of a policeman peering at her over the wall of the next stall. But when she realized that the toilet was empty and quiet, she slipped the laptop into the front of her drawstring pants and pulled them up, yanked down her turtleneck, stepped out of the stall to check herself in the mirror, and then scooted from the bathroom and out of the casino, hardly able to keep from running.

At Diamond Jim's Pawn, she slid the laptop across a counter to a man with a beard and a crossed eye. He skipped any kind of greeting as he examined the case. He opened the laptop, checked it out in less than three minutes, then said, "Two hundred dollars. Final offer."

Lutie felt her knees turn to rubber, imagined her face drain of color, and said in a weak voice, "I'll take it."

"You have sixty days to redeem it. After that, it's mine."

Lutie signed the card he handed her, using the name Norma Neal, the girl who had pierced her ears in the school bathroom. She took the receipt and the money in twenty-dollar bills, which she crammed in her purse as she left quickly, without looking back.

In exactly nine minutes, she entered OUCH! And grinned at Eddie, saying, "Payday came earlier than I expected."

Even though the Clark County Library was three times the size of the public library back in Spearfish, Fate had, by eleven o'clock, learned the layout of the place and spent time in every section from the children's collection to government publications. He'd seen black, white, and brown patrons, had heard people speaking Chinese, Spanish, Italian, French, Polish, Japanese, and two other languages not even the librarians could identify for him.

He'd listened to a dark woman wearing an old-fashioned nurse's bonnet and cloak reading a story about Florence Nightingale to a quiet huddle of children sitting on the floor. In the basement, he'd watched a blind man reading Braille; on the main floor, tucked into a corner, he'd seen the author of a novel signing copies of her books. And a young man wearing a uniform embroidered with Nature Preserve smiled at him as he led a group of young people into the special collections room.

Shortly before one-thirty, Fate had, as far as he could tell, outlasted everyone who'd been waiting with him that morning for the library to open.

He'd seen the woman with the wagon leave the browsing area first, followed not long after by the peace-shirted man, who had checked out several books on water management.

The Hispanic woman and her child had spent almost two hours in the young people's library before they left with three more Dr. Seuss books, which the child carried like found treasures.

When Fate went searching for the redheaded teens, he'd found them in curriculum materials where he'd handed the boy, Josef, a copy of *The Dictionary of Idioms* he'd discovered in the reference department. He learned that the brother and sister, from Poland, had been in the states for only three months, brought to Las Vegas by their parents, who were both structural engineers.

Josef, delighted by Fate's kindness, hugged him tightly, using every form of "thank you" at his command.

By three, Fate had amassed a stack of books at the table, where he'd remained for most of the day, books titled *One-Letter Words*; *This Is Your Brain on Music*; *The Selfish Gene*; *Why People Believe Weird Things*; *Parallel Worlds*; *The Little Book of Scientific Principles, Theories & Things*; and *The Book of Maps*.

He was just getting into *Mind Wide Open* when the rumbling of his empty belly sent him to the water fountain again, believing liquid could quiet the growl in his gut. Minutes later, he made a trip to the bathroom, where he peed and washed his hands.

Back at his table, "his place" for the day, he found in addition to the books he'd been reading a brown paper sack folded over neatly at the top, a sight that caused the hair on the back of his neck to rise. He looked around, the note left on Floy's car last night very much on his mind. But he saw no one nearby except for the library patrons at other tables, all of whom he'd noticed before his trip to the men's room.

Finally, he sat down. And with trembling fingers, his breath coming shallow, he opened the sack and peered inside.

The bag contained a package of peanut-butter crackers, an orange, and a small carton of milk, which did not have a photograph of a missing child, a boy named Fate McFee.

Lutie couldn't seem to get past many windows along the Strip without stopping to check out her reflection, thrilled with the image of the girl who stared back at her. A girl with coral lips tattooed on her neck, new studs in her ears, golden highlights in her hair, an airbrush tan, and a French pedicure done in black and white to match her newly "acquired" sunglasses.

As a silver stretch limo passed and parked at the curb beside her, she enjoyed a short-lived fantasy that it was stopping for her. Moments later, jarred out of that movielike reverie, she imagined that Brad Pitt and Angelina Jolie might step out, followed by their new children, who would parade by her like a row of ducks and ducklings. But when the chauffeur opened the door, a gaggle of giggling Paris Hilton wannabes spilled out and sauntered into Luxor, not one famous face in the whole bunch of them.

Though she'd gone the entire day without thinking of food, she was suddenly struck by the gnawing of her stomach. Down to her last two dollars and change, she decided to go into the next casino she came to, order whatever she wanted, then walk the check, as she'd done the day before.

But inside the Tropicana, she ran into a wedding party— a young man and woman wearing grass skirts, leis, and neck-laces of conch shell beads, both barefoot, moving across the casino floor toward the escalators. The bride wore a bikini top of ivory silk designed to match the garland of flowers encircling her head and the bridal bouquet she carried.

They were followed by the bridesmaid, quite obviously a sis-ter, and the best man, both dressed in island getup. After them came the wedding guests, which Lutie estimated to be nearly a hundred.

Guessing the ceremony would include a reception, Lutie de-cided to go for the food that would be available rather than take her chances downstairs at one of the restaurants, so she "hid" herself in the crush heading upstairs.

The Island Wedding Chapel, palm-thatched, blanketed with tropical foliage, included a waterfall and recorded Hawaiian music playing softly from concealed speakers. The chapel filled quickly with a few guests—including Lutie, standing at the back.

After the "I do's" and the traditional kiss, the bride's father invited everyone to a private dining room a short distance down a hallway for a reception honoring his daughter and her new husband on "this very special occasion."

A combo of musicians played inside a spacious ballroom with a gigantic chandelier shimmering above a polished dance floor. Round tables set with gleaming china and crystal as well as centerpieces of fresh orchids awaited the wedding party as servers filled flutes with champagne, while others began delivering plates with silver warming covers to the tables, each setting identifying guests by name with a place card.

Since Lutie knew her name would not be among them, she simply stepped inside the room to a line of food carts and helped herself to a plate, the wait staff too busy to notice or care.

In a food court across the street at the Showcase Mall, she devoured her feast. Chicken livers and water chestnuts wrapped in bacon, mahimahi, Hawaiian barbecued ribs, and chunks of grilled pineapple on skewers. And though she could not have put a name to all the food on her plate, she enjoyed every bite.

Finished, she crossed the street and headed for her meeting with Nechia, but when she found out the time—ten past three—she slowed her pace, reluctant to arrive earlier than she'd been invited.

Fortunately, she discovered the Carnival Court, a piazza just outside Harrah's with lots of action. A rock group played on a broad stage, kids danced in front of the bandstand, and a big circular bar was crowded with groups of mostly older teens and young twenty-somethings who laughed, moved in time to the music, and downed little bottles of beer stacked in buckets and fancy drinks served in tall colored glasses.

The bartenders, mostly guys, tossed bottles in the air and to one another, constantly flipping, spinning, throwing, and catching while they sang, danced, and kept the crowd entertained. When Lutie said something to a girl washing glasses behind the counter, a remark about the bartenders' tricks, the girl warned her that the word *trick* could get her dumped on if one of the dudes heard her use it. This, she explained, was a flair bar, and those "tricks" she saw were called "flairs."

"Oh, like Tom Cruise in *Coyote Ugly*," Lutie said.

"Tom Cruise was in *Cocktail*," the girl answered in exasperation, then turned and walked away.

When the best-looking of all the bartenders slapped a napkin in front of Lutie, he said, "What'll it be, sweetheart?"

"One of those," she said, pointing to a tall blue bottle in the hand of a smiling blonde seated at a bar stool nearby.

"You got an ID?"

"Not with me, but I'm twenty-one."

"Yeah, and I'm seven."

Lutie felt her face flush but hoped her new airbrush tan would hide her embarrassment. "Okay, I guess I'll have a Coke."

Just then, a handsome man, midtwenties, slid onto an empty stool beside Lutie. "Here, Octane, bring me two rum and Cokes. In blue bottles."

"Sure thing, T.," the bartender said as he swiped up a ten-dollar bill T. had rolled into a cigarette-size circle.

"Everyone here calls me T.," he said to Lutie. "What do I call you?"

"Lutie."

"Unusual name. Matter of fact, you're my first Lutie."

"Well, I guess that makes us even. You're my first T."

"Good. I like being first. You here on vacation, Lutie?"

"Sort of."

"Ah, a story here. And a mysterious girl to tell it."

"I'm here to meet my father."

"You and your father staying at Harrah's?"

"Yeah. Well, my father's not here yet, but . . ."

"So, Lutie, what are you? Fifteen? Sixteen?"

"Twenty-one," she said as the bartender put both drinks T. had ordered in front of him. This time, T. tossed a twenty on the counter.

"Keep the change, Octane."

"You know him?" Lutie asked.

"I know them all."

"So you're not on vacation. You live here."

"I do indeed live here, but I'm always on vacation."

Lutie tasted the drink T. handed her, then smiled. "I like it. Thanks."

"So what are you going to do if your old man doesn't show, Lutie?"

"What makes you think he won't?"

"Hey, girl. You can't fool an old fooler, didn't you know that? You're in some kind of trouble. I spotted that when I saw you walk in here."

Lutie didn't want to show that his remarks scared her, but she found herself pulling her bottom lip between her teeth, a signal that she was uneasy.

"Relax, honey. I'm a helper, not a hurter."

"Look, when my daddy gets here—"

"Well, let's say he doesn't. What are you gonna do then? Huh?"

"I've got to get back to college by the first of the month, so I'll stay here and play for a few days, then—"

"Honey, if you've ever been on a college campus, I'll chug this and eat the bottle." He held up his glass. "My guess is you don't have enough money to get a good swerve on."

"What does that mean?"

"I've got you figured for a runaway with a pile of baggage to carry around."

"Well, you've got me figured wrong."

"A runaway who doesn't have enough dough to see the elephant. And you can't get a job 'cause you're just a kid."

"I told you—"

"Probably don't have a driver's license, no ID. But T. can help you out with that kind of problem."

"Listen, I've got to go. I'm meeting someone in Harrah's and—"

"Yeah. I'll bet you've got a real important meeting to go to. But you remember this: T. can help you out with that ID. Make you eighteen or eighty."

"Thanks for the drink," Lutie said as she slid off the bar stool and started toward Harrah's.

"You bet. Now, come back and see me, you hear? I'm easy to find. And if you don't find me, I'll find you."

Fate was sitting on the hood of the Pontiac, but when he saw Lutie coming from a block away, he ran to meet her.

"Did you talk to Daddy?" he asked, his face flushed with excitement.

"No, not yet."

"Well, did that lady call the prison? Was she able to find out when—"

"Yeah, she called, but she won't know anything until tomorrow. Someone in the warden's office is going to get in touch with her then."

"So when did she say for you to come back?"

"She didn't set a time. Just said tomorrow."

"Well, guess we can survive another night in the car, huh, Lutie?" he said, an attempt to get more than a few words from her. He was much more accustomed to her anger than to this new quiet tone.

"You look different, Lutie. I don't know what it is, but you don't look like you did when—"

"I had my hair up this morning."

"Yeah," he said. "Guess that's what it is."

Lutie knew how little attention Fate paid to appearance; nevertheless, she'd made herself ready to meet him. Her tattoo was covered by her turtleneck; she'd hidden her stolen sunglasses in her purse; and she'd taken the temporary studs from the new holes in her ears. If he mentioned her tan, she could explain that away. She had, after all, been in the sun for two days, and he wouldn't, she knew, notice the highlights in her hair. But there was nothing she could do to hide her pedicure because of the flip-flops she was wearing. Fortunately, Fate hadn't noticed. Not yet.

"Here," he said, handing her the orange he'd received in his mystery lunch sack.

"Where'd you get this?" she asked.

"At the library. You won't believe this, but someone gave me some peanut-butter crackers and milk and this orange."

"Who?"

"Don't know. I got up to go to the bathroom; when I went back to the table where I was reading, there was a sack with this stuff in it."

"And you didn't see who put it there?"

"Nope. And I looked, believe me. Because of what you said about the note on the car. I thought at first that you might be right about someone setting us up, someone trying to get us in trouble, but—"

"Do you think it might have been one of the librarians?"

"Maybe. I don't know. Anyway, I ate the crackers and drank the milk, but I saved the orange for you."

As unaccustomed as she was to feeling guilt, Lutie couldn't help but regret that she'd spent the money from the pawnshop on herself and bought nothing for Fate, who'd saved her his orange.

"So, you want to move the car to the library for the night? The parking lot looked pretty safe."

"How far is it?" Lutie asked as she got into the Pontiac.

"Couple of miles, I guess."

"I don't think we have enough gas to go two miles."

"Hey, look!" Fate pointed to the gas gauge, which showed almost a quarter of a tank.

"No," she said, flicking her fingernail against the glass covering the gauge. "Something's out of whack."

"But when we parked here this morning, the needle was at empty, just like it was last night."

"This is crazy. Who would put gas in our car? And how would they drive it to a station when I've got the keys?"

"Just a second." Fate slid out and walked back to the cover on the car's gas tank. An empty industrial-size bottle of cooking oil was overturned on the curb. He picked up the bottle and sniffed the odor of gasoline. By then, Lutie was beside him.

"Here's how." He held out the bottle for her to smell.

"Fate, something really screwy is going on here. Rocks falling on the car, that note, this." She held out the orange. "And now, gas. Almost a quarter tank."

"Well, whoever is doing this stuff for us must not mean any harm. So far, he . . . or she seems to be looking out for us. I say let's go to the library, give it a try."

"Okay, show me how to get there."

At ten o'clock, with the car parked in the back row of the lot at the library, Fate peeled the orange, then handed it over the seat to Lutie.

"Don't you want any?"

"I'm not hungry," she said. "You eat it."

"So what did you eat today?"

"Oh, I had some chicken and stuff."

"You walk the check again?"

"Yeah."

"You know, Lutie, you're going to get caught doing that."

"Yeah."

"Maybe we ought to go to a shelter—"

"Fate, I told you we can't do that. If we do, we'll get caught and sent back to Spearfish."

"Well, maybe we don't have to spend the night. Maybe we can go to a shelter, get a free meal, and leave."

"I don't know. Let me think about it."

"You know, Lutie, when Daddy gets out, we won't have to worry about food and gasoline and beds to sleep in. He'll take care of us."

"And we'll all live happily ever after?"

"We can go to school, and have beans and corn bread, fried bologna, okra, and that dish he used to make. Goulash. Isn't that what he called it?"

"I think so."

"And we can go places. Maybe to the Grand Canyon. Take one of those helicopter rides. And go to the Hoover Dam. Did you know you can take tours of the dam and they're free? And we could go see the petroglyphs and—"

"The what?"

"Petroglyphs. They're drawings chiseled into the cliffs of the canyons centuries ago. Boy, they would be something to see. And we could do stuff you'd like to do, too. We could go to—"

From the front seat, Lutie, who'd been crying silently, could no longer hold back. A mournful sob escaped from deep inside her, followed by another and another.

"Lutie?" Fate sat up and leaned over the seat. By the pole lights in the parking lot, he could see her face twisted with grief, her sobs turned to wailing.

"What's wrong? Did I say something that—"

"Daddy's not coming back, Fate," she said.

"What? What did you say?"

Then, working for control, she said in little more than a whisper, "He's not coming back, Fate. Daddy's dead."

PART TWO

CHAPTER NINE

F OR THE NEXT few days, while Fate spent time at the library where they continued to park the Pontiac, Lutie walked the streets looking for a job. She first tried the upscale casinos popular with tourists: Bellagio, Luxor, Wynn's, and Rio. But before long, she was reduced to making the rounds of the seedy joints that catered to the down-and-out, small casinos selling cheap, watered-down booze; cockroach cafés and short-order diners smelling of onions, sweat, and stale grease.

But even the worst of the worst required documents she didn't have. And without a Social Security card she couldn't get a job washing dishes or taking out the trash. So on the fourth day she returned to the one place and the one person who had offered to help her.

When Lutie arrived at the Carnival Court one morning around eleven, T. didn't act at all surprised. In truth, he looked as if he'd been expecting her. Instead of sitting at the bar, he was at a table, where he ordered two screwdrivers. One for him; one for her.

He stood, pulled out a chair, and greeted her with a soft kiss on the cheek.

"Ah, sweet Lutie. Hey, has my favorite little girl been crying?"

Lutie had been trying since early morning to conceal her red nose and the puffiness beneath her bloodshot eyes with cover stick and dark foundation, but each time she'd applied more makeup, a fresh outburst of weeping had destroyed her efforts.

"You said you could help me get a driver's license. Were you kidding?"

"Guess that meeting you had the other day didn't go so well."

"I asked you if you were kidding," she said, an edge to her voice now.

"Do I look like a kidder? Here." He handed her one of the drinks. "Try this."

"What is it?"

"Orange juice and vodka."

"Isn't it a little early to be drinking?"

"They don't seem to think so." He gestured toward the bar, which was busy and loud. "Besides, didn't your mother ever tell you that orange juice is good for you?"

Lutie set the glass back on the table without tasting the drink. "So what do I have to do? To get the license."

"It's a snap. We'll take your picture and come up with a new name."

"I don't have any money."

"Have I asked for any?"

"So I'm gonna need to change my name?"

"That depends."

"On what?"

"If the law is looking for you."

Lutie hesitated, then took a long swallow of her screwdriver.

"You're gonna have to trust me, Lutie, or I can't help you."

"I might be in some trouble. See, this woman me and my brother were living with in South Dakota, she died. And we—"

"Did you kill her?"

"No! Why would you ask me something like that?"

"Hold on, now. I'm just trying to find out what kind of problems you're dealing with. That's all."

"She had a heart attack at a Wal-Mart, so . . ."

T. started laughing.

"What's so funny?"

"She died at a Wal-Mart?"

"Yeah, at the checkout line."

T. was hysterical, laughing so hard that he made heads turn. Wiping tears from his eyes, he said, "That's wild, Lutie. Too good for you to be making it up."

"Oh no. I'm not. But here's the thing. I lied to a policeman, then I stole her car."

"The dead woman? You stole her car?"

"Yeah. I had to, 'cause me and my brother, Fate, we had to get out of town before—"

"Then you're right, no question about it. The law is after you."

"Yeah." Lutie took another hefty drink. "And now . . ."

"You have a Social Security card?"

"No."

"Good."

"Why's that good?"

"Because your name has to be the same on both documents."

"Okay. How about Renee? I've always liked that name. Renee. I'll have to think about a last name, but—"

"See, babe, we'll have to use the name and Social Security number of someone who . . . well, someone who isn't with us anymore."

"You mean I'm going to use the name of a dead girl?"

" 'Fraid so. But you can handle that, can't you?" He watched Lutie drain her glass, then signaled Octane for another one.

"Now, how old do you want to be? Eighteen? Or eighty?" he asked, trying to lighten her mood.

"I haven't thought about it."

"Well, now's the time."

"I'll be sixteen on my next birthday, so—"

"Sixteen it is if you just want to drive. But if you want to be able to buy liquor or work in a casino, you have to be twenty-one."

"Think I look that old?"

"No, but my boy is good with a camera. If you put your hair back like this . . ." He swept Lutie's hair back from her face with his fingers. "There. You just aged a couple of years. Then we'll use a little makeup here and here."

When he ran a finger down her cheek, Lutie's eyes filled with tears again. She wasn't used to kindness from a stranger. She grabbed a napkin from beneath her screwdriver to blot her face, just as Octane put a fresh drink in front of her, took T.'s money, nodded, then retreated silently to the bar.

"You want to tell me about it? I'm a pretty good listener, so I'm told."

"No, not really," Lutie said as she started on her second drink of the morning. "My life just sucks so bad. I fucked over my little brother the other day, I got some bad news about my daddy, and I . . ." She hiccuped, wiped away new tears, then tried to smile. "Sorry. I didn't mean to dump all this on you."

"Hey, babe. I'm your friend. Who else you gonna talk to?"

"You and Fate, but he's only eleven. Actually, you're the only people I know here."

"Oh, I'm gonna fix that, sugar. You're gonna make lots of new friends in Vegas. I promise. Just leave it up to T. 'cause he'll never let you down."

*   *   *

98

Fate had spent most of the morning in the library, paying less attention to the books than the patrons, librarians, and staff, except for the hour or so he spent reading the Bible.

Each time he left his place at the table, pretending to go to the bathroom, search for another book, or get a drink of water, he quickly doubled back to see if he could catch someone leaving him another lunch sack or maybe a note with a warning or some directions to follow that would provide safety from detection for himself and Lutie.

But shortly before noon, with no apparent sign that his Samaritan was keeping him in sight, Fate left the library, heading for the campus of the University of Nevada at Las Vegas, which he'd just learned was only blocks away.

He was trying not to replay the news Lutie had passed on to him, trying not to think about his father dying in a prison hospital some thirteen hundred miles from Spearfish. But he finally gave in and pulled from a library shelf a copy of the *Merck Manual* and read about hepatitis—the symptoms, diagnosis, and treatment of the disease that had taken his daddy's life. And, oddly enough, Jim McFee had died on the same day that Floy Satterfield had dropped dead in Wal-Mart.

Then, for some reason he couldn't explain, Fate had taken a Bible from the religion section, where he read over an hour from the book of Exodus, the book that seemed most liable to provide an answer to the question bothering him most—the significance of the date on which both Floy and his daddy had made their exodus from this world less than twenty-four hours apart.

But the more he read, the more confused he became, so he put the Bible back on the shelf and left the library.

*   *   *

He found the Marjorie Barrick Museum, the place he intended to spend the rest of the day, on the eastern side of the campus. He studied first the section of the museum containing weaving and basketry, but when he came to the native Southwest displays of jewelry, his mind wandered back to the earlier hours of the morning, when he'd seen Lutie putting studs in the new holes of her ears.

That's when she'd told him about finding the laptop days ago, using the money from the pawnshop on herself—a pedicure, tattoo, airbrush tan, highlighted hair. She'd even shown him the sunglasses she had stolen. He'd listened to her without comment, which had only seemed to make her sadder. She'd even told him to get mad, throw a fit, asked him to try to make her feel worse than she did. But when he'd said nothing, just given her a hug, she'd cried harder than she had when she'd told him about their daddy.

Girls, he knew, were hard to figure out—sisters even worse—but, for this, he couldn't even guess how he should have responded.

Sure, he was angry, he was hurt, but it seemed a little late to express either emotion. The harm had already been done. And it came as no great surprise. Lutie was selfish, mean-spirited, and immature. But what could he do about it? Nothing except try to survive and see that she did, too. They didn't have much. But they had each other.

T. paid the taxi driver, then led Lutie into a place he called "the studio." Outside, the building looked abandoned—windows boarded up, graffiti sprayed on the brick facade, and a business name, long ago painted on the entrance, diminished by time and weather until all that remained were the indistinct letters *INC*.

The first room they entered, probably intended to be a lobby, was empty except for a couple of folding chairs; a wooden table scarred with initials carved into its surface, scores of cigarette burns along its edges, and a few porno magazines piled near the center; a trash can containing empty beer cans, takeout boxes, rags smeared with dried paint, and a stiletto with a broken heel.

"Philo?" T. yelled.

"Yeah," a voice answered from somewhere at the back of the building.

The smell of toner and cheap perfume overpowered the second room. Larger than the first, it was crowded with counters of cameras and film, hanging backdrops of faded canvas, miles of electric cord and cables, tripods, movable banks of lights, reflectors, and gadgets Lutie couldn't begin to identify.

Against the back wall, she saw clothing racks hung with costumes—maids' uniforms, slinky dresses and gowns, lingerie and shiny capes; shelves above the rack yielded a tangle of wigs, silk scarves, feather boas, exotic bras and panties, and net stockings.

One cardboard box on the floor was crammed with dolls, baby bottles, stuffed animals, rattles, bows of ribbon, lacy bibs, and panties for little girls. Another box held sex paraphernalia of the kind Lutie had seen at Sexual Pleasures, the shop she had stopped in a few days earlier.

"Hey, Philo, catch you in the middle of something?" T. said to a middle-aged black man who slipped into the room through a sliding door taped over with brown paper, a door he shut quickly behind him.

"I'm waiting for Biggy to change out a mike. This the girl?"

"Yeah, this is Lutie."

"Okay, let's get this done, Louie."

"Lutie," she said. "L-u-t-i-e."

"Sit here," he said to her as he twirled a round, backless stool to adjust the height.

Lutie did as he'd told her, then watched as he set up a tripod a few feet in front of her, loaded a camera with film, and clamped it in place on top of the tripod.

He was muscular, dressed in recently shined mules, starched and creased jeans, and a blue tank that showed off his biceps and a torso with well-developed abs. His head was clean-shaven, as was his face, which sported no metal, not even an earring. He had no tattoos Lutie could see, and his only jewelry was a large, gold, expensive-looking watch.

Behind Lutie he moved into place one of the backdrops, this one in a nondescript gray. After that, he went back to the camera, glanced at her through the lens, then said, "Tilt your head up. . . . No, not that high. . . . There. Now, Lutie, turn just slightly to the right. . . . Good. Perfect."

"You said you wanted this for a driver's license, right?" Philo asked T.

"Right."

"Okay." To Lutie, Philo said, "I want you to smile, but not smile."

"How do I do that?" Lutie asked.

"Act like you just smiled at someone you don't like—a phony smile, then slowly let it fade. I just need a couple of seconds. Think you can do that?"

"Yeah."

The camera clicked twice in rapid succession.

"Now I'll change the lights and we'll take the same shots from the other side."

"You look terrific, honey," T. said as he stepped up to smooth Lutie's bangs across her forehead. "Terrific. Beautiful."

"And twenty-two? Do I look like—"

Just then, through the sliding door came a very small young man, weighing at most a hundred pounds, face studded with metal, hair pinked, wearing jeans whose crotch fell below his knees and a shirt that said Jesus Saves. Through the opening behind him, Lutie glimpsed a naked man and girl on a bed; she was flipping through a teen magazine, and he was examining one of his toenails.

"Dammit, Biggy. Can't you knock?"

"Sorry, Philo, but I needed to ask you if you want Rita on top or—"

"I'm busy," Philo said, obviously unhappy with the disruption. "I'll be there in a minute."

After Biggy left the room, Philo finished adjusting a reflector, got the shots he wanted, then said, "That ought to do it, T. Unless you wanted something else."

"Yeah, since you're set up, it wouldn't take long for you to get a few more shots, would it?"

"What do you have in mind?"

"Something sexy." He turned a smile on Lutie. "You wouldn't mind that, would you, darlin'?"

"I don't know. Like what?"

"Well, like . . . oh, say, three or four shots of you nude, but just from the waist up."

"Now wait a minute," Lutie said. "You told me—"

"That money didn't matter, but this is a way for me to repay Philo for helping you out. And that's what this is all about, isn't it, sweetheart?"

"But I—"

"You gotta learn to trust me, Lutie," T. said.

"I do. But I won't do that. Not nude."

"Oh, come on, now. Stop worrying about your little tits. Just pull out whatever you stuffed your bra with this morning, hug a teddy bear, and I guarantee you, I sell that picture to ten guys, nine of them will jerk off before their pants hit the floor."

Lutie looked defiant. "I can find other ways to get an ID and a Social Security card. I don't have to—"

"How, huh? You gonna work in a car wash? Flip burgers in

some greasy spoon? Get real, Lutie. You pose for Philo, your bill is paid in full."

"Who'll you sell those pictures to?"

"What do you care, huh?"

"Well, I wouldn't want people I know to see them."

"Who do you know in Vegas? Your little brother, me, and Philo, who—by the way—isn't interested in girls, big or little. Ain't that right, Philo?" T. lit a cigarette, then said, "You don't appreciate what—"

"No smoking in here, T. It damages the equipment."

"Okay, but you know what I want."

"Yeah. I know."

As soon as T. went outside, Philo, his voice soft, his manner gentle, said, "You go ahead and get ready, Lutie, while I check things out in the next room. When I come back, we'll get the photos T. wants. Won't take a minute, then you can get dressed."

"Okay."

"And here. Take this." Philo handed her a worn-looking teddy bear missing an ear. "His name is Tanker."

Twenty minutes later, Lutie and T. walked out of the studio, she with a driver's license, a Social Security Card, and a new name—Belinda Ferguson; he with three photos of Lutie, her small breasts bare, a pout on her face, and Tanker the teddy bear held against her neck, hiding her new tattoo.

After Fate left the museum, he wandered the campus, uncomfortable at first, half expecting to be stopped, to be questioned by some higher authority. Inside the museum, he had been comforted to discover families with children his age or even younger, but out here, he saw almost no one younger than twenty, students—their arms holding textbooks, their backpacks stenciled with UNLV, the straps cutting into their shoulders with the weight of whatever the packs contained.

Perhaps he could claim to be a child prodigy, an avant-garde composer or a nuclear physicist. But he knew he'd never pull that off. First of all, he didn't have a student ID, he couldn't even read music, and the only physicist he could name was Stephen Hawking.

Fortunately, though, when nobody seemed the least bit interested in him, after he began to feel invisible except when he absently rambled into someone's path, he relaxed and began to explore more freely.

He avoided the law enforcement building, where he noticed a few men and women in police uniforms standing outside smoking, but ducked quickly into the law library and exited at his first opportunity. Then, on one of the pathways, he stopped before a large glass-enclosed bulletin board, where he discovered a printed list of scheduled exams and learned that the following Friday was the last day of the summer semester.

He followed three students, all girls dressed in shorts and flip-flops, notebooks and texts in their arms, into the building of communicative arts. But as the girls continued down the hall, he stopped at a closed door and looked through a small glass window into a darkened classroom where a film was playing to the few students inside.

"Excuse me," a woman said to Fate, who was blocking the door. When Fate followed her inside, he slid into one of the many empty desks at the back of the room and watched the movie, a documentary about a bicycle policeman on the streets of Seattle. The narrative was in English and Wolof, a language widely spoken in Senegal—a fact Fate would discover later when he returned to his books of trivia. But the title of the film, he found out when the movie had ended, was *Police Beat*.

He would have liked to stay while the credits rolled, but when the classroom lights came on, he left hurriedly, before being subjected to questioning by whoever was in charge of the class.

Not far away, on the northwest side of the campus, he discovered a recently constructed school. According to a sign over the entrance, this was the Paradise Elementary School, and from a note taped to the door, he found that classes for grades K through six would begin on September 5, just weeks away.

For the rest of the day, Fate imagined himself a student at Paradise Elementary School, a name that echoed in his head like the notes to a piece of well-loved music, one so familiar to him that he could sing it in his sleep.

In the Desert Garden, Fate found four teams of Scrabble players, their games set up on tables and benches shaded by a pergola thick with the smell of cape honeysuckle. He watched the play, strolling from one group to another. The players, mixed in ages, were quiet with concentration, but now and then one would look up and, smiling, ask if he played. When he answered that he did but admitted to being inexperienced, some acknowledged that they were new at the game themselves, then invariably gave him an invitation to join them any Tuesday or Friday at two.

They couldn't have imagined what their kindness, an invitation of inclusion, meant to him then.

A few blocks away from the campus, Fate passed behind a Chinese restaurant as an employee, a man of indeterminate age and Asian features, came out the back door with several large plastic bags, which he carried to a Dumpster in a nearby alley. When he saw Fate watching, he said, "Hi."

Fate nodded, then started walking away.

"Wait," the man called. "I'll be right back," he said, his voice without accent.

Fate, sure he'd done nothing wrong, nothing for which the man might mean him harm, waited while the man went back into the restaurant, returning minutes later with a Chinese takeout box and a plastic-wrapped napkin with chopsticks and plastic utensils.

"Thought you might like to try our Singapore noodles with shrimp. Best in the city."

"Well, yes, but—"

"We serve buffet every day until two when we close, reopen at five. Whatever is left on the lunch line, we throw out. And I believe you might like to try this."

"Thank you," Fate said, accepting the gift. "Thanks very much."

"No problem." Before he went back inside, the man said, "You come back tomorrow, and if you're lucky, we might have some mushroom beef left. Or maybe kung pao chicken."

"Well, I don't know if I'll be here. See—"

"I lived on the streets when I was your age. For three years."

Before Fate could respond, the man turned his back and disappeared inside the restaurant.

By the time she'd filled out job applications at Mandalay Bay, the Venetian, and the Tropicana, Lutie knew the chances of her being hired as a cocktail waitress were next-to-nothing. Either her new ID failed to convince the people working in employment that she was twenty-two or the size of her boobs, even enhanced as they were with paper towels, made her an unlikely candidate for the profession.

She didn't give up, not then, not until she'd tried at two more casinos, but at MGM, a hotel with over three thousand rooms, she applied for a job on the cleaning staff, the job of a hotel maid. If she was hired, she'd work for minimum wage plus tips, but she was told not to expect much. Gamblers checking out of the hotels, she heard, were not inclined to have more than change for the maids who cleaned their toilets, made their beds, and carried away their trash.

She agreed to a drug test, which involved nothing more than giving up a clipping of her hair. And she signed a form consenting to a background check, which, she trusted, would show no evidence of a felony conviction. Since "Belinda Ferguson," the new name on her documents, had died at age three, there was a strong indication she'd had no criminal history.

Lutie didn't know until the conclusion of the test, signing the consent, and the end of the interview that a job wasn't available then, wouldn't be available until at least the following month. And she and Fate couldn't survive that long without money.

Their needs, including toothpaste and deodorant, products they could share, and tampons, soon to be an immediate necessity for her, could be provided by some quick maneuvers at a grocery or drugstore, but food was a different problem.

Lutie knew she could manage to slip a couple of candy bars into her purse or pockets, maybe even a banana or two, but they couldn't get by for long on that kind of diet.

Then, sitting in "Central Park" at New York–New York, wondering what her next move would be, she saw two elderly women, both in polyester pantsuits, both with the same permed, short gray hair. Respectable-looking grandmother types.

"Excuse me, ladies." Lutie lowered her gaze as if she couldn't meet the eyes of these two strangers. "But . . . well, I was wondering, uh, hoping that . . . maybe you might, uh, be able to help me."

Stammering and with her fingers fidgeting with the straps of her purse, she trusted that her gestures would convey her humiliation in asking for help.

The taller of the two women put both hands on her belly bag, a protective measure. "Help you with what?" she asked suspiciously.

"See, me and my little brother . . . well, we're stranded here, but—"

"Stranded at this casino?"

"No. We're stranded in Las Vegas."

"Where are your parents?"

At this question, Lutie managed to work up a couple of tears. "They're dead."

"Oh, my," the other woman said.

"And we don't have any money for food or for a bus ticket to Sacramento, where our aunt lives."

"Where is this little brother of yours?"

"He's in a library. He loves books."

The belly bag woman, who'd been conducting this interrogation, whispered to her partner, "Remember what Walter told us about Gypsy kids? He said they work in groups—little con artists, purse snatchers, quick-change artists."

"Oh, give it up, Inez. You see a gang of Gypsies around here?"

"No, I'm not a Gypsy. Honest." At that declaration of truthfulness, Lutie squeezed out a few more tears.

"No, honey, I don't believe you are," the short woman said as she pulled her billfold out of her purse.

"You're so gullible, Molly."

"Might as well give it to her as to those damn slot machines."

"Okay, okay." Inez wasn't happy about this, but she unzipped her belly bag and took out three one-dollar bills.

"You're going to give this girl three dollars? You know what three dollars will buy in this town?"

"No, but I've only got seven dollars left of my gambling money for the day, Molly. If I give her that, then I'll have to start on the money I put aside for tomorrow and—"

"To hell with tomorrow's money. You could be dead by tomorrow. Give the girl some *real* money."

Minutes later, when Lutie walked away, she had forty dollars in her pocket and renewed confidence in her acting ability.

As she was passing a Denny's, she saw a Help Wanted sign in the window, but inside she discovered she'd be required to have both a TB and an HIV test to work as a food handler.

And though she felt certain she carried neither disease, nor did her three-year-old, long-dead cohort, Belinda Ferguson, she knew those tests would send her back to T. for more fake documents.

At the next shop she approached, a store that carried everything from lettuce to luggage, she momentarily gave up her newly created and only partially completed list of resolutions to be a better, more truthful person as she slid a box of tampons, a tube of toothpaste, and a package of Gummi Bears into her purse. But she bought, actually paid for, a denim backpack with a picture of Albert Einstein, a gift for Fate—$14.04 of Inez and Molly's money.

A few blocks off the Strip, heading back to the car at the library, she saw the Las Vegas Blood Bank with a notice that said, "Immediate Payment for Your Donation of Blood." But a Hispanic man working at a central desk in the lobby told Lutie she'd have to have a letter postmarked at least six months prior to today's date in order to provide proof of residency in Vegas.

Lutie didn't need a fortune cookie to tell her that she'd soon have another photography session with Philo . . . or worse.

As she gathered up the papers outlining the rules of the blood bank, she didn't, at first, see the handprinted scrap of paper that had seemingly been tossed beside her purse. She recognized the penmanship, the same as what had been printed in the note left on the hood of Floy's car, but the message she held in her hand now was different:

St. Vinsents Shelter, L.V. Bulvd. No.,
breakfast from 10½ to 11½ ever day

L.V. Reskue Misscion, W. Bonanza,
supper from 5 to 6 ever day

L.V. Salvacion Army, W. Owens No. L.V.,
free food ever day.

Just after they met back at the car, Lutie shared with Fate the
odd note she'd gotten at the blood bank. And since it was nearing six, they agreed to go to the Salvation Army for supper to
see if the meal was *really* free; and to look for the stranger who
continued to connect to their lives.

Lutie followed the directions Fate read to her from the street
map he'd copied at the library the day before, staying on Las
Vegas Boulevard until it intersected with Owens on the north
side of the city.

The shelter, they discovered, was only one of a number of
buildings in the Salvation Army complex, but after parking,
they simply followed the broken trail of the homeless heading in
the same direction.

Funny, Lutie thought, how quickly she'd learned the look
of the homeless. Regardless of how they were dressed, or how
clean they were able to keep themselves, independent of the
way they walked—sometimes bent by an unseen weight or
sometimes moving with a pretended pride—their eyes betrayed
them. Though they had no place to live, no place of their own
to come home to, desperation and humiliation had come to live
with them. And their eyes—dreamy, vacant, hopeless, lost, defeated—gave them away. Knowing this made Lutie wonder how
long it would be before she and Fate, a boy of eleven, began to
take on that look.

When they finally arrived at the shelter, they discovered that
a meal was, indeed, being served, and no one who ate was asked
to pay.

Their trays contained plates with a salad, baked chicken, pinto
beans, and sliced white bread spread with butter. They had their
choice of tea, water, or lemonade.

They ate at one of several long tables seating as many as ten, a table they shared with a family of three—the father and two especially quiet, small girls; an elderly man named Ray who kept up a constant conversation with a salt shaker, referring to himself in the third person; and a middle-aged woman wearing a soiled cotton hospital gown and a rather clean housecoat a size or two larger than she needed.

A man who appeared to be homeless himself delivered a blessing, interrupting the meal already half-finished by most. Even so, the majority stopped eating, then bowed their heads until "Amen" sounded from table to table.

The food was good and plentiful. Diners were invited for seconds; dessert was also available—one-layer chocolate cake served from a dozen cookie sheets.

Lutie, suffering from a reluctant appetite tonight, ate what she could. But Fate cleaned his plate, all the while describing the UNLV campus where he'd spent most of the day.

"And besides the museum, it has a recording studio, a café called the Book n' Bean, a fitness room, computer lab, more classrooms than I've ever seen, libraries—a whole bunch of libraries—and a mall with a flashlight thirty-eight feet tall. It weighs seventy-four thousand pounds and—"

"A flashlight?"

"It's called 'the Beacon of Knowledge.'"

"That's awesome," she said without a trace of enthusiasm. "You gonna have cake?"

Afterward, with Fate still jabbering about the university, Lutie drove them back to the library, where they'd parked for five nights without incident. And though they hadn't noticed anyone watching them at the shelter, Lutie had felt a presence she couldn't describe.

"So, you think maybe I can go to school there?"

"Where?"

"Lutie, do you listen to me? Ever?"

"Help me get our stuff out of the trunk."

"I told you, it's called the Paradise Elementary School, and it's right on the campus. An elementary school with a university all around it."

As they converted their seats to beds, Lutie realized that Fate's voice had an eagerness she hadn't heard from him in days.

"You think I can go there, Lutie? Now, it might be that only the kids of university students and teachers can be admitted. I don't know. And I suppose we'd have to have a real address to enroll, but—"

"We have one." Lutie pulled out her driver's license, showed it to Fate.

"Who is Belinda Ferguson?" he asked.

"That's me now."

"And you're twenty-two?"

"Don't I look it?"

"Where did you get this, Lutie?"

"Well, I traded some work for a guy who takes photos and makes documents like this. Whatever you need."

"What kind of work?" Fate asked suspiciously.

"I cleaned his studio."

"How'd you meet him?"

"Oh, it's a long story. But he gave me an advance against my first paycheck, and I bought you something." Lutie pulled a large sack from behind her seat and handed it to Fate.

"Gosh," he said when he pulled out the backpack. "This is keen, Lutie. Really keen."

"Fate, don't use the words *gosh* and *keen* in Vegas."

"Why not?"

"Makes you sound like the dweeb you are. No need to advertise it."

"Lutie . . ." Fate hesitated. "You didn't steal this, did you?"

"The receipt's in the sack. Go ahead. Look at it, I know you want to. And here's something else." She handed him a ten-dollar bill.

"Gosh, thanks, Lutie. I mean, thanks for the backpack. If I get to go to Paradise, I'll need this. All the students I saw on the campus today had a backpack."

"Oh, you're going to that school. Before long, we'll be in our own apartment, with a *real* address. Not this one." She waved the driver's license, then put it in her jeans.

"What about you, Lutie? What about your school, huh?"

"I'm going to check on that. I think I'll get my GED. That way I can keep a job and study at night."

As Lutie bunched up an afghan for a pillow, she said, "Fate, don't you think it's weird that Daddy and Floy died on the same day? I mean, I wonder if they died at the same time, at the very same instant? Like they had some kind of connection. You know what I mean?"

Fate avoided a direct response, choosing not to tell her that he'd read Exodus, looking for an answer to the same question.

"I don't know," he said.

"Yeah, I guess if there'd been a connection, it would've been between Daddy and Mom. Not Floy. She wasn't his wife, not his one true love."

"Lutie, you're not going to get all creepy on me, are you? Not like one of the Harlequin romance books you and Floy used to read?"

"No, but I just can't stop thinking about him. All the questions I've got in my head. For instance, they said he died of hepatitis. And I don't even know what hepatitis is. Do you?"

Fate gave Lutie a vague answer, saying there were different kinds of hepatitis, but he didn't tell her that because their father was a drunk, he had most likely died of hepatitis B. And he didn't tell her that from what he'd read in the library, their daddy's last hours—or days—were filled with agony . . . vomiting, diarrhea, a bloated belly, distended veins that ruptured, chest pain, the collapse of his kidneys. His skin the color of a yellow highlighter. And finally, drowning in his own blood as it filled his lungs.

"I just hope he didn't suffer," Lutie said.

"I don't think he did."

"Seems like we oughta do something for him, Fate. Don't you think so?"

"Like what?"

"I don't know. We didn't get to go to his funeral. We don't even know where he's buried."

"I saw a show on TV once, about old convicts who get sick and die in prison. Their bodies are sent home if they've got families, so they can bury them. But with Daddy, well, he's probably buried in the prison cemetery."

"That's what I mean. We couldn't have a funeral, but I think we should do something to say good-bye."

"You got any ideas?"

"Why don't we go to a church? I don't mean for Sunday school and all that, but let's just go into a church where we can sit and think about Daddy. Think about good times we had with him, like the time he played Santa for us when he put on a pair of old red long johns and—"

"Lutie, he was drunk. Don't you remember? He fell into the Christmas tree, broke most of the ornaments, smashed the box with the vase in it that he'd got for Floy. They had a big fight over it."

"Fate, you always remember the stuff that went wrong. Why don't you try to focus on the fun times, like our camping trip to the Badlands National Park. That was fun."

"Yeah, it was."

"Bet we could think of lots of nice memories."

"I suppose."

"Okay. Let's do it. Let's do it tomorrow."

"All right."

They were quiet for a long time, as if respecting each other's private thoughts.

Fate was hoping Lutie had fallen asleep when she said in such a soft voice, he could barely hear her, "You suppose he was thinking about us when he died?"

"Yeah. I bet he was, Lutie. The last thing on his mind would have been us. You and me."

CHAPTER TEN

LUTIE HAD TO wait six days for her next photo session while Philo finished a project in Los Angeles. Six long days and nights of dread, imagining what T. would ask her to do. So by the time she went to "the studio," she was a wreck. She knew when she'd told T. back at the Carnival Court that she needed more documents, even more than the last time, that she'd be required to show more skin than she had before. She just didn't know how much.

Philo wrote down what she said she needed: TB and HIV test results, a food handler's permit, a registration form and Vegas tag for Floy's car, and school records for Fate's fourth grade from Miami, Florida—a city about as far away from Spearfish as she could get. She asked Philo to show that her brother was an A student in advanced classes, which she assured him was the truth, a fact that mattered to Philo and T. not at all.

Lutie was so jumpy when they went back into the photography room that she wrapped herself in her arms as if she were freezing.

"Okay, sweet thing," T. said, "Philo's gonna use the same head shot he used on your driver's license for some of these forms that require a picture ID, then he's gonna shoot you in your little birthday suit."

"I, uh . . . I don't know if I can do this."

"Sure you can. Here." He fished a capsule from his pocket. "Take this," he said. "It'll help you relax."

Philo, setting up his equipment, said, "I don't think she'll need that, T. I believe I can get these without—"

"You shut your mouth, Philo. I'm still paying your salary, and don't you forget it," T. snapped. Then, to Lutie, he said in a softer voice, "Take this, sugar." He grabbed a bottle of water off a counter, then handed it to her along with the capsule.

While looking directly at T., without a glance at the water or the pill, she swallowed it.

"Good girl. Now—"

"Okay, T.," Philo said. "You got what you wanted; now, why don't you go out for a smoke and let me take care of this."

"Whatever you say, Mr. Tarantino."

As soon as the door closed behind T., Philo asked Lutie if she'd like to take a few minutes to get ready, then change behind one of the backdrops.

She nodded, already feeling the effects of the drug T. had given her.

"Take off all your clothes, then put these on." He handed her a pair of see-through thongs with black lace, then said, "And would you put your hair in two ponytails and tie them with these?" The bows he gave her to tie her hair were made of pink ribbon.

Minutes later, when she emerged, Philo was ready to shoot. He handed her a pacifier that looked like a small penis and asked her to hold it in such a way that she looked about ready to slide it between her lips.

Feeling as if she were floating somewhere above her own body, she did exactly as Philo asked, and he clicked off the shots in rapid succession. Then, when he asked her to take off the panties and let her hair down, she didn't give a thought to going behind the backdrop again.

"Would you like me to get you a kimono to put on while I get these next shots set up?"

"No. I'm fine."

Philo brought her a chair and asked her to sit down with a lollipop in her mouth and one hand holding an opened book, then he told her to touch herself while she tilted her head back, her eyes closed, her mouth open as if she were in a period of ecstasy.

"Lutie," Philo said in a voice just above a whisper, "you seem like a good kid . . . but most of the girls I meet are 'good kids' when they start. And this is none of my affair, but I'm going to tell you anyway. If you have to do business with T., and maybe you'll have to 'cause Vegas is a tough town to live in when you need help—stay away from the pills and the powder . . . the dope T. will offer you. Free. In the beginning."

"What did I take? Today."

"Doesn't matter much. Probably OxyContin. Next time it might be white bitch or devil's dandruff or ice. You might have to snort it, smoke it, or inject it. But you use it twice, use any of it twice, and you might never recover from it.

"Now this other stuff you do? Porno or prostitution or . . . worse, you might someday get over that. But dope? Chances are it'll destroy your life.

"And that's all I got to say about it 'cause you'll do what you want to anyway. At least, that's been my experience."

When she left, she had all the documents she'd asked for, but this time T. walked with her a few blocks. Time, he said, for them to have a talk.

"You know, Lutie, I'm taking a big chance on you. I could go to jail for the favors I'm doing for you."

With her high wearing off a bit, she said, "And I know you wouldn't do that unless you made some money off me."

"Pocket change. That's what I make off you. Pocket change. Hardly enough to pay Philo. And his kind of photography doesn't come cheap."

"So what is it you want?"

"More. I want more from you. I *expect* more from you."

"Like what?"

"Movies. Pictures. You're sweet, young, natural. Hard to find a girl who hasn't had a tit job yet. See, you look like the all-American girl. You say you're fifteen, but Philo can make you look twelve. Or younger."

"You're talking porno movies, aren't you? I saw that room with the naked man and woman on a bed, cameras set up, mikes. I know what goes on back there."

"Now, that's dangerous talk, Lutie. That kind of talk can get you in real trouble. Talk like that can get you hurt. Oh, yeah. That's dangerous."

"Dangerous? How?"

"Oh, if you talked about the movies we make at the studio, say something to the wrong party, well . . ."

"I'm not gonna tell anyone, T. I'm trying to stay out of trouble here myself. I've got a little brother to take care of and—"

"I know, honey. I know. And that's why I'm offering you this opportunity. You can make a lot of money. And you can make it fast in this business."

"I don't want to do that, T. Besides, I've got a job if I decide to take it."

"Yeah, I heard. Making beds and cleaning shit out of toilets at the MGM."

Lutie looked stunned. "How'd you—"

"Not much goes on in Vegas that I don't know about, darlin'. But let's get back to you. Here's the thing: Cleaning hotel rooms is never gonna let you put together enough money to get you and your brother into a decent place. See, you have to lay out a damage deposit, pay first and last months' rent, put down utility deposits. You have any idea how much you'd need to do that?"

"Well, I guess I hadn't thought of that."

"No, 'course not, but T. is trying to take care of you, see? And if movies aren't your thing, I can get you hooked up with something else."

"Like what?"

"Well, even with those little bitty boobs, I can get you a job as a stripper . . . or a pro."

"Pro? You mean a whore?"

"Now wait a minute, babe, you don't need to be so harsh with me. I'm trying to look after you here."

"Right."

"Hey, when you finally realize this stupid plan of yours ain't gonna work, when you finally see that you can't make enough money to live anywhere besides your car, when you reach the point where you gotta go Dumpster diving to feed you and your brother, you'll turn to some kind of business that'll help you get where you wanna be. And that's when you're gonna need me, old T., looking out for your best interests. Keeping you safe, healthy, and whole. You get what I'm saying?"

"I gotta go now, T."

"Okay, baby girl, but you'll be back. You'll be back to see me. And it won't be long, not nearly as long as you think."

Lutie went back to Denny's with her food handler's permit, which resulted in her first job offer, an eight-hour shift starting that night at eleven p.m. But she wasn't sure leaving Fate alone all night in the car was a good idea, so she said she couldn't start that soon.

She checked at a dozen casino restaurants, figuring that waitresses would make better tips there, but most had all the help they needed at the moment, and many already had a waiting list of potential employees. Even the two casinos that did have openings could offer her only night work, which, they explained, was the shift where all their new waitstaff had to start.

She filled out an application at a twenty-four-hour cleaners called Right Away when she saw a Help Wanted sign in the window, but the job was only part-time and the pay was pathetic. She tried for work at tourist spots; bars; flower shops; an import bazaar; a beauty salon where she was offered the job of janitor—shampoo and sweep-up girl, a position scheduled to open up in three weeks; upscale shops in the Fashion Mall and the Midway at Circus Circus.

When she passed a shop called Showgirl Costumes, she noticed a sign on the door, a sign that read, "25 sexy moves taught by a professional pole dancer. We help with costumes, jewelry, and job locations. All physical types considered." But when she tried to go inside, she found the door was locked.

A short distance away, she went into Biomedics, a blood donation center that paid for plasma. She spoke to a receptionist who gave her an information sheet that listed the regulations and payment disclosure: thirty dollars for the first donation; thirty-five dollars for all that followed.

On her way back to the car, she passed a narrow brick building, the Glenmoor Arms. When she saw the Apartment Available sign in the yard, she went in. The manager, a disinterested woman who appeared to be a little drunk, showed her the apartment, a one-bedroom efficiency with torn shades at the window, a bed with a bare mattress covered with stains, a kitchen with an oven missing its door, and a sink where ants marched from beneath a broken faucet.

The rent, the manager announced, was four hundred dollars, first and last month due upon occupancy, but that included water and trash pickup; a damage deposit of two hundred dollars, non-refundable if the renter owned a pet; no dopers and no noise after midnight.

When she reached the car, she was surprised to find that Fate hadn't arrived ahead of her, so she took the time to count the money left from the "donation" made yesterday by the gray-haired ladies. Almost three dollars, an amount that assured her that she and Fate would be going back to the Salvation Army shelter for a free meal that evening.

Lutie decided they would go to a Catholic church—not, she said, because of the denomination, but because the building was only two blocks from the library.

They arrived just after nine, found the front doors unlocked, the vestibule empty and silent. The nave was dark, lit only by gauzy diffused light coming through stained-glass windows and some candles glowing near the door.

One elderly woman was sitting in the back pew, her eyes closed as she ran the beads of a rosary through her fingers, her lips moving without sound as she prayed. Another woman, a young Latina, sat near the statue of the Virgin Mary at the side of the nave. Neither woman acknowledged in any way that Fate and Lutie had entered and seated themselves close to the front.

Fate sat still and stiff, his face registering nothing but discomfort that may have come from the unfamiliar surroundings. Or perhaps he was feeling the pain of his reason for being there—to remember good times with his father as a way of saying good-bye. A funeral of sorts, as Lutie had called it that morning.

The thought of death and funerals made him remember something he'd read in one of his fact books about the strange deaths of some popes. He recalled that John X was imprisoned and suffocated and John XIV was left to die of starvation in prison. He reasoned that prison had been no kinder to his father than to those unfortunate popes.

Just then he realized that Lutie was wiping tears from her face, making him wonder not why she was crying, but why he wasn't, so he willed himself back to thoughts of his father, searching for memories.

A ball game. His father had taken him to a semipro ball game in Rapid City, but what he remembered most about that outing was his dad getting drunk on beer and falling from a row of bleachers.

He quickly ran through the books of the Bible and the Ten Commandments, which he'd memorized at the Sunday school Floy took them to in Spearfish, then he backed up and went through the commandments again to count the number he'd broken.

A party. A surprise birthday party. They'd been living with a woman named Beverly, a woman his father had taken up with for a while. He recalled a cake with candles, a pretty woman giving him his first sip of whiskey, everyone yelling, "Surprise!" when his daddy walked in. But again, the memory dissolved with a picture of his father drunk, passed out in a recliner, vomit on his undershirt.

To quiet the films playing behind his eyes, he concentrated on the life-size crucifix attached to the front wall. Fate studied the figure with such fixed attention that he curled his fingers so that his nails cut into his palms, trying to imagine the pain Christ must have felt, hoping that his own pain would bring tears. But that didn't work, either.

Beside him, he felt Lutie's body shudder with weeping, saw her hand covering her mouth to silence the sounds of her sobs. He shifted then, put his arm around his sister, and pulled her close so she could cry into his shoulder.

But still he remained dry-eyed.

Though he couldn't remember his mother, her death, or her funeral, he tried to reach that empty spot deep within him that would forever remain a void, a feeling that sometimes made him sad enough to cry.

But he couldn't get there now.

He remembered reading somewhere that the number of Catholics in the United States was 66,407,105.

Finally, he tried to make his mind go blank, something he'd read about in a book on meditation. Concentrate on his breathing, focus on a pleasant scene, and when his mind wandered, bring the scene back and breathe.

And that's when he saw the image of his father, alone in a prison hospital as he suffered the throes of death—his mouth agape in agony, crying out for help but without the aid of sound, his belly bloated as his lungs filled with blood, the last gasp for air.

And with the vision of his father's swollen hand reaching out for comfort, the comfort of another's hand, the tears that Fate had tried to shed came. Not because he'd willed them, but they came. Streaming down his face and falling onto Lutie's hair.

CHAPTER ELEVEN

FATE HAD KNOWN from the moment he opened his eyes this morning that he was going back to Paradise to see what he could learn about the school. He hadn't mentioned it to Lutie, knowing that she wanted to be left alone when she woke up. Besides, he knew she had something on her mind, something she hadn't been able to share with him.

She was grieving for their father, no doubt about that. She'd always been a daddy's girl, and learning about his death had, in some ways, been harder for her than for Fate.

When Jim McFee had run off and left his boy and girl with Floy, he had broken Lutie's heart. And though she hadn't talked much about it, Fate knew she believed her daddy would come back for them soon. Fate, on the other hand, had come to believe as the months dragged on that his father cared so little for them that he would likely never show up again.

So now that Lutie knew she wouldn't see her daddy again, she was lost. And Fate knew that having a little brother to take care of wasn't making her life any easier.

That's why he was sorry he'd gone on and on about Paradise. She didn't need any more pressure right now.

He waited until she took off before he went into the library to brush his teeth and take his whore's bath, but he didn't stick around there long.

He reached the elementary school soon after nine, found the front door unlocked, and went inside as quietly as he could. He inhaled the odor of floor wax and chalk, the smells that always signaled fall to him, the time the new school year began. His favorite time of year.

He'd been upstairs, downstairs, and in the basement before he met someone on the main floor, not far from where he'd come in.

"Good morning, young man."

The man who spoke appeared to be in his midforties. He was dressed informally—cotton slacks, short-sleeved shirt, boat shoes with no laces. He came out of an office marked Principal and seemed surprised to find a visitor in the hall.

"Hello," Fate said.

"Mind if I ask how you got in here?"

"Through the front door."

"Ah, still the most popular entrance, I suppose, though we do have the occasional student who prefers to bust through a locked window or crawl up the fire escape, but that's usually a late night visit. And you don't strike me as that sort."

"No, sir."

"I thought that the front door would be locked, but a number of our teachers are here today getting ready for the new semester."

"Yes, I saw some of them in classrooms shelving books and decorating bulletin boards and—"

"So you've been touring Paradise."

Smiling, Fate said, "I saw the amphitheater, the swimming

pool, the computer lab and chemistry department and the band room and—"

"Do you play an instrument?"

"No, but I'd like to learn the saxophone."

"Excellent. Our music professor, Dr. Wintle, would—no doubt—like to teach you. He's the best."

"And you offer Latin and drama, and you have a chess club, and you teach geology."

"We lucked out this summer. We had a visiting lecturer from Austria who taught a two-week seminar in crystals."

"Wow," Fate said, then remembered Lutie told him only dweebs used the words *gosh* and *keen*, making him wonder if *wow* fell into the same category. "I went into the language lab and the library and I found the . . ." Suddenly his smile faded, and worry lines creased his forehead. "Was that okay? Going in and out of your classrooms, just wandering around without permission?"

"Absolutely."

"Are you the principal?"

"No, I'm her assistant. Excuse me for not introducing myself sooner. I'm Mr. Grove. And you are . . . ?"

"Fate McFee."

"Nice to make your acquaintance, Mr. McFee," he said, offering his hand. "Now, tell me. Did you like what you saw here today?"

"Oh, this is a wonderful school. The one I went to last year didn't offer much more than math, language arts, social studies, and gym. But here . . . well, I'd give anything to study here."

"What's stopping you?"

"I figure this is a private school with tuition and all."

"Nope. Public. No tuition, no fees, no uniforms."

"Then . . ."

"All you have to do to come to Paradise is to live within our zone."

"Oh."

"Where do you live now?"

"Well, my family isn't settled yet. Not really. I mean, we're not in a permanent place right now."

"I see." Mr. Grove had worked with kids long enough to know he was getting too close to that private place in troubled youngsters. "Well, when you're ready, we can have your school records faxed here, usually within minutes."

"Sure." Fate nodded. "The fax."

"I'm curious, Mr. McFee, about your grades. I'm guessing they're pretty good. Am I right?"

"They're good." Uncomfortable with talk that bordered on bragging, Fate looked at his shoes. "I make straight A's. And I'm in accelerated classes."

"That doesn't surprise me. Not at all."

Fate blushed but managed a timid smile.

"If you'll wait here, I'll get you a map of our zones."

"Okay."

Within moments, Mr. Grove returned and handed Fate a brochure called "Everything You Need to Know About Paradise."

"The map's in there as well as answers to some of the questions you'll think of later."

"Thank you."

"I look forward to seeing you at enrollment. And welcome to Paradise, Mr. McFee."

When Fate left the campus, he walked north on Swenson, an unfamiliar street, but he had no destination, had no reason to want one. He was content to let his mind take him back to Paradise, where he saw himself as a student, spending his days in classes learning Latin, studying art and music history, using a real telescope; asking questions about astronomy, mythology, the measure of force—the kinds of questions he'd longed to ask.

He would, in all probability, have teachers with PhD's. Not some coach who had to teach social studies and drive a school bus.

Fate knew, too, that he would explore the university campus every day after school, sneaking into classes of calculus, British literature, geology, Chinese, philosophy, world religions. He'd meet students from Bhutan, Eritrea, Guinea-Bissau, Andorra, and Nauru—places he'd only read about; he'd listen to professors designated as university scholars, those who held endowed chairs, maybe even Nobel Prize winners, as they explained why the dugong, the babirusa, and the goliath frog were disappearing from the world.

But he was abruptly pulled out of the fictional world where he'd been living for the past several minutes by a golf ball that came sailing over a chain-link fence several feet away, bounced three times, then rolled to a stop just at the toe of his right foot.

When he looked to see where it had come from, he saw a golf cart speeding across the grounds inside the fence, the cart coming in his direction.

The driver, a man nearing sixty, stopped the cart, got out, and, using his golf club, started searching for the ball by parting tall grass and smacking at low bushes.

"You looking for this?" Fate called, holding up the ball for the man to see.

"Imagine so," the golfer said, then walked to the fence and accepted the ball as Fate dropped it into his outstretched hand.

"Yep, see right there?" He pointed to three black letters printed on the ball: F.E.W. "My initials," he said. "Frederick E. Wing."

"What does the *E* stand for?" Fate asked.

"Never told, never will." He smiled, then took a money clip from his pocket, pulled off a one, and handed it to Fate.

"Son, you have any idea what this ball costs? Of course you don't," he said in response to the blank look on Fate's face. "It's a Pro V1. Most expensive ball made. A buck's a cheap price for getting this back. Now, understand, I've got a whole pocketful of these in my golf bag, but I'm having a good game. I can afford to take a stroke on this hole, and I will as long as I recover this ball."

He waved, his back to Fate as he dropped the ball a couple of feet inside the fence and gave it a whack that Fate thought must have pleased him when he looked over his shoulder and smiled.

"Thanks, boy," he said as he climbed into the cart, then drove away.

Fate spent the rest of the afternoon searching for misplayed golf balls. He figured any ball that landed outside the fence might mean more cash for him, so he looked through weeds, sand, and gravel, beneath bushes and the occasional tangle of vines. He paid special attention to the brand names on the balls and was particularly pleased when he found a Pro V1 or any ball with initials, believing that they might bring the best prices.

When a woman in a uniform and cap pulled up in a cart marked Wynn's Security, Fate felt tense for fear he had violated some law. When she motioned him toward the fence, he moved reluctantly in her direction.

"What are you doing?" she asked.

Fate held open the bag so she could see what was inside. "Figured I might be able to sell them."

"You can if they're in decent shape, but you won't get much for your trouble. There's a place called the Eighteenth Hole over on Hacienda Avenue that reconditions used balls if they're clean. But they won't give you much."

"How much?"

"Ten cents each, I think."

"I sold one a couple of hours ago for a dollar. One ball."

"Now, who the devil would pay you a buck for a—"

"Frederick E. Wing."

"Sure, I know Mr. Wing. He's been a member here forever. Rich, too, but so is everyone else who belongs to Wynn's."

"It was a Pro V and had his initials on it. And I've got lots more Pro V's in here, and most of them are initialed, too."

"Here." She reached across the fence for the bag. "Let me see what you've got in there."

As she raked through the balls, she would occasionally pull one out and read the initials. "B.J.H. That's Ms. Hendricks. She only plays with Lady Precepts. And here's one belongs to Jim Vanzant."

"You think they'd pay to get those back?"

"They might. Problem is, you can't get past the front gate, and the boys in the guardhouse for sure will run your little butt off if you stand out there trying to sell used golf balls back to their owners."

"Well, where is Hacienda Avenue?"

"A long walk from here. But I'll tell you what I'll do. I'll give you . . . oh, say, five bucks for the whole lot. That's more than they'll pay you at the Eighteenth Hole, I guarantee you."

"Then how much will you get when you sell them to—"

"Oh, I can't sell them, kid. I'd lose my job. But it'll make me look good if I hand Ms. Hendricks's ball back to her. She'll remember that when she gives out her Christmas bonus."

"Okay, it's a deal if you'll pay me five dollars for every bag I can fill."

"Well, you're quite the wheeler-dealer, aren't you, kid?" She grinned as she handed him a five-dollar bill. "All right, then. Guess we're in business."

"Yes, ma'am," Fate said as he pushed the money deep in his pocket. "We're in business."

CHAPTER TWELVE

THREE DAYS LATER, Lutie got a job at the Desert Palms Motel, a seedy three-story concrete-block building with plenty of desert but not a palm in sight.

Two girls had just been fired for selling drugs on the premises, which accounted for Lutie being hired on the spot. She'd been handed an ill-fitting uniform—a jumper and white blouse—and issued a badge bearing her new name, Belinda, a match to her fake documents.

The first time the boss, a Russian named Pavel, called out the room numbers "Belinda" would be responsible for cleaning that day, Lutie forgot who she was supposed to be and failed to respond, prompting Pavel to yell a repetition of his instruction. Not the best of beginnings to a new job.

Each girl was responsible for cleaning sixteen rooms a day, and though some of the women on the staff were in their sixties, Pavel called them all girls.

If the girls could finish their rooms before their eight-hour shift ended, they could leave. If the work took more than eight hours, they stayed until all of their sixteen rooms were cleaned. Regardless, they were paid six dollars an hour. Pavel paid no overtime, the girls received no benefits—no medical, not a day of sick leave, and the idea of a paid vacation was laughable. They had thirty minutes for lunch and two coffee breaks of ten minutes each, one at ten in the morning and one at two in the afternoon.

Lutie was surprised to learn that some of the cleaning women had been working at the Palms for several years, but since most were illegal, they were reluctant to change jobs.

On her first day, Lutie made friends with Urbana, a girl of eighteen from Cuba. On their morning break, they shared a cigarette at a table near the swimming pool, the water so fetid and dark that alligators could be hidden beneath the surface.

"You wanna try to stay away from Pavel," Urbana warned. "He's a free feeler. Grab your ass, rub your tits, do more if he corner you in a room alone. You always leaves the door open when you cleaning. If it close, we know he's inside and we come in to bring fresh towel. He got me alone once, but enough for him."

Urbana, several inches taller than Pavel and forty pounds heavier, laughed.

"When he wrestle me onto bed, I grab his nuts and squeeze until I thought they pop. He ain't touch me since."

After they each took a last puff of Urbana's cigarette and re-turned to work, Lutie put in practice some of the advice Urbana had given her, advice to help her finish her rooms in eight hours. And most of the shortcuts saved time and energy, depending—of course—on the condition of the room.

Most of the guests at the Palms did little more than litter the rooms with empty beer bottles and bones from the rib joint across the street. If they'd kept a dog in the room, the girls usually had extra messes to deal with, and if there had been a baby, they often had to contend with messy diapers left in odd places.

But the worst were women who tossed their used tampons under the bed or left their Kotex wadded into the bedding; men who left their used condoms between the sheets or peed into the trash cans.

The weirdest stories were passed around during the girls' lunch breaks: one who found all the drinking glasses stuffed with pickles; three newborn kittens, left in a cardboard box, taken home by Katrina, a maid who was going to try to bottle-feed them; a Gideon Bible covered with ketchup; and the tale, passed on for years, of finding a baby asleep in a closed dresser drawer. Maria, one of the older girls, claimed to have once found a condom, half-filled with semen, stretched over the mouthpiece of the telephone.

But for its failings—poor pay and lack of benefits, the boorish behavior of the boss and the guests—it was a job that Lutie McFee, aka Belinda Ferguson, needed right now in order to survive.

Fate was spending less time at the library and on the UNLV campus now that he was collecting and selling golf balls. He'd found another course, the Las Vegas Hilton Country Club, which he usually worked in the mornings, then returned to the Wynn course later in the day.

His trek between the two clubs took him past the Chinese restaurant, where he stopped in a couple of days a week to see his friend Chou, who always greeted him warmly and served him a meal.

And he'd found two more buyers for his golf balls: one a young caddy, the other a security guard at the Hilton gatehouse. On his best day, he brought in fourteen dollars; his worst day paid him a profit of three fifty.

But rather than give in to discouragement, he became more determined to help Lutie put together enough money so they could move into an apartment within the Paradise school zone. And time was running out. That's when he decided to extend his operation.

He'd seen a bushy-haired little man pushing a grocery cart filled with cans he picked up from the streets, alleys, and curbs, a guy who darted from spot to spot, his eyes seeming to zero in on aluminum from blocks away—cans poking from sacks, from mounds of sand, from overflowing Dumpsters.

One morning as Fate was on his way to the Hilton Club, he stopped the man to ask about the value of the cans, but the guy turned ugly, making threatening gestures, shouting furiously at Fate in a language he didn't understand. Clearly, Fate had encountered an entrepreneur carefully guarding his business, one he was not prompted to share.

But Fate wasn't about to be scared off by what he figured must be a lucrative enterprise.

Besides, since he was on the streets most of the day walking to and from golf courses, why not carry an extra plastic bag for wayward aluminum cans? He didn't think it would be too difficult to locate a place to sell them. And it wasn't.

That very day, he met a woman pushing a four-wheel walker with a large wire basket mounted on the front, a basket half-full of cans and bottles.

He introduced himself politely, learned her name was Gladys and that she used the walker for exercise following knee surgery. But once she had recovered enough to bend, she'd started picking up debris in her neighborhood, litter tossed from passing vehicles. Then she'd found that a recycling center would pay her fifty-five cents a pound for the cans. She said as a result, she could keep working her stiff knee, do what she could to clean up her street, and make a bit of money on the side.

She told Fate how to get to one of the recycling stations, they said their good-byes, and he was off, a sack in each hand.

By the end of the week, he had almost forty dollars in cash to hand over to Lutie.

One of Lutie's perks at the Palms was that she and Fate could manage a shower and shampoo a few days a week, those times when Pavel was away from the motel. She caught on quickly to his schedule: banking on Mondays, Rotary Club breakfasts on Tuesdays, and grocery shopping for his mother on Fridays. He was always gone for a half hour, usually more, plenty of time for Lutie to sneak Fate into one of the empty rooms.

Another plus was Maria, the oldest of the girls, a beautician before she left her home in Monterrey. She gave Fate a free haircut while Lutie cleaned a couple of Maria's rooms, a good trade for all three of them.

But best of all, Lutie made a friend. A best friend. She and Urbana spent their breaks together smoking cigarettes Urbana brought from home, secreted out of her brother's packs, or those left behind in the rooms after guests checked out. They shared lunches, too. Free sandwiches they got from a flirty boy named Sonny who worked in the kitchen at the Skillet, a café next door to the Palms.

Urbana lived with her twenty-three-year-old brother, Raul, and his friend from Colombia, Arturo. Both guys worked at a body shop a few miles from the Strip, and both sold drugs when their money ran low, which—according to Urbana—was often.

Once, a few weeks after Lutie started working at the Palms, she saw Raul when he came by to pick up Urbana. When he smiled and said hello to Lutie, she felt a jolt like an electric spark run down her belly.

The next day, Urbana said that Raul wanted to take her and Belinda out Saturday night, go to a few clubs, dance, have some fun. Lutie was shocked when she realized how long it had been since she'd been invited anywhere by anyone. But she'd never gone out with a man of twenty-three, had never imagined herself dancing with one as handsome as Raul, had never even gone dancing unless she counted the school dances she went to with Norma, the girl who had pierced her ears in the school bathroom.

"Yes!" she screamed, then she squealed, grabbed Urbana, and twirled her around. And now, finally, she trusted Urbana enough to admit that Belinda was not her real name, a fact that didn't faze Urbana.

"Do you know how it is, the salsa?"

Lutie's enthusiasm suddenly waned. She shook her head.

"Not to worry. I teach you."

And for the rest of the day, Lutie practiced her first salsa lesson as she danced in and out of rooms.

The girls who worked at the motel got paid every Friday, and though Lutie was desperate for the money, she always dreaded being alone with her boss. So each time she went to Pavel's office for her check, she made sure to keep the desk between her and the free feeler.

They hadn't gotten along since Lutie's first payday a few weeks earlier when she saw the salary he had inked in on her check, causing her dread of fighting off the hairy Russian to turn to anger.

The Social Security deduction was no surprise, but when she saw that he'd withheld ten dollars as a deposit on her uniform, she lost it.

"You can't do this!" she yelled.

"Of course I can. I do it to all girls who work for me."

"This rag wouldn't bring a quarter at a yard sale!"

"Every time a girl quit without she turn in her uniform, cost me money. Hundreds of dollars a year I am cost."

"Yeah, I know those trendsetting designers don't come cheap. And once you put on one of these"—she ran her hand across the bodice of her jumper—"you never want to give it up. I plan to be married in mine," she said as she stormed out of Pavel's office and slammed the door behind her.

But that wasn't the end of it. Since she had no bank account, she had to give up 20 percent of the total to cash her check at the PayDay Money Store.

Fate had made more selling golf balls and cans in a week than she had working at the Palms.

Lutie didn't tell Fate she was going clubbing on Saturday night. Instead she lied, said she would be in late because she and Urbana were going to a sneak preview that didn't start until midnight. Fate didn't believe her, but he knew she needed some fun in her life, so he didn't question her excuse. Nevertheless, that didn't mean he wouldn't worry about her. Lutie had a history of bad choices.

He stayed in the library on Saturday until after five, then hitched a ride with an old man driving a pickup who took him within a few blocks of the Salvation Army.

Lutie and Fate had become two of the "regulars" at the shelter, so he knew the menu tonight was beef stew, a thick slice of cheese, crackers, and rice pudding. His favorite night was Wednesday, when they served meat loaf, mashed potatoes, green beans, and sugar cookies, but the stew wasn't bad.

Fate knew several of the other homeless who ate at the shelter every evening: Luisa, who worked at a day care center, and her son, Diego, just a few months younger than Fate; Larraine, the woman who wore a hospital gown and a housecoat three days a week when she had dialysis; Sam, a chain-smoker with lung cancer and his two preteen girls, Emily and Ashley; Brother Evans, who was a homeless preacher; and Ray, the man who conversed with salt shakers, a Vietnam vet suffering dementia.

But tonight, when Fate walked in, he knew something was different. Couldn't be the food, because he could see pots of stew bubbling on the stove in the kitchen, and the pass-through had bowls of packaged crackers and a tray of sliced cheese.

No, the difference was in the sound—or lack of it. An odd silence had settled over the room. And just as Fate noticed candles burning on each table, Brother Evans stepped from the back of the room and asked those gathered to join him as he offered up a prayer for Sam, who had died that morning.

But instead of bowing his head, Fate scanned the crowd, his eyes coming to rest on Sam's daughters, Emily and Ashley, who were pressed against a woman dressed in a wrinkled gray suit with a briefcase beneath her arm. She had each girl in hand as if she expected them to bolt. Emily, the older sister, looked pale and tight-lipped; Ashley, the younger by a year or two, was crying quietly.

A chorus of amens rose when Brother Evans concluded his prayer. Then Ray, with a guitar strapped across his chest, began to play a song unfamiliar to Fate, with lyrics that sounded unsuited to the occasion. Ray was singing "Still in Saigon," and though his voice wasn't bad, the music suffered because the guitar was missing a string. But Ray seemed undaunted by the impaired instrument.

With the final note of the song, Sam's daughters were shepherded out the door and into a waiting car Fate could see through one of the shelter's windows. Word soon spread that the girls were headed to foster care.

After dinner, Fate caught a ride back to his "neighborhood" with Marvin, who returned occasionally to the shelter to help with the serving of the evening meal. Long before Lutie and

Fate had arrived, Marvin had stayed at the shelter for nearly a year before finding work as a truck driver, a job that afforded him personal use of the truck and enough money to move into a shared apartment.

Back at Floy's car, Fate found a package of cookies on the hood, his midnight snack. He and Lutie were regularly treated to gifts from their secret friend—fruit, doughnuts, packages of peanuts, candy bars, licorice. Once a flashlight, another time a tiny portable radio, but the reception was poor. And they had yet to see who delivered these treats to them.

But even cookies couldn't help Fate tonight as he struggled to find sleep. He was uncomfortable on his first night without Lutie, and he couldn't manage to let go of thoughts about Sam's daughters.

He wondered if they'd get to stay together with the same family or if they'd be separated. And the story Lutie had told him about kids in foster care kept bad images of Emily and Ashley replaying behind his closed eyes.

Sometime around three, Fate was awakened with the urge to pee. He crawled out of the car, barefoot and wearing only jeans, and had just unzipped his fly when an excruciating pain struck the arch of his left foot.

A slice of moonlight allowed him to see the scorpion he'd stepped on as it scurried away across the asphalt of the library parking lot.

He was unable to bear the searing pain without yelping in agony and hopping up and down on his one good foot. Minutes later, when he hobbled back to the car, his left foot was afire with fever and beginning to swell. He grabbed a bottle half-filled with Pepsi and poured it over the sole of his foot, but it only made the pain worse.

An hour later, worn down by pain and the circumstances of his life, Fate slumped onto one of Floy's afghans and gave himself to sleep, a sleep so numbing and deep that he didn't feel the hands that taped a roasted cockroach over the sting on his foot . . . nor did he feel the comforting gesture of a hand that softly patted his knee.

CHAPTER THIRTEEN

LUTIE COULD HEAR a voice calling to her, a female voice, but she couldn't identify the speaker. At first, she thought it was her math teacher back in Spearfish, then she believed it was Floy. But when she tried to open her eyes, a blinding glare forced them closed.

"Come on, girl. We got to put straight this room before he show up. The time almost six-thirty."

As someone vigorously shook her shoulders, Lutie tried to resist, flailing at whoever was bent over her, prodding her body to move. But her hands, curled loosely into fists, failed to connect with anything solid, letting her believe momentarily that she was dreaming.

"Wake up, Lutie. You better to wake up and help me."

Finally, through the opened slit of one eye, Lutie saw Urbana's face, out of focus, like looking at her underwater.

Lutie groaned, then turned her head away from the light coming through the window, her movement causing the bed beneath her to begin to spin. She opened her eyes against the pain building up behind them, to find herself in a room twirling like a Tilt-A-Whirl. With the bed and the space around it spinning faster and faster, she felt the bile surging inside her but was helpless to rise. And even if she could, her mind was so clouded that she didn't recognize the room and couldn't have located the bathroom, although she'd cleaned it and dozens of others exactly like it many times.

Finally, gagging, she managed to hang her head off the side of the bed, giving Urbana the warning she needed.

"Oh, no, you don't!" she yelled as she dragged Lutie from the bed, stood her unsteadily on her feet, and, by grabbing her from behind in a bear hug, pushed her forward into the bathroom. She shoved her into the shower stall under a stream of icy water just as the first of last night's liquor and food spewed from Lutie's mouth.

"Nasty," Urbana said as she jerked the shower curtain closed. "Nasty! Stay until you bring all up. You hear me?"

Twenty minutes later, Lutie stepped out of the shower, her body chilled and slightly blue in contrast with her face, which had taken on a greenish hue. With her teeth chattering, she gave herself up to the ministrations of Urbana, who dried Lutie's hair with a towel, wrapped her in a clean sheet, and led her back to bed.

Urbana, in the most motherly tone she could muster, said, "Now. You will live."

"What happened?" Lutie asked, her voice trembling and weak.

"You mean between time you danced salsa at Habana Heaven, show off your tits, and at two o'clock when Raul carried you from car to here?"

"Oh, God." Lutie covered her eyes with both hands and shook her head.

"You not a good drunk. Don't try again." Then Urbana handed Lutie a pill and a glass of water. "Take this. Feel better soon. Then we straight the room and go before Pavel come."

"Why are we here?" Lutie asked.

"Magda, night clerk at front desk, friend of mine. Gave me key to room."

"But—"

"Couldn't take you home. Don't want you little brother to see you like drunk."

"You look awful," Fate said when Lutie crawled into Floy's car. "And why aren't you working today?"

"I'm sick."

Fate was slumped in the backseat, his leg propped up on the front passenger seat.

"What's wrong with your leg?" Lutie asked.

"I got stung by a scorpion."

"God. I'll bet that hurt."

"Yeah."

"What's that on the bottom of your foot?"

"A roasted cockroach and a Band-Aid."

"What?!"

"Guess I fell asleep an hour or two after it happened. When I woke up, this is what I found." Fate bent his leg, twisting it so he could look at his foot. "It's a lot better now."

"You figure it was our guardian angel again?" Lutie asked.

"Who else."

"Did you see him?"

Fate shook his head. "I didn't even feel this happening." He indicated the Band-Aid. "It hurt so bad, I think I sort of passed out."

"Sorry I wasn't here."

"Why didn't you come home last night?"

"Home?"

"Well, why didn't you come back here?"

"Oh, after the movie me and Urbana went out to eat. She

bought me a dinner at a Cuban restaurant, then we went to her house and watched TV until two or three. We both fell asleep on her couch."

"So what made you sick?"

"The food, I think. It was real spicy."

Fate didn't believe her story but decided to let it go. He knew if he badgered her, they'd end up fighting, then she'd pout and give him the silent treatment for a couple of days. Instead, he grabbed his shoes and socks, getting ready to make his rounds of the golf courses.

"You think you can walk with your foot in that kind of shape?"

"Yeah. It's not bad at all now. Guess this really works." He pulled the Band-Aid loose and, with the dead cockroach stuck to it, tossed the mess out the window. "What are you going to do today?"

"Find a cool place and go to sleep."

"Go up to the second floor in the library. They have a leather chair up there, real comfortable. If you can get it before someone else, you can grab a book, pretend to read, put your head back, and sleep. I see people do it all the time."

"Okay. I think I will."

When Fate had put on his socks, he picked up one of his shoes, then ran his fingers inside the toe and pulled out some folded bills.

"Here's what I made yesterday. Nine dollars. Not a bad day, huh?"

"No. That's good."

"Let's count it all."

Like an eager banker, Fate looked forward to the time each day when they counted their money, watching their stash grow, even though it had been growing more slowly than he would have wanted.

"Not today," Lutie said, her voice void of any enthusiasm.

"Why not? We do it every day, Lutie. Why not today?"

"I just don't feel like it."

"Then give it to me. I'll count it."

"No, let's wait until—"

"What's wrong? Huh? You come up short?" Fate's suspicion about the money gave his voice an angry edge. "Did you buy something last night, something you don't want me to know about?"

"Like what?"

"Maybe the cigarettes I smell on your clothes. Or the liquor on your breath?"

"Goddammit, Fate, I don't have to answer to you."

"Give me that." Fate jerked Lutie's purse away from her, leaned away as she tried to get it back. When he unzipped it and pulled out the plastic billfold where she kept their money, she snapped at him.

"You know, I earned as much of that money as you did, so I had every right to—"

"This is it?" Fate held up the bills he'd taken from the slim wallet. "Forty-two dollars?" He was yelling now. "You spent thirty dollars last night? For a movie, a free meal, and some TV, you spent thirty dollars?"

"Fate, I . . . I didn't mean to. It just happened."

"Oh, really. How did it 'just happen,' Lutie?"

"I don't owe you an explanation," Lutie said with all the sarcasm she could muster. "I don't owe you anything. Just because you—"

"I hitched rides so I could get a free meal at the Salvation Army where, by the way, not that you'd care, there was a ceremony for Sam, who died yesterday morning."

"Sam? The daddy of those girls?"

"And while I was eating stew and crackers, you were having a real night on the town, weren't you? You get drunk?"

Lutie turned away, looked out her window without response.

"You did, didn't you? You got drunk and . . . what? Had sex? Bought drugs?"

Fate got out of the car, shoved the money deep into his pocket, and walked away without a word or backward glance.

Two days later, Lutie took the night-shift job at Denny's, and on her first night there, she made nearly thirty dollars in tips, the exact amount of money she'd spent from the "stash" she and Fate called their savings—which Fate had started keeping since Lutie's night out. If she could make that kind of money regularly and keep both jobs, she figured that by the time Fate's school started, they could be in an apartment.

Her optimism didn't last long, though. On her second night, she brought in a disappointing total of eight bucks, and from that she had to pay nearly three for a porcelain platter she shattered when it slid off a tray she was carrying.

But the job at Denny's offered a great advantage she hadn't counted on when she started. She got all she wanted to eat while she was there by meals returned uneaten to the kitchen when the eggs were overcooked or a steak was too well-done. And she managed to feed Fate every morning when she returned to the car without paying a penny for the food.

Of course, her new schedule left her tired, always in need of sleep. Within a week of starting at the restaurant, she had dark circles under her eyes, and by the end of each day, her shoulders slumped as exhaustion set in.

She started her days at six-thrity with the aid of a small travel alarm she stole at a hardware store. She liked to arrive at the motel by seven on those days when she and Fate could have time for a shower before she started work at eight. Her shift there ended at five, which was her bedtime. The only problem was the heat. The car was so hot until the sun went down, sleeping in it was impossible, so Fate met her at the car every day after quitting time at the Palms, then she drove them to the Salvation Army complex, where she slept using her afghan as a sleeping mat, beneath the shade of a stand of old cedar elms. Fate went inside for supper, then watched over Lutie as she was sleeping while he read by the glare of a flashlight.

He woke her at ten so she could change into her Denny's uniform, drive them back to the library parking lot, and get to the restaurant on time.

By then, Fate was ready for sleep, and though strange night sounds woke him in alarm, he was getting better at falling back asleep without too much trouble.

Once, when he was awakened by an unidentified noise near the car, he sat up in time to see a limping figure retreating into the tree line next to the library.

The next morning, he found two fresh apples left on the hood of the car.

CHAPTER FOURTEEN

AT FIRST FATE and Lutie hadn't talked much following their confrontation, but as time passed, they were able to get back to their frequent conversations about money. Always about money.

Only days before the start of the fall semester at Paradise, they had $334.92 saved, hardly enough to cover all the costs involved in getting an apartment.

Fate had a stack of free magazines he picked up in stores and from street racks. They were called Apartment Finders, and he checked and rechecked them, circling possibilities of places within the Paradise zone.

Lutie had so little free time that they seldom found an opportunity to go look at his choices, but it didn't take long for them to learn that the advertising in the magazines was almost always misleading.

If an ad included the phrase "Needs some TLC," they discovered that was code for "This apartment is unlivable," and "Cozy little nest" meant a place of comfort for mice, fleas, and bedbugs living in harmony in a one-room efficiency.

One flat they looked at was advertised as a "two-bedroom with loads of extras." They were not surprised to find that the "extras" included a refrigerator without a door handle, a dried pile of dog manure in the corner of one bedroom, and a battalion of cockroaches that had seized the kitchen in what had apparently been a one-sided invasion.

They went to see a two-bedroom mobile home because the ad for it said, "You'll find a warm welcome here." After they looked at it, they assumed the word *warm* referred to a recent fire that had scorched the trailer, most especially in the kitchen, but had covered the dwelling from end to end in soot and the smell of smoke.

They even took a chance on looking at a shared apartment that they could rent for only three hundred fifty dollars a month and required no damage deposit. What they found was an eighty-two-year-old man who kept over thirty cats—he admitted he'd lost count after Puff died. He called himself Darth, he was in a wheelchair, and he needed someone to feed the cats; cook his meals; unstop the toilet; pluck the stiff dark whiskers from his chin, whiskers he likened to the uncontrolled growth of Bermuda grass; and do something about the roof, which—judging from the number of pots, buckets, cans, and pans placed at various spots around the apartment—leaked from two dozen cracks in the ceiling.

One afternoon after Fate had almost nothing to show for his efforts to sell his golf balls and cans, he said, "Lutie, are we getting anywhere?"

"What do you mean? Getting where?"

"Well, we've been here for . . . what? Six, seven weeks? We're still living in the car, still eating at the shelter and whatever you manage to slip out of Denny's. We're not in school, and we don't seem to have much chance to get a place of our own. At least not in time for—"

"I don't see it that way, Fate. I know it's slow going, but we're getting there. And we're doing it all on our own. Besides, what choice do we have?"

"That's what I've been thinking about."

"A choice? Like what?"

"Well, maybe we should've stayed in Spearfish after Floy died. Sure, we would've gone on to foster care, but maybe we would've been lucky. Both of us might've gone with a nice family. A mom and dad who wanted us, *really* wanted us. A couple who would treat us well, buy us school clothes, maybe have a computer and lots of books. Maybe even a dog or—"

"Fate, what world are you living in? Huh? You're describing one of those sweet little TV series like *Seventh Heaven* or something. A make-believe life where everything works out, everyone is happy, everyone loves everyone. But life's not like that, kid. And it sure as hell isn't what foster care is like."

"But if we—"

"You go back if that's what you want. We've got enough money to buy you a bus ticket, but I'm not going with you. So you'd better think about this real hard. If you stay here, I'm going to get you in that fancy school and—"

"Paradise."

"Whatever. But if you go back, you'll be in Bernard Elementary again, you'll be living with a family that probably won't give a damn about you, and you'll be doing it all without me. So make up your mind. And do it now."

Fate chewed at an imaginary hangnail, an attempt to buy enough time to blink away tears, but when he finally turned to Lutie, one tear had broken free and was tracing a path down his cheek.

"I'm not going back without you, Lutie. No matter what happens."

*　　*　　*

153

Lutie had forgotten about the cotton taped on the inside of the bend of her elbow, a dressing she'd been wearing since she left the blood center early while Fate was still asleep in the car. She'd decided to forgo their showers in order to be at the center when it opened at seven, figuring she could still make it to the motel by eight.

She knew if she was late, she'd hear about it from Pavel, who kept a ledger, entering the times each of the girls came to work and the times they left work every day.

She was lucky this morning, arriving exactly at eight, just in time to join the girls circling Pavel as he called out their room numbers. As they went to the supply rooms to get their carts, she fell in beside Urbana, who had seemed cool toward her since the night they'd gone out with Raul and his roommate.

"How's things?" Lutie asked.

"Fine," Urbana replied. But something in her voice said she was not inviting conversation.

"Hey, Urbana, are you upset with me about anything?"

Urbana shook her head.

"You know, I'm sorry about getting plastered when we went out with Raul and Arturo, but I want you to know how much I appreciate you taking care of me, getting us a room, helping me sober up and all."

"Okay."

"How's Raul?"

"I don't see him much. He dating a girl he met at the Habana. He with her all time now."

"Guess I didn't make a very good impression, huh?"

Urbana shrugged.

"Come on, talk to me. Tell me what's on your mind."

"Okay, I tell you. Someone take money from my purse that night. Twenty dollars, lot of money to me. And the only times I leave my purse at table was with you."

"Oh, Urbana. I didn't take your money. I wouldn't do that. You're my friend."

"What I think, too, but—"

"Maybe I left our purses at the table when I was dancing. As a matter of fact, I was missing thirty dollars myself and I don't remember spending it for anything."

"Yes, Raul and Arturo pay for drinks, give us zip, buy the—"

"What's zip?"

"Crank. Crystal. You say you don't remember? Hell to dammit, Lutie, you the worsest drunk I ever know. But look like you make friend with the needle now." She touched the bandage on Lutie's arm.

"Oh, no. I gave blood this morning."

"I see. You a real . . . what you say, humantarium."

"Afraid not. I did it for the money. Thirty-five dollars. See, my brother and I are saving for our apartment."

They had reached the last rooms at the end of the hall, just before one of the outside entrances. Lutie would be working the rooms on one side of the hall, Urbana on the other.

"Let me ask you a question, Urbana. When Raul brought me to that room, did he . . . did we . . ."

"So you accuse him of what?" Urbana said, her voice rising with anger. "Fuck you while you pass out? You listen to me, little rat, my brother good man. He no take advantage of a cheap drunk like you. Do I know? Yes. I was with him when he carry you into room, put you on the bed. So now I know you take my money and you accuse Raul of—"

"No, Urbana. No! I'm not accusing him. Honest. I just needed to ask because—"

Urbana, turning her back on Lutie, knocked on a door and called, "Room service," the process the girls went through sixteen times each day.

Lutie did the same at a door directly across from Urbana's room.

Receiving no response, she used her key to open it, wedged her doorstop beneath the door, grabbed sheets and pillowcases from the cart, and went inside.

She didn't see the naked man hiding inside the darkened bathroom, didn't hear him remove her doorstop or close the door. But when she heard the lock turn, she walked to the end of the bed to see who was there, a pillow in one hand, the pillowcase she was changing in the other.

She tried to scream, but he was fast. She got out no more than a surprised yelp before he yanked the pillow from her hand, pressed it against her face, and shoved her back onto the bed, his body on top of hers.

She was screaming, but no sound escaped the pillow as he clamped it ever tighter over her face. Soon, she was fighting for breath.

As he yanked up the skirt of her jumper and tore off her underpants, she grabbed a hunk of his hair and pulled, but his hair was greasy, preventing her from keeping her grip.

He was inside her within seconds, his body slick with sweat as he lunged again and again. She felt as if he were splitting her in two.

She tried to concentrate on what Urbana had told her about Pavel: "You always leaves the door open when you cleaning. If it close, we know he's inside and we come in to bring fresh towel."

And now she knew Urbana was working right across the hall, knew she must notice that Lutie's door was closed. Surely she would use her key, come in and help her.

But the door never opened even though she heard the wheels of Urbana's cart as it moved on to the next room.

CHAPTER FIFTEEN

LUTIE NEVER RETURNED to the Desert Palms, even though she had a few days' pay coming. After the rape, she'd recovered her own clothes from the girls' dressing room, then showered, scrubbing herself raw, shampooing her hair until the bottle ran dry.

Finished, though still feeling putrid, but believing she was as clean as she'd ever be, she'd set fire to her uniform in the bathtub. She'd waited until it was fully aflame, dark smoke billowing, then walked unhurriedly out of the building seconds after the fire alarm sounded, setting off the sprinkler system in the halls, the lobby, the office, and all the rooms.

She'd spoken to no one when she left, even the few, which included Urbana, who'd run for the exits.

She'd surprised Fate, who was still in the library following his whore's bath, reading before he started his day in the streets. She'd told him she'd been let go at the motel, saying little in answer to his questions, simply explaining that business had dropped off and since she was the last hired, she was the first fired.

She'd spent the day alone while Fate was taking care of his business of collecting golf balls and cans. Sitting in the shade of a tree on the library lawn—never nodding off, though she was more tired than she'd been in her entire life, never shedding a tear despite the feeling of intolerable anger and unbearable sadness—she'd stared soundlessly at a scene only she could see.

That evening when she and Fate went to the shelter for supper, she ate nothing, but the look and smell of the food sent her running for the bathroom twice to throw up.

She'd worked only two hours of her shift at Denny's that night, telling the manager she was too sick to stay, then she'd driven the car back to the library parking spot without a word to Fate.

He'd known, of course, that beyond losing her job at the motel, something else had gone terribly wrong for her, but he hadn't asked. He knew her so well, knew she would tell him when she was ready. Not before.

Now, only days later, Lutie was working her full eight hours at Denny's, but she was only going through the motions. Her personality had changed—her real smile had faded, replaced by one that was wooden and forced; her quick, funny comebacks to her favorite teasing customers were no longer quick or funny, leaving her conversation flat, lacking spirit. She felt, without caring, that she was old, worn out, hollow, and used up. She knew, at just fifteen, that she was damaged. Beyond redemption.

Without the benefit of the washers and dryers she'd used at the motel, her clothes and Fate's were dirty and wrinkled, but she didn't seem to notice or care when she wore a blouse with yesterday's ketchup or a pair of pants with dried splatters of grease down the legs.

Her new personality and appearance soon resulted in fewer tips at the restaurant. And with the loss of her income from the Palms, the savings she and Fate had worked so hard to put together began to suffer.

She went to sell blood again, but her weight had fallen to one hundred and eight, two pounds below the hundred and ten limit, so she was turned away. She tried panhandling once more, this time an older couple walking the Strip, but she couldn't manage a convincing performance and came away empty-handed and embarrassed.

One morning, when she was sitting in a park she'd recently discovered, a disheveled middle-aged woman and a young girl parked their grocery cart and squeezed in on the bench beside her.

"Pretty day," the woman said. "I'm Fiona, and this is my daughter, Pammy. She's deaf, but she can sign and she's pretty good at reading lips if you talk slow."

"Hi," Lutie said.

She would have known they were homeless even without seeing their belongings heaped into the cart. She would have known because of their eyes—hopeless and defeated. Even the girl, who couldn't have been as old as Fate, had eyes with the look of the lost, the forgotten.

"Want some pizza?" Fiona asked. "We have pepperoni. I think it has extra cheese, too." She reached into the grocery cart and took from the top a package of greasy newspaper, peeling back the stained pages to reveal an almost whole pizza. She held the paper out to Lutie, an offering. "Help yourself."

"No, thanks. I just ate."

"You go to St. Vincent's for lunch?"

Lutie shook her head, then was struck by the knowledge that this woman, this stranger with everything she owned stuffed into a rusted grocery cart, had recognized her as homeless, too. She realized that her own eyes had taken on the look of desperation that belonged to people who had no shelter, no job, no money. People without hope.

Fiona broke off a piece of pizza for her daughter, then one for herself. "We usually go to St. Vincent's, except for those days when we have a hankering for pizza. If we time it right, we're among the first waiting at the Dumpster behind Mama Roma's at one-thirty when they start clearing out their lunch buffet. Right around one-thirty. You oughta try it."

"Yeah."

Fiona wiped her mouth with the back of her hand, then said, "So, honey, how long you been on the street?"

Fate, alone while Lutie was working her shift at Denny's, wondered if he'd ever be comfortable with night sounds. Sirens, barking dogs, falling tree twigs, breaking glass, a crying child, fighting cats. And tonight, the sound of distant laughter woke him.

He didn't know what time it was; the clock in the dash of the old Pontiac hadn't worked in years. But he could tell from the color of the night sky that dawn wasn't far away. Knowing Lutie's shift was about to end, knowing she'd soon be back to the car, eased his tension, letting him doze off again.

Minutes later, the car was jarred by a concussive blow accompanied by an explosive sound.

Yanked from sleep, he jerked himself upright to find three boys, older teens, staring at him through the windows. Two were standing beside the back door; the other one was on the hood of the car.

"What do you want?" Fate asked, his voice giving weight to his fear.

"Sucker act like he don't know what we want," said the teen nearest the door, causing his cohorts to laugh.

They were black or Hispanic. Fate couldn't tell for sure on the darkened parking lot despite the light poles ringing the property. They were all dressed pretty much the same: baggy jeans, black T-shirts covered by red jackets, and bandannas on their heads.

The one on the hood threw him a sign, prompting the others to do the same—keeping their index fingers and pinkies straight while curling the other fingers and thumbs into their palms.

"Get your skinny white ass out here."

"No."

"No? Did he say 'no' or did I just imagine that?"

"I think the punk said 'no.'"

"I don't have any money, if that's what you want."

"Sure you do. Only question is, how much and where's it at?"

"You think my sister and I would be living in this car if we had money?" Fate was trying to sound tough, but for a skinny eleven-year-old, "tough" was hard to pull off.

"You don't come out, we gonna bring you out, and you're not gonna like what happen to you then."

All pretense of "tough" drained from his voice, Fate said, "Please don't."

The boy on the hood jumped up and down again, making the same explosive sound that had awakened Fate.

He was so startled by the noise, he yelled, "Stop that!"—appropriate under other circumstances, perhaps, but certainly not this one. Three boys—almost men—threatening a scared child who was in no position to issue orders, a child about to wet his pants.

"He want you to stop, Carp. Can't really blame him, nice vehicle like this."

"Hell, we couldn't get twenty dollars for this heap of metal even if Zee Dee high on ugly dust. Now, we played with this white boy long enough."

As one boy forced opened the back door, Fate slid to the other side of the car, just as the door on that side opened. When hands grabbed him by the back of his neck, he struggled with his feet and fists to stay in the car but was no match for the force of the boy, who dragged him out and stuck a gun in his face.

"Now, you little bastard, empty them pockets. And don't give me no shit. Say one word, it'll be your last."

"Okay," Fate said as he pulled change from one pocket, then reached for the other, which was empty.

Then something happened so fast that Fate wouldn't be able to recall all of it until later.

"Cops!" yelled the boy on the hood as he jumped off the car and ran toward the tree line.

The boy with the gun tucked it into the waist of his jeans, then headed toward an office building in the distance. The third ran toward the Strip as a police car with sirens blasting and lights flashing pulled into the library parking lot.

The policeman in the passenger seat jumped out and went after the boy with the gun, while his partner pulled out to follow the one running toward the Strip.

Within thirty seconds, all the noise and action had moved on, leaving Fate alone, his heart pounding, sweat spilling into his eyes.

He could think of only two scenarios: The police would come back to question him, or the gang would return and kill him. He wasn't crazy about either outcome, so he did what most eleven-year-olds would do. He hid.

He found a spot behind a thick hedge that ran along the front of the library, where he worked to bend his body into the smallest shape he could, then pulled loose a couple of branches of greenery to give himself a vantage point so he could see the car.

All he could pray for was that Lutie would beat the police and gang to the car. And this time, God said yes.

When Fate saw her turn the corner heading toward the library, he left his hiding spot, yelling at her.

"Run, Lutie! Run! We have to get out of here fast."

"What's the hurry?"

"Come on! We've got to go. I'll tell you why later."

Hearing something new in his voice, something Lutie had never heard before, she started running. They reached the car at the same time.

"A gang tried to rob me, one of them stuck a gun in my face and . . ."

Lutie started the car.

"Then the police came and—"

"The police?! What'd you tell them, Fate? What'd you say about us?"

"They didn't ask me anything, they just took off after those guys, but they'll be back, Lutie. Trust me, the police will be back to ask us—"

Lutie had heard enough to know they had to get the hell away from the library. She gunned the car, squealing around corners, running stop signs, working her way into heavier traffic. She wasn't sure where she was going, but she knew for sure she would never again let her little brother spend another night sleeping in a car all by himself. Never again.

"Where are we going, Lutie?"

"He actually pointed a gun in your face? A real gun?"

"Yeah."

Lutie didn't want him to know that she felt as though her heart were in her throat, didn't want him to know how much she wanted to stop the car and cradle him in her arms.

"So, do you know where we're going?" he asked again.

"No, dick-head. I don't have a clue."

CHAPTER SIXTEEN

THE MOTEL LUTIE moved them into was called the Gold Digger Inn, the cheapest place she could find: $19.95 per night or $10.00 for three hours. The Digger, as the locals called it, was most popular with long-distance truckers. They could park their rigs on the huge lot behind the motel for no charge, gamble in the Digger Casino, have a meal of all-you-can-eat pancakes any time of the day or night for ninety-nine cents, or take their pleasure with the prostitutes who roamed the premises 24/7.

The girls and women plied their trade in the Digger for the johns willing to pay not only for their services, but also for the cost of a three-hour room, or they performed their work in the truck's cab, usually on the sleeping berth behind the driver's seat.

Lutie and Fate's room held no surprises, but for the price, they hadn't expected any. They had shelter. A door with two locks, a window air conditioner that actually worked, two beds—real beds with pillows and covers—clean towels, a toilet, a tub, and a TV. After the way they had been living, they no longer took such amenities for granted.

Unfortunately, there was almost always the noise of a bed headboard bouncing against the walls on either side of their room or the one above them. Occasionally, they were awakened by a crash of glass from the parking lot, and on their second night there, they heard three gunshots nearby.

The biggest disappointment of all, though, was that living at the Digger removed Fate from the Paradise school zone. But he didn't say a word about his letdown. He knew Lutie was doing what she could to keep him safe at night while she was working at Denny's. Besides, now that they were paying twenty dollars a night for the motel room, they couldn't possibly put together the six or seven hundred dollars they figured they'd need to rent an apartment in the Paradise zone.

Fate spent the first week of living at the Digger trying to work his way into a job. The library where Lutie had parked Floy's car had been within walking distance of the two golf courses where Fate had made money selling golf balls. But here, on the east side of the city, there were no golf clubs, public or private, so he had to depend on collecting cans, and the nearest recycling station was miles away. As a result, Lutie drove him there every few days, the backseat and the trunk filled with boxes and plastic sacks of aluminum cans.

Sometimes, he actually lost money because of the driving distance and the rising cost of gas. But he didn't mention that to Lutie. Truth is, they had talked only when necessary since the day she quit working at the Desert Palms. Sometimes she took two or three showers a day, and he occasionally heard her groaning in her sleep. Odd and sad behavior for her, but when he'd asked her to tell him what was wrong, he never got an answer.

In his walks looking for cans, he located three elementary schools within a mile or two of the Digger. And though he tried to avoid comparing them with the Paradise, his effort was useless.

One was a brick building constructed in 1940, according to a plaque near the door, but time had dealt with it harshly. Several trailers and one prefab formed a disjointed square at the back of the school. One of the trailer doors had been ripped from its hinges; Fate peeked inside just long enough to see that it was being used as a crack house during the summer recess.

Another, Martin Luther King Elementary, was a three-story concrete-block structure, but all the windows on the first floor were covered with bars. He wondered if the bars had been added to keep students in or to keep intruders out.

The third school was long and lean, one story decorated with graffiti. By looking through grimy windows, he located the library, a room about twice the size of his and Lutie's room at the Digger. The shelves lining three walls were only half-filled with books. A world map pinned to a bulletin board had been torn in two, the floor was covered with stained carpet, and the chalkboard contained a message that said, "liberiuns wo'nt give head."

Suddenly, the face of a black man appeared on the other side of the windowpane; a second later, the window flew up.

"Whatcha want here?" the man asked. "Whatcha lookin' for?"

"Nothing, really. But I might be going to school here this year, so I was curious about the library. I like to read."

"You going to come to school *here*? Why?"

"Well, my sister and I live in the Gold Digger Inn, and it's not so far from here."

"No, it ain't far at all. Just the first stop along the line."

"The line of what?"

"You stay there and watch me, let me show you the line." The man, with salt-and-pepper hair—more salt than pepper—stood a broom he was holding in the corner, then erased the comment from the board. He drew a star on one end and said, "This is the Gold Digger where you livin'. Right?"

"Yes, sir."

The man then made a star a couple of feet beyond the first one. "There the school where we standin' this minute." He put down a third star past the center of the chalkboard. "This is the jail. County jail 'bout five mile from here." Finally, he drew the fourth star at the far end of the board, put down the chalk, and turned to face Fate. "That"—he tapped the final star—"the prison."

He paused, waiting for his lesson to sink in. "That the line, boy. You come to this school, it only be the second stop on the line. You hear what I'm sayin'?"

"Yes, sir, I do."

Three days later, on Fate's fourth visit to the school, Joshua Washington, the only janitor at James Baldwin Elementary, gave Fate a job—a secret job, in case any of the teachers or staff showed up and asked about the boy. Should that happen, Joshua said he'd tell them Fate was his grandson, another secret between the man and the boy.

Fate had to take care of all the jobs that involved bending, as Joshua had arthritis in his spine. And there were plenty of jobs that required bending: holding the dustpan while Joshua swept debris into it; pulling up all the rubber mats used in the gym for floor exercises, then taking them outside to be hosed down; lugging boxes of textbooks to the rooms where they would be used. Joshua was happy to pay Fate three dollars a day from his own pocket and share the lunch his wife sent with him every day. Though this was the time of the year when Joshua's job was most demanding, it would provide work for Fate only until school started.

But there was a catch. In addition to Fate's help for six hours a day, he had an assignment to read many of James Baldwin's books, a grand assignment for a book lover who had never read any of Baldwin's work. Not so for Joshua, who had read them all, some several times over. For instance, he'd read *Notes of a Native Son* seven times and *Go Tell It on the Mountain* four times.

He told Fate that at home he had all of Baldwin's books, which he kept on a special shelf with a framed autographed picture of Baldwin dated 1975, when he spoke and signed his new book, *Just Above My Head,* in a bookstore in Harlem while Joshua was there visiting his sister.

Each time Fate finished one of Baldwin's books, he and Joshua would discuss it for days. Once, following a brief rainstorm, Joshua reclaimed one of Baldwin's lines: *"God gave Noah the rainbow sign, No more water, the fire next time!"*

Fate sometimes thought that God was looking out for him and Lutie. The notes left for them, and the food they found on the hood of the car and in the library. All of that came from someone. And if it didn't come from God, then maybe Fate's mother was watching over them or maybe even Floy. But he felt pretty certain that it wasn't his daddy because he didn't figure Jim McFee had the status of an angel.

Anyway, whether it was a guardian angel or fate or just plain luck, he had traded the Clark County Library several miles away for the Gold Digger Inn, the James Baldwin Elementary School, and Joshua, a new and badly needed friend.

Joshua told him about the teachers he'd be with in most of his sixth-grade classes, talked about the ones who couldn't or wouldn't even try to hide their bigotry, told him about the big, tough-talking gym teacher who was the sweetest, most caring, most accepting of all, gave him a heads-up on those teachers who hated their jobs and those who loved teaching.

Joshua also told him about the students who'd be in his classes, told him the ones to steer clear of—the "hotheads," he called them—boys who fought with their fists, boys most likely to have a knife, and the ones who managed to get guns into the school despite the metal detectors. Joshua had found a half dozen or so hidden around the building—taped to the backs of toilet tanks or on the tallest shelves in the supply room. Once he even found one wired to the bottom of a teacher's chair. Said he'd found Rugers, Colts, Smith & Wessons, and even a TEC-9, "the cop-killer gun," Joshua called it.

"Some of these boys is just plain crazy, few of the girls, too. Me and my wife, Doreen, raised three girls. No boys. Each time Doreen got pregnant, I was wishing and praying for a boy, but the Lord knew what was best, 'cause our girls turned out fine. Two of them finished high school, and both of them went off to college."

"What about the other one?" Fate asked. "Your third girl? Is she still in school?"

"Bea. Honey Bea, I called her. She died. Fifteen years old and she died."

"Was she sick?"

"Drive-by shooting. One crazy boy in a car full of crazy boys just driving around to find someone to shoot. My Honey Bea walking with a bunch of kids going to the mall. And the boy who shot her? Didn't even know her. Didn't even know her name."

Joshua turned away, picked up a bucket of soapy water and a mop, then headed down the hall. "This school got a lot of them crazy boys. You best to steer clear of them hotheads, Fate."

"Yes, sir. I'll try. I'll sure enough try."

Lutie was barely holding on to her job at Denny's. But if she knew it, she didn't show it. *Most* of the time she came in to work her shift, and usually she wasn't more than an hour or so late. But since she didn't have a phone, and probably wouldn't have thought to call if she did, her coming in for work was a crapshoot.

And though her body might have been there, her mind wasn't.

She always seemed to find herself reliving that day at the Desert Palms.

She screwed up orders—serving well-done steaks when the customer had ordered rare; making mistakes in tabulating the bills; forgetting to refill drinks; overlooking her tables stacked with half-eaten meals, spilled coffee and milk, crumbs on the booths. And worst of all, she kept calling the boss Stan when his name was Steve.

When she got off work in the morning, she'd bring Fate some breakfast, then crawl into bed for the day, sleeping until her next shift at Denny's.

But all that changed one night when one of the cooks, a young guy named Johnny Viper, said, "Hey, girl, what's going on with you?"

"What do you mean?"

"You look like shit. Sick?"

"Yeah. Sort of."

"Ain't none of my fucking business, but I got something that'll make you feel good no matter if you've got the measles or if you're sick in your head."

"Really?"

"Real fuckin' really. Meet me out back when you take your smoke break."

And that's what she did.

Her first few "buys" were free, but once she was hooked, she had to start paying, so by the time school started, almost all her tip money went into Viper's pocket, cash that Fate didn't know about.

The day school started, they had a little less than two hundred dollars, but Lutie had a surprise for Fate. She'd noticed that his shoes were so small for him that he'd sliced the seam down the back so his heel could stick through. And every pair of pants he owned were at least two inches too short. So she went to the

Catholic Charities, where she picked out some used shoes and clothes for her brother.

She thought at first that he'd be excited when he woke up and found "new" clothes laid out on her bed, but as she placed them there, she saw them for what they were: athletic shoes that had been the rage four or five years ago; a shirt that had been patched on the elbow; a pair of slacks that a banker might wear.

When she turned to wake him, she found that he'd gone to sleep reading his tattered copy of the Paradise Elementary School brochure, and she knew the clothes weren't going to raise his spirits at all.

He ate the Danish she'd brought home from Denny's, washed it down with a small carton of milk she kept in a cooler.

When she waved him off to his first day of classes at James Baldwin Elementary, he managed a tight-lipped smile in return. And even in the used clothes she'd bought, she thought he looked fine.

But when he came in that afternoon, he looked anything but fine. He had a cut over one eye, blood dripping from his nose and lip, both knees of his banker's slacks torn out, and one sleeve of his shirt ripped off.

"Fate! What in the world . . . Are you all right?"

"Well, I had a little trouble, as you can see. But it's a wonderful school. Intellectual atmosphere. And very friendly. I obviously made a good impression and gained so many new friends."

CHAPTER SEVENTEEN

Lutie hadn't slept at all the night before, wrestling with her decision. But by the time the sun came up, she knew what she had to do.

Fate was still sleeping when she left the motel room. She had cleaned his wounds and bandaged them the day before, but there was no cover for the bruises on his face or the swelling of his upper lip.

She found T. at the Carnival Court, having a drink at the bar with a young redhead wearing a low-cut tank top that barely covered the nipples of her crafted breasts. When he noticed Lutie standing a few feet away, he wasted no time in reaching her.

"Sweet little Lutie," he said as he wrapped her in his arms. "I've missed you, darlin'." With just a look, he sent the redhead away.

"I've got to talk to you," Lutie said.

"Then let's take a table so we don't have to put up with the same old lies the drunks at the bar love to tell."

He pulled out a chair for Lutie, then scooted his close to her.

"So, precious girl, how's life treating you?"

"Not so good." She bit her lip, a sure sign of tension. "I've got to get seven, eight hundred dollars. Today."

"Whoa, baby, whoa. What makes you think you can pull down that kind of money in a day?"

"I'll make one of those movies for you. A porno film."

"Well, honey, it's not all that easy. See—"

"I can do it. I can do whatever you and Philo want me to."

"Let me explain this to you. Philo's finishing a project today, which means that as soon as it's in the can, he'll start a new one."

"Then it's the perfect time for me."

"I doubt it. I leave the casting up to Philo, so I imagine he's already made up his mind about who he's using."

"But maybe not. Call him, please. Call him now and just ask him, T. I *really* need that money."

"You're a girl in a hurry, aren't you? What's the matter, Lutie? You got a habit now? Little coke problem?"

"This is not about that."

"Then—"

"My brother, Fate. We're living in the Gold Digger and—"

"Oh, shit. You *are* in trouble. I've had three girls attacked there in the past couple of years. One of them lost an eye, another died. Stabbed in the chest. Sweet Jesus, Lutie, why would you even consider moving in there?"

"The motel's not the problem. It's the school Fate's going to. He got beat up yesterday, the first day of classes."

"So you need this money to—"

"To move. To rent a place close to a different school, a school Fate's visited. It's Paradise Elementary, but the Digger's not in their zone. So will you call Philo? Ask him to put me in this new movie?"

"Honey, you need to understand something. Philo's good at his job. And he's fast. But these films aren't shot in just one day."

"How long does it take?"

"Four days, five. It takes as long as it takes, so you probably wouldn't get paid until sometime next week."

"Then can you loan me the money now and when I finish the film—"

"I don't know, Lutie. That doesn't sound like such a good idea to me."

"Why not?"

"Let's say I give you seven bills, and you go on a coke binge. You don't show up to film, the money's gone, and I'm left holding the bag. An empty bag."

"That won't happen, T. I promise you that won't happen."

"Well, if Philo's lined up Ebony and Lingo, they might be able to cover for you when you fuck up—no pun intended." T. grinned at his own cleverness. "They're two of the best. Ebony knows her way around, guess she's made eight or nine pictures for us, and Lingo—"

"T., I won't lie to you. I've never done it with a girl, but—"

"Piece of cake, Lutie. Piece of cake. I'll show you a couple of videos at the studio and you'll know exactly what to do. Hey . . ." His brow wrinkled when an unpleasant thought struck him. "You're not a virgin, are you?"

"Hell, no!" She tried for a look of defiance, but when she saw the picture of the rapist in her head, she asked T. if he'd get her a screwdriver while she went to the ladies' room.

"How about I get two screwdrivers?" he said. "Start this day off right for the both of us."

While he was at the bar, Lutie made a dash to the bathroom, where she snorted a dime of coke inside one of the stalls. Then, at a large mirror over the sink, she made a quick check for telltale signs of white powder on her face before she returned to the table. T. was waiting there with their drinks.

"What happened, sugar?" He reached across the table and

brushed away one speck of white just above her lip. "You stop in for a little pick-me-up?"

Pretending not to understand the question or deciding simply to ignore it, Lutie said, "So, will you call Philo now?"

"I already did." T. raised his glass, waited for her to do the same, then said, "Here's to our new porn princess." As they toasted their new venture, T. slid seven hundred dollars across the table to Lutie.

At the studio, Lutie met Ebony, a statuesque beauty whose skin was the color of coffee, and Lingo—tall with a sculpted body and a gay partner, Brice, who did hair and makeup for the cast.

Philo had the three "stars" disrobe in their dressing rooms, then, wearing kimonos, come to the studio bedroom, where he told them the story line of the movie, a plot featuring a married couple—Ebony and Lingo—bored with their sex lives until they hire a young live-in housekeeper, who would be played by Lutie.

When Philo had them remove their kimonos and pose in various sexual positions for Polaroid shots, Lutie was so uncomfortable and embarrassed that she wanted to run. But she didn't. She knew she had no choice. If she didn't make this film, she and Fate would soon be living out of a car again, and he would still be going to James Baldwin Elementary, where his next beating might be worse than the first.

After Philo finished with the still photos, he thumbtacked them to a bulletin board, then sent the actors to the fitting room, where a Vietnamese woman was waiting. She had them try on costumes, which she measured, marking seams with chalk, pinning up hems, adjusting straps, belts, chains—and doing her work without speaking a word.

From there they returned to their dressing rooms, put on

their street clothes, and met with Philo again so he could give them their scripts. He told them to memorize their lines for tomorrow, the first day of shooting, because he would not tolerate an actor who didn't know his or her lines. He said their day would begin at eight o'clock, not a minute later, and told them to be prepared to stay late, as he planned to finish this film in three days.

On her way to the Digger, Lutie stopped at Denny's, where she bought fifty dollars' worth of coke from Viper with the money T. had given her, flashing—without intending to—the entire seven hundred not only to Viper, but to another guy working in the kitchen.

When she got back in her car, she snorted a few lines to try to ease the ugly memories of the pictures she'd just posed for, knowing that the next three days she'd be doing more of the same. And probably worse.

By the time Lutie got to their room at the Digger, she'd come up with a story to tell Fate, a wild tale that was certain to arouse his suspicion, but she couldn't think of another explanation for the money in her purse. Besides, even if he didn't believe her, he'd be so thrilled to learn he was going to be a student at Paradise, he might not throw too many questions at her.

"You're going to what!?"

"Be in a commercial. A toothpaste commercial."

"And you're going to make six hundred dollars?" The look on Fate's face, something between a sneer and a grin, told Lutie he didn't believe her.

"True." She crossed her heart, a sign of gospel fact. "And I'll get another six hundred if they like it." Anticipating an extended interrogation, Lutie jumped in with the lines she'd rehearsed after she'd left Philo's studio. "See, when they make a commercial, they test it out in a certain area. The Northeast, for example. Say, Maine and Illinois and New York. Like the thirteen colonies."

"Lutie, Illinois wasn't one of the thirteen colonies."

"Yeah, but you get the idea. So, if the commercial does well there, then they'll show it in the South, maybe, then the West, and so on."

"But actors, real actors, have to audition. Some guy doesn't just walk up to you and offer you a job in a commercial without even—"

"Listen, Fate, it's kind of like what's-her-name being spotted at a drugstore by some talent agent. Next thing you know, she's a movie star. That's kind of how it happened to me, except I wasn't in a drugstore. I was walking into the Gap because they had a Help Wanted sign in the window and—"

"Lutie, if you think I'm going to believe this, then you—"

"Well, maybe you'll believe this." She pulled six one-hundred-dollar bills from her purse and slapped them down on the nightstand between their beds. She'd hidden the other fifty inside the zippered pocket of her jeans, money she'd need for her next buy from Viper.

"But you haven't even started filming yet," Fate said as he spread the bills across his pillow.

"He paid me up front. 'Up front.' And the first thing we're going to do is rent us a nice place in the Paradise zone."

Fate's eyes grew wide with the realization that one of his dreams was about to come true. He grabbed up the bills, yelled, "Yippee!" and began jumping up and down in his stocking feet, first on one bed, then on the other.

"Quit, before you fall. If you hurt yourself, some of this money'll go to pay a doctor's bill."

"Okay," he said, short-winded by his excitement. "When can we move?"

"As soon as we find a place, but I'll be filming the next three days, and the director, a man named Philo, said I'd be working late. Maybe real late."

"What about your job at Denny's?"

"I guess I'll get there when I get there. If we finish filming at ten, I'll have plenty of time to change into my uniform and get to work on time. If we film past ten, I'll just be late. I'm going to talk to Viper tonight, see if there's any way he can cover for me if I'm late."

"So when do you think I can start school?"

"I think you ought to let those bruises fade first; otherwise, you'll start at Paradise looking like a punching bag. I don't care how highfalutin that school is, there'll be boys who'll want to prove how tough they are by beating the crap out of the new kid, especially if he's already black-and-blue. Besides, we have to move first so you'll have an address in the zone. How about we look for a place on Saturday and you start your classes on Monday?"

"That sounds great. Just great." Then he leaned across the space between them and gave Lutie a hug. "Thanks," he said, his voice constricted by the lump in his throat, the way he felt when he was about to cry.

"So what do you think?" Lutie asked.

"Well," Viper said, "you can probably get by with coming late once or twice. After that, you're history here."

"That's what I'm afraid of."

"But look at it like this, Belinda. Working here, whether it's waiting tables, cooking, washing dishes . . . they're all shitty jobs. So if you lose this one, you just move on to the next."

"You're right." Lutie flashed him a smile. "Thanks for making me feel better about it. Now, the next problem is finding a decent place, an apartment close to the school Fate's going to."

"What school's that?"

"Paradise Elementary."

"Yeah? Guess if you've got to go to grade school, that's a good one. But what do I know? I quit after the fourth grade."

"You're kidding."

"Nope."

"How'd you get by with that?"

"Had a guy I know make up a phony death certificate."

Lutie started laughing.

"Yeah," Viper said. "I think I died of polio. Can't remember. Polio or measles. School even sent a letter of condolence to my mom."

"What'd she do?"

"Nothing. She didn't give a shit. Long as she had her Marlboros and a bottle of vodka, she stayed happy."

Rodney, the night-shift dishwasher, reached behind Viper for a stack of plates. " 'Scuse me, Belinda, but I heard you say you wanted a place close to the university."

"Yeah."

"Well, my brother and his wife live in that area. They got a pretty nice apartment, think they pay like four hundred a month. I could ask them if there's any vacancies if you want me to."

"I'd sure appreciate it, Rodney."

"Where you and your brother living now?"

"We have a room at the Gold Digger Inn out on North Main."

"Girl I knew was murdered there couple of years back. Guy slit her throat."

"Oh, man. I want to get out of there. Soon as I can find a place, I'm gone."

"I'll talk to my brother when I get home, see if he knows about a vacancy at the Regency where they live. You have a cell phone? I can give you a call."

"No, but just call the motel. Ask for room one thirty-eight."

"Will do."

"Thanks, Rodney. Thanks a lot."

"You bet."

"Order's up," Viper said. "Table four, two ham-and-cheese omelets."

"Got it," Lutie said as she picked up the plates and headed for table four, sidestepping three drunk boys, much too young to be able to buy booze. Just old enough to drink it.

CHAPTER EIGHTEEN

LUTIE'S FIRST DAY of filming had left her feeling raw—the best word she could think of to describe the humiliation of what she'd done. Raw flesh, raw emotions, raw images playing in her head, images she couldn't seem to shake even with the high she was feeling from her dwindling stash of cocaine.

She'd gone through most of it during the breaks they took when Philo had to reset the lights or when he needed to adjust his camera or tinker with the tripod. But she hadn't needed to worry about hiding her habit. Ebony, Lingo, and Brice had their own stash and used it openly in a small canteen with tables, chairs, coffeepot, and fridge, a room just a doorway away from the set and out of Philo's view.

But as degrading as some of the acts she'd already performed in front of Philo and his camera had been, she'd felt even worse when, during their lunch break, Philo had come into the canteen for a cup of coffee. When he'd glimpsed her snorting coke at one of the tables, he'd turned away quickly, pretending he hadn't seen her, but not before she saw the expression on his face, an expression of both sorrow and disappointment. A look she'd seen before on her mother's face when she'd caught her in a lie.

Now, even though it was dark, she'd parked the car as far from their room at the Digger as she could. She didn't want to take the chance that Fate might not have closed the curtains. She could only imagine how he'd feel if he saw her in the parking lot taking a hit.

Besides, she needed a little extra time before she went in and faced him, fearing that something in her behavior or the way she looked would communicate to him what she'd been doing.

She tried to think of how their conversation would go, the questions he'd ask about filming a toothpaste commercial, about the story she'd tell, the lies she'd have to come up with. But the coke she'd just snorted screwed up her thinking, so she gave it up, deciding that she couldn't control whatever talk took place between her and her brother.

Instead, she concentrated on what she wanted more than anything just then: to brush her teeth and take a shower, the water as hot as she could stand it. She checked her watch, relieved to find that she had plenty of time to clean up, get into her uniform, and get to Denny's on time for her shift.

When she finally felt she had pulled herself together, she locked her script inside the glove compartment, then dropped her keys into her purse. It hadn't taken her long to discover that she didn't have many lines to memorize. Her character was more interested in action than conversation, but the script told her where to stand, when to crawl onto the bed, and what to do with both Ebony and Lingo once she had placed herself into the correct position.

Just as she started to get out of the car, she saw two figures approaching, two men, she thought, but she couldn't make out their features in the dark.

When she realized they were coming for her, she locked the doors, then fumbled inside her purse for the keys. But the weight of her key chain caused them to sink to the bottom of her bag, burying them with a charm bracelet, tampons, hair clips, tissue, combs, tubes of lipstick, gum, a spiral notebook, and three pens.

Just as they reached the car, she saw that one of the men was Rodney, the night cook who'd offered to help her find an apartment. The other was a guy she hadn't seen before. He was big, maybe two eighty, over six feet tall, wearing a T-shirt that said, "The Lord Sees What You're Doing."

"Hey, Lutie," Rodney said.

"I told you my name is Belinda."

"Yeah, I know what you *said*, Lutie."

She hadn't realized until then that her window was down a couple of inches, not enough for Rodney to get his hand through, but enough that they could talk without yelling.

"What do you want?" Lutie asked.

"We was in the neighborhood, thought we'd pay you a visit."

He didn't wait for her response but tried her locked door. "Let me in, baby. We need to do some business."

"What kind of business?"

" 'Bout some blow I got for you. Me and my bro there, Huff, we gonna give you a good price."

"Sorry, Rodney, but I don't have any money. Maybe when I get paid, I can—"

"Hey, white sugar, you got six bills in that bag." He gestured to Lutie's purse. "I seen 'em when you made a buy from Viper. So you can let me in, or you can pass the money out to me, but either way I'm gonna get it."

"Huh-uh. That money's gone. I put it all down on an apartment today."

"You jackin' me 'round now, Lutie. And that's a mistake. A big mistake."

"No, really. I found a place over on—"

"You was makin' a hump flick today, girl. Puttin' that cooch out there for that fag."

"How do you know that?"

"I got ways. Now, you gonna give me the money or am I gonna have to come in there and take it? Your choice."

Lutie rolled her window closed and tried again to snag her keys, but Huff, with a metal pipe the size of a baseball bat, struck Lutie's window. She screamed, but the sound was trapped inside the car. She hit the horn, causing several of her neighbors at the Digger to look out their windows, but a quick look at what was happening was enough to cause them to close their shades.

She kept honking, though, until Huff shattered her window, peppering her with shards of glass, one embedding itself in her cheek, another in her arm. Others rained in, striking her mostly in her face.

When Huff reached into the car, trying to pry her purse from her hands, she sank her teeth into his arm, biting down into his flesh until she brought blood, dripping from his arm and smearing across her mouth and chin.

"You bitch!" He jerked his arm out to inspect his wound before Rodney pulled up the lock and opened the door. He grabbed Lutie's purse, fished inside her wallet, and pulled out the six hundred dollars he'd come for, then tossed her purse into the backseat.

"Now," he said. "Since you done caused us so much trouble, believe you better pull down your pants and show us what you got down there. See if we want some of it."

When he grabbed her arm and pulled her to him, she spat in his face.

"You shit-head!" she screamed. "You rotten shit-head!"

Furious now, Rodney swiped at her spittle with his shirtsleeve, then pulled her out of the car. When she fell onto the concrete parking lot, she heard the crack of a bone but didn't feel the pain. Not for several seconds. Then she saw a finger hanging at an odd angle.

Huff, savage now, drew back his foot and kicked her in her rib cage, the side of her head, her shoulder, her hip, while Rodney was working her jeans off despite her kicking at him, clawing his face, throwing ineffectual punches, though she put as much energy as she had into each one.

Then she heard Fate.

"Lutie," he hollered, "where are you?"

"Here, Fate. Here. Help me!"

When Fate rounded the last row of parked vehicles and saw what was happening, he threw himself into the middle of it, doing little harm but knocking Huff off balance enough that he fell and sprawled backward, striking his head on the bed of a pickup parked beside Floy's car.

"Leave her alone!" Fate shouted as he jumped on Rodney's back.

Rodney could have handled the boy with no trouble, but he wasn't prepared for the dog. She didn't make a sound until she bounded over Lutie, going for Rodney's throat. A low growl came from deep inside the rottweiler as she began to shake Rodney like a cloth doll.

But when a man near the back of the car said, "Draco. *Basta!*" the dog let go of Rodney immediately, leaving him coughing and rubbing at his neck as he picked himself up. He and Huff backed off some twenty, thirty feet before they turned and ran, the sound of their feet slapping pavement growing fainter as they distanced themselves from the dog.

Fate watched until their attackers disappeared in the distance, then he turned toward the man who was approaching, a limping man with dark eyes and a rottweiler named Draco.

CHAPTER NINETEEN

DO NOT TO be ascared of me," the limping man said. "I am Juan Vargas, your friend." Silence. "You understand what it is I say?" Still too traumatized to speak, Fate nodded.

When Juan cut the engine fifteen minutes later, Fate pushed himself high enough to look over the seat in front of him, where he was met with a slobbery lick from the rottweiler, who occupied the passenger seat. But instead of seeing what he had expected to see—a hospital— he saw a modest house, dark inside and out.

He had a dozen questions for Juan Vargas, who had driven them there after finding the keys in Lutie's purse, but he hadn't asked them. Not once.

Lutie, still unconscious, had made no sound as she was lifted into the car by the man and the boy. Even with broken bones, torn muscles, and a damaged face—a face Fate could hardly recognize—she'd made no sound.

Fate, squeezed into the back floorboard to be near her, pulled off his T-shirt, wet it with a stale Coke from a three-day-old bottle, then—with great care—sponged her face and neck, hoping the cooling cloth would rouse her. She remained silent and unmoving. Watching the rise and fall of her chest, he knew she was still breathing, but she looked so small, so wounded, he feared she was near death.

Juan gave a one-word command to the dog, *"Quédate!"* then went to the door and knocked. Seconds later, a light came on near the back of the house, then the front, and finally on the porch. Within moments, a large man in a bathrobe came from the house and accompanied Juan to the car.

The porch light—one single yellow bulb—was so faint that Fate could not make out the features of either man as they lifted Lutie from the car, but as he followed them to the house, he studied Juan Vargas from the back. He was a powerfully built man from the waist up: broad shoulders, thick neck, muscular arms that bulged beneath his faded denim shirt, ripped near one elbow, stained with fresh blood.

In contrast, the lower half of his body looked thin, almost frail. His jeans, much too large for his frame, were held up by a leather belt with JUAN hand-tooled across the back, causing his pants to pucker around his small waist and thin hips.

Atop his long black hair, bound into a single braid that reached his waist, he wore a Panama hat, the brim tattered, the crown bent and soiled.

He was tall but looked even taller because of his Western boots, which Fate guessed to be made of snakeskin. The heel of the boot on his bad leg had been built up by an inch or so, most likely to lessen his limp, but when he walked, putting weight on that leg, his foot turned in so that with each step he took, he pitched sideways.

As Fate followed the trio inside, he saw a plaque over the door: "Dr. Hector Morales, M.D."

The first two rooms they passed through, a living room and

a dining room, looked ordinary except for several large framed circus posters decorating the walls.

As they passed a closed door in the dining room, the doctor called, *"Rosa, te necesito."*

Fate heard a woman's voice from the other side of the door: *"Sí, ya voy. Un momento."*

At the back of the home, they entered what appeared to be a well-equipped doctor's office—counters with bottles of various-colored liquids, cotton balls, bandages, trays of instruments, glass-fronted cabinets neatly arranged with medications, blood pressure cuffs hanging from hooks on the wall, X-ray equipment, an examination table . . . and more circus posters.

The doctor turned on a bright light, which illuminated the table and afforded Fate his first look at the face of the man called Juan Vargas.

His skin, the texture of leather, the color of rich brown tobacco, was a geography of lines that intersected like roadways on a map. His eyes were as dark as heartwood, and if what Floy often said was true, something about eyes being windows to the soul, then this man's life was filled with sorrow born of regret and disappointment.

A scar through one of his heavy black eyebrows had turned the hair white along both sides of a fold of flesh used to close the wound. He had a thick mustache badly in need of trimming, and though his cheeks showed the stubble of several days' growth, Fate could tell he had once, long ago, been a handsome man. But now, he was old. Perhaps, Fate thought, as old as thirty.

As the doctor, who had changed into a pair of white scrubs, was working his freshly washed hands into a pair of rubber gloves, a slight woman with white hair slipped into the office through a side door. One of her cheeks was still showing creases from the pillow she'd slept on, but her green eyes, nearly the color of her scrubs, were alert.

She and Juan exchanged greetings with the warmth of old

friends who haven't been in touch for a long time. After she washed her hands, she, too, put on rubber gloves. And as she approached the table, she noticed Fate for the first time, acknowledging him with a smile, a smile that quickly faded when she saw Lutie stretched out on the table. Involuntarily, she patted Lutie's shoulder as she bowed her head in a short prayer before making the sign of the cross.

While the doctor began his examination of Lutie's head where her hair was matted with blood, Rosa monitored the girl's blood pressure and checked her heart rate. When she produced a clipboard with a form attached to it, she wrote down numbers as she repeated them in Spanish to her husband.

Fate was certain that such middle-of-the-night intrusions were common occurrences in that house—a child running a high fever, an elderly man gasping for breath, a mother of four with pneumonia, a teenager suffering a stab wound. And he was certain that no one was turned away.

The doctor adjusted one of the overhead lights, then leaned down to get a closer look at a deep gash running from Lutie's jaw to her ear where dried blood had pooled. A knot nearly the size of an avocado seed appeared on her forehead just at her hairline, and one of her eyes, now the color of a plum, was swollen shut.

While Rosa was setting up for an IV, the doctor opened Lutie's mouth and retrieved a tooth barely attached to her upper gum. Using his fingers, he inspected the inside of her cheeks, then examined her tongue to find that she'd bitten through it on one side.

As he began to unbutton her blouse, he spoke to Juan, who immediately led Fate from the office to the living room, where they sat side by side on a couch.

"You're very worry about your sister, but my friends, Dr. Morales and his wife, a nurse, they will to take good care of her."

"They will take good care of her," Fate absently corrected Juan's English, a matter of habit.

"Yes, I don't speak the English quite good, but Spanish I know."

"And I don't speak Spanish."

"But we will find a way, Fate, to talk one to each other."

"How do you know my name?"

"I hear Lutie call your name much times." Quickly, Juan corrected himself. "Many times."

"My sister . . ." When Fate began to cry, Juan put his arm around the small, shirtless boy and pulled him close. "I'm afraid that Lutie . . . I'm afraid she'll die."

"No, no. Lutie strong girl, and my doctor and nurse friends don't let her to die. Trust this, I tell you."

With a bit more control now, Fate said, "How did you know about us? Your notes, the food . . ."

"Fate, we have later for to answer questions. For now, you rest. You have not to fear, but to rest. Only to rest."

"But—"

"I wake you when it needs."

And Fate, his body heavy with fatigue, his mind clouded with doubt, his eleven years feeling like ninety, leaned his head on Juan Vargas's shoulder, closed his eyes, and gave himself, at last, to sleep.

CHAPTER TWENTY

FATE, LUTIE, JUAN VARGAS, and Draco left Rosa and Dr. Hector's home just after dawn on a Tuesday, and though they'd spent only four days and nights there, Fate could hardly get through the good-byes, mostly because of Rosa. She had become, for him, as close as a woman could to his notion of a mother since his own had died before he had memory.

Rosa was always available to assist her husband in his practice, but somehow she managed to find time for Fate. In her small library, quiet and comfortable, she had created a space that seemed spiritual, though there were no religious symbols in evidence—no crucifix, no statues of Mary, no paintings of Jesus, no lectionary stand holding a Bible.

There, Rosa introduced Fate to writers he didn't know: César Chávez, Gabriel García Márquez; to the poetry of Pablo Neruda; to the art of Diego Rivera; and to the music of the Mexican cellist Carlos Prieto.

But her favorite writer was Sandra Cisneros, whose piece titled "Salvadore, Late or Early," only two pages long, was the most beautiful prose Fate had ever heard. He especially liked the sound when Rosa read it aloud.

In addition to sharing her books, her music, and her art, she invited Fate to the kitchen to talk while she cooked, and to him, her cooking became an art as her beautiful small hands mixed, kneaded, beat, sliced, and diced.

She told him how she and Dr. Hector had met, both of them working at the same circus in order to pay for their medical training—he as a physician's assistant, she as a nurse practitioner while working on her RN. She talked, too, of their meeting Juan Vargas, an aerial performer, watching him fly through the air a hundred feet above the earth without a safety net below.

But when Fate asked how Juan came to live on the streets of Las Vegas, Rosa gave brief, vague accounts, telling him Juan would open that chapter of his life when he was ready.

Every night, Rosa came to the room where Fate slept, to read to him her favorite stories by her favorite writers. Then when she finished, she would kiss him on the cheek and whisper, "May God keep you in the safety of His arms."

Yesterday, the day before their departure, Juan and Fate had gone to the room at the Gold Digger where Lutie and Fate had been living. At Juan's polite invitation and with his help, Fate had worked through the rubbish that had piled up since they'd moved in. He rounded up Lutie's cosmetics, teen magazines, shoes, clothes, hats, belts, and scarves—most shoplifted, a few actually paid for. He emptied what was left in the glove compartment after it had been ransacked; then boxed up his own books and a small bag of his clothes.

After they'd packed them in the trunk of Floy's Pontiac, they drove two blocks, where they transferred Lutie's and Fate's possessions into the trunk of Juan's Lincoln Continental, cavernous when compared with the Pontiac.

The car, Fate learned, was an '88 and might have been valuable if not for the dents and dings the body had suffered through the years. But though it looked pretty shabby outside, the inside was roomy, the upholstery looked and smelled new, the floorboards showed no sign of dirt or sand, the dash was clean of dust, and even the ashtrays were empty and shining.

Juan, not much of a talker, had explained a bit of the automobile's history, but mostly he let the car do the talking for him. He was proud of the old Lincoln, and keeping it spotless was important to him.

Fate had known without being told that Juan was moving them out of the Gold Digger. Perhaps he planned to take them in, maybe share his apartment with them. Fate didn't figure he had a house, but a small, inexpensive apartment seemed likely.

When they finished the transfer and a last look through the trash of the Pontiac, Juan tossed the keys onto the dash, then slid under the wheel of his own car and pulled away.

"What about—" But Fate didn't get to complete his question.

"We don't need it anymore. This"—he patted the steering wheel—"will be the better car for the trip. Her name is Matilda. Good tires, license tag legal, registration legal, and more resting bed for Lutie."

Fate could have asked then, could have asked where they were going . . . and why, but he didn't. He felt safe with Juan, the first time he'd felt safe since Floy died.

Juan drove several miles out of town to a spot on the bank of Callville Bay where he lived in a tent surrounded by brush and young saplings, almost hidden from view. Living in a tent, away from the streets of Vegas and the people who wandered those streets, seemed to be a step up from living in a stolen car, so if Juan was moving Lutie and Fate into the tent with him and Draco, Fate would be glad.

But that wasn't part of the plan.

Juan kept his tent just the way he kept his car: spartan, spotless, and organized. Beside a sleeping bag, he had a small cooler, a box of books, and another of clothes, neatly folded and well arranged. A shoe box contained his toiletries. The only object that seemed personal was a framed photograph of a younger Juan, his arm around an older man who favored him, a man Fate guessed to be his father. The picture stood on several glass bricks to serve as a table only for the photo. Fate noticed that when Juan packed the picture, he placed it carefully among his folded T-shirts for protection. Finally, Juan packed a twenty-pound sack of dog food and a large plastic bowl, and they drove back to Dr. Hector's house, Fate already dreading the next morning's good-byes.

He hadn't slept well that night, knowing it was likely the last night he would ever spend in that house, in the doctor's office, Rosa's home. The last night she would come to his room, read to him, tuck him in, and whisper her prayer. When he finally did fall asleep, it was Rosa he was thinking of.

The plan was to leave just after dawn, so everyone was up except Lutie. She had regained consciousness shortly after being placed on the examination table, but because of the pain, Dr. Hector had kept her sedated, as she was now for the trip they were about to undertake, a trip whose destination was still unknown to Fate.

Dr. Hector went over his instructions for the third time, handing Juan the plastic bag containing antibiotics to fight infection, pain medication Lutie would need regularly for the next two or three days, fresh bandages and astringents for cleaning her various wounds.

The men loaded Lutie into the spacious backseat of Juan's Continental, a move they accomplished under the direction of Rosa, who had spent hours the previous day turning the backseat into a hospital bed so that Lutie could ride comfortably and safely on the trip. She had even made a bed out of old rugs and blankets for Draco, who would alert Juan if Lutie needed attention.

Rosa had packed a plastic box filled with fruit, *gazpacho español* soup, lemon chicken, *buñuelos*, and *sopa da plátano*, a dessert she had made for supper the previous evening and which Fate had liked so much, he had taken three helpings, only after Rosa insisted.

When it was time to say good-bye, Rosa hugged Fate tightly to her chest and whispered to him, "If you ever have need of me, no matter the time, just call." She slipped into his hand a closed envelope, then kissed his cheek and whispered, "May God keep you in the safety of His arms."

Fate waved as the Lincoln pulled away, but the features of Rosa's face were distorted because of the tears in his eyes.

He waited until they passed a sign that marked the city limits of Las Vegas and another that urged visitors to come back soon and often.

Finally, it was time to ask.

"Juan, where are we going?"

"Oklahoma," Juan said. "We go now to Oklahoma."

PART THREE

CHAPTER TWENTY-ONE

Fate, slumped in the passenger seat, his head resting against the window, had been asleep for almost two hours when Juan pulled into a QuikTrip.

"Where are we?" he asked.

"Just east of Flagstaff. But my blue baby here"—Juan patted the dash of the Lincoln—"she likes to having her belly full."

A rustling sound from the backseat caught Fate's attention.

"Is big sister awake?" Juan asked.

"No."

"Well, time for her medicine, I have to peeing, Draco, too, and Matilda wants gas. Kill four birds with one rock, huh?"

"Two birds, and it's stone, not rock."

"You gonna mess with my English all the way to Oklahoma?"

Fate grinned. "Probably."

"I tell you what. You talk your English and I'll talk mine."

"Speak, not talk."

199

Juan shook his head in mock disgust. "This gonna be one long damn trip."

"Why don't you go to the bathroom; I'll give Lutie her medicine."

"Okay," Juan said as he got out of the car. "But remember, Doc said one of the blue ones, two white. You don't confuse."

"I won't."

With Juan's seat empty, Draco jumped into it and started to whine.

"It's okay, girl. He'll be back."

After Fate gathered the pills, a bottle of water, and a straw, he got into the back, making room for himself on the seat beside Lutie. He studied her for a few moments, watching her eyelids flutter in sleep, wondering what she might be seeing behind those delicate, paper-thin layers of flesh, both purpled now with bruises.

"Lutie, it's time for your medicine."

She opened her eyes as far as the swelling would allow and said, "I'm thirsty."

Fate inched his fingers beneath her head and lifted it until her lips found the straw. With each pill she swallowed, she grimaced.

"Is your throat sore?"

"Everything is sore," she said as Fate lowered her head back to the pillow. "When did I get out of the hospital? Or was it a clinic?"

"Just this morning."

Since the attack, Fate had talked to Lutie several times, so he wasn't as frightened by her confusion now as he had been at first. Dr. Hector had explained to him that the drugs and the concussion, though mild, would leave some blank spots in her memory for a while.

"Where are we now?"

"In Arizona."

Fate could see in her expression that she was trying to piece together bits of information, trying to get what she *could* remember in the right order.

"Are we still with that man? That Italian guy?"

"His name's Juan, and he's Mexican, not Italian."

"Oh, yeah. That's right. Juan. So where is he?"

"He's gone to the toilet. Do you need to go, Lutie? I can help you if you do."

"Help me?" Fate heard the fear in her voice. "I'm not paralyzed, am I?" Seized with alarm, the notion that she might not be able to walk, even though she had walked several times while at Dr. Hector's, she slapped at her thighs with her good hand. "I can feel my legs."

"No, no. You aren't paralyzed. Just stiff and sore. The doctor said you would be for a few more days."

"Then why would I need you to help me?"

"I just meant I could walk you to the bathroom."

"Then do what? Wipe my butt? *No,* thank you! If I need to go, I can get there by myself." But to make sure, she lifted her legs one at a time, the effort causing her to groan, a sound that drew Draco's attention. When she draped her paws over the seat, her face staring into Lutie's, the girl was startled.

"That's Draco," Fate said. "Juan's dog."

"God, it looks like a beast."

"She's just big. She rides back here with you to make sure you're okay, kind of like your own warning system on this trip."

"Now, tell me again where we are?"

"Arizona."

"And where are we going?"

"Oklahoma."

"Why?"

201

"Juan has family there. He thinks they'll let us stay with them, take care of us."

"But I was taking care of us, Fate. I had a job, money for our apartment, and—" A memory suddenly broke through, her breath coming hard as she tried to remember. "My purse! Where's my purse, Fate?"

"It's safe, in the trunk, Lutie."

"Are you sure? You'd better make damn sure because all our money's in it. That black purse with a silver lock."

"I'm sure." And he was sure that the purse was in the trunk, but he was also sure the money was gone; sure, too, that the white powder in the plastic bag was coke. But he knew this wasn't the right time to talk about that. He didn't think Lutie was ready to handle that subject just yet. "For now, you need to relax, leave worrying to me until you feel better. Can you do that?"

"But you've got to get my purse out, look inside the billfold, and count the money."

"I will."

Drawing a deep, slow breath now, her eyes blinking as her medication kicked in, she said, "Fate, do you remember . . ."

He waited for her to continue. Finally, she said, "That day." She was beginning to drift away, though she seemed to be trying to hold on to the moment of memory, to pull herself back from the waiting fog.

"What day?"

"We were, I think we were making mud pies, because . . . because we were locked out of the house, but . . ." Her eyes glazed over, then closed, making Fate think she'd gone to sleep.

But she surprised him.

"Seems like we were living with Bona or Meverly then."

"Maybe it was Mona or Beverly," Fate said.

"Yeah. The one who bleached her hair and turned it orange. Well, when we went in the house, all that mud, she . . ."

Before she could put it all together, she was out, her body limp against the sheets of the bed Rosa had prepared for her.

"Sleep, Lutie. Everything's going to work out."

As he brushed a stray lock of her hair away from her face, he realized he didn't really believe what he'd just said.

They were going to travel over a thousand miles with a man they hardly knew, going to a town they'd never heard of before, to join a circus family who had no idea that two kids, Lutie and Fate McFee, were about to come into their lives.

Then Fate smiled when he remembered what Floy used to say when he'd tell her about one of his bizarre plans to change the universe. She'd look at him as if he were more or less a regular person and say, "Now, what could go wrong with that plan?"

Nevertheless, he stroked his sister's arm and said in a whisper, "This will all work out fine, Lutie. Just fine."

For the next couple of hours, Lutie and Draco slept while Fate and Juan had occasional conversations—brief, stiff talk limited mostly to the scenery, the traffic, the weather—all crafted to avoid revealing anything personal. But that was about to change.

"Tell me about the circus, Juan."

"Ah, Rosa been talking, right?"

"I asked her about the posters in her house. The circus posters."

"So what do you want to know?"

"Everything."

"I could talk all the miles to Oklahoma and still not tell everything."

"Then talk real fast," a comment that made Juan laugh, but not loud enough to wake Lutie.

"You been to circus, right?"

"No."

"You have never saw circus?" Juan looked dumbfounded.

"Seen, not saw."

"Sorry, Professor McFee."

"The circus never came to Spearfish; I guess because the town's too small. One came to Rapid City last year, but we didn't get to go. The woman I told you about? Floy? She didn't have enough money."

"You seen circus on TV, though. Right?"

"Saw, not seen."

"Saw, seen. I saw what I seen, I seen what I saw. What's difference?"

"You're right. What's difference. Now, tell me about the circus."

"My family in circus for many generations. Parents, aunts, cousins, uncles, brothers, sisters. See, Fate, circus is like a . . . *tribu*. Is it right? *Tribu?*"

"Sounds like you might mean tribe."

"Yes! Tribe. So babies grow up in circus tribe. Become acrobat, cook, rigger, animal trainer, clown, trick rider, aerialist. And whatever parents do, the childs—no—the childrens must become better. Like *mi bisabuelo* Hernando Vargas, he—"

"Whoa. '*Bisabuelo*'?"

"What you call father of father of father of son?"

"Oh, great-grandfather."

"Right. My greatest grandfather performed in Mexico. So did *mi bisabuela*, uh, greatest grandmother. Then they come with four babies to circus in U.S.A. But three babies died from the big disease. Very big."

"Flu? The Spanish flu?"

"*Sí*. But remember this, Fate. Flu come from Spain, not Mexico," Juan said defensively, then waited for affirmation of his opinion before continuing.

"Okay. I understand."

"Good. Everywhen something go wrong, people scream, 'The Mexicans did it! The Mexicans did it!'" Juan used the high-pitched voice of an angry, frightened woman, making Fate grin.

"So your great-grandfather worked in the circus. In Mexico and in America?"

"Oh, he was good aerialist. Traveled all over U.S. with the Greatest Show on Earth."

Fate's eyes showed the impression Juan's remark had made on him. "You mean Barnum and Bailey?"

"Barnum and Bailey. That's right."

"Wow."

"Then Mr. Barnum died, big changes. My greatest grandfather and wife go to Ringling Brothers with only one baby, my grandfather Julio, who become *great* aerialist. He married my grandmother Sim. Mama Sim. They had six childrens and—"

"Six?!"

Smiling, Juan said, "Mexicans love to make love."

"Were all six aerialists?"

"No, no. Only two. Brother-and-sister act. Very popular, but Great Depression hurt much the circus, so the big family all worked at circus, taking up tickets, juggling, selling *palomitas de maíz*, popcorn. See, my English not so bad, huh?" Juan was lost in some old memory for a moment. When he returned to Fate, he smiled. "The others did what they could do to make money."

"Hard times."

"Yes. Very hard. Magda, who did aerial act with her brother? She killed during a show. She flied . . . flewed?"

"Flew."

"She flew without net when they doing a difficult exchange. Big act. Paid good money. My papa, Raynoldo, was her partner, her brother. He never ever talk about the accident."

"Maybe it hurts him too much to remember."

Juan got quiet again for a while, leaving Fate to wonder what he was thinking. Finally, he said, "My papa got married at nineteen. Gabriela, my mother, was just a girl. They had four kids, boom, boom, boom. I'm the youngest.

"By then, my family owned some land, some animals, so started their own circus. One ring, then two, now five. Vargas Brothers Circus. Five rings. Wait till you see. Where to look first? Here?" He pointed out the driver's window. "There?" He gestured out the passenger's window. "Five rings, all at same time."

"And you became an aerialist like your father, grandfather, and great-grandfather."

Draco suddenly popped up, standing on her hind legs, her paws draped over the back of Juan's seat, and barked once.

"Uh-oh. Lutie needs something," Juan said.

And he was right. She was awake when Fate turned to check on her.

"I have to pee," she said. "Real quick."

After two stops in New Mexico—one in Gallup, the other in Albuquerque—Juan decided that they'd had enough for one day on the road. And as tired as he was, he could only imagine how Lutie must have felt.

Each time they'd stopped and helped her to the bathroom, he'd thought they should have followed Rosa and Hector's advice and put off the trip for a few days.

And as much as Juan dreaded going back to Oklahoma, his reluctance growing stronger each hour, he knew if he didn't go then, he wouldn't go at all. Ever. Best, he finally decided, to get it over with. Not only because of the boy and his sister. But what he, Juan Vargas, faced back home.

About a hundred miles shy of Clovis, he rented one room with two double beds at a Days Inn. After he and Fate helped Lutie into the bathroom, she took a shower and changed into a nightgown, then limped to bed holding on to Juan's shoulder. By the time he gave her the pain pills, she was hurting so much that she gritted her teeth.

He waited until her pain subsided, then said good night.

"Where are you going?" Fate asked. He had assumed Juan would be staying in their room.

"Sleep in the car," he said. "Right outside your door. If you need me, knock on the window. I can be here fast as this." He snapped his fingers to indicate his speed.

"But you've been in the car all day. You need to stretch out, get comfortable. Don't you think—"

"My Matilda is plenty comfortable, Fate. Besides, she loves me." Juan laughed and slapped Fate on the shoulder.

"Juan, if it's the money, we can pay some of it."

"No, little man, I got money. I just like the outside." He opened the door, but before he left, he said, "*Hasta mañana*. Early."

As soon as he was gone, Lutie said, "Fate, put that bottle of water here on the nightstand."

"Sure. How you doing?"

"You just told the Italian guy we could help him with the price of this room."

"Yeah. I have a little more than thirty dollars."

"Have you forgotten about the six hundred bucks in my purse? I told you about that, didn't I?"

"Yeah. The toothpaste commercial."

"Then—"

"Lutie, I might as well tell you now, I guess. But please, please try to stay calm. You've been in bad shape; getting upset won't do you any good."

"What are you talking about?"

"The money, Lutie. It's . . . well, it's gone."

"Gone? What do you mean, 'gone'?"

"I'm so sorry."

"Did you lose it?"

"No."

"Did I? Maybe in that friggin' car wreck?"

"You weren't in a car wreck."

"So how did this happen?" She held up her splinted fingers, held out her arms, both cut, bruised, and bandaged, pulled her hair back to reveal the silver dollar–size bald spot where her widow's peak had been, then brushed back the thick mane on the side that she used to try to hide most of the stitches running down her cheek. "If it wasn't a car wreck, how did I get so messed up? Huh?"

Ordinarily, she would be in a rage now, arms flailing as she stomped around the room, stopping from time to time to make a point, using every cuss word she knew while making up a few new ones, and throwing a shoe or a Coke can, whatever was handy at whoever was in her line of fire.

But she was too weak now, too sore and immobile for a rage. All she could manage tonight was a feeble bluster, and even that lacked the familiar Lutie force she could call up without hesitation or real provocation.

"You were beaten, Lutie."

"Beaten? But you told me I'd been in a wreck."

"No, for some reason you *thought* you'd been in a wreck. Dr. Hector said it was a substitution for what really happened, something you weren't ready to face. He said it might be best to let you believe that for a while. Until you were stronger."

"Beaten? Who did it?"

"Two kids. One of them was named Rodney. I think they intended to kill you."

"Oh, God. I . . . yes, I remember." She let her body go limp—a gesture of defeat and the result of Percocet. "He took my purse, pulled me out of the car by my hair, then . . . That's all I can think of. The rest is gone."

"Good."

"Good? Fate, are you crazy? We had over six hundred dollars." She was beginning to slur her words now. "We had a chance—"

"No, I meant that it's good you don't remember the rest. I can't see how it would help you right now to remember all they did to you."

Suddenly, she began to tremble. Believing she was having a chill, Fate grabbed another blanket from the closet. "Was I . . . was I raped again?" Even as she was drifting into the fog of the drugs, she couldn't let go without knowing. "Was I, Fate? You have to tell me the truth. You have to."

"No, Lutie, you weren't raped." He spread the blanket over her from chin to toes. "But why did you say 'again'? Have you been raped? Ever?"

Lutie's lips formed a word, but she issued no sound as her eyes slid shut.

"Please answer me, Lutie. Have you been raped?"

"Just a bad dream. I guess." She gave herself up to an artificial sleep then, a sleep only drugs could produce.

Fate paced the floor awhile. When he was certain Lutie had gone under, he slipped out the door, easing it shut behind him.

He found Juan on the hood of the Lincoln, leaning back against the windshield while he smoked a cigarette and gazed at the sky.

"What are you doing?" Fate asked as he boosted himself onto one of the car's fenders.

"Looking for answers." He pointed to the sky.

"Finding any?"

"Nope."

"Did you know that the star closest to our sun is Alpha Centauri?" Fate asked.

Juan said, "Do you know that star is more than four light-years away from our Earth?"

"Well, did you know that if you started on a trip to Alpha Centauri when you were just a baby, and traveled ten thousand miles per hour—"

"That after passing nearly fifty thousands of years, you would be only halfway to there," Juan said.

Both man and boy studied each other then as if they were looking at a specimen of life rarely seen on Earth.

And perhaps they were.

CHAPTER TWENTY-TWO

TYPICALLY, LUTIE WAS the last one to crawl out of bed, growling and grumbling her way through her morning routine but always finding ways to make everyone within earshot miserable. But not today.

She got up before Fate, washed her face, brushed her teeth, and dressed, all without waking him, even though every movement brought fresh pain to some part of her body. Then, energy spent, dressed in jeans and T-shirt, she crawled back into bed.

For the next hour or so, she slept fitfully. Awake, bits and pieces of the beating she'd taken played and replayed in her memory. Asleep, her dreams reconnected her to the porn film, pulling up images of herself, first with Ebony, then with Lingo, images that bled into more dreams, each driven by greater shame and humiliation than the last.

She was relieved when Juan tapped at the door, waking Fate. A new day. Fresh. Clean. Untouched.

But given the right time, the right circumstances, she knew she'd find a way to screw it up.

After Fate unchained the lock, Juan came in balancing a tray of doughnuts, bananas, and hot chocolate.

"Sorry to wake up you, but we got another far day. Not so long as yesterday, but far."

"How long?" Fate asked.

"I think a little less of five hundred miles. How're you feeling, big sister?" She didn't speak but tried to smile, an effort that caused her mouth to hurt. "Not ready to running a marathoner yet, huh?"

"Marathon," Fate said.

"My English professor," Juan said to Lutie while he cocked his head toward Fate. "How 'bout some breakfast?"

Fate took a doughnut for himself, then offered one to Lutie, but she closed her eyes, turned her face away.

"Where'd you get this stuff?" Fate asked as he reached for another doughnut.

"Down in the lobby. Free. A breakfast continental, they call it."

Fate let that one go. He didn't want to throw too much at Juan too fast. His abuse of English had been going on far too long to improve much.

"Have you gave her morning medicine yet?" Juan asked Fate.

"No, I just got up."

"So, I will do now while you eat." Juan dug around in the plastic sack until he came up with two bottles. He shook out one blue capsule, two white. Lutie swallowed them by sipping bottled water through a straw. Drinking directly from a container was impossible because of the stitches in her lip.

When she finished, Juan put his hand to her forehead. "You feel some warm, Lutie. Maybe you have the fever. I call Dr. Hector now."

Juan spoke Spanish after he reached the doctor, a way—she believed—that was meant to keep her in the dark. Ordinarily, she would have pitched a fit, would have demanded to know why she was left out of a conversation about herself. But she was too tired, her mind too foggy, to jump into the middle of that fight.

After the call, Juan went to the car and returned with a box containing more medical supplies. After he filled a syringe, as the doctor had instructed, he injected Lutie in her hip. Odd, she thought, that she felt embarrassed when Juan had her lower her jeans and panties, considering that only days earlier she'd been filmed naked, acting her part in sex scenes that left her feeling dirty and degraded.

Minutes later, she was only slightly aware of Juan re-dressing her wounds before being helped to the car with Fate on one side, Juan on the other. And in the last moments of her consciousness, she felt Draco's tongue lick her hand before she bedded down beside her.

Lutie was still out when, a hundred miles down the road, Fate was wrapping up his tell-all to Juan. He hadn't left anything out: being abandoned by their father, then living with Floy until she died. Stealing her car to get to Las Vegas, learning their dad was dead, living on the streets, getting free meals when they could. Just trying to survive.

When he finished, Juan took a firm hold of Fate's shoulder and gave it a squeeze.

"Life has not dealt you good cards. Not yet. But I'm—"

"Dealt," Fate corrected. "Life hasn't dealt. See, dealt is the past perfect form of the verb deal."

A groan from the backseat put a temporary halt to their conversation.

"Is she awake?" Juan asked.

Fate took a look at Lutie, who was sleeping soundly. "No. Maybe she's just dreaming."

"I'll check fever again when we stop to eating. You hungry?"

Fate shook his head. "Juan, how did you keep up with us?

Back in Vegas? You were always just where you needed to be when we had trouble. How did you do that?"

"I have crystal ball," Juan said, grinning.

"No, really. Like what were you doing at that construction site where we hid on our first night in Vegas?"

"You mean one being builded on Harmon Avenue?"

"Yeah. Why were you there?"

"Had a job. Night watchman."

"You're kidding."

"Nope. Had a cot on floor three. Seen you come in, seen Lutie turn car lights off. Watched you give the place the one-over."

"Once-over."

"Then you decided for Lutie to parking. Good place, too, 'cause that Pontiac hided from the street."

"Then you're the one who dropped rocks on our car."

"I know when construction crew come, they call police and haul you to juvie, put you in system. I figure anyone work too hard to be not seen, need help. Besides, I would lost my job if boss founded you there."

"And the note? About parking at the library. That was you, too?"

Juan nodded.

"Then how did you find us when we moved into the Gold Digger Inn?"

"Ah." Juan tapped his head. "Detective work. Rodolfo Acosta took over."

"Who's Rodolfo Acosta?"

"Famous Mexican actor. Always play detective."

"Okay, but how did you keep up with us?"

"I think, 'Now, Rodolfo, where would two kids go if they ascared, but had no money? Cheap place, but room with door and locks.' Did not take long for this detective to come up with answer. Gold Digger Inn. Cheapest motel in all Vegas. Dangerest but cheapest. So, me, Rodolfo, and Draco find your car. Case closed."

On hearing her name, Draco's ears perked up, causing Juan to reach back and rub the rottweiler's head. "My detective dog."

"But why did you do all that for us, Juan?"

"All what?"

"The warnings, the notes, food . . ."

"Why not?"

"You've been on the streets for a long time, long enough that you've seen a lot of people in trouble. Even kids. Did you help them the way you've helped us?"

"I try. Sometime I can. Sometime I can't. Help not always what peoples want. Sometime running-away kids just keep running. Sometime peoples crazy. Sometime they ascared of law, might be to thinking I taking them to jail."

"So you try to help them because . . ."

"Paying back. I tell you this story. My friends, Rosa and Dr. Hector, going every week to clinic on bad side of town to help homeless who sick, hurt, need medicine, doctoring. One night, Rosa saw me there on sidewalk. Filthy, drunk, old blood on my face, head. Clothes got stink with sick on pants, hair got bugs. No peoples want to touch me.

"But Hector and Rosa touch me, take me to center for detoxing. Month later, Hector come for me. Take me to their home, Rosa feed me, give me clean bed, and they take me to meeting."

"What kind of meeting?"

"Meeting for drunks, meeting for dopers. Give me book to read, let me hear stories by peoples like me. All stories different, but same. We drink, try to quitting but drink more. Again and again. But in meetings, we learn we cannot to quitting by ourselfs. Need help from Higher Power."

"Is that God?"

"Maybe God, maybe Buddha, Muhammad, Creator, Virgin Mary mother of Jesus. Maybe just friends or all peoples in meetings trying to help each others. Listen: *Dios déme la serenidad para aceptar las cosas que no puedo cambiar, el valor para cambiar aquellas que puedo, y la sabiduría para reconocer la diferencia.*"

"What does that mean, Juan?"

"I asking for courage to be changing things I can change. Like you and big sister."

"But me and Lutie, we aren't drunks or addicts."

"Not yet. But you live the streets in Las Vegas, can do bad things to you. Make sick your mind. You try to be better peoples, then one day you give up. Juan do not wants that for you and big sister."

"So you are helping us because . . ."

"Paying back."

At their next stop, Juan took Lutie's temperature again, then, obviously concerned, went inside the Stop and Go where he'd parked and placed another call to Dr. Hector. When the conversation ended, he filled a plastic cup with crushed ice, bought a roll of paper towels, and hurried back to the car.

There he wrapped a few towels around a handful of ice and gently washed Lutie's face, reddened now with fever.

She opened one eye, forced a crooked smile despite the stitches in her lip, and said, "Thanks, Angelo. That felt good."

Juan turned a puzzled look to Fate, who said, "She thinks you're Italian."

"Oh." Juan shrugged, as if he were accustomed to strangers mistaking him for "Angelo."

He wet some towels with the last of the ice and placed them across her neck. After he injected her again with Rocephin, he added a yellow capsule to her blue and white ones as Hector had just advised, then he got them back on the road, pushing Matilda faster than he had been.

"How high is her fever?" Fate asked.

"Too high."

"Is she going to be okay?"

"Sure. We must only need to get her to Hugo."

"Does every circus have a doctor?"

"No. Too much expensive. Circus use doctors in the towns where circus is booked. But not to worry. Good doctor in Hugo. We be there soon."

"Juan, tell me about the place where we're going. Hugo."

"A small town, especially when all the circuses are on road."

"All? What do you mean, 'all'?"

"Five circuses winter in Hugo."

"Why?"

"Circus only stay on the road for six months or so. When weather is good. But the animals must to being housed in winter, and Hugo has good winter, not many snows, not many ices. Very nice. How you say word for good air, good weather? Huh?"

"Climate?"

"Ah, yes. In Spanish is *clima*. Climate in Hugo is better for animals. So a owner of some circus find enough land for crew, performers, animals, outbuildings. Word moved to more circuses, and them come to Hugo, too. They stay from October to April, then go on road for about six months before they come back home."

"Home?"

"Yeah, much circus people buy homes there. Kids go regular to school; the others all work through winter to being ready for next circus season."

"Who keeps the babies, the little kids, while the circus is traveling?"

"Oh, kids go, babies, too. Remember what I tell you about the circus family, the tribe? The other folks keep check on teenagers 'cause, well, they got sex on their thinking. Anyway, the teenagers take care for toddlers, and grandmas take care for babies."

"What about school?"

"Each circus has teacher. Maybe two. The kids in class every day. So because students leave regular school early and return weeks after school starts, the circus teachers make sure their kids staying up to their sniff."

"Snuff."

"Up to their snuff. Why? Because of good teachers who travel with them."

"Will the circus be in Hugo now?"

"Maybe. You know if they back as soon as we get close."

"How?"

"So many ways. Many. Roar of tigers, lions, bears. Moaning and bawling sounds of camels, trumpets of elephants. Donkeys braying, horses whinnying."

Fate could tell that Juan was reliving a pleasant past but saying nothing about his homecoming.

"And good smells. Popcorn, fried onions, cotton candy. Animals' odors. To me, is wonderful. The smell of life."

"Juan, why did you leave the circus?"

"Oh, I'll tell for another time." Juan hunched over the steering wheel as if he needed to concentrate more on his driving. "Better check on big sister. That fever."

"Okay, but when did you leave Hugo?"

"Why you got so many questions?"

"Well, fair is fair. I told you about me and Lutie, so why don't you—"

"I leave Hugo, my family, fifteen years ago," Juan said, keeping his eyes on the highway so Fate couldn't read his expression.

"And when was the last time you came home to visit?"

When Juan didn't answer, Fate wondered if it was because he didn't want to or because he was tallying up the time.

Finally, he said, "Fifteen years ago. The day I left."

Both were quiet as Juan maneuvered Matilda around eighteen-wheelers, cutting lanes to avoid slower vehicles. Once, caught behind two slow drivers, Juan passed them on the right shoulder, causing Fate to close his eyes.

Finally, to break the silence and because of his unlimited curiosity, Fate asked, "What'd you do, Juan? In the circus, I mean."

"Oh, lots of jobs. Circus need animal trainers, truck driver, ringmaster, cooks, clowns, jugglers, trick riders, midway novelties, roustabouts—"

"Yes, but what did *you* do?"

"I was aerialist."

Fate's excitement was obvious. "Tell me about being an aerialist."

"Maybe another time. I need map. Please look there." Juan pointed to the glove compartment.

"Sure."

Juan didn't need a map. The route was imprinted on his brain, in his heart. But the boy's request, "Tell me about being an aerialist," blew away years of sand and silt under which Juan had buried his memories. And he wasn't ready to dig them up.

CHAPTER TWENTY-THREE

JUAN PULLED INTO Hugo shortly before eleven that night. The few businesses that dotted Main Street, those that weren't shut down and boarded up, were closed for the night, with the exception of a bar where three pickups and a motorcycle were parked. A neon sign in the window said, ALVA AND ROY'S TAVERN.

When he reached the residential part of town two blocks away, all the houses were dark except for one.

"Mama Sim always leaves her front light on in case somebody needs her. And with a family the size of ours, someone always needs her."

The porch light, a bare bulb hanging just above the steps, exposed a wooden swing and three plastic lawn chairs as well as several coffee cans holding plants beginning to wither in the unrelenting late summer Oklahoma heat.

When Fate and Juan helped Lutie from her backseat bed, Draco leapt out and made a beeline for a different kind of bed—a patch of colorful zinnias, where she squatted to do her job.

The front door was opened by a small elderly woman in a blue nightgown, her hair half-covered by toilet tissue wound around her head, held in place by a bonnet of sheer pink net.

"Who's out there?" she called with curiosity, but without a trace of fear.

"It's me, Mama Sim," Juan answered. "It's Juan."

The elderly woman, interrupted while saying her rosary, used it to make the sign of the cross, then kissed the beads in her hand.

"Come up here. Let me see your face in the light."

Juan took the stairs slowly, helping Lutie, who groaned with every step she took, as Mama Sim moved eagerly toward the edge of the porch to meet them.

"Oh, my sweet baby is back," she said as she reached for him, placing her hands on either side of his face, then kissed his cheek. "I've prayed for the day," she said, "when you'd show up on this porch. And here you are—not in the light of day, but the middle of the night. Sometimes I believe the Lord plays harmless little games with us so He won't get bored."

"I got some people with me," Juan said as he and Fate succeeded in lifting Lutie to the top step.

"Yes, I see that."

"They're kids, Mama. Brother and sister. He's Fate; she's Lutie. But she's hurt, maybe real bad. Can you call Doc Adams? Get him to coming over and taking care for her? He always come, day or night."

"Honey, Doc died six, seven years ago. A great loss to all of us. We got another boy here now, calls himself a doctor, but he looks to be fifteen, he doesn't make house calls, he's only in the office three days a week, and his home phone number is unlisted. But I hear he's a hell of a golfer."

"Hector patched her up in Vegas, but now she got fever."

"Doc Hector," Mama Sim said, clearly pleased by his memory.

"Well, she's had the best of the best. Now she'll have to settle for second best, I guess."

"Who's that?" Fate asked.

"Me, sweetheart. That's me. Now you two get her in here while I heat a pan of *sopa*. Just made it tonight. But don't you dare let that mangy-looking creature in my house," she said, gesturing toward Draco. "I can forgive that beast for what she's done to my zinnias, but I can't abide having her in my home. You hear?"

Without waiting for an answer, she disappeared into the house, and not more than a few seconds passed before they heard pots, pans, and dishes banging around in the kitchen.

Fate and Juan guided Lutie across the porch to the front door. Fate could feel the heat of her body against him, even through her clothing, but he wasn't prepared for the heat he felt when she settled her face on his shoulder.

"She's burning up, Juan," he said, hearing the panic in his own voice.

"I know. But Mama Sim, she know what to do. Trust me."

Juan used his foot to prop open the screen door so they could get through without losing their grip on Lutie.

"She doesn't weigh more than a *colibrí*," Juan said.

"*Colibrí*. Does that mean feather?"

"No, *colibrí* is a bird. Looks like a thumb. Claps its wings too fast to count."

"Hummingbird."

"Yes!" Juan said with misplaced pride, since it was Fate who had translated the word, but Juan was beginning to feel that they were a language team.

"And they *flap* their wings, not clap."

"How do you know, Professor? Maybe they *clap* because no other bird can *flap* fast as they can. Watch out for table behind you."

Mama Sim stepped into the kitchen doorway, wiping her

hands on a fresh apron tied around her nightgown. "You say her name is Lutie?"

"Lutie McFee. And I'm her brother, Fate."

"Well, you're both welcome in my house, Mr. Fate McFee. My name is Simona Rosales Anahi Citalalli Guadalupe Salazar Vargas, but everyone calls me Mama Sim. I hope you will, too."

"Yes, ma'am, I will. 'Cause I don't think I'll be able to remember all your other names."

"Fine. Now, while the kitchen stove is doing its job, I'll have a look at your sister."

"I think she's pretty sick."

"Looks like you're probably right."

They followed Mama Sim into a room that was mostly bright yellow: the bedspread, wallpaper, decorative pillows, curtains, rug, and lamp shades. All yellow.

Mama Sim turned back the covers so Juan and Fate could position Lutie on the bed. As the old woman brushed the girl's hair away from her face, she said, "Now. Suppose you tell me what happened to this child. The whole story."

Fate had dozed off on the couch in the living room when a woman in green pajamas and white tennis shoes came through the front door without knocking.

"Hi. Who are you?" she asked with either anger or suspicion. He couldn't tell which.

"Fate McFee."

"Whose car is that parked out front?"

"Juan's."

"Juan who?"

"Juan Vargas."

"Our Juan Vargas?" she said, her voice rising a decibel.

"I guess so."

"Where is he?"

"Back in that bedroom." He gestured toward a closed door just down the hall.

"Where's Mama Sim?"

"She's in the bedroom, too."

"Well, is he hurt or drunk or both?"

"No. He's helping take care of my sister."

"What's wrong with her? Your sister."

"She got beat up."

"Was it Juan? Is he the one beat her?"

"No! He's trying to help her."

"Honey, I hate to tell you this, but if Juan is involved in any way, you're in for a terrible disappointment."

"Why do you say that?"

" 'Cause Juan spreads disappointment like a cat sheds hair."

"He's never disappointed me."

"He will."

"I don't think so."

"Ah, to be young again when everything is possible." She ruffled his hair. "You're a cutie," she said, then started for the bedroom. "I'll see if I can help Mama."

"Ma'am, is she your grandmother?"

"Yes."

"Then Juan is . . ."

"My little brother."

"Oh."

"Well, I might as well play my part to get this prodigal son scene over with. Anyone tell you where to sleep?"

"No."

"Right up these stairs." She opened a door, turned on a light switch, and said, "You'll find some blankets folded on top of a cedar chest, but I doubt you'll need them. No bathroom up there; it's down here at the end of the hall."

"I'll be fine. Thank you."

"And if you're hungry, I smell Mama's avocado soup on the stove."

"Ma'am . . ."

"I'm Esmerelda, Essie for short. Don't get excited if you hear us yelling. A good chance this homecoming is gonna go haywire. Most things do when Juan's around." She smiled at Fate, ran a finger down his cheek, and said, "Good night."

"Night, Essie. And thanks."

Ten minutes later, Fate was asleep in the upstairs bedroom, Juan was pacing the living room after being banished by Mama Sim, and the women were trying to wrestle Lutie out of her clothing despite the good cussing they were getting for their trouble.

CHAPTER TWENTY-FOUR

Fate had awakened in the middle of the night; the clock on the dresser said 3:18. But since the room seemed so little used, he didn't know if he could trust the clock, obviously manufactured in an earlier era. When he looked out a window near the bed, he figured the time must be pretty accurate because of the position of the moon.

He was surprised to find that someone had removed his shoes and socks and slipped off his jeans, all without waking him, then folded his clothes neatly on a chair near the bed. He pulled on his jeans, then headed down the stairs in the dark to Lutie's room, where a night-light burned.

He found her asleep, the flesh on her cheeks and forehead cool to his touch. Mama Sim was snoring softly in a rocking chair near the bed until Fate stepped on a creaky board in the old wooden floor.

"She's better," Mama Sim whispered. "Can you tell?"

Fate nodded as his eyes filled with tears.

"Let's go to the kitchen so we won't wake her."

"When did her fever break?" he asked as he took a seat at the kitchen table.

"After Essie and I got her in a cool tub of water. She didn't like it, but we managed. She's got a lot of fight in her for such a little thing. And a mouth that would outdo any sailor I've ever known." Mama snickered. "I'm not likely to forget our two-on-one skirmish." She held out her arm, which had been raked by Lutie's nails and the outline of what appeared to be the girl's teeth—at least the ones she still had.

"But she was out of her head, so I didn't take any of it to heart. And while we had her in the tub, after she calmed down a bit, we washed her wounds. By the time we dried her and got her back in bed, she let us re-dress her injuries without a word, took her medication, and she's been asleep ever since. One or more of the kicks she took bruised her bladder or kidneys. It'll clear up in a few days, most likely. Not much to do about her ribs or her finger. Time will heal those."

"What about her face?"

"Well, she's not going to be happy about the scars. Looks like Doc Hector had to put in twenty-five, thirty-five stitches to close that deep cut on her cheek. Her lip? I don't think that's gonna be noticeable in a few weeks. Hector managed to close that cut with no more than a half-dozen stitches. He does good work, but he had a real mess to deal with. Now, that front tooth she lost, the dentist here, Dr. Slice, can replace that as soon as her lip heals."

"What about the concussion?"

"Hard to say how much of her confusion is caused by the concussion and how much is due to all the medicines she took for the trip. But I'm going to start weaning her off the drugs tomorrow. I'll feel better, though, when the circus gets back in a few days, 'cause one of the jugglers used to be a nurse and he'll—"

"When? When will the circus be here?" Fate asked.

"Raynoldo, my son, called this morning, said he thought they'd be back in two or three weeks."

Fate's excitement was too great to be confined to a kitchen chair. As he jumped up, he said, "Does Juan know?"

"Now, you sit. Let me fix you a bowl of soup. I've raised enough boys to know you're hungry even in the middle of the night."

"Okay, but I want to see Juan. Be the first to tell him about the circus coming back. He'll be so glad."

"Juan knows already. I told him." Mama pressed Fate back into his chair, then took a seat opposite him. "Fate, I think there's some things you don't know about Juan. But I guess now's the time for you to hear them. Okay?"

"Okay," Fate said with reluctance in his voice. He had a strong feeling that whatever he was about to hear wasn't going to be good.

"Juan's mama and daddy, Gabriela and Raynoldo, were divorced when he was just a baby. Gabriela took him and the older kids back to her people in Mexico. I don't suppose Juan spoke a word of English until he was twelve, thirteen when he ran away and came back here to his papa. Raynoldo.

"Now, Ray is a good man, but demanding. Very demanding. Especially when it comes to performing. You see, Ray was probably the best aerialist in North America when he was younger.

"So he started working with Juan; and because Juan was his son, he wanted . . . no, he demanded the boy to be even better than he was. And Juan didn't disappoint his papa. Juan took to that wire just like a baby to his mama's breast. The wire, the danger, the applause. See, it was in his blood, Fate. The blood of his grandfather, his father, and now him. The son.

"By the time he was seventeen, he was *the* great aerialist, even better than his papa. But all that fame, the praise, the press, the girls. Oh, my God, the girls! They were crazy for him. But somehow, I guess it wasn't enough. And that's when the trouble started."

"What happened?"

"I was still on the road back then, and I think we were in Arizona. Kingman. Anyway, Juan took Ray's pickup and drove to Las Vegas to see this fancy show called a circus, but it's not a real circus. Not one animal in the whole show."

"Cirque du Soleil?"

"Yes! And after that, it was all Juan could talk about. Cirque this; Cirque that. Breakfast, dinner, supper. He even went to cathedral to ask God's help. Can you believe? Praying to be in a circus when you're already in one of the best in the world?

"But his papa would never consent, would never give his blessing to allow Juan to leave. See, Fate, to us, this is not just *a* circus, but *the* circus. The circus of our family."

"Your tribe."

"That's right. We've been here, here with this circus, for sixty years. I first performed with a hoop when I was just a little girl. Then I was a tumbler; after that, a clown. But the first time I climbed on the back of a horse, the deal was done. I performed with horses for over twenty years. Still be doing it, too, but for a beautiful little pinto I named Princess. And she was, too. A real princess.

"Spirited, bold, brave. More dare than brains, I suppose. One night in Toledo she tried a jump. Broke one of her legs and one of mine. I bawled for a month. But that was the end for both of us. I cried so hard they had the doc give me a shot. Slept for three days."

Mama Sim got up from the table then, ladled soup into a bright red bowl, and put it in front of Fate. She handed him a soup spoon and a stack of warm tortillas.

"Now. See if you don't like that, huh?"

After the first taste, Fate grinned.

"See what I say?" Mama asked. "Won first place ribbon at the fair with my avocado *sopa*. Three times. Beat out last year by the mayor's wife. No doubt she cheated.

"You know what? Once I was in the Safeway grocery store and she was there, too. I watched her exchange all the small eggs in a carton with extra large in another. Saved her thirty-four cents. She's a woman with no principles. No ethics. Such a woman would certainly cheat at a county fair to get a first place ribbon."

"So," Fate said, "you were going to tell me about Juan's trouble."

"Oh, my mind wanders down odd paths. But I don't care. Some of the paths of my imagination are so much more interesting than the one I'm really on.

"But, I will tell you this tonight because it will be the elephant in the room for days when the word spreads that the circus is coming back and that Juan is home. See, it was no secret, Juan was his papa's favorite child. But when Juan left, his papa rarely spoke of him again. Especially after Juan became such a huge hit with Cirque du Soleil."

"And Juan never came back for a visit. He told me that."

"No, after the accident, he—"

"Is that what happened to his leg? An accident?"

"Juan was doing an act with Cirque, fell forty feet. No net. He was in the hospital for more than three months. In a cast, actually in several different casts, but nothing worked. And you can see how that left him. A cripple.

"Twenty-two years old and a cripple for life. Ray sent me and Essie to Las Vegas to get him, bring him home. But he wouldn't come.

"He had too much pride, he said, to come back and become a juggler or a clown. So we came home without him. By then, he was a drunk, a doper, living on the streets. All his talent gone to waste, his dreams a nightmare."

Mama Sim pulled a tissue from her apron pocket and wiped her eyes.

"Never figured we'd see him again. And I doubt we would have if not for you and Lutie. I hoped he'd stay, at least long enough for him and Ray to put all that behind them, 'cause one's probably gonna carry the other to the cemetery someday. But he said he won't be here long enough for that to happen."

"What do you mean, 'long enough'?"

"He hasn't told you that, either, has he?"

"Told me what?"

"He's leaving before his papa brings the circus home."

CHAPTER TWENTY-FIVE

FATE HAD GONE back to bed after finishing his soup, but he didn't do much sleeping. He had a lot to think about now that he knew Juan was planning to leave before long. He wondered if his friend was going to return to Las Vegas, and if he did, would he want two kids tagging along. Maybe, he thought, Juan was going to dump them on Mama Sim the way Jim McFee had dumped them on Floy.

In the early hours of morning, Fate heard voices downstairs, which prompted him to dress and tiptoe down to the kitchen, where he heard Juan and Mama Sim talking in hushed tones, sometimes in English but also in Spanish. He took a quick peek into the room where he saw Juan leaning against the kitchen counter, watching Mama Sim at the stove pour pancake batter onto a cast-iron griddle. Though he knew he shouldn't eavesdrop, he stepped back, pressing himself against the wall so he could listen without being seen.

Juan asked, "You know what he'd do if he seen me here? Nothing," he said in answer to his own question. "He wouldn't say any word. Just pretend not to see me, not to hear me. Just act like I be a ghost. Just the way he act on the day I told him I was leaving."

"You don't know that," Mama Sim said. "It's been fifteen years. A man can change a lot in fifteen years."

"Not him. Not Raynoldo Vargas."

"Oh, he hasn't changed, but you have? Is that what you're telling me?"

"I made many mistakes, Mama. I did, but—"

"Yes, you did." She turned then, using her spatula the way an irate teacher might use a ruler to chastise a student. "When you left here, a young stud, you knew everything. Dropped out of school in the ninth grade—"

"*Décimo,*" Juan corrected.

"Okay, tenth, if that makes you feel any smarter. Said this circus was a waste of time. Wasn't anything left for you to learn here. Like to broke your papa's heart."

"But I was just a kid, Mama."

On a roll now, she acted as though she hadn't heard him. "You said you knew all you needed to know to make a name for yourself in the big time." She shook her head, turning back to flip pancakes. "Cirque du Soleil," she said, her face squinched up as if the words had left a bad taste in her mouth.

"I was a . . ." He struggled to find the word, then gave up. "*Gilipollas.* I was a *gilipollas.*"

"I see you haven't made much progress in learning English, either. Yes. You were an asshole."

"But I'm sorry."

"Remember when me and Essie went to Las Vegas to bring you back after your accident? Found you sleeping on the streets, lice in your hair, vomit in your beard, head messed up with that dope and cheap wine. Not a soul out there who cared if you lived or died. You remember that?"

"Yes," he said, turning his head away from her in shame.

"You know who sent us to find you, bring you back?" Without waiting for an answer, she supplied it. "Your papa, that's who. Have no idea how he knew you were in trouble. But he knew.

"Maybe he had a dream about you, or maybe some old friend called him. More likely it was God who told him to find his son and bring him home. But did you listen to us? No! Said we should mind our own business, let you mind yours."

"But I am different now. I do not drink, do not do drugs. Got my head straight; got my life right."

"You got an apartment?"

"No."

"Stay in a homeless shelter? Get a bed in a flophouse when you panhandle a few dollars?"

"No panhandle. No stay in flophouse or shelter. I have good tent."

"Oh, honey. Why don't you come home, stay with us? We're the only family you've got. And there's always work in a circus. You know that. And Raynoldo, he's not getting any younger. But most importantly, we love you. We want you with us."

"What would you have me do, Mama—sling hash in the cook-house? Help the roustabouts hammer stakes for the tent? Sell tickets? Be a barker?"

"Juan, it's not what you want. I know that, but it's—"

"Mama, I was great aerialist. Maybe best in whole world. Can you think how I would feeling to ring the cookhouse bell for breakfast? Hear some rigger whisper about me? Hear his friends talking about me, how I think I too good for circus, so I go to Las Vegas to become star, but come away with nothing but cripple leg? No, I cannot to do that. If I can no perform, then—"

"Okay. I understand. But will you talk to your papa? Try to make things right between you? Can you at least do that?"

Before Juan could answer, Mama Sim turned away from the

stove to put a plate of pancakes on the table. And that's when she saw Fate standing in the kitchen doorway.

"Well, good morning, little silent one. You sleep well?"

"Yes. How about Lutie?"

"Hardly moved all night. Feeling better today."

"That's good news."

"Say, how you like to go over to winter quarters with me after breakfast?" Juan asked. "Let me show you around."

"Sure. I'd like that. I'd like it a lot."

The winter quarters for the Vargas Brothers Circus was only three blocks from Mama Sim's house, so Juan and Fate walked, with Juan filling in a bit of Hugo's history, pointing out where various performers lived, where the old high school had been located before a fire destroyed it in 1982, the original Vargas land where zebras, llamas, yaks, giraffes, and horses were housed until the circus outgrew the land and new structures were built elsewhere.

Just as they walked across a cattle guard under a brightly painted sign that said, VARGAS BROTHERS CIRCUS, Fate was startled by the roar of an animal.

"What was that?" he asked.

"Tiger."

"Is the circus back?"

"No, not yet. But not all animals go on road each year. Some pregnant, some ill, some in accident. Or sometime just too old."

"What happens to them then?"

"They stay here until ready to be back on road. Stay with us until taken by zoo or animal shelter. Or until they die."

"Really?"

"Sure. They give us best years of their lives. We give them comfort and love."

235

"Love?"

"Fate, you cannot to perform with elephant for twenty, thirty years without finding to love it. We celebrate when they have babies, we sad when they lose they mates. We cry when they die. They might have three tons, but they our pets just as much as cats or dogs. They just can't curl on our laps to sleep."

"Is that where the tiger is?" Fate pointed to a barn with a sign above the double doors that said, CAT HOUSE.

"Come on," Juan said. "I show you."

They entered an immense structure partitioned into large cages— clean and roomy—most bigger than the places where Fate had lived.

"This is it. Home to tigers and lions." All the cages were empty except one where a mama tiger was nursing two cubs. She didn't rise at the appearance of the man and boy; instead, she let out a menacing growl that seemed to say, "Okay, guys. That's about close enough."

"She's beautiful," Fate said. "I wonder how old her babies are."

"I'm guessing four, five weeks."

In the EQUINE BARN, they encountered one horse, pregnant and glad for the company. As she reached the fence of the enclosure, she put her head over the top rail for a scratch behind her ears and maybe a treat. Juan supplied both, rubbing her head and producing a carrot from his pocket.

"You came prepared, didn't you?"

Before Juan could answer, the barn door swung open. A boy with a pitchfork and a head of frizzy red hair said, "Who are you?" with an air of authority in his voice.

"I'm Juan Vargas. And this is my friend Fate McFee."

Unable to hide his suspicion, the boy asked if they had permission to be on the winter grounds.

"Well, I think so. I Raynoldo Vargas's son, Mama Sim's grandson," a reply that seemed to let the boy relax.

"Who are you?" Juan asked.

"I'm Johnny Leon Conner."

"You Dub Conner's son?"

"He's my daddy."

"Well, I be damn. Never figured Dub to saying 'I do.'"

"You know him? My daddy?"

"My running buddy, boys together. We fish, chase girls, play flag football. Even went to jail together. Cellmates for a night. And he—"

From outside the barn, they heard a man's voice. "Johnny? You better not be hidin' from me or—"

"In here, Daddy. In here with Sarah and an old friend of yours."

When the door opened, a redheaded man in starched khakis with Vargas Brothers Circus embroidered onto the shirt pocket squinted into the darkness of the barn, then turned on the overhead fluorescent lights.

"Juan? Juan Vargas, you SOB! Is that you?"

"Damn sure am, Dub."

The men walked toward each other, shook hands rather awkwardly, then gave it up and embraced the way true friends do when they've been apart for years.

"I knew it," Dub said. "Told 'em, 'He'll be back one day,' and sure enough, here you are." Only then did he notice the boy behind Juan. "This your boy?"

"Wish he was, but no. He's my friend. Fate McFee, meet Dub Conner and his boy, Johnny."

The boys, struck by shyness, mumbled, "Hi," while studying their shoe tops.

"I know where your boy got red hair," Juan said, "but does he got your temper, too?"

"No, my wife put the quietus to that. But he got his blue eyes, his smarts, and his love of horses from her. Sarah, there"—he gestured toward the mare—"she's his."

"Looks like she ready to foal," Juan said.

"She is." Johnny rubbed the horse's muzzle. "Couple more weeks."

Dub said, "I just put on a pot of coffee. Come down to the cookhouse, Juan, and let's catch up. Got time?"

"Plenty of time." Then, to Fate, Juan said, "You want to seeing the cookhouse?"

"Well . . ."

"Can he stay with me?" Johnny said. "I'll show him around." Then, to Fate, "Want to?"

Fate smiled and nodded.

"Okay, then. He belong to you for a while. Besides, I don't think your dad want you to hearing some of the shenanigans we did when we were kids." Juan looked at Fate for confirmation. "Is it right? Shenanigans?"

"Right."

After Juan and Dub left the barn, Johnny stood the pitchfork up, leaning it against Sarah's stall.

"What do you do with that?" Fate asked.

"I've got to muck out some of the pens. Hey, you wanna go bike riding?"

"I don't have a bike."

"We've got lots of 'em down in the prop shop. Come on."

As they jogged across the lot, Fate asked, "Do you get to travel with the circus?"

"Yeah, but not this year. My dad had surgery about a month before the circus went on the road, so he needed me to stick around, help him out until he's a hundred percent again. Mom didn't go this year, either. Said she had too much to do in the costume shop, but I think she just wanted to be here in case my dad needed her."

Fate followed Johnny into a metal building with six-inch steel center columns spaced out the length of the structure, which looked to Fate to be as long as a football field and a lot more fun.

Each side of the building was separated with partitions made of chain-link fencing with storage bins located from floor to ceiling, all with neatly lettered signs describing what was contained inside: tools, electrical wiring, hoses, pumps, air hoses, tires, oil, saddles, bridles, drills, nails.

Fate took his time reading the signs, looking over the materials he passed, but Johnny shot ahead.

"Hurry, Fate. The good stuff's down here."

And he was right. All that clowns could need was at the far end of the building: musical instruments, hats, row after row of miniature cars, buses, police cars, fire trucks; juggling pins, costumes, rubber chickens, gloves, wigs, shoes, rubber noses, racks of bicycles, unicycles; plastic swords, guns, knives.

"Look," Johnny said. He had on a green wig, a fake yellow nose, a fireman's hat, and rubber shoes twice as long as his feet. His appearance was a signal to Fate that they could put on anything they wanted.

And they did. As a bald-headed ballerina, as a construction worker with a yellow hard hat and polka-dot work boots, and as myriad other incarnations, until Fate, as a policeman, "shot" Johnny as a threatening gorilla, who twisted, gasped for breath, and expired in a B-movie death scene.

"Hey!"

The man who'd stepped inside the building, dressed in the same uniform as Dub, was obviously an employee of the Vargas Circus.

"You boys ruin those outfits, Essie and Katy'll be on you like sunburn on the Fourth of July."

"Okay, Lymon."

"And put all that stuff back where you got it, you hear?"

"Yes, sir."

After Lymon drifted away, the boys got out of their costumes. As Johnny shook the dust from the gorilla suit, he said, "Lymon's grounds supervisor. He never goes on the road, but stays here to keep an eye on the equipment and the animals. He can tell just by looking if one of the animals is sick."

While they were folding costumes and stacking them as neatly as teenage boys could fold and stack anything, Fate said, "What grade are you in, Johnny?"

"Seventh. This was the first year I've ever started school on opening day. See, when we go out in March, we don't come back until October."

"How do you make up all that work?"

"Oh, we have teachers who travel with us, make sure we stay up to grade level so when we return, we aren't behind."

"Are you? Ever behind, I mean?"

"Shoot, no. We're almost always a little ahead. And I don't mind school here in Hugo, mostly because of Mrs. Gee."

"Who's that?"

"Mrs. Gee? She's the greatest. And pretty, too, like a movie star. But she's tough. Won't let us get by with anything. She seems to know when we're not doing our best work. Kind of like a fortune-teller."

"Do you have a fortune-teller in the circus?"

"Lady Scharinda. But I stay away from her."

"Why?"

"She scares me."

As Johnny stacked the last of the costumes in the bin, he said, "Let's take one of the clowns' cars down to the lake. Want to?"

"I didn't know there was a lake around here. Will your dad care?"

"He won't even know."

They tried the fire truck and ambulance, both with dead batteries, before they got the double-decker bus running.

"Hop in," Johnny said. "I'll drive us to the lake; you can drive back."

As they raced through the camp, they passed the welding shop, the painting barn, electrical repair, and the general repair garage. When they got close to the elephant quarters, Johnny slowed, then stopped.

"Hey, Greta," he called, then whistled. From inside the barn he heard the trumpeting of an elephant, followed by another, sounding closer than the first. Then, from the opened sliding door, a huge elephant came out, the weight of her footsteps so heavy that the ground beneath the boys' feet sent a quiver up their legs. Greta was followed by a young elephant not even half her size but moving fast to keep up.

When they reached the fence, their trunks found the openings and Johnny's pocketful of peanuts.

"Here, Fate." He poured half the nuts into Fate's hand.

"What do I do?" Fate asked.

"Just open your hand for Trini, the baby. She'll find them."

As Trini's trunk reached Fate's hand, he giggled at the sensation of elephant flesh against his own, a sensation he'd never dreamed of having. But when all but the last peanut was gone, Trini accidentally nudged it from Fate's hand, causing it to fall to the dust, beyond the reach of the baby's trunk.

Fate stepped a foot out of the bus so he could bend, twist himself into a position to retrieve the peanut, and offer it to Trini. She repaid him by gobbling it and then, at the boys' quiet applause, raised her head to the admiring crowd of two. The elephants locked trunks and bowed.

"Wow," Fate said.

"Yeah. They've been practicing so they can go on the road next year."

As the boys settled in the clown bus again, they heard Dub yell, "Johnny, where the hell you think you're going?"

"Hey, Dad. Thought I'd show Fate the lake."

"You muck out those pens yet?"

"No, sir."

"Then park your bus, grab your pitchfork, and get to work."

"Aw, shoot."

"Maybe Fate can come back tomorrow. Spend the day, have supper with us. That sound okay with you, Juan?"

"Sure."

While Johnny drove the bus back into the building, he asked Fate how old he was.

"Almost twelve."

"Then we'll be in the same grade, same classes."

"I'm not sure I'll be here when school starts."

"Why not?"

"Well, it's complicated. But I hope it works out."

"Oh, me, too. Then, next October, we'll go on the road together with the circus."

"That would be great. Just great."

CHAPTER TWENTY-SIX

LUTIE STAYED IN bed until almost ten-thirty, would have stayed longer if she hadn't run the risk of peeing on the mattress. She made the trip to the bathroom in absolute silence, but then force of habit took over and she unthinkingly flushed the toilet, the sound reverberating upstairs, downstairs, front, and back.

She hurried back to bed and pretended sleep when, ten minutes later, Mama Sim tapped on the door, entering with a tray of hot tea, orange juice, scrambled eggs, crisp bacon, and a short stack of pancakes.

"Good morning, Lutie." Mama Sim arranged the pillows at the girl's back and adjusted the covers across her chest. "How you doing this morning?"

"Okay."

"You look better. The bruising around your eyes is starting to fade. Did I hear the toilet flush?"

"Sorry, I forgot."

"Maybe I ought to put a sign in there. Do Not Flush. We've got to make sure your urine's clear."

"Where's Fate?"

"He went to the winter quarters with Juan."

"Oh." Lutie sipped at the tea, then said, "Can I ask you a question?"

"Sure."

"Are you Juan's mother?"

"No, sweetheart. I'm his grandmother, but thanks for the compliment. His mother left here years ago. Took all the kids. I think Juan was two, maybe three. Last I heard, she was still in Mexico. Tampico, I believe."

"Why did he come back?"

"He wanted to be with his father, Raynoldo, my son. And he wanted to work in the circus. He was just a teenager when he ran away from Gabriela, his mother. He started school here in Hugo, but that lasted only two or three weeks. Guess that's why his English is so bad."

Lutie pushed her eggs from one side of the plate to the other. "I think you forgot my blue pill."

"They're all gone, Lutie. You took the only one left last night."

"Can you get some more?"

"No, Dr. Hector sent just enough meds to keep you comfortable for the trip, but now it's time to taper off. Don't want you to get hooked on drugs, do we?"

"What about the white ones?"

"You have the last one on your tray. There, by the spoon. Take that and you'll be done with them, too."

Lutie swallowed the pill and managed a few bites of egg before she quit. "Sorry," she said, "but I'm just not hungry."

"Yeah, narcotics kill your appetite, but now that they're gone, you'll begin to eat again. Just takes a couple of days for them to work their way out of your system."

"I wonder if you've seen my purse? It's black with a shoulder strap and a silver clasp."

"Not that I've noticed. Honey, would you like me to unpack for you? Most of the drawers are empty, and that closet's got plenty of extra space."

"I guess not. I suppose we'll be going back in a few days anyway. No sense in packing twice."

"Back? To Las Vegas, you mean?"

"Yeah."

"Well, I guess that depends on how long it'll take you to mend."

"But like you said, I'm getting better every day."

"You have something waiting for you in Vegas? A job? Boyfriend? School?"

"A job."

"Chances are we can find something for you to do here. In the circus."

"I don't think so. The circus life, well, it just doesn't interest me much."

"Yeah, it's not the job for everyone. Up at four, travel for a couple of hours, four more hours to set up. Then as the last performance ends, we start reloading the tent and everything in it, hit the road, then start all over again the next morning. Some love it; some hate it, like Juan's mother, Gabriela, if you know what I mean."

"I think I do."

"Okay," Mama said as she gathered up a glass, an empty soda can, a straw, and a hand towel. "I'll be in the kitchen. If you need anything, give me a whistle. I'll give you time to eat whatever you can, then after your bath, I'll re-dress your wounds."

"Thanks."

As soon as Lutie heard Mama Sim banging around the kitchen, she crawled out of bed, put the tray on the dresser, and, as quietly as possible, upended the garbage bag she'd packed in. Somewhere she was going to find her purse. Rodney had stolen her money, but maybe she still had some drugs she'd bought from Viper.

The bag contained mostly clothing—lots of underwear, a bathing suit, flip-flops, costume jewelry, a diary, some belts, a framed photo of her receiving a first place trophy for some gymnastic competition, a few teen magazines she'd swiped from Wal-Mart.

But no purse.

She left her stuff wherever it landed, then—energy spent—limped back to bed, fell asleep as soon as her head rested on the pillow, and had no recollection of Mama Sim coming in to remove the tray.

She was too worn out to hear what was going on, too weak to care. All she wanted to do was escape, and the best way to do that right now was to sleep.

After Fate volunteered to help muck out the pens, Johnny got him a pitchfork, and between the two of them, the work went fast. They cleaned the cages of a giraffe nursing a tender knee; two zebras—the female in heat; several camels banged up in a mishap from their last show. Johnny seemed to take the work in stride, but Fate was like a child in a surreal world where unicorns waited to make his dreamscape real.

Finished, Johnny got permission from his dad to take bikes to the lake so he and Fate could seine minnows for a fishing trip the next day.

Three hours later they returned, their jeans wet up to their knees. They both smelled of fish, their shirts and faces were splattered with mud, and small twigs were twisted into their hair. Their faces, sunburned, sprouting fresh freckles, and plastered with smiles, showed Dub how the day had gone.

Perfect!

"Sorry, Dad," Johnny called. "We didn't mean to be gone so long, but we followed Big Foot's tracks for almost a mile"— a comment that sent both boys into spasms of laughter.

Dub grinned. "Did you catch him?" He'd heard about Big Foot many times before. He'd tracked him even when he was a boy.

"Not yet, but maybe tomorrow."

"Fate, Johnny's mom talked to Mama Sim about that fishing trip you guys got planned for tomorrow. Wondered if you could have supper with us and maybe spend the night."

"What did she say?" Fate asked.

"She said it was okay with her."

The boys yelled, jumped up, and bumped chests as they'd seen pro athletes do.

"Can we sleep outside, Dad? In the tent? Please?"

"I don't see why not. If the weather's good."

More celebration. "It's settled, then," Johnny said. "What time will you be here?"

"I don't know. It depends on what Juan wants me to do and how my sister's feeling."

"What's wrong with your sister?" Dub asked.

"Lutie? Oh, she was in an accident."

"Well, that's too bad."

"Thanks."

"Come as early as you can," Johnny said, almost pleading.

"Why aren't you in school?" Fate asked.

"We're out for a teachers' meeting. Three days."

"Okay, I'll see you tomorrow as soon as I can get here."

The boys waved as Fate took off running across the grounds.

When Fate tapped on Lutie's door, he got no response, so he started to turn away when he heard a sound inside.

"Lutie, it's me. Can I come in?"

"Yeah."

He was surprised to see her sitting in the rocker, her face turned away from his as she looked out the window. But even more, he was shocked to realize how frail and gray she looked.

She'd washed her hair and changed into a faded gown he'd never noticed before, probably something brought to her by Mama Sim or Essie.

"You feeling any better?" he asked.

"Have you seen my cheek?" she asked, her voice flat, without inflection that would give away her mood.

"No, it's been bandaged since . . . well, when all this happened."

Now, without another word, she turned to him, straight on, revealing her ravaged cheek, a deep cut, an insult to the newness of a fifteen-year-old's face. A crevasse where none should be, the cut from just outside her eyelid to her lip. Inches of flesh separated by a sharp blade, held together now by black thread and medicated with a deep red application, a red that seemed more ruinous than blood.

She held absolutely still, eyes unblinking, as Fate examined her face. She was so silent, so still, she might have been a young woman posing for a painter of fame in an earlier century.

Fate worked hard to keep his expression steady and calm, to show none of what he was feeling or what he guessed she must be feeling.

"You want to throw up, don't you?" she asked.

"No, Lutie. Honest, I—"

"Don't lie to me, jerk-head. I know how it looks. It's mine, you know."

"Don't you think maybe it looks worse to you than to anyone else?"

"Oh, please. Don't try that crap with me."

"I think you're trying to rush it. After all, you still have your stitches. Nothing good happens fast, you know."

"Listen, goofy ass, one more phony comforting word and I'll give you a scar that will make this one look like body art.

"You know, there's not a TV in this whole damn house. Not one. I haven't seen *The Jerry Springer Show* since we left Spearfish. So what am I going to do but eat and sleep? And not that it's any of my business, 'cause I'm only your sister, but where have you been all day?"

Suddenly, Fate was a boy again, relieved of talk about scars and conversations meant to make him feel guilty.

"I went to the winter quarters with Juan and met a boy my age. Johnny Conner. He lives out there in a trailer with his mom and dad. They'd be on the road with the circus right now, but his dad had an operation a few weeks ago.

"Lutie, you should see all this stuff out there. They've got everything for clowns: unicycles, big rubber shoes, wigs, makeup, fake noses, stilts, costumes for firemen, policemen. Johnny dressed up in a gorilla costume and I shot him 'cause I was a policeman.

"We rode around in a clown bus, I saw a tiger and two cubs, real ones; a mama elephant and her new baby; a giraffe taller than this room and—"

"Whoopee!"

"I can't wait to take you out there. You'll love it."

"I'd rather walk into a hive of bees."

"And we seined for minnows. You know what that means?"

"Fate, I so don't want to know what that means."

"'Cause tomorrow we're going fishing and I'm going to stay for supper and spend the night."

"Is this supposed to be thrilling news to me?"

Fate's enthusiasm faded as quickly as it had enveloped him. He got up from the rocking chair and walked across the room to the window, looking out at Mama's flower garden.

"You know, Lutie, I've never spent the night with a friend. I've never gone fishing or been asked to supper. You know why?"

"Could be 'cause you're such a dork."

"No, it's because I've never had a friend before. Never."

CHAPTER TWENTY-SEVEN

THE NEXT MORNING, when Mama Sim brought in the breakfast tray, Lutie pushed it away, claiming she couldn't eat.

"What's the problem?"

"I'm sick, that's the problem. I told you I need some more of those pills."

"I could get you a Tylenol," Mama said. "It might take the edge off your discomfort."

"Dammit, I don't have discomfort; I have pain."

Eyeing empty suitcases and bags on the floor, their contents left wherever they'd landed as Lutie had tossed them out late last night, Mama said, "Looks like you decided to unpack after all."

Lutie glared but said nothing.

"Did you find what you were looking for?"

"You know I didn't."

"Why, Lutie, how would I know that?"

"Because you took it, you Mexican bitch."

Mama pulled herself to her full height, looking as if she'd grown by a couple of inches. She closed her eyes to count silently to ten, her habit since childhood. But Lutie's accusation made her so angry, she barely made it to six.

"Now, you listen to me and listen good, because I won't say this but once. You were welcomed into my home, brought here by someone who cares for you. I've done all I know to do to make you comfortable and help you to heal. I've treated you with kindness and respect.

"You may call me Mama, Mama Sim, or Mrs. Salazar Vargas, but if you ever call me a Mexican bitch again, or refer to me with any term of disrespect, you'll find your baggage in my front yard, where you may retrieve it, then move on.

"In the meantime, you may help yourself to anything in my kitchen, but I will not be serving you meals in bed again. And I expect you, beginning now, to clean up after yourself and to help out with chores.

"Have you got that straight?"

"Yes," Lutie said with a look of shock on her face.

"Yes, what?"

"Yes, Mrs. Salazar Vargas," she said with as much sarcasm as she could manage given the ass stomping she'd just gotten.

"The Tylenol is in the left-hand drawer of the kitchen cabinet," Mama Sim said as she left the room.

Lutie stared at the closed door for minutes, feeling angry, sad, guilty, and miserable. Finally she covered her head with the blanket and began to cry. She didn't know how long she'd slept when she heard Fate's voice.

"Lutie? You okay?"

When she lowered the blanket, he could tell she'd been crying. "What's the matter?" he asked.

"I feel like shit, and that old woman won't give me any more of my pills. *My* pills. She probably took them herself."

"Why would she do that?"

"Never mind. What do you want?"

"I'm going over to Johnny's and I won't be back until tomorrow morning, so I came by to say good-bye and see if there's anything you need."

"Yes! I need my purse. See that?" She pointed to the mess on the floor, on the dresser, the rocker, the bedside table, and a small chest. "I went through it all. No purse. You told me it was in the trunk."

"It was."

Lutie's eyes brightened a bit. "You think it's still there?"

"No, it's here." He went into the closet, reached behind a stack of blankets, and retrieved her purse. When he handed it to her, she was practically bouncing on the bed.

"Why'd you put it there?"

"You were so worried about it, I thought maybe I should hide it."

Lutie checked the billfold. Empty. She shook out some loose tissues, which yielded a dime. She removed her cosmetics, a plastic claw for her hair, a broken comb, and a half stick of gum. When the purse finally looked empty, she upended it on the bed. No fake tube of lipstick filled with rolling papers; no sunglass case with a rolled-up plastic bag of pot concealed behind the cheap leather lining; no silver compact with a hidden compartment of coke.

Nothing.

"You took my stuff, didn't you, Fate?" He could hear the familiar tone of anger building in her voice, but this time he was determined not to back down.

"If you're talking about the marijuana, the coke, and the pills, yes. I threw them away."

"Where?!" Now her anger was moving into rage territory.

"I threw them in a trash barrel at a QuikTrip in Arizona while Juan was inside paying for gas."

"You had no fucking right to do that, you stupid little prick. It was mine!"

"Well, it's not yours now, and you might have a hard time hooking up with a pusher out here."

"Don't bet on it, asshole."

"Lutie, this is the time, the perfect time, for you to get yourself straightened out. You've been off that crap for days now."

"No, you fool, I've just been taking a different kind of dope that you and Juan gave me all the way from Vegas to right here in Boondock, America. And then Mama Simple took up where you left off. Can't say they'd be my drugs of choice, but they gave me a nice buzz before they knocked me out."

Lutie shifted into a different position on the bed, pushed the whole mess she'd taken from her purse into a pile, and began to conduct one more thorough examination with the thought that she'd missed something. Something important. And she had.

"Where are Floy's keys?"

"In her car."

"And where the hell is her car?"

"Juan left it in Las Vegas. Said he was afraid it wouldn't hold up for the trip."

"So you just let him walk away from *our car*?"

"It wasn't ours anyway. It was Floy's."

"Yeah, and she probably needs it about now, huh?"

"Lutie, I didn't know what to do. You were hurt. Hurt bad. I thought you might die. But here was a man who offered to help us, so . . ."

Fate sat down in the rocker and ran his hands through his hair as she'd seen him do hundreds of times before.

"Well, what's done is done," she said. "We can't change that. And by now, Floy's car's been stripped or stolen or hauled off to the junkyard or a police compound. So we're going to have to figure out another way to get around."

"To get around where?"

"Vegas, stupid. Las Vegas. We've got to stay on the move or—"

"Lutie, maybe going back there, back to Vegas, isn't our only choice. Have you thought of that?"

"Where do you want to go?"

"I don't know. But why can't we stay here for a while? We're not in any special danger here, are we?"

"Fate, by now we've broken so many laws, they can send us to prison if they find out who we are."

"They? You mean these circus people?"

"No. The law."

"But we're not even sure the law is looking for us. And if they are, why would they be looking down here in Oklahoma?"

"Fate, I hope you don't think I'm going to make my home here in Circusville, U.S.A."

"But it wouldn't hurt for us to stick around here for a while, would it? Just until we decide where we want to go. Besides, it's better than living in a car or staying in a motel like the Gold Digger. We're clean, we get three meals a day. And we're safe, Lutie. We're safe."

"Fate, I'm not going to settle for being safe. I'm going to be somebody. And that damn sure ain't gonna happen here in Dorktown."

CHAPTER TWENTY-EIGHT

Though Fate's day had started off badly—a confrontation with Lutie was never a good beginning—he decided to let it go. To dwell on the ugly, hurtful words she'd spat at him would change nothing between them, but it could spoil his time with Johnny if he kept thinking about what she'd said.

After Dub learned that Fate had never fished before, he decided to go out with the boys to anchor his old johnboat over the hole he baited every New Year's Day with their Christmas tree. Both he and Johnny had taken some monster crappie from the spot, and the occasional bass or catfish, too.

Knowing that Fate would be unfamiliar with the awkward feel and sometimes stubbornness of a rod and reel, he tied a couple of cane poles to the side of the boat. After they gathered up the minnows they'd captured yesterday, and a can of worms they'd dug when Fate arrived, they set out with the lunch Katy had packed them and had their lines in the water ten minutes later.

For the first hour or so, Johnny caught a couple of crappie and Dub caught three, plus a two-pound bass. Fate lost six hooks, broke his line four times in the brush beneath the boat, and cast twice into a weeping willow tree at the edge of the bank.

His first catch of the day was the jeans he was wearing; his second was Johnny's cap, which caused Dub to exchange Fate's rod and reel for one of the cane poles he'd been wise enough to bring along.

Fishing now with live bait was a different ball game. Fate was so squeamish about baiting his hook with a worm that he tried several times to do it with his eyes closed. The result? Some punctured fingers. But after he landed his first fish, a perch about five inches long, he learned to thread a worm onto a hook with more ease and less pity. The trick, he decided, was not to think of the worm's mom.

Once, at Dub's suggestion, he tried to bait a minnow, but it slipped from his fingers into the water. He held a firmer grip on the next one he grabbed from the minnow bucket, but when he realized that he'd hooked the tiny fish in the eye, he went back to worms. Unfortunately, the image of a blind minnow swimming helplessly somewhere in the lake came to his mind several times during the day.

They started in on the lunch Katy had prepared for them a little early, so by ten o'clock not even a crumb of angel food cake was left in the basket.

They fished through the afternoon; their stringers grew heavy with fresh fish, but it was thirst that finally forced them to head in. They'd been as greedy with their bottled drinks as they had been with the sandwiches, pickles, potato salad, chips, and cake.

Dub cleaned the fish at a makeshift sink with a garden hose hooked to it behind the house, performing a special kind of post-mortem procedure that Fate didn't care to watch.

So while they had time, before the sun set, Johnny took Fate to his secret spot, a tree house he'd built himself. The steps were sturdy lengths of scrap wood Mr. Wooten had given him at the lumberyard. Each piece, about sixteen inches long, had been nailed every foot or so from the bottom of an ancient misshapen tree to nearly the top, a sixty-foot wild oak that Johnny claimed to be a hundred years old.

The "house" he'd built near the top felt secure, but Fate, not crazy about heights, didn't spend much time looking down.

The room—the only room—wasn't tall enough for either boy to stand in, but Johnny had bought two old beanbag chairs at a garage sale for a dollar each, so the "accommodations," as Johnny liked to say, "were pretty danged comfortable."

He'd tacked up three pictures of *Playboy* Bunnies on the walls and a newspaper clipping of his T-ball team. He had an orange crate turned on its side to serve as a library for his books—all sci-fi—and from behind the crate he took out his collection of treasures, which he kept in a lidded tin box that had once held cookies, according to the logo stamped on the lid.

But now it held unique marbles, rusted keys, a packaged condom, a robin's egg, an empty brown medicine bottle, an antique glass doorknob, a girl's pair of pink underpants, a broken pocket watch, a school picture of a girl with a ponytail, and a letter he'd written her but never sent.

"Do you love her, Johnny?"

"I saw her feet once. She was barefoot, playing in mud with her little brother. Mud squishing between her toes, her nails painted pink. She has the prettiest feet I've ever seen, so yeah, I guess I might love her."

"Did you tell her?"

"Heck, no! And you're the only person I've ever told, so if anyone finds out . . ."

"Sure. It's our secret, then. Forever."

They fumbled a handshake they'd seen basketball players use on TV, but they messed it up so badly that they fell back on their beanbags, laughing. Fate laughed so hard, he had to work to regain his breath. But he didn't care.

He had a friend, his first—a *best* friend who took him to his tree house and showed him his secret love letter.

He couldn't remember ever feeling so happy before in all his life.

"Now, let me show you the best of all." From beneath the treasure box, he removed a magazine called *Sizzle,* which was full of girls advertising themselves as dates. Some wore panties and bras, some just panties, and some were entirely naked—one with gigantic breasts, both held to her mouth so she could kiss the nipples.

"I didn't know girls did that," Fate said.

"Well, there's the proof."

As Johnny turned the pages and the boys pored over the photos, several crowded onto each page, Fate saw a naked girl with small breasts posed on a chair with her head tilted back, her mouth open as she touched herself "down there." The girl in the picture was Lutie.

Since Johnny paid more attention to one of the girls with her butt pointed to the camera, Fate hoped he wouldn't recognize Lutie when he finally met her. But just to be sure, when they heard Dub call to them from the house, Fate lagged behind his new, best friend and carefully tore out the page with Lutie's picture and folded it into his pocket.

The happiness he'd felt moments earlier was replaced now by dread.

CHAPTER TWENTY-NINE

AFTER DINNER WITH the Conner family, Dub helped the kids put up the tent in the backyard while Katy brought out sleeping bags and pillows. Johnny found two flashlights and sent Fate to the shed for insect spray.

The boys said good night and headed outside with Boggle, Scrabble, a stack of comic books, chips, cans of sodas, and what was left of Katy's pie.

"Hey, are you all moving out or just planning on spending the night?" Dub asked.

"Just one night, Dad."

"Well, don't stay awake all night. You can help me fix some fence early tomorrow. I've got to go to Ardmore in the afternoon."

"Okay."

"Maybe I can help you," Fate said.

"You don't want to do that," Johnny said. "He only pays two dollars an hour. Not even minimum wage."

"Oh, you don't have to pay me. I don't have anything else to do."

"Then you're hired. Good night."

As soon as the boys got settled in the tent, Fate said, "Listen. Just listen to that."

"What? I don't hear anything."

"Night sounds. It's so quiet out here you can hear the tree frogs, crickets, locusts."

"My dad loves those sounds, too." A minute later, Johnny said, "Tell me about your dad. What's he like?"

"Oh." Fate took some time here; he had a decision to make. Finally, he said, "He's quiet. Real quiet."

"And your mom?"

"She's a lot like yours. She's pretty, she likes to cook, I think, and she's crazy about my dad. She worries too much, though, about me and Lutie."

"Mothers are funny that way, aren't they? The first time I rode an elephant, my mom went ballistic."

"You rode an elephant? Wow. I'd like to do that."

"If you come with the circus next season, chances are you might get to if your mom'll let you."

"What do you do in the circus, Johnny?"

"Once the tent is up, I help with the bleachers, the seats, the ring curbs, then I sell big top novelties before and after the show. I ride a horse in the spec and I—"

"What's a spec?"

"Spectacular. It's the introduction when all the performers and all the animals except the cats parade around the rings. I've gotten to do some clowning when they need me, and I help break down when the show is over. My mom does stunts on horseback. She's really good, too. Seems like she communicates with the horses. My dad, he's the troubleshooter. If anything goes wrong in traveling, setting up, the performance, or breaking down and reloading, it's his responsibility to get the problem fixed. And fast."

Johnny paused just long enough to catch his breath. "Hey, you want to play some Scrabble?"

"Okay, but I'm warning you, I'm really hard to beat."

"Yeah, we'll just see about that."

Fate won both games before Johnny said, "I'm not sure you're that good. Could be you're just lucky. Luckier than a three-peckered billy goat. That's what my dad would say. I've got to take a leak."

"Me, too."

"Come on."

Fate followed Johnny to a rock ledge about twenty feet away from the tent. Then Johnny said, "Hold on." He went back, grabbed two of their empty soda cans, scrambled down the ledge, and set the cans up on wooden fence posts about three yards away, then went back to where Fate waited.

"Here's the rules: The one that pisses closest to his can wins. And if you knock it down, you get a prize. Ready?" Johnny asked.

"Yeah."

"Okay." Both boys pulled their penises out of the flies of their pajamas as Johnny counted, "One—two—three—go!"

Fate was the fastest starter, but the best he could manage was about two feet short of his can. Johnny, with more pressure, hit his can and knocked it over.

"Yes!" he yelled, pumping his fist in the air like a pro athlete.

"You win," Fate said.

"Then that makes us even."

"Huh-uh. I won two Scrabble games, you won only one pissing contest."

"Yeah, but the night's not over. We might have to pee again. But we have to do it before my mom gets up. My dad wouldn't care. Hell, he'd probably try to beat us both, but my mom would think it was sinful."

"Do you believe that, Johnny?" Fate asked as they crawled back into the tent. "That it's a sin?"

"Peeing to hit a can? No way. But there's other things I think are sinful. Like killing someone or committing adultery, but I don't think I have to worry about that till I get married."

"What about telling a lie?"

"A fib or a really big lie you'd tell your folks or your best friend?"

Fate was quiet for a while, then he said, "Johnny, I've got a confession to make."

"I hope you haven't killed anyone."

"No. But I lied to you about my mom and dad."

"What? Are they divorced?"

"No. They're both dead."

Johnny sucked in his breath. "You mean you and your sister are orphans?"

Fate paused, looked away, then nodded.

"Is that why you're with Juan Vargas?"

"Yeah."

"So he brought you here because of his grandma? Mama Sim?"

"Because of his whole family, I guess, except for his father."

"What do you mean?"

"I don't know. Some trouble he had with his dad a long time ago. So he plans to leave before the circus comes back. Before he has to see his dad again."

"Then where will you go when Raynoldo comes back?"

"I don't know. If I had my way, I'd stay here. I think with a little practice I could take you in a pissing contest."

CHAPTER THIRTY

LUTIE HAD JUST finished her shower, put on her pajamas, and gotten into bed with one of the books Essie had left with her. At first, Lutie had put them in a drawer in the nightstand, never intending to open the drawer or the books, but today, sleepless and bored, she'd pulled one out and started to read.

By the time she quit reading that night, she'd read almost a hundred pages. She'd lost herself in the story, a kind of magic to become someone else, to be living a life not her own, to be in a place she'd never been before.

An escape.

She'd also discovered that she didn't have to read about a princess or a famous singer or a spoiled rich girl. For instance, in *Plainsong*, the main character was seventeen-year-old Victoria Roubideaux, who was pregnant, broke, and alone. A girl even worse off than Lutie herself.

In many ways, Lutie found that Victoria was not so different from herself, except for the pregnancy. At least Lutie didn't have that to worry about. She hoped.

She was so charmed by the girl's name that she said it out loud just to hear the sound, though she might have liked it even more if she had not pronounced the last name "Rowbeedux."

After she'd readjusted the pillows and turned off the bed light, she didn't hear the faint raindrops fall because Mama Sim had been running her bathwater.

Mama Sim closed the shade in the bathroom, took off her blouse and bra, then bent over the sink to wash her face. As she reached across the mirror for a hand towel, she glimpsed her reflection and wondered, as she often did, who that old woman was staring back at her.

If Gilberato were still alive, but hadn't seen her since 1979, the year he died, would he recognize her should they cross paths? If she were paying her check for the dinner she'd eaten alone at El Tequila's, their favorite restaurant in Austin, and if she'd dropped some coins he would pick up and put in her palm, would he know who she was, would he say her name, whisper, "Simona," over and over the way he had each time they'd made love?

"Old woman," she said, admonishing herself for such fool-ish thoughts, making sure not to look at her reflection in the mirror again after she'd shed her skirt and panties. If she got depressed seeing the deep wrinkles in her face, the sagging flesh on her neck, and her white hair, which had once been thick and raven black, how would she feel if she glanced at the rest of her aged body?

As she eased into the bathwater, she remembered the bath of her wedding night. Gilberato had undressed her, then him-self, and carried her to the tub, which looked as if it had been frosted with whipped cream because he'd poured an entire bot-tle of bubble bath into it. Once they were both in the tub, he'd popped the cork on a bottle of champagne. He'd said that since their honeymoon would last only one night in a nice hotel in Nuevo Laredo, it should be a night to remember.

And it had been.

Even now, almost seventy years later, she could recall every detail. The soapy bubbles clinging to her nipples when he'd lifted her from the tub, causing them both to laugh as he'd carried her to the bed in the four-star hotel they couldn't afford. But, oh, what a night they'd had.

Mama Sim put her head back against the cool enamel of the tub and closed her eyes, which somehow made the memories more vivid. Many minutes later, she was brought back to reality by the sound of the light rain beginning to fall.

She wondered if the girl two doors away was asleep, the girl who had called her a Mexican bitch. Mama Sim had raised her children, some of her grandchildren, and two of her sisters' children, but she'd never dealt with a girl like Lutie. If only, she thought, she could figure out what possessed this girl, why she was so damn angry. Was it a boy? Her parents? Her home? Everybody, girl and boy, man and woman, she'd ever spent much time with would eventually talk about what was important to them.

Not Lutie. At least not yet.

But maybe if she caught her at the right time, in the right mood, Lutie would let down her guard and talk about what had led her to become this hateful person who had the ability neither to accept joy nor to give it.

Perhaps there was still enough time before she moved on.

Essie, who lived next door to her grandmother, was drinking a cup of tea at the kitchen table while helping her youngest, eight-year-old Morrell, with his homework. Tiki, her daughter who would soon be a teenager, had finished her school assignment and was reaping the reward: TV until nine o'clock, so she could watch her favorite show, *Grey's Anatomy*. The volume from the set, still too high even after Essie had told her twice to turn down the sound, was the result of a hearing problem Tiki had had since birth.

Essie, only two years older than her brother, Juan, was the watchdog of the Vargas family, which included their spouses, ex-spouses, children, siblings, and—on occasion—their dogs and cats.

No one had made the decision that Essie would live next door to Mama Sim; everyone simply accepted the living arrangement when Essie divorced her husband, Carlos, after she caught him in bed with one of the Chinese tumblers.

And now, with Mama Sim widowed for over twenty-five years, suffering from diabetes, and having survived one stroke, Essie was content to stay in Hugo year-round so she could take care of her and run the costume shop.

Before anyone in the circus family made a major decision, they went to Essie for advice. Not just because of Mama Sim's age and medical condition, but because Essie had a head for knowing the best advice to give. She wasn't bossy or mean, but she was stern. And sometimes that's just what was called for, especially with the younger ones.

She was asked out from time to time, but she always said no. For some reason she didn't like the idea of her kids, especially Tiki, watching her pretty herself up for some man. And the way some divorced mothers thought it was okay to bring their men home to their bedrooms late, counting on the kids to be asleep, counting on the man to get up and out early the next morning, that just wasn't her way.

She yelled at Tiki for the third time to turn down the volume on the TV, and the girl finally did as her mother had asked. That's when Essie first heard the rain.

*   *   *

By the time Dub unplugged the coffeemaker in the cook-house and turned out the lights, he knew they'd waited too long. The rain had already started. He and Juan had heard the distant rumble of thunder a couple of times but figured if they were going to get any rain, they'd be lucky. Hugo hadn't had a drop for over three months.

"Come on home with me, Juan. You try to make it to Mama Sim's, you might have to swim."

"I no want to wake Katy."

"It's not much past eleven. She won't be in bed. Besides, she baked pies today. I hid one from the boys, figuring they'd take the other one to the tent. And I was right."

"Okay. For Katy's pie, I do it."

Jogging from the cookhouse to Dub's trailer, they stopped to peek inside the tent. Fate and Johnny were asleep, wrapped in their sleeping bags.

"They're out like a light. Don't even know it's raining," Dub whispered.

As they went up the steps to the wide porch Dub had built around the trailer, Katy, with a smudge of chocolate frosting on her upper lip, met them at the door with an armload of towels.

"Looks like we might have chocolate cake, too." Dub kissed away the chocolate, then tossed Juan some towels.

"The boys okay?" she asked. "I thought they might come in when it started raining."

"They're fine," Dub said. "Now, let's have some of that pie I hid and some chocolate cake if you haven't eaten it all."

"Does Raynoldo know you're here, Juan?" Katy asked as she sliced desserts and poured coffee. "You haven't seen him in a long time, have you?"

"No, but I must to be going before he comes."

"Does Mama Sim know you're going?"

"Yeah. She not happy with me about that."

"What are you gonna do about Fate and his sister?"

"I think Fate could want to staying here forever. But Lutie, now she some kind of pistol. If I say to her, 'We leave tomorrow,' she say, 'Why not tonight?' She some kind of pistol, but I no understand what kind."

"Have you given any thought to leaving them here?"

"I think Mama Sim would keeping them, but she too old, too not well."

"You'd probably be surprised at all she does," Katy said. "Your grandmother's got more energy than I have."

Just then, a flash of lightning struck nearby, so close they could hear wood splitting in the tree that was hit. At that second, the electricity went out, leaving them sitting in the darkness.

The bolt of lightning struck so near the tent that Fate felt the earth quiver with the force. And what had started as a sprinkle, then become a shower, now was coming down hard, like marbles hurled from the sky, the drops as big as quarters.

"Oh, my God," Fate yelled as he fished around in the dark for his shoes and one of the flashlights.

"What's going on?" Johnny asked, much slower to wake than Fate. "What're you doing?"

"I can't find my other shoe." Fate had already wiggled out of his sleeping bag, located a flashlight and one shoe. When he swung the beam of the light toward the opening flaps of the tent, he spotted the mate and slipped it on without taking the time to tie the strings.

He was already scrambling out of the tent when Johnny sat up, rubbing his eyes. "Where are you going, Fate?"

"I've got to get to Mama Sim's. Fast."

"It's pouring out there. Let's just go in the house."

"No. It's my sister, Lutie."

By now, the rain was pelting the tent so hard that some of Fate's words were getting lost in the noise.

"She has tonitrophobia."

"What? What does she have?"

But Fate was already on the run, too far away for Johnny to hear him even if he had replied.

Just then, Katy opened the front door and yelled, "You boys get in the house. Now!"

"I'm coming, Mom, but Fate's gone."

In the few seconds it took Johnny to race from the tent to the covered porch, he was soaked.

"What did you say? Where's Fate?"

"That's what I was trying to tell you. He's gone."

Fate was halfway across the winter grounds when a series of lightning strikes created a thunderous roar that seemed to go on and on. As soon as the thunder quieted, Fate screamed, "Lutie, I'm coming! I'm coming, just hold on!" knowing there was almost no chance she could hear him from that distance.

But one creature did.

When Draco heard Fate's voice, she didn't hesitate. She crawled from under Juan's Lincoln, where she had taken refuge from the storm, ran to the door of Mama Sim's house, and stood on her hind feet, scratching and barking for attention. When no one came to answer her call, she took off. She crossed the porch in one graceful stride, made a beautiful flying leap clearing all five steps, and went streaking across the yard, disappearing within seconds into the deluge.

Lutie, close to losing her battle with full-scale panic, was sitting on the floor by her bed, arms wrapped around her knees, pulling them to her chest. Her eyes were clamped shut as she rocked back and forth in the coal mine darkness of the bed-room, wailing like an animal in distress.

At the edge of hysteria, she was trying to focus on an old memory: a doctor; her dad; and herself at five or six, in a hospital emergency room.

She couldn't remember all that had happened back then, the first time she'd had a seizure. But she did recall that her mother had already died, and for some reason, she was alone at home when a powerful storm struck—constant lightning and violent crashes of thunder that rattled the windowpanes.

Her father had found her convulsing in their living room, then rushed her to the hospital. The doctor who examined her had explained that tonitrophobia—fear of thunder—could, in extreme cases, cause seizures and, though extremely rare, could result in death.

He had encouraged Lutie to practice controlled deep breathing and told Jim McFee to make sure his girl wasn't left alone during storms. She would need, he said, someone who could calm her, hold her close, make soothing sounds, all to reassure her that she was safe.

But now she *was* alone, she couldn't control her breathing, she had no one to hold her, to soothe her with—

She began screaming again when a powerful crack of lightning struck so close by that the room blazed momentarily with light and the air exploded with a furious blast of thunder, which caused Lutie to fall back, prostrate on the floor, her body stiffened beside the bed.

Katy followed Johnny as they ran from the house to Dub's small workshop behind the trailer.

As soon as the shop door opened, the wind blew them inside, where Dub was showing Juan his newest project: restoring a '67 Mustang.

"Fate's gone," Katy said.

"Gone where?" Dub asked.

"He said he had to get to Mama Sim's," Johnny said. "Something about his sister."

"Lutie? What is wrong?" Juan asked.

"I'm not sure. He said something about her having some kind of disease. It sounded like tonytorbia."

"Fear of thunder," Juan said. "Fate told me."

As Juan raced toward the door, Dub yelled, "Catch!"

Juan turned in time to see a flashlight coming at him. After a left-handed catch, he was gone.

Mama Sim, moving as quickly as she could, fumbled her way out of the tub, then—knowing her path even in the darkness— reached the towel rack. She called to Lutie, "I'm on my way, darlin'," as she made a few swipes with the towel, half drying herself before she pulled her cotton gown over her head.

Lutie had stopped screaming but was now making a whimpering sound, like a dog taking a beating.

Mama was making her way down the hall to Lutie's room by letting her fingers trail the wall to tell where she was, when she accidentally knocked loose a framed photograph, which crashed on the floor.

The noise set Lutie to screaming again, but not for long. She soon resumed her whimpering sound.

"I'm here, Lutie. Standing here in your door. Where are you?"

Lutie couldn't speak, couldn't make herself find words, but continued whimpering, letting out an occasional sob.

Mama followed the sounds Lutie was making, got down on the floor, and gently pulled the girl with her under the bed, where she held her in her arms and started humming a wordless tune as she stroked her hair.

*   *   *

When Fate got into waist-high weeds, Draco disappeared. All but her tail. It stood up like a beacon for Fate to follow. "Atta girl, Draco," Fate said. "We're not far now. I recognize those boulders."

Draco wagged her tail at the sound of Fate's voice.

When at last they reached Mama Sim's house, everything about it looked different in the night. He'd never seen her place after dark without the porch light burning and more light shining from inside through the shades.

He and the dog took the steps three at a time. Not surprised to find the front door unlocked, Fate went in, with Draco right behind him. Fate called Lutie's name first, but when there was no answer, he was sure he heard singing coming from her bedroom, so that's where he followed the beam of his flashlight, with Draco following.

"Mama Sim," he called as he swung the beam of light around the room. "Lutie . . . ?"

"We're here, Fate," Mama said. "Under the bed."

Fate bent and aimed the light beneath the bed, where he found Lutie wrapped in Mama Sim's arms. Mama was humming a tune as she continued to stroke the girl's hair.

Fate scooted around to the other side of the bed, then squeezed himself in beside Lutie. He held one of her hands while Mama Sim held the other and continued to hum the song she'd been singing. Fate started to speak but decided against it, as Lutie seemed to be calming down. Draco walked around the bed and found room to lie down at Fate's back.

"I smell wet dog hair," Mama said.

"Well, Draco is a little wet."

Mama decided that this was not the right time to make any more of the smelly, muddy dog, so she went back to her humming.

Minutes later, they heard the front door open and then close, followed by the uneven gait that could only belong to Juan. He flashed Dub's light around Lutie but didn't see the crowd under the bed; he did, however, recognize Mama Sim's humming.

"What the hell you all be doing under the bed?"

"Lutie feels safer here."

"Okay. Yes. Okay."

Juan settled in the rocker, its squeaking falling into the rhythm of Mama's song.

The storm was moving away now, but it bowed out with one last, low rumble of thunder. Distant as it was, however, the sound brought a short, shrill scream from Lutie and a rather sad-sounding whine from Draco. But with Mama Sim holding her on one side and Fate on the other, the girl quieted quickly.

Juan hadn't been in Lutie's room long when Essie came in from next door. She carried an umbrella the wind had turned inside out and wore curlers in her hair.

"Hey! Where are you, Mama?"

"In here. Under Lutie's bed."

"Now, why wouldn't I have guessed that?"

As Essie walked into the room, the electricity was restored. "See," she said, "I bring the light." Five seconds later, the lights went out again.

"Oh, turn the lights back on, sister," Juan said. "You got the power."

"Shut up, Juan." While they were in the kind of argument they'd enjoyed since they were kids, someone else entered the darkened house.

"Mama? You here?"

As much as Juan hated the timing, the lights came on as his father, Raynoldo, walked into the bedroom. But he didn't ask why so many were huddled together under the bed; he didn't ask about Draco, who got up and came around to smell this intruder; he didn't even call to his mother again.

Raynoldo couldn't speak, couldn't take his eyes from the man sitting in the rocker. Juan, his son, was home.

CHAPTER THIRTY-ONE

Juan and his father stayed in the kitchen, each finding ways to avoid conversation as one by one the others left the room.

Mama ran Draco out of the house but didn't bother with a mop to clean up the mud the dog, the boy, Juan, Essie, and Ray had tracked in. Instead, she went to bed and pulled the covers over her ears. She'd wanted to stay, wanted to overhear what was being said in the kitchen, but she knew Juan and Ray wouldn't talk until they were alone. If they talked at all. She took her rosary from the nightstand, then fell asleep while she was praying.

Essie went home, explaining she'd come over to check on Mama Sim when the electricity went out. A quick peck on her daddy's cheek and she was gone.

After the storm moved on, Fate made sure Lutie was okay, then helped her into bed.

"Guess Juan didn't plan on this," he said.

"Plan on what?" Lutie asked.

"I told you. Juan wanted to be out of here before his papa

came home. They had a blowup fifteen years ago when Juan left home, so I can't imagine what kind of homecoming this is going to be."

"So we're not going to get out of here until Juan's settled up with Ray? That sucks so big-time."

"I don't know, Lutie. Maybe Juan will leave tomorrow, maybe he'll stay a few more days."

"Well, when he goes, we're going with him. Right?"

Fate's response of "Probably" left more doubts than Lutie liked, but he turned off the light and left the room before she had time to nail him down to something more positive.

Since Lutie's room was nearest the kitchen, she might have been able to hear the exchange coming from next door. But after her night of terror, she collapsed into sleep, missing the entire late night conversation between Juan and his father.

Both father and son endured an uncomfortable silence as they sat at the kitchen table watching their coffee cool. Finally, Ray asked, "What are you doing here?"

"The boy and his sister were in trouble. Didn't know where else to take them. She was hurt. I knowing Mama Sim would help her."

"They yours? Your kids?"

"No. Just two kids. Lost. Try getting through hard times. We be leaving soon."

"Never figured you came to stay." Ray pulled a pouch of tobacco from one pocket and his pipe from another. "I'm going to the porch. Have a smoke."

"Where you coming in from?" Juan asked as he followed Ray outside.

"Lawton."

"Not like you to leave the show on the road."

"Nope."

"Then . . ."

"Heard you were here."

"How you hearing that?"

"Cat trainer in another circus has a buddy in ours. Word travels."

"Or Mama Sim calling you with the news I'm here."

Ray shrugged.

"So you knowing I'm here. But why you came? Try to talking me back into family?"

"You were never *not* in this family." Raynoldo sounded very powerful now that he was at the edge of anger. "Never! You can't cut the ties of family just because you run away."

The sound of a pickup in need of a new muffler pulled them away from their conversation. Seconds later, Dub drove up, parked, and came to the porch.

"Everything okay over here?" he asked.

"Yeah. She asleep," Juan said.

"Well, Ray, didn't see you there." They shook hands. "This is a surprise."

"Thought I'd take a break."

"Have a good season?" Dub asked.

"Not bad. But we sure miss you."

"You miss me? Let me tell you the most exciting thing that's happened here since you've been gone. Johnny built a tree house where he keeps his girlie books, and Katy stepped on a copperhead. Both survived."

"Have a chair, Dub."

"Naw, I better get back. Katy was worried sick about Lutie, and if I don't come back soon, she'll imagine the worst."

As Dub climbed back into the truck, he said, "You all come out tomorrow. I've got some fencing to do in the morning, but it won't take me more than a couple of hours."

"Will Katy make that chocolate cake?" Ray asked.

"It's already waiting for you." As he drove off he called, "Take it easy."

"He's one in a million," Ray said. "One in a million." He tapped the burned tobacco off the end of the porch, then said without a glance at Juan, "Come on. We're goin' for a ride."

"Where to?"

By the time Ray drove his pickup across the cattle guard at the entrance to the cemetery, the rain had let up and the clouds had cleared. The moon cast a dim illumination across the graves.

Neither of the men had spoken since they'd left Mama Sim's porch, nor did they have anything to say after Ray parked and they started across the cemetery grounds.

Ray led the way with his flashlight, being careful to avoid stepping on graves as they entered a section apart from the others: Showman's Rest—the last stop for those who had traveled the long and winding route of the circus world.

When Ray directed the beam of his light on an extraordinary tombstone, he said, "Your uncle Pasqual. My brother." The granite image of a powerful man snapping a whip above his head watched warily as a tiger jumped through a hoop that appeared to be in flame. "Cat man for more than forty years."

The next grave was marked with the headstone of a costumed woman riding in the curve of an elephant's trunk. "My sister, Fabiola. Killed at nineteen when one of the elephants slipped, broke a leg, and fell on her."

Atop another marker was the ringmaster, a figure of a life-size man dressed in a tuxedo, tipping his hat, and bowing to an invisible audience. "Here, my older brother, Ricardo. Ringmaster in Mexico and every state in America."

Farther along the row, Ray stopped, made the sign of the cross, then focused his light on a remarkable stone, the statue of a man in leotards balanced on a high wire stretched between two platforms. "Papa. My papa," Ray said, then wiped his face with the sleeve of his shirt.

Juan followed his father in silence from row to row as Ray pointed out the graves of more cousins, aunts, uncles, nieces, and nephews, along with friends of many decades, all cast in the roles they had performed: clowns, riggers, jugglers, bareback ballerinas, acrobats, carpenters, cooks, flying trapeze performers—two killed in a midair collision—tumblers, painters, rough riders, concessionaires, stock managers, animal trainers, and, finally, a brightly colored popcorn wagon, empty now. Beneath its wheels were words carved in granite: "The tent has folded. The show has moved on."

Ray switched off his flashlight as the eastern sky was turning with the hues of blue, violet, and pink, introducing with a golden glow the sun of a new day.

"You've seen this place before, I know, but it meant little to you then."

"Papa, I was seventeen when I left."

"Oh, yes. I remember. You were a boy, too young, I suppose, to understand what this means. Too young to see that we aren't just a family. We are a tribe. A tribe of people who love the thrill of facing wild animals, who find joy in walking a wire suspended far above the earth, who love the freedom of swinging through the air. For us and for them who rest around us now, the circus is in our bones. It is and has been our life.

"Not the kind of life that comes from shooting piss in your arms or stuffing powder up your nose or drinking poison from the gutter that is your bed, a fire that drives you to crawl through the garbage of other people's lives."

"I no do drugs, I no drink alcohol. I no do those things for years."

"Then where have you been?" Ray asked with surprise. "Why have you not returned to us?"

"Papa . . ."

"You have family here. Family who loves you, wants you to be with us all the way. Even to this place." Ray waved his hand across the cemetery, the graves lit now by the first brilliant shafts of sunlight. "Then we will be with you. We will be always together. But until you can do that, you're lost to us."

Ray stared at his son for a moment, then turned and started back to his truck.

CHAPTER THIRTY-TWO

Mama Sim, always the first one up, was shocked when she walked into the kitchen before six and found Lutie making coffee.

"People won't believe me when I tell them I found Martha Stewart fixing breakfast in my kitchen."

"Not funny," Lutie said.

Mama Sim dampened a sponge and wiped coffee grounds spilled on the cabinet and the floor. "Have you ever made coffee before?"

"No."

"I smell coffee," Raynoldo said as he ambled into the kitchen with the early morning stretches and yawns. "And I want some right now."

Lutie filled a cup and handed it to him, the coffee thick with grounds.

"My name's Raynoldo, but I answer to Ray, too," he said. "And you are . . ."

"Lutie McFee."

"The one under the bed last night. You're Fate's sister, huh?"

"He was supposed to be named Fale, after our grandpa, but someone made a mistake on his birth certificate and crossed the *l*."

"Yeah, that's the way it goes. If we're not able to make our own mistakes the minute we come into this world, we don't have to wait long. Someone will come along and make them for us."

"Seems that way," Lutie said.

"Looks like someone beat the hell out of you."

Without giving it thought, Lutie absently touched her bandaged face.

"You been out to the winter quarters yet?" Ray asked Lutie.

"Ray, this is the first day the girl's been up since she got here."

"Hell, Mama, I'm not going to put her on the back of a wild stallion. I was just gonna ask her if she'd like to ride over there and have a look."

"Yeah, I would," Lutie said.

"Then let's eat and get out of here before Mama thinks of a dozen chores she needs done."

Just then, the front door opened and Juan walked in.

"You're up early," Mama said.

Juan glanced at his father. "Went to take care of that torn fence back of the monkey cage."

"Dub feeling okay?"

"I didn't see him. I was gone before he got up."

"We're going out to the quarters pretty soon," Mama said. "Wanna go back with us, show Lutie around?"

"Well . . ." Juan shot another glance at his father but couldn't get a read on what he was thinking. "I was gonna—"

"Can I go, too?" Fate asked, standing in the doorway, already dressed.

*   *   *

Lutie and Mama Sim rode to the winter quarters with Juan in his Lincoln, which Mama observed was "the size of a hearse," while Raynoldo and Fate walked. Ray said he'd driven so far and for so long, his butt cheeks had grown together. "Here I am," he said, "a man looking seventy in the eyes, and I put so many miles on my behind, I don't even have a crack anymore. Now, what's old Harve down at the mortuary gonna think about that when he pulls off my britches to hose me down before he sticks me in the ground? Probably tell everyone in town that I didn't have no butt crack. Harve can't keep his mouth shut."

Fate liked Raynoldo from the minute he walked in. He was funny and he didn't even have to work at it. He just liked to make people laugh. Fate had expected a grumpy, gruff old man who scowled all the time, a man who had little to say beyond a complaint. But he wasn't like that at all.

When Ray and Fate reached Dub's trailer, he was sitting on the porch, trying to work a burr out of Draco's tail.

"Draco told me you were coming, she just didn't know you'd be so slow. Good to sleep in your own bed again, Ray?"

"The best, Dub. The best."

When Katy and Johnny came out of the trailer, Fate was faced with the moment he'd dreaded: Johnny's first meeting with Lutie since Fate had seen her picture in the sex magazine in the tree house. But when Johnny clearly didn't recognize her, Fate sighed with relief.

"Hi," Johnny said after the introduction, then he flew off the porch, grabbed Fate, and the two of them took off . . . running, leaping, laughing about nothing more than the joy of being together.

"Ray, it's good to see you," Katy said. "How did it go? Good season?"

"More rain than we needed, but nobody got hurt, the animals

stayed healthy. But we missed you all. It just all runs smoother when Dub's in charge."

"Still a sweet-talking man. That might get you a hot banana muffin." She came down the steps and gave Ray a hug as Juan pulled up with Lutie and Mama Sim. "How you doing, Mama?" Katy asked.

"Katy, this is Lutie, Fate's sister."

"So I finally get to meet Lutie. You all come in and I'll put on a fresh pot of coffee. Got some muffins 'bout to come out of the oven, too."

"Thanks, Katy. But we're just gonna show Lutie around some, then get her back home before she tires out. This is her first day out of the house."

"Now hold on, Mama. I'm not against waiting for a muffin," Ray said.

"Your brother told me you'd been in an accident, Lutie."

"Yeah."

"Well, don't overdo yourself today. Better to get too much rest than not enough. I'd best go check on those muffins. You all change your minds, come on back. I've made enough to feed the whole circus. By the way, when will they be back?"

"Be a few more days," Raynoldo said. "I just needed a break. Got close enough to Hugo to drive home for a day, now I'll go back and round them up and bring them back."

As soon as Katy went back inside her trailer, Juan loaded up his passengers, which now included his father. But just before he pulled away, Dub stopped him, leaned against the driver's door. "Say, Juan. I think Big Foot's been messing around here again."

"No kidding? You see him?"

"No, but I saw his tracks."

"Where?"

"Out behind the monkey's pen. And you'll never believe this, but that son of a gun fixed some torn fencing back there."

"I'll be damned. You be careful, Dub. Stay alert. No telling what Big Foot'll be into next."

Dub slapped Juan on the shoulder and grinned. "Thanks, partner."

As Juan drove, Ray pointed out the welding shop and the elephant grounds, where Lymon, the groundskeeper, waved as he was hosing down Greta and her baby.

"That big building's where we keep the props," Ray said. "See, the circus has a different theme each year, so the props and costumes pile up. And there's the cat house. We have a lion and her two cubs in there now. That building is the paint and repair shop. Busiest place on the grounds during the winter when we're putting next year's show together."

"Anyplace you'd like to stop and look around, Lutie?" Juan asked.

"Not really."

"Let's take her to see the horses," Mama said.

"You like horses, Lutie?" Ray asked.

"I don't know. I've never been around a real one."

"Well, here's your chance," Ray said as Juan parked outside a barn. "Come on."

Lutie was glad she'd worn the ugly rain boots Mama had found for her; otherwise she'd have sunk to her knees in mud getting from the car into the barn.

As a brown-and-white horse came trotting toward them, Lutie backed away from the fence. "I didn't know they got so big."

"Lutie, this is Sarah. She's about to have a baby," Ray said.

"Can we watch?"

"Might can if we know in time. Here." Ray filled Lutie's hand with chunks of apple he took from his pocket. "Feed her one of these. Just hold it in your palm."

"Will she bite me?"

"Naw. She'll love you."

Lutie inched her way toward the fence and held out a piece of apple for Sarah, but when the horse lowered her head to take it, Lutie jumped back.

"Sorry," she said. "She scared me."

"Try again."

This time, Lutie was determined. When Sarah took the apple from her hand, the girl giggled. "It tickles."

She fed her all the apple, one piece at a time, then she imitated Mama and rubbed Sarah's muzzle.

"Hey, Lutie. Come out here," Fate called. He was driving one of the clown's police cars. "Get in. I'll take you for a ride."

"No. It's all muddy."

"Okay, but you'd like it, I promise."

Then Johnny pulled up beside him, driving the fire engine. He said, "Let's go."

After the boys took off, Ray said, "You wanna get on her, Lutie?"

"Ray, I'm not sure that's a good idea," Mama Sim said. "She hasn't been out of bed for . . ."

But Ray was already putting a bridle on the horse. When he opened the gate for Lutie and followed her in, he lifted her onto the back of the horse, took the reins, and led them around the ring. Lutie looked stiff and scared at first, but once she caught on to the rhythm of Sarah's gait, she was fine.

Katy came in behind them, so they didn't see her until she spoke. "Looks like they get along."

"Yeah. I think they do."

"Here's your muffin, Ray."

"What a sweetheart."

"Okay, Lutie, that's probably enough for one day. After all, she's gonna be a mama before you know it," Mama said.

"You don't think I hurt her, do you?"

"Why, how would you hurt her?"

"My weight. I mean, my weight might be too much for her right now."

"Yeah. All hundred pounds of you."

"So what do you all practice in there?" Lutie asked as she pointed to one of the largest structures on the grounds. A sign over the door said, RING BARN.

Ray said, "Come on. I'll show you."

Mama Sim, Lutie, and Juan followed Ray into a space that looked like a huge auditorium, except there were no bleachers. The floor was hardwood, resembling a basketball court.

"We have to take our shoes off in here so we won't scratch the floor."

"Why's that?"

"Well, for one thing, the acrobatic troupes work out their routines here, so the floor has to be absolutely level and clean. A tiny chunk of gravel tracked in could cause an accident.

"The plate swingers can't take their eyes off the other performers, their bamboo, or their plates. If they had to look down, even for a split second to make sure of their footing, good chance we'd have thousands of pieces of china sailing through the air.

"Same with the perch pole—three guys depending on each other and a perfectly clean floor."

But Lutie's attention had already moved on through the wires, cables, pulleys, cords, and cages, where she imagined costumed men and women sailing through the air as they twisted, turned, spun . . . their fingertips so carefully timed and trained to find a slender pole that would not wait, other fingers that could not wait to be joined with them.

"What's that?" Lutie asked. She pointed to balance beams of varying heights, starting with two feet off the floor to one that looked to be fifty feet high.

"The wire walkers start when they're young, working out on

the beams closest to the floor," Ray said. "Then, when they've managed that, they move up to the next, and so on.

"Now, the walkers work up there," he continued, "most with a net to save them if they fall. But some, the really great walkers, work without a net. Finally, all they have between their feet is that narrow piece of wire and fifty feet of air over a polished floor."

"That's what Juan did. Best wire man I ever saw. Best in the whole world until . . ." Mama Sim left "until" hanging in the silence that followed.

"The wheels of destiny," Juan said, an attempt to change the subject from his crippling accident. "Faster and faster they spin until you think they spin from earth to sky. There"—he pointed to the next ring—"the flying trapeze, the rings—three, four, five. Where to look? Here—" He walked into ring one. "Or here." He stepped over the ring curb into the next ring. "Or should you watch the tumblers and teeterboard?" He waved his arm over ring five. "But if you watch the destiny wheels, you can no watch the elephants dance, can you? Oh, Lutie, no way can I tell you how so much movement, so much color, the danger and excitement can make you feel. You sitting in the section E, row two, try to thinking what your life would be to live it in such a way. Feeling like heaven, I think.

"But, you see what happen? We get it right, put it in motion, then see how long it take before we mess it up. Mess it up real bad."

"Juan," Mama whispered, "you ought not to talk like that to her. She's just a kid. She's not even old enough yet to know what she thinks or why."

"I know, Mama, but I ascared she be too old now. Her life cut out for her already. The boy, too, unless something change in their living, we know how it all going to be for them."

"Shhhhh. She'll hear you."

Both Mama and Juan looked around for Lutie but didn't see her. "Where did she go, Juan? Outside?"

"Maybe. I guess she got to feeling boring."

"Bored," Mama corrected.

"Hell's bells. Now you correcting me, too."

"I'll bet she went over to the prop tent to see the clown getups Fate told her about."

"Or she might be on her way to the house."

They walked together. Neither of them noticed Lutie as she mounted the highest of all the balance beams, her eyes fixed in concentration.

CHAPTER THIRTY-THREE

Back at Mama Sim's, after supper was finished, Fate and Essie's kids, Morrell and Tiki, did the dishes while Mama sterilized her "instruments" and gathered up the supplies she would need for the "operation."

The stitches in Lutie's face were coming out this evening; the operating theater would be Mama's kitchen; the procedure would be performed on the breakfast table, which Essie had covered with a bleached white sheet.

Juan, following Mama's directions, had used a pair of pliers to bend the needle so that it resembled the shape of a quarter-moon. Tweezers, scissors, and the needle had been boiled in a pot on the stove and shared space now on a tray with gauze, tape, cotton balls, and bottles of alcohol and peroxide.

Ray had replaced the batteries in one of his flashlights, and Essie had brought a magnifying glass she would hold while Mama removed the stitches.

Finally, everything seemed to be in place and everyone had been assigned a task. Mama, of course, was the doctor; Essie, her nurse. Morrell and Tiki fought for the position of nurse's aide. Ray would hold the flashlight, and Morrell, after losing his battle with his sister, was given the magnifying glass to be used when Mama was doing the close work.

As Lutie crawled up on the table, she asked, "Mama Sim, have you ever done this before? Taken out stitches?"

"Honey, I've delivered babies, then stitched up the episiotomy."

"What's an epositonimy?"

"Just before a woman gives birth, she's cut from her vagina to her—"

"Whoa," Morrell said. "Too much information."

"Morrell, 'vagina' isn't a dirty word."

"No one in my Sunday school class has ever said it. Let's just stick to church words."

"I've stitched all kinds of wounds, Lutie," Mama said. "Feet, arms, fingers—"

"I don't give a damn about all that," Lutie said. "Just tell me if this is gonna hurt." She glared at Fate as she spoke. "I might need something for pain."

"No, you won't."

"We ought to tell her the truth," Tiki said. Then she smiled wickedly at her little brother. "What about the time Morrell got one of his balls cut and—"

"Tiki, if you're going to tell this story, use proper terms."

"Okay. He got one of his testicles caught on the wire we use to keep the field gate closed, and you had to sew that up. All that blood . . ."

"You're just telling this story to embarrass me," Morrell said. "Mama, make her stop."

"Okay, Lutie. You just lay back, take a couple of deep breaths, and close your eyes. Ray, I'm going to start down here by her lip and work upward, so put the light right . . . there. Perfect. Now, Essie, use a cotton ball and clean the cut with peroxide."

With the scissors, Mama cut the top of each stitch. Only the last two made Lutie grimace.

"Damn," she said. "You told me this was painless. It's not!"

"You're doing real good, Lutie. Morrell, hold that magnifier over that area right there." Mama used the tip of the scissors to point out the spot she couldn't see clearly. "Fine."

"Okay. All of the stitches are cut, so now I'm ready to pull them through with these tweezers. You might feel a little pinch or two, but it goes pretty fast. You ready?"

"Yeah. Get this over with."

"All right. Essie, dab one of those cotton balls with alcohol and swipe up that bloody spot."

"Hey, if I'm bleeding, then maybe you're taking these stitches out too soon."

"No. It's time. But when I pull the suture through, it can make a fine cut into the skin. That's all."

Mama continued to pull out the suture Dr. Hector had used to close up this nasty cut. And though they knew it would look better as time went by, Lutie would always have a scar on her face.

"Okay. That's it. Looks pretty good, too. And every day, it'll look better than the day before."

"Give me a mirror. Let me see."

"Tell you what. I'm gonna clean this up with some more peroxide, tape a layer of gauze over it, and let you see it after it heals some more. It'll look a lot better then."

"But I—"

"Please, Lutie. Trust me. When you get back from the dentist on Monday, me and Essie have planned something nice for you and you'll think, Wow. Just trust me."

"Why should I? You said this wouldn't hurt."

"I think it looks good, Lutie," Fate said.

"But it's not your face, is it, butt-head?" Lutie stomped off to her bedroom and slammed the door.

"What's wrong with that girl?" Mama asked.

Fate said, "She's mad at me."

"Why is she mad at you?"

"I'm not sure. Could be anything, I guess." Though he didn't feel right lying to Mama Sim, he didn't want to tell her about the drugs he'd emptied from his sister's purse on the trip from Las Vegas.

He supposed she'd find out about Lutie's fondness for drugs soon enough, if she hadn't already.

CHAPTER THIRTY-FOUR

Early the next morning, Juan woke to the sound of Draco's tail slapping against the side of the tent. Ordinarily, the dog, nearly as dependable as an alarm clock, wagged her tail at six-thirty, give or take a couple of minutes. Regardless, it was her way of saying, "Let's get this show on the road and some break-fast in this pan."

Juan could tell, though, judging from the light of dawn, that it wasn't close to six. But when he heard voices and felt Draco crawl out of the tent, he knew she was off to find out if those voices came from people who might have food and might be willing to share it with her.

"You're up early," he heard his papa say.

"Couldn't sleep." Lutie's voice.

"Looks like I'm waking up the whole bunch," Ray said. "Even got Juan's dog out of bed."

"Get down, Draco. Go away," Lutie said.

"You don't like dogs?" Ray asked. "I thought all kids liked dogs."

"I'm not a kid."

"No?"

"I'm sixteen. Almost."

Lutie sat on the porch steps, Draco curled up by her feet. Raynoldo was loading stacks of cardboard boxes from the porch into the bed of his truck.

"You ever have a dog?"

"Once. Stray we named Bingo. But we didn't get to keep him very long."

"What happened?"

"Woman we were staying with took him out in the country and dumped him."

"Why?"

"He tore up her house shoes, peed on her rug. Besides, he needed a rabies shot and she said she didn't have the money."

"Well, maybe you'll get you another Bingo one of these days."

"I don't want one. Dog's too much trouble."

"Yeah, they can be, but there's lots of strays out there looking for a home. I see them dead on the highways ever' day."

"Guess they should've learned to stay away from the road."

"Oh, you're a tough one, aren't you, Lutie?"

"I get by."

"But not without help, huh?"

"What do you mean?"

"Mama told me Juan brought you with him from Vegas because some men beat you. Took your money."

"That was Juan's decision, not mine. I didn't ask to come here."

"Yeah, you're tough all right."

Lutie shrugged, then watched Ray load the last of the boxes.

"You leaving today?"

296

"Yep. Got a few more shows to do before we wrap up the season."

"I guess circus is hard work. Packing up, moving all the time."

"We like the life. But after the last show, we're always glad to head home. Get the kids back in school, see family, old friends again."

"So when will you be back here?"

"Few days. But you'll know we're close long before you see us."

"How come?"

"You'll hear us coming! We take the elephants out of the trucks soon as we pull off the highway, let them parade into town. Horses, too. Llamas, yaks. We pull the covers off the cat cages so folks can see the tigers and lions through the bars. Clowns ride down Main in their miniature cars and buses.

"The folks come out to see us, stand on their porches and wave, holler. Whistles, horns honk. Performers wear their costumes, throw candy to the kids waiting by the side of the street. Oh, it's quite a show."

Even from the distance of his tent, Juan could see his father smiling, lost for a few moments in memories of other homecomings.

"You really like it, don't you," Lutie said.

"All I've ever known, all I've ever wanted to do. Hate to think about giving it up, but that's the way life works."

"What do you mean? You gonna quit the circus?"

"Might be able to hang on another year, but that's about it, I think."

"Why?"

"Look at me, girl. I'm an old SOB. Almost seventy, arthritis getting worse every season. Can't trust my eyesight the way I need to. Mostly aches and pains that come with the years. I ain't complaining. Man gets to work at something he cares about his whole life . . . can't ask for more than that.

"Things would be different, I guess, if I had a wife, but . . ."

"What happened to the one you had? Juan and Essie's mom?"

"Gabriela. She came to this country with me many years ago. We had babies, and our circus family, but Gabby? She never took up with the life, this country. So she went back to Mexico.

"Then, one by one my kids came back to me when they got older. First Armondo, my oldest boy, then—"

"Where's Armondo?"

"Killed. Vietnam. Essie came next, Juan soon after, only son I've got left. The way he's living, though, that ain't no good." Ray opened the hood of the pickup to check the oil.

"I'm never gonna have kids."

"Why not?" Ray asked.

"I don't want to take care of anyone but myself. Once Fate's old enough to be on his own, I'm gonna live by myself, make my own decisions. Do what I want."

"Well, you're young yet. Might be you'll change your mind someday."

Mama Sim came out the front door with a thermos jug and a brown paper sack. "Morning," she said. "Lutie, I didn't know you were up. Feeling okay?"

"Yeah."

"Ray, I fixed you a couple of sandwiches and some boiled eggs for your trip."

"Mama, I'm not going cross-country this time. I'll be in Tah-lequah before noon."

"I've never let one of you drive away from here without you have something to eat and drink on the road. Don't need to start changing my ways now."

Ray slammed the hood, wiped his hands with a dirty towel,

then shoved the towel into a bucket in the pickup bed. He gave his mother a hug, then roughed Lutie's hair.

"You girls be sweet now."

"When will you all be coming in?" Mama asked.

"Depends on what happens with our contract in Stillwater."

"I might not be here," Lutie said.

"Where you planning to go?"

"Wherever Juan is headed."

"Oh." Ray leaned against the pickup fender, took off his cap, and ran his fingers through his hair. He had the look of a man who'd had too many disappointments in his life. "I'd hoped he was home to stay."

"Lutie, do you and Fate plan to stay with Juan?" Mama Sim asked.

"Nope. I don't think he wants a couple of kids to take care of."

"Any chance you might change your mind about going with him?"

"We need to move on, get settled in some city so Fate can get back in school."

"What about you?"

"I'm not sure, but I don't think I'll go back to school. Seems like a waste of time."

"You need to save time? You got something to do right now? Some job you want to try?"

"If I can't be a model, I'd like to be a dancer, maybe an actress. I wouldn't mind being a movie star."

"You could stay here," Mama said. "I mean, until you decide where you're gonna go, what you want to do. Stay with us. Me and Raynoldo, Essie and her kids."

"If you wanted to, you could work in the circus," Ray said. "Try it out for a year. On the road for the season, then in school the rest of the time."

"What would I do in the circus? Sell popcorn, cotton candy?

Learn to ride an elephant?" She laughed, then shook her head, an indication that she'd already dismissed Ray's suggestion. "No, I guess we'll move on."

"What about Fate?" Mama asked. "That what he wants?"

"He'll do what I tell him to."

"But do you think he'd like to stay with us?"

"Doubt it. I think he'll stay with me."

"Well, you said you didn't want responsibility for anyone. Here's your chance. Leave him here, then you can go off without anyone to worry about."

Lutie started chewing on a loose piece of skin on her knuckle, letting Mama and Ray wait for a response. Finally, she said, "I'll ask him."

Ray opened the door of his pickup, but before he got in, Juan came from the direction of his tent, rolling up the sleeves of his shirt.

"You taking off now?" he asked his father.

"Yeah. I need to get back before our afternoon show."

"Ray, I forgot all about that laundry you brought home. It's in the dryer now. Lutie, will you come in and help me fold it?" Then Mama shot the girl a look that said she didn't have a choice.

As soon as the screen door slammed behind Lutie, Ray got his pipe and tobacco off the pickup dash, lit up, then eased himself up on the Chevy's fender.

"We wake you up?"

"I been awake since Draco left the tent."

The dog, hearing her name, came to sit at Juan's feet, looking earnestly into his face as if following the conversation.

"The girl told us you were leaving soon," Ray said. "Sounds like she intends to go with you."

"That's my plan. Can't say about theirs. If they want a ride somewhere with me, I'll take them."

"You going back to Vegas?"

"Expect so. I like the weather. There's work. Not a bad place for me."

"Someone lives in a tent, no family, not many friends, be my guess. Just you and your dog there."

"That's about it."

Ray took a puff of his pipe, then leaned his head back and blew smoke into the clear morning air.

"I'm going to tell you something you don't know."

"Okay."

"I sent Mama and Essie to find you out there, in Vegas, bring you home. I'd heard about your accident, so I figured you'd come back here. Waited over a year for you to show up. But you didn't. So I asked them to go get you, bring you home."

"They found me. Living on the street, strung out on crack, cheap wine. Whatever I could get. Lice in my hair, my pants soiled. They didn't tell you because they didn't want you to know how I ended up."

"Ended up? Hell, boy, you haven't ended up yet, have you?"

"Oh, I'm not messed up anymore, been clean four, five years now. Work when I can, but that's about it. Seems pretty 'ended up' to me."

"You're still young."

"I don't see much in my future to be excited about."

"No reason you can't work with me. I need someone to—"

"What? What do you need, Papa? Sword swallower? Fire eater? You want me to feeding the cats, clean their cages? Or maybe direct traffic, make sure all vehicles in handicapped parking has a sticker?"

"Hell, Juan, you ought to know that I wouldn't—"

"Here's what I know. Circus isn't such a good place for a cripple to work."

"Someone has to run the circus. It don't run by itself. I can't do it forever, and I'm not sure Dub wants to take over for me."

"Oh, I see. You want me to *run* it. Do the advance work, the billing, ordering. Make sure all contracts are signed and take care . . ." Juan walked a few feet away, stared down the road for several moments, as though he might be considering Raynoldo's proposal. But then he wheeled, faced his father, and said, "No! See, here's what you can't understanding. After you've been at the top, it's damn hard at the bottom."

"But it doesn't have to be that way."

"Sure it does, Papa. My leg is never going to get better. I never going to do high wire again. My life was up there." Juan gestured at the sky. "And it's still up there, so far above the crowd I can't even make out their faces. But I can hear them. . . .

"Look, you were right. See?" He pulled up his pant leg to reveal the place where his kneecap used to be. "If I'd listened to you when you told me to stay here with the family, I'd still have a whole leg."

"But you wouldn't have been the star I saw, working that wire, a hundred feet in the air. No net, no fear. Joy."

"What are you telling me?"

"I went to Vegas, Cirque du Soleil, and I watched you. I knew then you were right to leave here, to try for something bigger. Your dream, I guess you'd call it.

"Why? Because you were the best."

CHAPTER THIRTY-FIVE

LUTIE TAPPED AT the opened door of the costume shop, waited, then knocked, louder this time. She thought about turning away, going back to the house, and taking off the bandage by herself. In case she looked like a creature in a horror movie, she wondered if she might handle the shock better if she saw it alone.

Then from somewhere in a back room, she heard Mama Sim's voice and the sound of laughter coming from Essie.

But when she walked in, saw what the large front room of the shop held, she forgot momentarily why she was there.

Racks and racks of hanging garments stretched from wall to wall, and as she inched her way up and down the rows, she couldn't keep her hands from touching clothes she'd only dreamed of wearing. Body-hugging leotards in brilliant reds, royal blues, forest greens, designed with starbursts of rhinestones that reflected light, glistening like jewels; kimonos of sateen in black and silver with ribbons in colors of sunset orange and turquoise; bell-bottomed jumpsuits of bright yellow spandex splashed with sequins and amethyst; velvet ball gowns with swirls of sunstone, the fabric so soft and enticing that Lutie rubbed it against her face.

She discovered sparkling costumes for flamenco dancers, fairy-tale characters, angels, Gypsies, flappers, queens and their courts—all decorated with gleaming crystal drops, delicate lace, and beads of red and green, strands of fringe, tiny gemstones glimmering like diamonds and rubies.

On the back wall, she found shelves that reached from floor to ceiling, some crowded with shawls, boas, sashes, masks, wigs, gloves, scarves, and exotic fans. Others held crowns, nurses' caps, berets, cloches, top hats, sailors' caps, and safari hats.

After she made sure she was alone in the costume room, she put on a black-and-gold butterfly mask edged in red fake fur, a mask that hid the bandage on her face. Then she added a shoulder-length black wig and topped it with a green jeweled headdress adorned with the midnight blue plumage of a peacock's feathers. Finally, she draped a black boa around her neck, pulled on a pair of gold silk fingerless gloves, and at a full-length mirror struck the pose of a model.

"Very nice," Mama Sim said. "Absolutely lovely."

Startled to find Mama Sim standing behind her, and embarrassed to be discovered in costume, Lutie began removing the outfit she was wearing, putting everything back where she'd found it. "I'm sorry," she mumbled.

"For what? Trying on a few things? Goodness, child, nothing wrong in that."

"Did you make all this? The clothes, the hats . . ."

"Essie and me work on the costumes pretty much the year round. We have two women who help us from the first of the year until the circus goes out in March. That's crunch time. But stuff like the fans, wigs, the masks, and gloves, we buy."

"I've only seen clothes like these in the movies."

"Did you get a chance to look at everything?"

"When I came in, and heard you somewhere in the back, I started nosing through these. Guess I lost track of the time."

"Aw, I've been known to play dress-up out here when I'm alone. I'd hate for anyone to see this bag of bones in a sexy leotard, though I practically lived in them for nearly thirty years."

"I'll bet you like making costumes like this." Lutie pulled out a fringed flapper dress.

"I have fun with Essie, but performers having their costumes fitted can be a pain in the butt. 'Can you take it in about two inches?'" Mama said in a falsetto voice. "'I don't like this neckline.' 'Why is this so long?' They drive us nuts."

Lutie smiled. "Sounds exciting to me."

Suddenly, Mama Sim pressed her hands against Lutie's cheeks. "Your teeth! Oh, honey, your teeth. They're beautiful! Dr. Slice outdid himself."

"Yeah, I wasn't so sure about going to a dentist named Slice, but you were right. He's good."

"Come on, darlin'. Let's go get that bandage off. See what you look like now."

"Is this why you asked me to wait to see my face? So Dr. Slice could finish up first?"

"Well, that . . . and because Essie planned a little surprise for you."

"Really?"

"Let's go back and let her work some of her magic."

Mama Sim led the girl into one of the back rooms, where Essie was bent over a sewing machine.

"Look who's here," Mama said.

"I heard you two talking," Essie said. "Lutie, let me see those teeth."

When Lutie smiled, Essie squealed and clapped her hands.

"You're beautiful! Now let's make you even more beautiful. You ready?"

"I guess. I couldn't go to sleep last night for thinking about this."

"You worried?"

"Some. I'm afraid of what I'm going to look like."

"Here," Essie said as she turned a barber's chair away from the mirror.

"You're still not going to let me look?"

"Not until I'm finished."

"Okay."

When Essie gently peeled away the bandage, Lutie looked for some reaction, but Essie's expression didn't change.

"Close your eyes."

Lutie did as she was told, but with reluctance. Even though she couldn't see herself in the mirror, she wanted to feel more a participant in this event. With her eyes closed, she felt shut out of the action.

As Essie patted a flesh-tone concealer over the scar, Lutie said, "That's an odd sensation. That place feels numb."

"Yeah, it will for a while, then the feeling will return."

Essie took her time blending the foundation for Lutie's face. She dabbed a bit on, stood back to take in the color, then blended in a bit of pale yellow, which helped to correct a slightly bluish cast. Finally satisfied, she looked to Mama Sim for approval. Smiling, Mama gave Essie a nod.

To give Lutie some badly needed color, Essie brushed her cheeks with a soft coral blush, her eyelids with light brown to accentuate the green in her hazel eyes. She used a thin pencil of eyeliner on Lutie's top and bottom lids and dark brown mascara on the eyelashes. For the last step, she drew the outline of the girl's lips in dark rose, then filled in her inner lips with a pale pink lip gloss.

Pleased with the results of the makeup, Essie turned her attention to Lutie's hair. She trimmed it, shaped it to fall softly around the girl's face, then back-combed it a bit to add some height.

When she was finished, she opened one of the drawers at the makeup counter, where she'd hidden her surprise: a hat she'd made for Lutie. Beaded with aurora borealis rhinestones in a rainbow of colors, the hat also had a thin veil of elegant gold threads.

As soon as Essie finished fitting the hat on Lutie's head, she turned the chair so Lutie could see herself in the mirror.

At first, Lutie was speechless. Then she got up and leaned closer to the mirror, slowly turning her head from side to side.

Mama Sim said, "What do you think?"

"Well, I don't look much like Paris Hilton, but I guess I shouldn't have expected too much."

Dub and Juan were walking out of the welding shop when Dub saw Lutie disappear into the ring barn.

"Hey, there goes your girl."

"Lutie? No."

"She just went into the ring barn."

"Why the hell would she going in there?"

"Don't know, but I've seen her come out of there twice in the last couple of days."

"Believe I go seeing what she's up to," Juan said. "See you later."

As Dub started for his trailer, Juan walked down to the ring barn, but when he got there, he hesitated outside the closed door, wondering if he was doing the right thing. Finally, his decision made, he opened the door as quietly as he could, then made sure it didn't slam behind him. Once inside, he tiptoed as best he could, to stand behind a canvas draped near the entrance. When he peeked out, his eyes scanned the length of the enormous enclosure until he finally spotted Lutie on the balance beam.

CHAPTER THIRTY-SIX

LUTIE HAD JUST left the ring barn when she heard the crunch of gravel behind her, someone or something running, drawing closer to her with each footfall. When she turned, Fate jumped at her, roaring and clawing the air, an animal closing in on his prey. As he pounced, he wrinkled his nose and hissed.

"What are you supposed to be?" she asked. "I'm guessing a lion."

This was not the stunned, terrified response Fate had hoped for. "No, Lutie," he whined. "Can't you tell the difference between a lion and a tiger?" When she turned and continued walking, he got in front of her, skipping backward toward the road. "Where you been?"

"Costume shop."

"Why?"

"Mama Sim asked me to."

"Why?" He was clearly in a playful mood this morning—little brother pestering big sister.

"Essie took my bandage off."

309

"Why didn't she take it off at the house?"

"Fate, would you stop with the questions? You're getting on my nerves."

"You look really good. I can't even see your scar. But you have lipstick on your teeth. Here." Fate stopped skipping and made a move toward Lutie, pretending he was going to rub off the lipstick.

"Stop!" Lutie swatted his shoulder.

"Know where I'm going?" he asked.

"Probably."

"Where?"

"Fishing with Johnny."

Fate picked up a handful of small flat stones and began trying to skip them across the ground.

Lutie hadn't thought much about the change in her brother until now, but in her recollection of the past week, she realized he was different. He hadn't been slinking off to be alone with his books of facts or playing Scrabble and Trivial Pursuit by himself. He hadn't expressed any new fear of global warming, either. And then it hit her. He no longer reminded her of a forlorn, eccentric old man. No, he looked and acted like an eleven-year-old boy. He was, for the time being, a kid again.

"Did you know Raynoldo left this morning?" Fate asked. "He went to catch up with his circus."

"I know," Lutie said. "I saw him before he left. And I talked to Juan. Found out he's heading back to Vegas in a couple of days. He'll give us a lift."

"Back to Vegas?" Fate's voice was beginning to flatten out.

"Yeah."

Her response brought him to a stop in the road.

"Lutie, I don't want to go back there."

"Listen, Fate, we'll do it differently this time."

"No. I won't go back."

Lutie was far more stunned by the firmness she heard in his

voice than she had been during the abbreviated tiger attack minutes earlier. Still, she thought she could persuade him.

"I've been writing down some ideas, making a list of ways to make it easier on us this go-round."

"I don't care about your list."

"I think—"

"Lutie, you don't seem to be able to see what we have here. Something we've never had before. A family!"

"What?! We had a family," she said defensively.

"Not really. Oh, you did, but only until you were six. When Mom died. I never did because I can't even remember her. Here's what I do remember: you and me and Daddy living with any woman who'd put up with a drunk and two kids. But they didn't make us a family."

"You had me."

"And you had me. But we needed more. A family who went on picnics, argued over who was next in the bathroom, hugged, told lies, laughed. Even if we'd just had a dad who—"

"You *had* a dad!"

"Did I, Lutie? Did you? Did he ever come to see you in a tournament? I was there. Where was he? Did he ever come to school for parents' night or to see one of us in a Christmas play?

"He never took me fishing; we never played catch, not that I would've been any good at it. He took me to a hockey game once, but he got drunk, got in a fight, and we were thrown out.

"He didn't have a clue about our birthdays. We always had to tell him, hoping for some special gift, something other than a last minute stop at the IGA for a box of Cracker Jack, or a key ring. I was a seven-year-old who didn't own a key. One year, I think I was nine, he gave me a Gideon Bible from a Days Inn where he'd passed out the night before."

"The way you tell it, he was *always* drunk."

"Come to think of it, sis, I can't recall that you ever had any friends stay over except for that girl who'd been in juvenile detention for trying to steal her stepmother's car."

"You're making this sound as bad as you can, aren't you?"

"Can you make it sound any better?"

Lutie wheeled and stomped away. Before she reached the cattle guard at the entrance to the winter quarters, Fate caught her, grabbed her elbow, and turned her toward him.

"But here, Lutie," he said, making a sweeping gesture to include not only the circus grounds, but the whole town, "I feel like I'm part of a family. And get this: They care about me. And they care about you even if you have acted like an asshole."

Lutie's eyes flared with anger. "Fate, you talk like you're living in some fairy-tale world where everyone is just so *nice*." She pulled at the word *nice*, twisting it with her lips and tongue, trying to make it seem ridiculous.

"Hey, I like that. Fairy-tale world. It is, you know, 'cause I don't just have a family, I have a friend, too. A real friend. A *best* friend. He can throw better than me, but I can run faster than him. We both have the same favorite color—purple, because Donatello was the Ninja Turtle we both liked best. Johnny's someone I can talk to about anything. He keeps my secrets, I keep his."

Her face showing her impatience, Lutie said, "Are you finished? Or do you plan to go on with this bullshit until I fall down at your feet crying, asking your forgiveness for not seeing things the way you do?"

"Yeah." Fate ran his hand through his hair. "I guess I've said all I have to say."

"Finally! Now, I've listened to your story. You listen to mine.

"Forget what happened in Vegas before and think about how different it'll be this time. We won't have a car, for one thing, so we won't have to worry about the cops picking us up or some thugs coming after us 'cause we'll be living in a nice place. Not like the Gold Digger.

"See, I'll check the newspaper every day, and those free apartment guides, too, and I'll answer the ads where someone is looking for roommates to share a house. Or an apartment. Whatever. Then we—"

"What a great idea. Unless we end up with a pervert child molester. Or a serial killer. Or maybe that nutcase you picked up in Wyoming. The hitchhiker who intended to choke you to death and wanted me to—"

"Oh, don't be so dramatic."

"When we move in with this cannibal or slasher or ax murderer, what do we do for money? Or is he going to let us live there free if we like being sodomized and having our flesh burned?"

"I'm going to ignore that."

"Thought you would."

"We tell *her*, our nineteen-year-old roommate who is a college freshman from Vermont, that if she'll pay the first three months' rent, then we'll pay the next three. That'll give us ninety days to put the money together. You can go to school, work in the afternoons and on weekends. I'll work full-time. Believe me, Fate, this can happen. I just know it."

"What makes you so sure?"

"Because I learned a lot about how to survive when we were there."

"But you didn't learn the most important lesson."

"Which is?"

"We can't take care of ourselves without help."

Lutie's demeanor changed with the anger that seemed to burn from inside her. "I could have taken care of me," she said, her words clipped with indignation.

"Oh, here we go again with that 'You should have stayed in Spearfish' speech."

"Well, there's the question. Why didn't you?"

"I wanted us to stay together. Still do. Why? Because I love you."

"Here's some news. I don't know how I feel about you right now."

She'd hurt him then, she could tell by the look on his face, the look of a whipped dog. Of course, she'd wanted to injure him, but she hadn't intended the wound to cut so deep. She turned and started toward the house.

"Lutie, what's pushing you to leave here, to go back to Vegas? What was so wonderful there?"

"I told you before, Fate. I'm not going to settle for what most girls do—marriage to some jerk and a bunch of squalling kids. That's not what I want. I want to be the girl people notice, the girl people talk about."

"Yeah, you want to be popular. No, famous." Fate grinned, but something in his smile suggested it was coming from a darker place. "I remember how you used to pose in front of Floy's long mirror. Said you were going to be a model. But from what I can tell, you started at the bottom."

She stopped, caught her breath as her skin paled. "What are you talking about?" she asked.

"This." Fate pulled the porn page from his pocket, the page he'd torn from Johnny's sex magazine with Lutie's naked photo. He unfolded the paper and held it up for her to see. "And how about your movie debut? The movie you made in Vegas. Let's see, what was the name of that film? Wasn't it *Charlotte the Harlot*? Not a very imaginative title, but it rhymes."

Neither she nor Fate moved as minutes ticked by, not even when an old pickup honked as it passed them. With their gaze fixed on each other, they waited to see who would strike next.

Finally, Lutie crumpled. "How did you know?"

"I found your script in the glove compartment of Floy's car. Did you do all those things, Lutie?" He was into it now, zeroing in on her humiliation. "Did you really let a man—"

"Don't." She closed her eyes, stepped back, and crossed her arms over her chest. Defense.

Breaking a sweat now, even though the day was cool, Lutie felt a weakness in her legs that made her think they might not hold her up. She staggered once as she turned, then walked away from Fate without looking back.

CHAPTER THIRTY-SEVEN

Wʜᴇɴ sʜᴇ ɢᴏᴛ back to Mama Sim's house, Lutie was surprised to find it quiet, even in the kitchen, where the family
always seemed to gather. Nevertheless, she hurriedly checked all
the rooms to make sure she was alone. For what she was about
to do, she didn't want anyone trying to talk her into changing
her mind.

She made a quick trip to the shed behind the house, where she
found a ratty-looking suitcase covered with dust, cobwebs, and
a sticker that said, "*Omnibus de Mexico.*" Not much, but a step
up from the black plastic garbage sacks she'd traveled with from
Spearfish.

After wiping down the suitcase, she carried it to her bedroom.
Inside, she found an empty tube of toothpaste, two dead spiders,
a man's sock, and an old studio portrait, color tinted by hand,
which resulted in faces that didn't look quite real. The focus of
the picture was an unsmiling but beautiful girl holding a baby
with two children beside her. Lutie guessed the woman to be
Juan's mother, Gabriela, and the infant in her lap to be Juan.

When Lutie cleaned out the suitcase, she tossed the sock, toothpaste, and spiders in the trash but took the photograph to the kitchen and left it on the table.

The foul odor coming from inside the suitcase made Lutie suspect it hadn't been opened since the time Juan ran away from Mexico and showed up at Mama Sim's years ago. Hoping to overpower the smell, Lutie upended a container of talcum powder Essie had given her, then started packing. She wanted to get away before anyone discovered she was leaving.

When she'd left Floy's, packing had been easy; she'd simply thrown all she owned into garbage bags. But this time was proving to be more complicated. Since she would be hitchhiking, she intended to travel with only the suitcase and her purse. That meant not only putting aside the clothes Essie and Mama Sim had given her, but leaving behind more than half of what she'd brought from Spearfish.

Finally, she decided she was taking too much time deliberating, so she threw in what the suitcase would hold; then at the last minute she put in a snapshot Dub had taken of Fate holding his first fish.

Finished, she sat cross-legged on the bed with a notebook and pen to write a short letter.

Fate,

By the time you read this, I will be gone. I didn't know untill today that you knew about some of the things I did when we were in Vegas. I'm so ashamed of being in that movie most of all. But I feel even worse that you know. My only excuse is that I wanted you to go to that special school out there, Paradice. I probably could have made the money another way, but I didn't know how.

We will probably never see each other again so I want you to know that I understand why you hate me. I've given you plenty of reasons to feel that way. But the worse thing I've ever done, you don't even know about. I've never told anyone.

What you said about staying here with a nice family and haveing a best friend is a good plan. Staying with people who will take care of you and give you a good life is something I couldn't do. I'm sorry.

Lutie

"Lutie?" Mama Sim called when she and Essie got back to the house. "Lutie, you here?"

Essie, carrying a sack of groceries, said, "Guess she's gone for one of her walks."

"Oh, it feels good to get out of those shoes," Mama said.

"Your feet aren't swelling again, are they?"

"No. And I don't need another lecture about using too much salt. I hate that salt substitute. It tastes like a salt lick."

"Now, how would you know about a salt lick?"

"You forget that I was raised on a farm before I ever saw a circus. Any kid spent time around cows has tasted a salt lick."

"I'd better get some of this stuff in the fridge," Essie said as she headed for the kitchen.

When the front door slammed, Morrell came busting into the living room. "Where's Mom?" he asked.

"In the kitchen putting my groceries away."

"Mom," he yelled. "Did you remember to get some jelly beans?" As he disappeared down the hall to the kitchen, Mama settled on the couch with a pillow behind her back.

"Mama," Essie called, "you'd better come here."

"I'm awful comfortable right here where I am, Essie."

"Okay, but there's something here you ought to see."

Mama Sim heard something in Essie's voice that seemed a bit odd, so she pulled herself up and went to the kitchen.

"Now, what is it I should see?"

Essie held out the photograph of Gabriela and the children. "You have any idea where this came from?"

"Where'd you get it?"

"Someone left it there. On the table."

Mama turned over the photo to find stamped on the back, badly faded and stained, this copyright: *Ciudad Madero Fotografía.*

"My mom," Essie said as she pointed to each person in the picture. "That's Armondo, that's me. The baby is Juan."

"Do you suppose he put it here?"

"Could be."

"I'm going to see if Lutie talked to him."

Mama found Lutie's door closed; she tapped, then opened the door a crack. "Lutie, you asleep?" When no sound came from inside, Mama pushed open the door and went in. The bed was made, but a folded stack of clothes lay near the headboard, causing a dark look to cross Mama's face. She opened the drawers in the chest. Nothing. In the closet, she found empty hangers. *"Dios santo!"* she whispered.

She hurried to Fate's room. The door was open, but clearly he wasn't there. Just as she turned to leave, she saw the note on his bed. Her lips moved as she read it, her expression turning to one of anxiety. Bad news. Now and then she spoke, though she was unaware of the sound. "Paradise," she said. Then, near the end, "I'm sorry."

Unseen, Mama slipped on her shoes, grabbed her keys, and tiptoed outside. After she'd gone quietly down the porch steps, she hurried to her old GMC pickup, cranked it up, and was flying down the road toward town.

*   *   *

At the Good Old Days Antique Shop, Mama made a quick stop. Cash Abernathy, the owner, sat out front in a patched red leather recliner beneath an awning shading the building.

"Howdy, Mama," Cash said.

"You see a girl pass by, sixteen, small, brown hair?"

"No, Mama, don't believe I seen her."

"Think hard, Cash. She's wearing low-rise jeans that barely cover her hipbones and a red T-shirt that's way too short, so she's showing lots of skin. From here to here." Mama used her hands to illustrate how low the jeans were, how short the tee. "And her belly button's pierced. She's got a silver ring through it."

"Oh, her. Yeah, I saw a girl like that. She was carryin' a suitcase."

"Which way'd she go?"

"Down there to the bus station."

"Thanks, Cash."

The bus station smelled of dirty feet, onions, and Old Spice. A fat woman was sleeping on one of the benches, her dress pulled up to reveal several pounds of cellulite around her upper thighs. Mama, in a gesture of kindness, pulled the dress down to cover the unpleasant view, a slight disturbance that caused the woman to say "Bird shot," or "Bird shit," in her sleep. Mama didn't know for sure what she'd heard.

A family of Mexicans she didn't recognize sat wedged together on another bench. Mother, father, and seven children, all awake, silently watching the door as if they feared a lynch mob or the law would burst through at any minute.

At the counter, a lone agent was looking at pictures in *Hustler* magazine.

"Where to?" he said without looking up.

"I'm not going anywhere," Mama said.

"Then why are you here?" he said, his eyes never straying from the *Hustler* women.

"I'm looking for a girl."

"Yeah? So am I."

"She was here. Sixteen, low-rise jeans, belly button—"

"Was pierced. Had a silver ring in it. No hooters to speak of, but good-looking ass for a short girl."

"Where'd she go?"

"Out the door."

"I mean did she go north or south? East? West?"

The agent sighed and closed the magazine. "She wanted to know if I'd give her a ticket for some cheap ring she was wearin'. Hell, it wasn't worth five bucks."

"Did you see which way she went when she left here?"

"Look, lady. I sell bus tickets. I ain't a damn detective."

At the four-way stop at the end of Main, Mama saw Dub's pickup coming from the opposite direction. She stopped her truck in the middle of the intersection and flagged him down.

When he saw the expression on her face, he knew there was trouble. "What's up?" he asked.

"Lutie's run away. I'm afraid she'll hitch a ride."

"I just came from Idabel. She's not out that way."

"Then she either took 70 toward Durant or the Indian Nation."

"I'll take the turnpike; you take 70."

"Let's go."

Just west of town at the entrance to a deserted drive-in, Mama spotted Lutie getting into a vintage car with Texas plates. She sped around the car and slid to a stop only inches from the fancy front grille. Then she got out of her truck and hurried to the driver's side, where she found a boy who looked to be in his late teens behind the wheel.

Rolling down his window, he yelled, "You idiot! What the hell is wrong with you? You almost hit my car."

"Get out of this car, Lutie."

"Do you have any idea what kind of car this is?" the boy said. "It's a perfectly restored 1969 Pontiac GTO."

Mama pointed to the suitcase on Lutie's lap. "Know what she's got in there? Snakes—rattlers, copperheads, cottonmouths—"

"What?!"

"She's taking them to her daddy. He's a preacher at one of those churches where they handle snakes to prove that God will protect them."

"She's lying," Lutie said. "This is filled with clothes. Here. I'll show you." When she put her thumbs on the flimsy locks, the boy slapped one hand on top of the suitcase, holding it closed; with the other, he opened the passenger door. He shoved the suitcase out of the car first, Lutie next.

As he backed up, then burned rubber speeding away, Lutie picked up her suitcase, shot a vicious look at Mama Sim, and said, "I'm leaving here, and no matter what you do, you won't be able to stop me."

Thunder rumbled in the distance.

Mama said, "Storm's headed this way."

When Lutie saw streaks of lightning in the west, she became agitated, crawled into Mama's truck, and yelled, "Come on!"

As soon as they were inside the old GMC, Mama said, "I read your note."

"I don't suppose it mattered to you that the note I wrote was *for Fate*, not you."

"When I went to your room, saw that you were gone, I was in a panic. Looked all over the place. Went to Fate's room, where you left the note."

"So you were in a panic because I'd gone. You know how much I believe that? Not . . . one . . . bit." She drew out the words in order to make an impression. "He had a choice. He could go with me or stay with you. I really wasn't much surprised when he chose you."

"Why?"

"He hates me."

"Fate? He doesn't hate you, Lutie. He loves you. Adores you. No, Fate's not your problem."

"And I suppose you know what my problem is?"

"I think I do. I'm no mind reader, but I believe I know what's tearing you up."

"That's so lame."

"Might be. But I can tell when something's gone bad."

"You mean like me."

"That's right."

"And how can you tell?"

"Because of how you treat people. Seems the nicer to you they are, the meaner you are to them. Oh, you let them see another side of you, but then you push them away. Never let anyone get too close to you."

Another bolt of lightning, closer this time, produced a soft, rolling sound of thunder. Lutie scooted a bit closer to Mama.

"Look, Lutie, you act like everyone hates you. But that can't be true, can it? That *all* of us hate *you* all the time? I mean, we've got our own troubles, lots of problems in our own lives every day, so we don't give much time or thought to hating you."

"Maybe not everyone at the same time, but—"

"Yeah, I think you're right. There's only one person who hates you *all* the time."

"And who would that be, Miss Know-It-All?"

"You."

"What the fuck is that supposed to mean?"

"It means that you're your own problem. You hate yourself so much that you hate everybody else."

A blazing lightning strike that seemed to electrify the heavens created a thunderclap that rolled across the earth, making the old pickup shudder, causing Lutie to let Mama wrap her in her arms and pull her even closer.

"What happened to you, Lutie? What happened to make you hate yourself so?"

"I don't hate myself." Lutie tried to act as strong and sound as furious as she had earlier. She even tried halfheartedly to pull back, but Mama held her firmly in her arms. "I do *not* hate myself," she said again, hoping to sound confident and secure. But she sounded more like a frightened child.

"Tell me what happened, darling."

At first, Lutie said nothing, holding her resistance as long as she could; but finally, she said, "I don't know."

"You probably do, but you've pushed those memories and those pictures that made you feel so bad, you've pushed those way back here." Mama tapped the back of Lutie's head. "Or maybe you wrapped them up in an ugly little pouch and put it behind your heart. But either way, you've tried to bury it. So maybe now's the time to let it out. Because if you don't love yourself, you won't be able to love the ones who love you."

Mama held Lutie so close that she could feel her heart pounding, the resistance still holding her back. Then, in the blink of an eye, she felt Lutie's body go limp as she let down the years of barriers she'd worked so hard to build up.

"I let her die," Lutie said, her voice so soft and broken that Mama wasn't sure what she'd heard.

"What did you say?"

"My mother. I let her die."

"Why don't you tell me how that happened," Mama Sim said, trying to sound as natural as she could.

"She had that disease. A phobia, terrified of storms. She had seizures sometimes. Once, she lost consciousness. So my daddy told me that when a storm came, I was supposed to get in the closet where Mama hid so I could hold her, talk to her. Try to keep her calm.

"That worked, too. It always worked until that day. The day she died."

"And you think it was your fault?"

"Yeah. I was in my room playing and I didn't go to the closet as fast as I should have. But I went. Closed the door, put my arms around Mama, and said the kinds of things that I always said before." Lutie was struggling now, trying to talk despite the weeping that distorted her words. "Then there was a tremendous crack of lightning and the thunder just exploded. Like a bomb. The light in the closet went out."

Lutie was sobbing now, trembling violently, causing Mama to hold her even tighter.

"I felt my mother stiffen for a few seconds, heard her gasp for breath once or twice, then she went limp in my arms. I was only six, but I knew then she was dead. And I knew it was my fault."

CHAPTER THIRTY-EIGHT

Fᴀᴛᴇ sᴇɴsᴇᴅ sᴏᴍᴇᴛʜɪɴɢ was wrong when he rounded the corner and saw Mama Sim's house. Too many vehicles were parked in her driveway and yard: Dub's pickup; Katy's VW van; Juan's Continental; even Essie's Dodge Neon, which she always parked next door in her own driveway. And near the front porch steps, Fate saw Johnny's bicycle. But nowhere did he see Mama's GMC.

He tried to make himself believe they were all at Mama's because of the storm that had passed over nearly an hour ago. The rain had been accompanied by lightning and thunder, which might have caused Lutie a few rough minutes, but this storm—fast moving—was nothing like the fierce one that had struck a couple of nights ago.

And even if it was Lutie's phobia about thunder, Essie and some of the others knew what to do. No, something else was going on, something that caused a burning sensation in the pit of Fate's belly.

Morrell, who was never still, was sitting on the porch swing with Tiki, neither of them talking as they watched him coming toward the house. And when Johnny saw him, he didn't run to meet him as usual, but bent to adjust a spoke on his bike, an easy excuse not to look into Fate's eyes.

"What's going on?" Fate asked.

To add to his discomfort, nobody spoke.

"You all just hanging out?"

After several minutes of silence, Johnny said, "Maybe you ought to go in and talk to Juan or Essie."

When he stepped inside the front door, Fate knew without a doubt that he was going to be hit with bad news. Any movement and conversation that had been going on came to a sudden halt, as if everyone in the room were frozen in a photograph. Dub was caught sipping lemonade; Katy stopped as she was about to turn a page in a magazine. Only Juan met Fate's searching eyes.

"Let's go up to your bedroom," Juan said.

Without another word, the two of them climbed the stairs to Fate's room. When they sat on his bed, Juan pulled the note from where Lutie had left it and handed it to Fate.

As he read, he would, from time to time, shake his head and speak, as if he were talking to his sister. "I knew you did it for me, Lutie. I knew that." And as his eyes welled with tears, he whispered, "Of course we'll see each other again."

When he finished reading the note, he looked briefly at Juan as if he were about to ask a question, but instead he read the message from Lutie again. Finally, he let the paper slip from his fingers and float to the floor as his chest fell and his shoulders sagged—his spirit crushed by loss.

Juan gripped Fate's shoulder, but the boy seemed not to notice.

"This is my fault," Fate said, openly admitting his guilt, the guilt he'd been trying to run from all day. "When I told her I loved her, she said she didn't know how she felt about me, meaning she wasn't sure if she cared about me or not. I was hurt. I was mad. And the only thing I could think of was to hurt her worse than she'd hurt me. So I did.

"I said every mean thing I could think of. I made her feel horrible. Humiliated. I told her I knew about some sex pictures she posed for in Vegas, told her I knew about a porn movie she made out there."

When Juan tried to put an arm around Fate, offering comfort, he pulled away, knowing he was not deserving of comfort . . . or pity.

"I talked to her like she was . . . like she was nothing. That's why she ran away.

"She's gone because of me."

Just before sunset, the sound of Mama's GMC brought everyone inside the house rushing to the porch. Though the light was dim, they could see no one but Mama, the driver, in the truck. Dub stuck one hand in his pocket, slid the other around Katy's waist; Morrell and Tiki pressed themselves against Essie's sides; Juan folded his arms across his chest and leaned against the porch railing, while Johnny straddled his bike, hunkering down over the handlebars.

Fate flew off the porch and across the yard. When he reached the opened window of Mama's truck, he saw Lutie curled on the front seat, asleep, her head resting in Mama's lap. But before he could speak, Mama put her finger to her lips.

As she slid as gently as she could from beneath Lutie, the girl slept on, undisturbed by Mama's movement or the sudden silence of the old pickup. Mama walked around the truck with one arm around Fate's shoulders as she guided him toward the house.

"Is she okay?" he asked.

"Yes, Fate, she is. But right now she's exhausted, and I think the best we can do for her is to let her sleep."

"But what—"

"I know you and Lutie have a lot to talk about. So much to say to each other, but this isn't the time for it. Okay?"

"Sure, but can you tell me why she ran off?"

"I could, but I won't. That's something she'll have to tell you herself."

"I just need to know if she left because of me."

"Do you trust me, sugar?"

"You know I do."

"Then let it be for now."

When Mama reached the house and started up the porch steps, she was peppered with questions until she assured them all that Lutie was okay, asleep in the truck.

"Juan, will you go out and get her while I turn down her bed? And do your best not to wake her."

As Juan started for the truck and before Mama could get inside the front door, Johnny said, "Did you have to rescue her?"

"No, Johnny, I hate to disappoint you, but I didn't have to do battle with anyone. But I did get to her just after she'd hitched a ride with a boy not much older than she is. No telling what might have happened if I hadn't gotten her out of that car before the kid took off."

"What was he driving?"

Mama smiled at the question, even though she tried not to.

"I was just wondering," Johnny said, an attempt to somehow divert attention away from a question that he knew must have sounded silly. "It doesn't really matter, though, does it?"

"You know, it could have made a difference, because his car looked . . . what's that term? Souped up? Yes, that's it. That vehicle looked souped up to me. It was real shiny like a new car, but it wasn't. He told me it was a restored Pontiac GTO . . . 1969."

"Oh, my God. The Judge."

"He was a judge?" Mama asked with surprise.

"No, ma'am. The car is called the Judge."

"I see." Mama nodded as if Johnny's information were fascinating. But when she saw Juan coming toward the house carrying Lutie in his arms, she went inside to ready the bed.

"You all know about the Judge, don't you?" Nobody responded. "Believe me, the GTO is a real bad boy," Johnny said to those on the porch who were interested in his knowledge about cars. Unfortunately for him, no one was.

When Juan came up the porch steps with Lutie, Fate opened the door for him, then followed them into the house, down the hall, and into Lutie's room.

Mama Sim took off the girl's shoes, pulled the covers up to her shoulders, then smoothed her hair as it fanned across the pillow.

Then she, Juan, and Fate stood quietly watching Lutie sleep for a while. But when Mama and Juan finally left the room, Fate stayed, taking a seat in the rocker, where he would remain until his sister woke up.

Juan had heard Fate and Lutie talking since just after sunup, though from where he sat in the living room he couldn't have made out the words even if he'd wanted to. He'd dozed off a couple of times during the night, but when Fate left Lutie's room a few minutes past eight and closed her door quietly behind him, Juan was wide awake.

Obviously surprised to find his friend on the couch, Fate swiped his sleeve across his red eyes, then said, "Are you up early or late, Juan?"

"Aw, just thought I will be sticking around for a while."

"Why? See if me and Lutie were going to try to kill each other?"

"Never thought that."

"Well, we didn't fight."

"No?"

"She talked; I listened. Learned something about her I never knew before."

"And?"

"We're okay." The boy smiled then, a smile that made him look even younger than his years. "Yeah, we're okay."

Juan nodded. "Good."

"You're both up," Mama said with concern as she padded into the living room in her robe and house shoes. "Is it Lutie?" she asked Fate. "Has she—"

"She's fine. Probably gone back to sleep."

"You two talk? About stuff?"

"She told me about our mother."

"That's what I was hoping for." Mama grabbed Fate in a tight hug. "Now," she said to Juan, "you start the coffee?"

"Made a pot a few hours ago."

Mama made a face. "I'll put on some fresh," she said as she started for the kitchen. "Can't stand stale, cooked coffee. Biscuits or pancakes?" she asked as she shuffled from the room.

"How 'bout huevos rancheros?" Juan answered. "Or *migas*?"

"Might have known better'n to ask," she called back.

"Save me some," Fate said to Juan. "I'm going to bed for a little while."

"Will do it. Good night. Or good morning. What do gringos say?"

"I don't know. Am I a gringo?"

"Aw, hell. Go to bed."

Fate gave Juan a high five and then, running barefoot, took the stairs to his room two at a time.

Juan thought about going to his tent for a little morning nap to make up for the sleep he'd lost, but the promise of one of Mama's Mexican breakfasts was too good to pass up. Just then, the phone rang where it sat on the end table beside the couch.

"Who'd call this early except for your papa?" Mama yelled. "Get that, Juan. My hands are sticky."

"Hello," Juan said into the receiver. He listened a moment, then said, "Yes, I am Mr. Vargas, but I think you be calling for . . . No. Central time here, but is okay."

Minutes later, after he'd let the caller talk, Juan's look of confusion turned into an expression of disbelief. Finally, he said, "Say again, *por favor*."

CHAPTER THIRTY-NINE

JUAN HAD BEEN asleep for an hour or so when Draco heard Mama Sim's front door screen slam, causing the dog to race from the tent where she'd been trying to rouse Juan since he'd bedded down.

With the tent flaps left open by Draco's sudden departure, Juan looked out to see the dog following Lutie from the porch to the road and off toward the winter quarters grounds.

More curious to see if Lutie was heading for the ring barn than he was interested in trying for more shut-eye, Juan let the girl and dog get a good head start before he crawled from the tent and took off down the road far behind them.

Once Lutie reached the grounds, she didn't seem at all secretive about going directly to the ring barn, didn't even look around to see if anyone might be watching her. She'd been in and out so often in the past few weeks that she felt totally comfortable about being there.

Her only concern was to make sure Draco didn't dart inside when she opened the door. Juan couldn't hear what she said to the dog, but whatever it was brought Draco's tail to a standstill and caused her head to droop. Minutes later, when Juan slipped quietly inside, his dog was gone, having spotted a squirrel and taken up the chase.

By the time Juan reached his hiding place and hunkered down in a spot behind the bleachers, Lutie had already stripped down to her leotard, removed her shoes and socks, powdered her feet, and mounted the highest balance beam.

Even though she seemed to have no idea she was being observed, she began to perform as if before spectators. She slowly raised one arm above her head, her fingers slightly curled and pointing skyward; with the other arm she made a graceful flourish, sweeping her hand elegantly from left to right to include her entire make-believe audience.

With both arms moving at the same moment, it seemed as if a puppeteer had pulled ever so gently on strings attached to her hands. When at last her arms were outstretched at shoulder height, palms down, she was a lovely statue, head held high on her long, slender neck, eyes fixed on a point somewhere in front of her that only she could see.

Juan had watched her for only moments before he felt, once again, his amazement at seeing such talent, realizing that every movement was done without any apprehension, but with absolute focus and confidence.

Then, her gaze never wavering, she moved forward, the motion so imperceptible that only trained eyes saw her left foot shift position as it found by familiar feel the beam beneath it. In full control, she shifted forward with astonishing concentration and polished gestures. Right foot, then left, her feet finding their way without hesitation until she reached the near midpoint of the beam.

She stopped, waited for the Zen moment of perfect balance, the instant of flawlessness, physically and mentally, and when it came to her, she performed a forward handspring, then—without pause—two more. And although each was perfect in itself, all three seemed to be of one unbelievable piece.

Before Juan had even blinked, she suddenly took two quick steps forward, then went into a series of backward handsprings—three of them. Faultless.

Finally, with total ease, she landed a dismount that was executed immaculately. Moments later, she turned toward Juan's hiding place and bowed. As he stepped from behind the bleachers, he began clapping. Too excited by what he'd just witnessed, he lapsed into Spanish without realizing it.

"*¡Magnífico! Increíble! Glorioso! He estado observando, pero—*"

"Whoa. English, *por favor.*"

"I been watching you many times, but did not knowing until today how big your talent. Is *magnífico!*"

"Yeah, I got that part. I don't know about magnificent, but I figured I must have given you a good performance because this is the first time you've applauded."

Juan looked confused. "You mean that you been knowing about me being here times before today?"

"Sure. You're not very good at being quiet, Juan. And you always 'hide' in the same place." Lutie nodded to the bleachers. "Of course I knew. But until now I've just been working to get back in shape, going over and over each movement. See, it'd been months since I'd been on the beam."

Lutie reached for her jeans, but before she stepped into them, Juan said, "So, you want to returning to the beam?"

"No." She looked up, far above them, at the high wire suspended near the top of the ring barn. "I want to try that. The wire."

Something in her expression, a look Juan had not seen before, told him this girl had reached some kind of breakthrough. Her eyes had come alive, her face showed him for the first time that she had hope. Or at least the possibility of hope. And though he couldn't have known it, his own face was animated with excitement, an excitement he hadn't experienced in years.

"Will you help me?" she asked.

"Help you?"

"Be my coach."

"*Entrenador?*" Juan asked. His smile spread with each thought racing through his mind. "Okay, big sister. Get up there and show me what you got."

"Whatcha up to?" Essie asked as she walked into Mama's kitchen.

Mama, at the sink peeling potatoes, said, "Starting supper."

"I smell meat loaf."

"It's in the oven. Gonna fry up a skillet of onions and potatoes. You and the kids might as well come over to eat with us. Thought I'd make a salad, maybe open up a jar of green beans."

"The ones we canned last summer?"

"I guess."

"Want me to fix a salad?"

When Mama didn't answer, Essie asked, "What's on your mind? I mean, besides green beans."

"Your papa called a little while ago. Said they wouldn't be back soon as he thought. He worked out the Stillwater contract for two days, then he plugged in Cushing and Shawnee, a day each since they're close. So they won't be here until next Thursday."

"And you sound worried because?"

"I could tell Ray wasn't feeling his best when he was home a few days ago. Arthritis is getting the better of him. Looked like he'd lost weight, too."

"I noticed he wasn't getting around as well as when they went out last March."

"But the main reason he called was to see if that fella with the Shriners Circus had phoned. What's his name? Strong?"

"Stone."

"Yeah. James Stone. Your daddy seemed to think he would have heard from him by now with a final offer."

"No one else knows about that deal, do they? 'Cause Papa is having a devil of a time worrying about everyone else. I mean, if the Shriners buy Papa out, not everyone with Vargas Brothers is going to have a job. Shriners performers, riggers, stock men, costumers—they're already in place. So how many of our people will they take on if this deal goes through?"

"You know I haven't told anyone, but the word's gonna get around. That's for sure."

"What word?" Juan asked as he came into the kitchen.

"Aw, we're just running some gossip back and forth."

"Something smells good."

"Your papa called. Said he'd tacked on a few more dates, so they won't be back as soon as he thought. Maybe next Thursday."

"By the way," Essie said as she washed a head of lettuce, "when are you leaving? I heard that you told Papa you wouldn't be here when he gets back."

"You trying to run me off?"

"No. You've behaved yourself pretty well. Better than I expected."

"I'll be taking off before long, but right now I be helping Lutie out to do something."

"What's that?"

"Oh, I'm trying to teaching her how to ride the horses."

A couple of seconds later, they heard Lutie come in the door singing.

> I think I know you from somewhere
>> Are you from a room in my mind?

I think you know what I mean,
        but I'm afraid you won't like what you
find.

She continued humming until she stuck her head in the kitchen. "I'm gonna take a quick shower, then I'll set the table. Okay?"

"Okay," Mama said.

As soon as they heard Lutie shut her door, Essie said, "Well, what's gotten into our little firecracker?"

"You got me," Mama said. "But whatever it is, I'll take it."

Juan didn't say a word as he grabbed a slice of raw potato and stuffed it in his mouth.

CHAPTER FORTY

For the next week, Juan worked with Lutie two or three times a day for as many hours as he could stay with it while she made her transition from the beams to the high wire. He wasn't surprised by her toughness—she'd shown him enough of that characteristic to ease any doubts he might have had.

But now, watching her struggle hour after hour until the soles of her feet blistered, he became aware of a different kind of resilience in the girl. He saw her prick first one bubble of watery liquid, then another, squeeze each one dry, slap on yet another Band-Aid, and be ready to get back to the wire.

She just wouldn't give up . . . on anything.

Even when he barked out the same instructions for a difficult movement once too often, he was likely to be rewarded with a good cussing. But she'd stick with his direction until she got it right. And once she had the "how to" down, she owned it. Forever.

On that first day, the morning Lutie had started to train, Juan suggested she begin with the low wire, which wasn't more than a couple of feet off the ground. But she'd have none of that. Instead, she climbed to the highest wire. And though the height made her dizzy when she first looked down, she wasn't afraid. Instead, she felt she was finally in the place where she was meant to be. If not at the top of the world, then at least closer to the top than she'd ever been.

Even when she took her first fall from the wire into the safety net rigged up some thirty feet below, she dropped with such surprise and speed that she had no time to be afraid. And even before Juan had told her how to flip from the net to the ground, she seemed to know instinctively how to accomplish the move in such a practiced way that it not only looked graceful, but appeared to have been planned.

Somehow, they'd managed to practice under the radar of everyone except Mama Sim, but she didn't tell anyone, not even Essie, the one person she shared almost all her secrets with. And though Fate and Johnny spent most of their time together on the winter quarters grounds, they gravitated to the other end of the property, where they had access to the clown cars and costumes, Johnny's tree house, and Katy's cookies, cakes, and pies.

So Lutie and Juan—student and teacher—were left alone and undisturbed as they reached out together, hoping to snag an impossible dream.

"Listen," Essie said. "Did you hear that?"

Everyone at the table stopped what they were doing—passing potatoes, buttering biscuits, stirring sugar into tea. They listened. And they listened as one.

A moment later, Morrell broke into a smile. "I hear the drum," he said.

"And a tiger," Tiki added. "I heard a tiger growl."

Juan stood up, his food untouched. "They're coming home."

Like a herd of sheep, everyone at the dinner table jumped up and followed Juan to the front porch.

"The circus," Mama said to Fate and Lutie. "The circus is here."

And sure enough, within minutes they saw the elephants coming down the road, each connected to another by its trunk twined around the tail of the one before it, with showgirls dressed in sparkling costumes perched upon their backs.

Behind the elephants, they saw the cat cars, tigers and lions pacing behind their bars as if they knew they were almost home. The horses, two abreast, had costumed women standing on their backs, no saddles, no blankets, only the reins for the riders to hold on to.

"That's what I used to do," Mama said to Lutie. "I always rode into town standing atop my horse, me in something red and gold, Prince with gold braided into his mane."

Then came the clowns, some doing tricks for the folks on their porches to see, others speeding in circles in their miniature vehicles.

Johnny raced from his dad's trailer, crossed the winter quarters grounds, and pounded down the road, yelling, "Fate! They're here!" By the time he reached Mama's yard, he was breathless, more from excitement than from his long-distance sprint. "See that?" he asked Fate, pointing to a miniature fire truck driven by a clown dressed as a fireman. "It's just like the one we wrecked last week," he whispered.

Behind the clowns came the acrobats, some walking on their hands, other men balancing women upon their shoulders; some of the girls—most in their teens—paraded past by doing handsprings, both forward and backward. Then came the women from India, spinning their plates at the ends of bamboo poles;

and the jugglers, tossing their pins incredibly high without dropping even one.

Fate was speechless as he watched the constant procession of llamas, sheep, zebras, camels, and donkeys. From time to time, a troop of Chinese men and women on unicycles would dart across the road, some balancing exotic-looking objects in their hands and on their heads.

Following the long line of animals and performers came the passage of campers and vans. Then a cavalcade of trucks carrying equipment—the big top, cook's tent, rigging, cables, electrical supplies, canvas, netting, cotton candy and popcorn machines—all decorated with stars, banners, streamers, and some with more costumed performers riding on the cabs and fenders.

As the last of the circus vehicles passed the house, heading for the winter quarters to unpack for the next few months, Ray pulled into the driveway in his pickup and honked. He was smiling and waving until he saw Juan standing on the porch.

As those who circled Raynoldo dispersed, the kids heading to the circus grounds, Essie back to the house, only Mama, Juan, and Ray were left standing in the yard. After Mama gave Ray another hug, she said, "We've got a God's plenty of food on the table, honey. Why don't you come in and eat while it's still hot?"

"I'll be in as soon as I unload the pickup bed. If I put it off now, I won't get it done for days."

"Let me help," Juan said.

"Didn't expect to see you here. From what you said to me last week, I thought you'd be back in Vegas by now."

"Well, I got the sidetracked."

As Mama started up the stairs, Ray called to her, "Mama, did that guy call me back?"

"Which guy?"

"From the Shriners. James Stone."

"No. I figured he'd call you. You didn't lose your cell phone again, did you?"

"Nope. But he didn't call me."

"Maybe he needs more time."

"He's had plenty of time. Said he'd call me back last week."

"He didn't phone here. Now, hurry up and get in here for your supper."

As Juan and Ray started unloading the truck and hauling small pieces of equipment to the garage, Juan said, "He called."

Ray looked confused.

"Stone, the Shriners' guy. He called."

"Did he—"

"He thought he was talking to you."

"And you didn't tell him the difference?"

"I tried. At first, I tried. But when I finding out why he is calling, I acted like I am you."

"Why? You didn't screw up the deal, did you? We've been negotiating since last May, when I decided it was time to sell out, and we're close to agreeing on a price. I don't want to let this get away from me."

"Sorry, Papa."

"Sorry for what?" Ray asked, his voice giving away his suspicion.

"I told him I'd changed my mind. Did not want to sell. Circus too important to our family."

"You told him that?! Without talking to me first?"

"It is best, I am thinking, for you to keep Vargas Brothers Circus."

"Dammit all to hell, Juan. I can't do this anymore. It's too much for me."

"Yes, I know."

"Then—"

"Let me show you something, then we will talk."

"Well, you damn sure better have a lot to say."

CHAPTER FORTY-ONE

Mama Sim's house came to life on the night the circus returned. Everyone knew she missed being on the road, so at the end of each tour, they brought the trip to her, making gifts of their stories from the towns where they'd performed.

When Fate and Lutie met the Vargas clan, they were amazed by the number of cousins, uncles, aunts, nieces, nephews all crowded into one house, all talking at once—a situation that made it easy for Lutie to slip out unnoticed.

Half an hour later, Juan whistled for quiet. Because he wasn't comfortable making an announcement, he'd had Lutie write down for him what he wanted to say. As soon as he had everyone's attention, he began to read Lutie's message written on an index card.

"Welcome home," he said, which caused a widespread response. "You've been missing." When he noticed a look of confusion on several faces, he looked at the card in his hand more closely. "Sorry. You've been missed." His correction was met by smiles from the adults and giggles from the kids, who knew

English well. "Because of your homecoming, I have planned a surprise for you tonight." Some in Juan's audience clapped, others raised their eyebrows at his strange news, and several broke into puzzled conversation with whoever was standing nearby.

"I know you're all tired and probably ready to get to bed, but before you begin to break up this party, please follow me to the ring barn, where a treat awaits you." Finished, Juan smiled and bowed to rousing applause.

"Good job, Juan," called one of the cousins from the back of the room. "You planning to go into politics?"

"This year? No. Next year? Maybe."

As they poured out the front door and across the porch, Mama Sim saw Raynoldo sitting in the swing, smoking his pipe.

"Come on, Ray. Juan has a surprise for us at the grounds."

Ray's smile didn't quite manage to suggest happiness. "Juan's already given me one surprise today. I think that's enough."

"No, it's not. Now, give your son a chance. Surely he deserves that."

Mama went down the steps and started across the yard with the others, but then she stopped to turn and stare at her son. Finally, he got up and reluctantly fell in with his kin.

"Hey, Johnny," Fate called as he and the Vargases approached the ring barn. "What're you doing here?"

"I'm not sure. My dad told me to meet him here, but I can't find him." Johnny looked over at the Vargas family as they made their way inside. "What's going on?"

"We don't know. Juan said he had a surprise over here. Have you seen Lutie?"

"No, but I might have missed her. Maybe she's already inside."

"Well, come on. Let's see if we can find her," Fate said.

"I want to know what the surprise is."

Fate and Johnny, among the last to enter, sat in the center section behind Ray and Mama Sim. Fate, looking over the crowd, didn't see Lutie or Juan. He was just about to ask Mama about them when a spotlight came on, shining into the center of the middle ring.

Johnny followed the beam of light to one of the light boxes, where he saw his dad. "What's he doing up there? He never does any tech, that's not his job."

"Shush," Mama whispered.

Seconds later, Juan stepped into the spotlight holding a mike and wearing the ringmaster's top hat, prompting whistles and cheers.

This time he spoke without the benefit of notes.

"Ladies and gentlemen, boys and girls . . . I have not the gift for to speaking, but what I say to you is coming from my heart. Some months ago I was lucky to meeting a boy and girl in Las Vegas. Fate and Lutie are their names. Why was I lucky? Because they have teached me much about what is important. Like the Vargas Brothers Circus . . . and family."

Juan smiled at the roar of applause.

"Now I have the chance to help teaching these boy and girl. You will see in a minute about what I am saying. Fate has listen to me tell about myself, and in my talking, we both have been learning more about what make a family to love each other.

"And Lutie has listen to me tell about wire walking. As you will be seeing, she already has been having the talent, but I am lucky in being able to help her training for the wire.

"Okay. Enough for my talking."

A male voice in the family yelled, "Yes, Uncle Juan, enough for your talking," which caused more laughter.

"I giving you Miss Lutie."

And with that, the spotlight drifted upward until Lutie was illuminated, standing on one of the platforms at the end of the high wire. She was wearing a brilliant blue leotard with a matching headband covered in rhinestones.

"Oh, my God," Fate said, causing Mama to turn to him and, smiling, pat his knee.

"It'll be all right," she whispered. "Don't worry."

"You knew about this?" Raynoldo asked her. "What the hell has been going on here?"

"Just watch," she said.

Lutie began much as she had on the balance beam when she had performed for Juan a couple of weeks ago. She raised one arm toward the ceiling while she made a flourish with the other, letting her hand drift from one side of the center section where the family was seated to the other side.

Then she made her first step onto the wire, never wavering in her balance as she took the next step. Now she was clear of the platform, nothing but air between the slender cable she stood on and the net far below. She kept her head high, her eyes straight ahead.

She moved forward in a graceful, perfectly paced stride to near the midpoint of the wire, where she stopped, again waiting for that moment of certainty, and when it came, she performed a flawless forward handspring. While she waited for the applause to die, she stood absolutely still; then, when silence returned, she walked the rest of the wire to the other platform, where she picked up a rope she had placed there earlier.

Sensing that Lutie was preparing to try something dangerous, Fate leaned forward and whispered to Mama Sim, "What is it? What is she going to do?"

"Watch, honey. Just watch."

As Lutie started back across the wire, she held the rope in one hand. But near the center of the wire, she transferred one end of the rope to her other hand, and Fate understood what she was holding. A jump rope.

Standing as still as a sculpted figure, she waited as the people below sat transfixed. Finally, she swung the rope, and just before it reached her feet, she jumped. Her timing was unerring, her balance perfect. She jumped again and again, then dropped the rope, which fell to the net below.

The audience went wild—whistling, stomping, shouting, applauding—all anticipating the end of her performance. But they were wrong. As soon as they realized more was coming, they quieted. That's when Juan slipped into the empty seat beside his father.

Moments later, Lutie's body tensed slightly, a sure sign that she had something else to show. With the beauty and grace of a ballerina, she began to lean back, slowly, slowly, until suddenly she was all motion. With an uninterrupted series of backward handsprings, she moved across the wire to the platform, where she raised both hands and then, smiling, bowed to those seated below.

"Yes, Juan. She is amazing. Can't argue with that. A talent like hers comes along once in a lifetime. I thought I was good, thought you were great, but that girl will make us all look like amateurs if she stays with it. She's only fifteen, though. A child. Next week she might be in California, next month in Las Vegas. Next year, a mother. No telling."

"No, I think she really be wanting this. Think of it—a triple somersault. Not only forward, but backward, too. Have you ever seeing aerialist do such? Huh, Papa? Have you?"

"Look, Juan. She would sell some tickets, no doubt about

that. She'd be great for the business, wonderful publicity, a good-looking girl that age. But what I'm trying to tell you is that ticket sales is not our only problem.

"I won't lie to you, say we're making the kind of money we were until a couple of years ago. Gas has gone up, feed for the animals is sky-high now, equipment costs are out of sight, so we make do when we can by repairing the older pieces rather than buying new. But parts are harder to get, and even when we can find them, we pay through the nose. Wages are higher, too, but the raises I can afford aren't what they should be.

"Anyway, all that aside, here's the problem. Right here." Raynoldo tapped his chest. "It's me. And don't you say a word about this to Mama Sim. She'd drive me crazy trying to take care of me and I'd—"

A look of alarm crossed Juan's face. "What is it? Your heart? Blood pressure? Papa, do you have a cancer?"

"No—hell, no! I'm not sick, I'm just old. Worn out. Arthritis, bad eyes, bad balance. Can't even get a hard-on anymore. Old man's ailments, that's all. But it's enough to let me know that the time's come to get out of the business. Time to let go of the circus."

"You can't be doing that! Remember what you tell Lutie? I was hearing you. You talk to her about the parade of homecoming through town. The people coming out to watch elephants, horses, clowns. The performers in costumes, neighbors clap and waving because they happy to have back the circus.

"You tell to Lutie the circus all you ever been wanting to do, that you be hating to giving it up. You say, 'A man can't want more than to do work he loves.' For you, Papa, that love, that work is circus."

"What I meant, Juan, is—"

"Oh, I know what you mean 'cause you say to Lutie that 'Juan the only son I got left.' You tell to her that 'the way

350

Juan living ain't no good, but guess he doing what he wanting to do.' Bad choice, you thinking. Well, now I thinking bad choice, too."

"So let me understand what it is you—"

"And you say, 'Hell, boy, you have no ended up yet.' So now I start figuring that you be having the right answer. I have no ended up yet. I want to be coming back to circus."

Ray looked as though he'd just recovered from a knockout—eyes glazed, mouth agape, expression dazed. Finally, he said, "But you told me you couldn't come back, couldn't live at the bottom after you'd been at the top."

"Right! That's right! But I can train the next one to be making it to the top. Lutie. And I can running the circus for you if you teaching me."

"Are you sure, son? Sure you're going to stay with us now?"

"Yes, Papa. Because circus is more than business, more than giving fun to people buying tickets. Circus is family. Circus is tribe. And I am part of our tribe."

Sometime after ten, the visitors had all cleared out. Mama Sim had gone to bed not long after Ray turned in; Lutie and Fate sat together on the porch swing, with Draco curled up between them, sleeping, her head resting on Lutie's lap. Juan was stretched out on the porch steps, smoking his last cigarette of the night.

In her pajamas now and with her hair still wet from a long hot shower, Lutie kept the swing moving with her bare feet.

"I just can't believe I didn't know you two were spending that much time in the ring barn," Fate said. "I mean, I'm down at the circus grounds every day."

"But you and Johnny were having too much fun to be paying attention to us."

"Well, it was amazing to see you up there on that wire, in the spotlight. I still don't know how you did that, Lutie."

"Because she's the real deal," Juan said. "Your big sister is an honest-to-*Dios caminante del aire*."

"What does that mean, *caminante* something?" Fate asked.

"Wind walker."

"That's nice," Lutie said as she rubbed Draco's head. "Wind walker. Makes me sound like I have some kind of magic powers."

"I thinking maybe you do," Juan said.

"So are you saying she's going to be in the circus, Juan?"

"Why don't you asking her?" Juan said.

"As long as you're here, Fate, and as long as Juan is going to stick around to coach me."

"I'm here to stay," Juan said.

Lutie said, "Then me, too."

"That makes three of us," Fate said.

"Okay, now that's settled, I'm going to bed. You going with me, Draco?"

Draco opened her eyes to give him a look, then yawned and put her head back on Lutie's lap.

"That's some kind of loyal, huh? See you in the morning."

Juan started for his tent, but when he was only steps away from the porch, Fate yelled, "Watch out!" saving him from stepping into dog droppings.

Juan waved.

"Night, Juan," Lutie said.

"He's some great guy," Fate said as they watched Juan crawl into his tent. "Lutie, did you know that when a dog poops, it attracts a hundred forty-four flies?"

"Get outta here," she said as she swatted at him. "What'd you do, dingbat? Count 'em?"

"And did you know that houseflies hum in the key of F?"

"Only if they have perfect pitch."

"Don't know about that."

"Gotcha! Finally found something you can't tell me." Suddenly, Lutie pointed to the edge of the mowed yard and just beyond, where the weeds had partly taken over.

"What?"

"Fireflies."

"We been here all this time and you just now noticed them?"

"Guess I wasn't out here at the right time."

"They love nights like this. Warm, moon and stars covered with clouds, no outdoor lights. The stage is all theirs."

"Did you ever see a firefly in Vegas?"

"No decent firefly would ever spend a night in Vegas."

"Do you remember once when we were living with Beverly? We had twin beds, but you were afraid of the dark, so as soon as she shut the door, you got in bed with me. Beverly wouldn't let us leave a night-light on, said it ran up her electric bill. So we got out of bed one night, emptied safety pins she kept in a jar, then slipped out the window in our sleepers to catch lightning bugs."

"You know, Lutie, there's something familiar about that story."

"Oh, we stayed out a long time. Caught a zillion of those little bugs."

"And when we crawled back to bed, that jar of bugs lit up like a forty-watt bulb."

"But the next morning, we found the jar filled with water. Beverly had come in and drowned all our bugs. She was such a bitch. The only reason she worried about her electric bill was because of the money she spent on gin."

"Hey," Fate said, "let's get a jar—"

"Get two. With lids—"

"And see who can—"

"Catch the most—"

When Fate came trotting from Mama's shed with two empty lidded jars, Lutie got serious. She made Fate take off his shoes and socks so he wouldn't have an advantage. And their spoken but abbreviated challenge began. The dew made the grass slick, so now and then one of them would take a tumble, while the other called out, "Two." Then Lutie stepped on a goathead sticker, which cost her precious moments to extract it.

"Five!" Fate yelled.

On her feet again, Lutie made a single, then a double catch. "Three!" She crawled under a barbed-wire fence, got three more low-flying critters. "Six," to which Fate answered:

"Eight!"

Brother and sister, both barefoot, she in pajamas and wet hair, running, jumping, shouting, "Fourteen!" then skipping, crawling, laughing, yelling, "Nineteen!" darting, dancing, twirling, "Twenty-three!" dashing, skipping, soaring, "Forty-one!" until finally both fell on their backs into the dew-covered grass, breathless, light-headed, and giggling like the children they'd hardly ever had a chance to be.

As the jars sparkled yellow, lights on—lights off, they stared at the sky just as the clouds parted and a quarter-moon showed itself.

They were content to lie side by side, their backs soaking up the dew, their breathing returning to normal, their eyes heavenward. Silent. And smiling.

At last, Lutie said, "I'd better get to bed. Juan told me to be up by six for weight training."

Fate rolled onto his side so he could see Lutie's face. "What are we going to do with these lightning bugs?"

"Only one thing to do," she said as she unscrewed her lid. "Let them go."

"Yes. Let them all go free."

The small creatures left the jars leisurely, seemingly un-changed by their brief confinement, then flew away . . . rising, gliding, glittering, as the boy and girl, still lying in the grass, watched the golden flashes rise in the stillness of the night.